PENGUIN MODERN CLASSICS

THE FORTUNES OF RICHARD MAHONY

AUSTRALIA FELIX

Ethel Florence Lindesay Richardson was born in Melbourne in 1870. Her Irish grandmother, a devotee of Handel, called her son Henry Handel and from him Richardson took her pen name.

Her father, Walter Lindesay Richardson, was born in Dublin and emigrated to Australia in the early 1850s. Her mother arrived at about the same time and Ethel was born fifteen years later. When she was three, she and her younger sister were taken to England, but while there her father learnt of the collapse of his financial affairs and returned to Australia.

Ethel Richardson spent an unhappy childhood, some of it at a select girls' boarding school, depicted by her in *The Getting of Wisdom* (1910). In 1888, nine years after her husband's death, Mrs Richardson took her daughters abroad so that Ethel could continue her musical studies in Leipzig. She spent most of the next sixteen years in Germany, where she met and married J. G. Robertson, later to become first Professor of German Literature at the University of London. In Leipzig, she experienced failure as a musician and turned to writing. Her first published novel was *Maurice Guest* (1908). Later, in England, she began *The Fortunes of Richard Mahony* (1917-1921), visiting Australia in 1912 to refresh her Australian memories. After her husband's death in 1933, she moved to Sussex, where she died in 1946.

HENRY HANDEL RICHARDSON

THE FORTUNES OF RICHARD MAHONY

Australia Felix

With an Introduction by
LEONIE KRAMER

PENGUIN BOOKS

Penguin Books Ltd,
Harmondsworth, Middlesex, England
Penguin Books,
625 Madison Avenue, New York, N.Y. 10022, U.S.A.
Penguin Books Australia Ltd,
Ringwood, Victoria, Australia
Penguin Books Canada Ltd,
2801 John Street, Markham, Ontario, Canada
Penguin Books (N.Z.) Ltd,
182-190 Wairau Road, Auckland 10, New Zealand

First published by William Heinemann Limited, 1917
Published in Penguin Books 1971
Reprinted 1975, 1977, 1979

Introduction Copyright © Leonie Kramer, 1971

Made and printed in Australia
by Alexander Bros Pty Ltd, Mentone, Victoria

CIP

Richardson, Henry Handel.
Australia Felix.

(Penguin modern classics).
First volume in the author's trilogy The fortunes
of Richard Mahoney.
Previously published, Ringwood, Vic.: Penguin Books,
1971; originally published, London: William
Heinemann, 1917.
ISBN 0 14 003338 6.

I. Title. II. Title: The fortunes of Richard
Mahoney. (Series)

A823'.2

INTRODUCTION

Until 1929, when the publication of *Ultima Thule* completed the trilogy *The Fortunes of Richard Mahony*, Henry Handel Richardson considered herself a failure. Her two earlier novels *Maurice Guest* (1908) and *The Getting of Wisdom* (1910), had aroused only temporary interest, and some speculation about the author. The first two volumes of the trilogy *Australia Felix* (1917) and *The Way Home* (1925) were possibly too remote from each other in time of publication, and too inconclusive to warrant serious critical attention. Richardson herself recorded that opinion on *Australia Felix* 'ranged from "a dull but honest volume" to "might have been written by a retired grocer" ', and that *The Way Home* 'was pronounced "intelligent but dull", "a thick crumby slice of life, but no story" '. Her character Richard Mahony, she reports, was thus dismissed: ' "Mr Richardson has lost all control of his hero. . . . The situation has become so stupidly hopeless that it ceases to interest the most sympathetic reader . . . it is difficult to believe he has taken any trouble to arrange his thoughts or construct his character . . ." ' Even Nettie Palmer, who was later to become Richardson's most ardent and persuasive advocate in Australia, wrote of *The Way Home* that '. . . at worst it might be considered rather too much like a historical picture – a little flat and lacking in atmosphere'.

The original failure of these two books is easily enough explained. Neither is self-contained. *Australia Felix* abandons Richard Mahony at a point where he imagines that a chapter of his history is complete, and that he has 'got off scot-free' from his colonial experiences. But for the reader this can at best be an inconclusive pause in a narrative whose future is unpredictable, and was in fact far off. *The Way Home* ends on a downward turn of Mahony's fortunes, but even the knowledge of his financial ruin hardly prepares one for the complete disintegration of his personality which is the subject of *Ultima Thule*. Nor is there sufficient impetus in *The Way Home* to compensate for its incompleteness, and even when it is viewed in its proper perspective as the central movement of Mahony's life, it is still the least compelling of the three sections, though it was Richardson's favourite one. It is not surprising that its failure convinced Richardson that she was 'as far from making good as ever', and that, after nearly thirty years as a novelist 'there was nothing for it . . . but to resign myself to failure *in perpetuum*'.

*

Ethel Florence Lindesay Richardson was born on 3 January 1870 in Melbourne. Her Irish grandmother, who was devoted to Handel, called her son Henry Handel and from him Richardson took her pen name. In 1940 Richardson explained herself thus:

I was bent on keeping my identity a secret. There had been much talk in the press of that day [i.e. at the time *Maurice Guest* was completed] about the ease with which a woman's work could be distinguished from a man's; and I wanted to try out the truth of the assertion.

Her father, Walter Lindesay Richardson, was born in Dublin, studied medicine in Edinburgh, and emigrated to Australia in the early 1850s in the hope of making his fortune on the goldfields. Her mother arrived from Leicester at about the same time. Ethel was born fifteen years after her parents' marriage, at a time of prosperity for them. When she was three, she and her younger sister were taken to England, and while they were there her father learnt of the collapse of his financial affairs, and returned abruptly to Australia, as Richard Mahony does at the end of *The Way Home*. Thereafter Ethel Richardson was a victim of his financial and psychological instability, as he took his family from place to place in a vain attempt to recoup his losses and recover his professional and personal prestige. Almost every year saw a move to a new house, as he wandered about Victoria in search of his lost hopes. He died insane in 1879, and was buried in the small country town of Koroit in the Western District of Victoria.

Ethel Richardson's Australian childhood gave her memories of the Australian countryside that lived with her for the rest of her life; a love of books that she attributed to her father's passion for reading; experience of the tensions and anxieties of family life, and an unusually mature view of the suffering and misery that are part of that experience; and a conviction, gained largely from her experience of boarding school, that she did not conform to the comfortable pattern of youthful pleasures and interests which seemed to satisfy her fellow-pupils. She presents her view of herself as an adolescent schoolgirl in *The Getting of Wisdom*. This novel and the closing sections of *The Fortunes of Richard Mahony*, where she appears as Cuffy, are her only substantial fictional recollections of her Australian youth.

In 1888 Mrs Richardson took her two daughters abroad, so that Ethel could continue her musical studies at Leipzig Conservatorium. She spent most of the next sixteen years in Germany, which became and largely remained her spiritual home. In Leipzig she met J. G. Robertson whom she married in 1895, and who became first Professor of German Literature in the University of London. In Leipzig too she experienced failure as a musician, and her own account of these years clearly suggests that she turned to writing as a refuge from the public life of the executant musician. In Germany, both before and after her marriage, she absorbed with relish the musical and intellectual life of the day, and her mind was stimulated and nourished as it had never been before. She read widely in European literature, and in the late 1890s, under the influence of her husband's suggestion that she should turn her experience of the musical life of Leipzig to good account by writing about 'a musician who failed to make good', she began *Maurice Guest* (1908). The sense of rootlessness and insecurity, and, in her musical and literary interests, of isolation from her fellows, that had marked her childhood in Australia, vanished in the active cultural life first of Leipzig, and then of Strasbourg.

The pattern of Richardson's life changed again, however, when her husband took up his appointment in London in 1904. From then until her death in 1946 Richardson lived in England. After the formative, full years in Germany, life in England more and more became a withdrawal into solitude. In the guarded seclusion of her London study she began work on *The Fortunes of Richard Mahony*, which was to occupy nearly twenty years of her life. In 1912, when *Australia Felix* was completed though not yet revised, she made a short visit to Australia to refresh her memories and to check certain details that she had written into the novel. She did not return to Australia again. After her husband's death in 1933, she moved to Sussex, where she died in 1946.

Australia had given her an understanding of the restlessness and suffering that were Mahony's destiny; Germany had widened her intellectual interests and enabled her to find her vocation; England gave her the isolation and stability she needed for writing. It is open to question whether any of the three countries between which her life was divided gave her a home. It is at least possible to speculate that the rootlessness she describes so well in Mahony, she understood with her heart as well as her mind.

*

Henry Handel Richardson began her literary career as a translator, first of J. P. Jacobsen's *Niels Lyhne* (1896) and then of Björnson's *Fiskerjenten* (1896). At the same time she produced a few critical articles on music and literature. Some time in 1906 or 1907 she began work on *Maurice Guest*. It is a compelling story of a young Englishman who comes to Leipzig to study music. His love affair with a passionate and possessive Australian girl absorbs and finally obsesses him, so that his work is destroyed, and he becomes a helpless victim of his own jealousy and fear. Richardson fills the novel with detail about the musical life of Leipzig, and the book is charged with the excitement of student days, over which the shadows of failure and despair gradually lengthen. Though it is essentially a novel about passionate love and jealousy, it also offers some comment on the distinction between genius and talent. Maurice Guest is unable to meet the demands of a musical career; and Richardson emphasizes his failure by contrasting it with the success of the brilliant but arrogant Schilsky, whose ruthless drive and selfishness win him success in music and love.

Richardson began her autobiographical novel *The Getting of Wisdom* 'partly as a relief from that book's [i.e. *Maurice Guest*] growing gloom'. By contrast it is a light novel. It relates the escapades of an adolescent girl at boarding school, but essentially, as its title suggests, it is about the difference between learning and wisdom. Laura Rambotham, Richardson's fictional version of herself, is a 'writer in the making'. As Richardson later wrote:

. . . in her small way the child came up against some of life's knottiest problems: crime and punishment; the workings of sex; passionate love. She was driven to ask herself Pilate's hoary question about truth; to put her faith to the test and find it wanting. Also, by dint of sad experience she discovered, unaided, the art and craft of realistic fiction.

Once again, as in *Maurice Guest*, though in a very different temper, Richardson is looking at the relationship between art and life. Laura Rambotham is bewildered by the apparent inconsistency of a world which demands one kind of truth from the artist, and another from real life, and which rewards the artist's lies with praise, and the ordinary person's lies with censure.

The years between *The Fortunes of Richard Mahony* and her last novel, *The Young Cosima* (1939), saw the publication of a number of short stories, most of which were collected in *The End of a Childhood* (1934). The title story in this book carries on the account of Cuffy's childhood from the point where she had left it at the end of *Ultima Thule*. In *The Young Cosima* Richardson turned to historical sources once more, this time to reconstruct the history of Wagner's relationship with Cosima Liszt and Hans von Bülow. And here again she turns to the problem of the artist, seeing in Wagner the man possessed by his genius, driven on against his will by the demands of his art. Wagner tells of his sacrifice:

Free will? There's no such thing: not for the artist. Of all living mortals he's the most unfree; stands powerless in the face of his own powers.

One cannot, of course, ascribe Wagner's views to Richardson. But *The Young Cosima* draws attention yet again to her preoccupation with the artist's role, and with the inner forces that bring a man to success, and whose absence spells artistic and personal failure.

By the time Richardson wrote *The Young Cosima*, she had exhausted the materials that her own life and experience could supply. In each of the earlier novels she had been steadily driving back into her past for the substance of her fiction. Her years in Leipzig and a youthful passion gave her the factual and emotional sources of *Maurice Guest*. In *The Getting of Wisdom* she reconstructed and shaped four years of her school life. In *The Fortunes of Richard Mahony* she journeyed back further still, into her family's past and the history of her country, and to her own earliest memories.

*

The Fortunes of Richard Mahony is without question Richardson's most important work. It covers some twenty-seven years of Mahony's life, from his arrival in Australia in 1852 to his death. In the first volume Richardson links Mahony's personal history closely to the history of the colony of Victoria, and of Ballarat in particular, in the years from 1852 to the later 1860s. The controlling force and centre of *Australia Felix* is, arguably, not the character of Mahony, but the life and history of the colony. Richardson's thorough and systematic account of the development of Ballarat from a ramshackle mining community into a provincial city is more than mere background to Mahony's personal history. Colonial life is the source of his prosperity and an important reason for his incurable dissatisfaction with whatever happens to be his present state. It is, in effect, the condition of his existence: and while Richardson makes quite explicit the weaknesses and conflicts, the ambitions and ideals, and the changing, indefinable aspirations which are at the centre of Mahony's character and personal relationships, these are not permitted to overshadow the social and environmental influences which are at work upon him. Thus Mahony, a severe critic of the feverish, grasping ambition of the goldfields, and the fecklessness and instability of the diggers, is himself as much a victim of the gambling instinct as are those he despises, and just as little able to control his conflicting passions as the most ignorant miner. In *Australia Felix* Mahony is a point of reference for the history of a period in which so many gave themselves thoughtlessly into the hands of fortune.

But when (in *The Way Home*) Mahony travels for the second time from England back to Australia, Richardson does not attempt to sustain the historical background of the narrative. Instead she concentrates on the social environment in which Mahony lives as a prosperous medical practitioner in Melbourne. He does not belong, nor aspire to, 'the stylish set' that revolved around Government House. His social life is that of the small intellectual group whose centre is Bishopscourt. Here Mahony discusses the lively intellectual issues of the day, particularly the debate between science and religion provoked by the publication of Darwin's theories.

By eliminating historical events, and concentrating upon Mahony's social contacts, Richardson narrows the range of the novel in such a way that she is able to close in on Mahony. This effect is reinforced by the chronology of the trilogy. In *Australia Felix* she covers some fifteen years of Mahony's life. The time-span for the rest of the novel is twelve years – approximately eight years for *The Way Home* and four for *Ultima Thule*. In this last volume she moves closer still to Mahony's inner life, so that gradually even the landscape becomes a subjective reflection of his state of mind. Thus, by narrowing her perspective from the broad historical view offered in *Australia Felix* to the more concentrated social context of *The Way Home* and finally to Mahony's psychological world, Richardson conveys through the design of the novel an essential part of its meaning. It is an accurate reflection of Mahony's increasing preoccupation with his mental states, and gradual separation from the historical events and environment which have shaped him.

In another way too, the structure of *The Fortunes of Richard Mahony* reflects the dilemma of the wayward man who is its centre. Looked at from one point of view, the novel is the fullest and most coherent expression in Australian fiction of the divided sensibility which is the persistent affliction of migrant populations and expatriates. At the beginning of the novel Mahony arrives in Australia as an adventurer. He affects an attitude of critical superiority to the raw society of the goldfields, and is patronizingly indulgent towards the miners' struggle for justice epitomized in the account of the Eureka Stockade. By the end of *Australia Felix* he has acquired enough wealth (as did so many of his real life contemporaries) to return 'home' after some fifteen years in exile to what he still calls 'the dear old mother-country'. Up to this point Mahony's migrant story is comparable to that of the squatters in Henry Kingsley's *The Recollections of Geoffry Hamlyn*, whose sole purpose for migrating is to make enough money out of the colony to be able to return to a comfortable existence in Devonshire.

But the next phase of Mahony's career, recorded in *The Way Home*, is a study in disillusionment. The one thing Mahony has not been able to predict is the effect upon him of his years at the end of the world. He has forgotten the simple fact that it is often harder to go back than to go on. His memories of the past do not match the present reality; England, whose greenness and tidiness he had pined for after the boundless, undefined, straggly, dry Australian landscape, seems small and cramped. After the open cheerfulness of his Australian friends (crude though he often found them) the English seem enervated by provincial snobbery, and paralysed by the pointless polite formalities of their existence. So he returns to Australia, longing, as he would never have believed possible, for the sun.

When, at this period in his life, Mahony finds himself a rich man, he again does what others of his time and since did in real life. He sets off on the grand tour of Europe. From this he is recalled to Australia by the collapse of his fortunes, this time compelled back to the adopted country to which, ironically enough, he would have returned voluntarily. By this time Mahony is already losing the battle against his environment. Though without stating it directly, Richardson makes it plain enough that Mahony has been captured by Australia, and that he is enslaved as much by his failures as by his successes. So it is that in the end the country of his exile becomes his last home and his obscure but permanent resting-place.

The geography of the novel, then, reflects the complex vacillations of Mahony's attitudes. Ambition drives him from England, and nostalgia drives him back. The next movement is from failure in England to triumphant success in Australia. His very success drives him back to Europe once more, and his final exile begins, not with ambition and hope, but with disaster and despair. From despair to total defeat is the record left by *Ultima Thule*. In meticulously depicting the divided loyalties of Mahony, reluctantly and painfully surrendering his homeland and yielding to the fatal enticements of an alien world, Richardson points to the complicated mixture of love and hatred, admiration and fear which is to be found even in the modern inheritors of Mahony's world.

The writing of *Australia Felix* was, for Richardson, a major research undertaking. She was once asked whether she considered herself to be a realist, to which she replied: 'Perhaps you might call me a "realist", if by that word you mean some one who endeavours to set down the truth as she sees it!' But her answer is not quite accurate. For she aimed both to tell the truth as she saw it, and to tell the truth as it was. So she prepared herself for the writing of *Australia Felix* by reading a collection of important histories and memoirs of Victoria and the gold-diggings in the 1850s. She noted even the smallest details of the dress, language and habits of the diggers, and collected in meticulously indexed note form far more information than she was able to use.

Writing about the methods of modern novelists in *The Experimental Novel*, Emile Zola describes at some length how a naturalistic novelist would go about writing a novel on theatrical life. He would first, argues Zola, set out with this general idea. Then he would make notes about everything relevant to the theatrical world. He would interview people, collect their stories, pictures and expressions. He would then consult documents. And after all this, he would visit the theatre himself, examine it minutely, and accumulate first-hand knowledge to support his research.

In that passage Zola might be describing Richardson's approach to the writing of *Australia Felix*. In her years in Germany she read widely in European fiction. In Jacobsen's *Niels Lyhne* she had found 'a romanticism imbued with the scientific spirit and essentially based on realism'. The scientific spirit expresses itself in her methodical and detailed descriptions of the goldfields, and even in her determination accurately to reproduce the contours of the landscape. The evidence of her diary shows that when she visited Australia in 1912, one of her aims was to check the details of her descriptions of Ballarat. For example she made the train journey from Ballarat to Melbourne that Mahony in *Australia Felix* made, and noted in her diary the precise point in the journey at which he would make the speech she had already written for him.

Of equal interest, however, is her way of using the historical material she accumulated. Sometimes it is possible to trace in the text of the novel the exact sources of her descriptions. Sometimes the exact wording of a phrase or sentence is derived from her source. This is true even of the descriptions she carried into the novel from her own diary. Her method is rather to accumulate and organize fact than to absorb and recreate it. When, for example, she gives a full description of the contents of Mahony's store in *Australia Felix*, her method recalls Balzac's patient accumulation of detail.

The effect of this practice is, of course, the creation of a world undeniably clear in its outlines, and solidly authentic. It raises, however, the difficult question of significant detail. Zola distinguished between Balzac and Flaubert on this point, seeing in the latter a 'discreet equilibrium' between descriptive detail and character. Zola's formula for the control of detail – that it should always complete or explain a character – would disallow some of the description in *The Fortunes of Richard Mahony*, perhaps particularly in *The Way Home*, where the lengthy account of Mahony's English experience, presented in considerable detail, does not seem justified by the relatively small gain in knowledge of his character. In this section there is the added difficulty that Richardson has committed herself to stock notions about English and colonial attitudes, and these are never explored in sufficient depth to expand one's view of Mahony's inner conflict. Much more effective are those passages, of which the Proem to *Australia Felix* is the most notable example, where Richardson controls the details by a point of view, thus giving them a meaning and shape without sacrifice of accuracy.

To observe the operation of Richardson's 'scientific spirit' in *The Fortunes of Richard Mahony* is to be reminded that only part of the novel is to be accounted for in this way. Though as has already been suggested, the relationship of historical and social context to Mahony's development varies within the novel as a whole, *The Fortunes of Richard Mahony* remains *his* story. It is *his* fortunes that are its subject. At the level of material facts, the trilogy progresses with chronological exactitude from beginning to end. But another order of facts is embodied in the structure of the novel, the mental facts of Mahony's progress towards insanity. The external events of the novel, accurate and realistic in themselves, are at the same time a means of projecting the internal events, and the chronology of these is not nearly so simple.

Mahony's mental chronology cuts across the actual time-scheme of the novel in *The Way Home*, which in terms of his mental journey should be called 'The Way Back'. The way home, it turns out, is the way to rejection and disillusionment, and to the discovery that the past is irrecoverable. It is a nightmare journey back into his own past. Only when Mahony arrives at the threshold of his childhood in Dublin does he realize that he has postponed his journey back for so long because he has 'a nervous aversion' from returning. He emerges from this underworld, feeling, as James Joyce did, that he was one of the living returning to the dead.

In Edinburgh where he had been a medical student his experience is the opposite. Here he is a 'shade permitted to revisit the haunts of men'. His lost youth, in the form of his successors, rebukes him with opportunities lost and hopes unfulfilled, and conscious of his deficiencies, he retreats from making contact with the eminent men of his profession. And even while Mahony pauses, ruminating on a vanished past, he is being propelled into a future which, like the past, will swallow up his hopes. At this point the forward pressure of the novel shows very clearly Mahony's indecisiveness, and his very limited capacity for self-analysis.

Yet he is not without aims or ambitions. When speculations in shares bring him wealth, he spends his money on books, and his leisure pondering current controversies, annotating 'The Book of Genesis', considering papers for the medical journal, and actively exploring spiritualism. Yet none of these activities is productive. He is constantly frustrated by his own inadequate grasp of reality. His pride makes him aspire to conditions beyond his capacity. He is a dreamer whose dreams refuse to take on definition; a romantic whose aspirations remain distant clouds.

Richardson establishes the central problems of Mahony's character by presenting a whole range of other characters whose lives impinge on his. The most important of these is, of course, his wife Mary. The course of their relationship clarifies Mahony's strengths and weaknesses, and plots his deterioration. As his character weakens, so Mary's gains in strength, until finally their roles are reversed and he ends in the kind of dependence on her that, from the beginning, he expected to be her relationship to him. Perhaps Richardson's dedication of *Ultima Thule* to Mary Mahony may be taken as acknowledging the reversal of their responsibilities. From this, Mahony's most intimate relationship, Richardson moves out to his friend of the early days, Purdy Smith, to his wife's family the Turnhams, to his Ballarat friends the Ococks, and further still to his employee in the store Hempel, and to patients and casual acquaintances such as the chemist Tangye. This large range of characters, all carefully delineated, is however marshalled to testify to Mahony's character. Each, from his different vantage point, as friend, relative or acquaintance, has something to contribute to the explication of Mahony's character. He is reflected in a number of different mirrors, carefully angled and placed.

Up to this point, where Richardson concentrates on the establishment of Richard Mahony's character by means of a number of reference points outside him, the realistic method serves her well. The sheer weight and accuracy of details of landscape, history, society, conversations, and events of daily life, create the conviction that substantial and reliable actuality is being described. Richardson has the capacity to direct her reader's sympathies, to place him firmly within the conflicts of the main characters, sometimes to be made irritated and impatient by Richard's moods, tantrums, complaints and pompousness, sometimes by Mary's obstinate common sense, taste for trivialities, and short-sighted pragmatism. These shifts in sympathy are managed without any direct intervention by the author. Richardson had learnt the lesson of European naturalism well. It had reinforced her attachment to literal fact, and to objectivity. There is truth in Nettie Palmer's statement that 'there seemed a dogged determination in her to pursue the method beyond the customary bounds' . . . and her explanation of this is compelling:

Or perhaps it would be truer to say that she was so absorbed by her own experience and had brooded so long and deeply upon it that she could hardly imagine going beyond it for materials for her art.

When she did go beyond it, in *The Young Cosima*, she found it 'a very heavy job', and the novel bears witness to her labour.

For a long time, however, Richardson did not disclose that her own experience was involved in *The Fortunes of Richard Mahony*. When Nettie Palmer visited her in London in 1935 she recorded her insistence that '*Maurice Guest* and *Mahony* are works of fiction'. When in 1940 Richardson wrote some notes on her books for the *Virginia Quarterly Review* she said that 'except for a vague memory, the only material I had to draw on was about a dozen old family letters'. It was not until she began writing her fragment of autobiography *Myself When Young* (1948) (which was cut short by her death), that she revealed that Richard Mahony was a portrait of her own father. Recent research has disclosed how closely Richardson kept to the actual chronology of Walter Richardson's life, and makes it clear that the novel is as much fictional biography as it is history. Its structure, therefore, is controlled both by the actual historical events which form its background, and by the events of Walter Lindsay Richardson's life with which they interlock. Richardson has used the facts to guide her steps through a past of which she had no first-hand knowledge. Her claim of objectivity extends to her insistence that she speaks in the novel for the generation about whom the book is written, and that it is *their* view, not her own, that the novel advances.

There are, however, difficulties in regarding the novel with quite the detachment Richardson herself demands. Even had she not confessed (again in *Myself When Young*) to the truth of her husband's assertion that in drawing the portrait of Richard Mahony 'I had drawn no other than my own', one could hardly fail to see it, together with her other novels, as the expression of certain consistent preoccupations. One key to these is the extent to which Richardson departs from the known facts in *The Getting of Wisdom* and *The Fortunes of Richard Mahony*. *The Getting of Wisdom* contained, as she herself said, 'a very fair account of my doings at school and of those I came in contact with'. By any ordinary standards Ettie Richardson was a success in the last five years of her school life. She was intelligent, and regularly carried off prizes. She excelled at tennis, and was a promising pianist and composer. In her last year at school she earned reviews in the main Melbourne papers for the performance of one of her own compositions. Yet in the novel her academic success is only glancingly (and somewhat slightingly) referred to, she is pronounced a failure in sport, and her musical achievements are not mentioned at all. The chief successes which, as a schoolgirl, Ethel Richardson scored, are omitted from her autobiographical fiction. The whole emphasis of the novel is placed upon her failure in human relationships, her sense of isolation from her fellows, and her conviction that she was considered 'odd and unaccountable'.

Similar omissions of fact support the main bias of *The Fortunes of Richard Mahony*. It seems clear from recent research that in the early 1870s, when Walter Lindsay Richardson was prosperous, and in his earlier days in Ballarat, he was an active man in certain areas of public life, and a man with a wide circle of friends. It is true that both in *Australia Felix* and *The Way Home* Richardson refers to his outside activities, and to the fact that he was in demand for his musical skills and speech-making. But these minor successes are given much less weight than his psychological difficulties, and the uneasiness with which he handles personal contacts. Similarly, Mahony's aspirations to intellectual activity are constantly frustrated. He never turns his ideas into actuality. Walter Richardson, on the other hand, did contribute to scientific journals; and the intellectual interest Mahony shows in spiritualism was, for Richardson, a real one. He was President of the Victorian Association of Progressive Spiritualists, and a contributor to its journal. So it seems that in dealing with her father's past, as with her own, Richardson has censored or considerably restricted those facts which bring her subjects into too easy a relationship with their fellows, or offer them the comforts of worldly success. She seals them within their conviction of their own uniqueness and difference from others; giving to Laura Rambotham the kind of failure which might be the beginning of the discovery of herself as a writer; and to Richard Mahony the failure which ends in total psychological and spiritual defeat.

Richardson was nowhere more explicit about her intentions in *The Fortunes of Richard Mahony* than when, in her article for the *Virginia Quarterly Review*, she wrote:

So far, all the novels about Australia that had come my way had been tales of adventure, and successful adventure: monster finds and fortunes made in the gold fields, the hair-raising exploits of bush-rangers, and so on. But there was another and very different side to the picture, and one on which, to my knowledge, no writer had yet dwelt. What of the failures, to whose lot neither fortunes nor stirring adventures fell? The misfits, who were physically and mentally incapable of adapting themselves to this strange hard new world? I knew of many such; and my plan was to tell the life-story of one of them . . .

That is not to be taken as an exact reflection of the nature of Australian fiction at the time Richardson began the trilogy. Her knowledge of the literature of her own country was slight; as late as 1930 she wrote to Nettie Palmer: '. . . am beginning to feel that I really know something of Australian writers at last – by name at least.' While it was true that there were many success stories of life in the Colony – Magwitch in *Great Expectations* typifies one kind of legend about the prospects of making a fresh start and striking wealth – the dark side of the picture was presented by such writers as Marcus Clarke, Price Warung, Henry Lawson and Barbara Baynton. In any case it is questionable whether Richardson would so readily have turned to the theme of failure had she not already explored it in *Maurice Guest* and experienced it in her own life.

For she was a very introspective writer, for all her objectivity. She traced her understanding of the destructive love so meticulously dissected in *Maurice Guest* to an adolescent passion she herself had experienced. It also has clear affinities with the passionate attachment to a school friend which casts a sombre shadow over the last section of *The Getting of Wisdom*. Her representations of jealousy and emotional deprivation have the force of actual experience, not of acquired knowledge. As such, they have a very different tone from those passages in which she describes Mahony's intellectual speculations, or even his religious gropings. Possibly because she is in these instances attempting a historical reconstruction, her writing has a cool, calculating impartiality very different in pace and temper from the tension of the prose in parts of the earlier novels; but certainly there are occasions in which Mahony's morbid sensitivity is described with an insight that can only be the result of personal suffering. In 1912 Richardson stood outside the post-office in Koroit where her father had died, and asked herself:

Why do I feel so strongly about him? An early Victorian man, with all the prejudices and limitations of his time. But I see him as a seeker, with all the higher needs in him crushed physically, dissipated mentally, dazed and confused by the ultimate demands of life. He was never once equal to it,

In *The Getting of Wisdom* Laura Rambotham too is confused, young though she is, by the demands of her fellows. One of the lessons she learns is that while lying in real life earns the contempt of one's fellows, lying in fiction is essential for their approval. Even in this light treatment of a schoolgirl's life, Richardson sets the one against the many, the 'seeker' against the 'demands of life'. Again in *Maurice Guest*, her hero's personal qualities are unequal to the demands he and the world make upon them. He fails as a musician (as Richardson herself had done) and as a lover, and finally destroys himself, yielding to the desperate remedy from which Mahony manages to pull himself back. In each of these novels Richardson draws deeply on her own inner emotional experience as well as on her knowledge, first-hand or acquired, of the external circumstance of the world she creates. In each case it is the suffering of failure, the acute isolation of the individual who cannot find comfort in his fellows, that she most powerfully conveys.

If Richard Mahony's failure were merely a matter of worldly misfortune, the naturalistic method that Richardson chiefly employs might be adequate to her purpose. But Mahony is susceptible to forces larger than himself, and it is clear from her own comments and from the epigraphs to each book of the trilogy that Richardson sees him as representative of the common fate of humanity. She sees him, as Hardy sees his characters, battling a destiny to which, in the end, he must succumb. (It is interesting to note that she admired 'intensely' Hardy's *The Dynasts*.) Hence the novel is designed, not simply in terms of the chronological progression of historical and biographical events, nor in terms of the more complex history of Mahony's inner life, but as a pattern of interlocking ironies. One's attention is drawn to this underlying pattern by the titles of the trilogy and the separate volumes. Mahony's fortunes are misfortunes, and even his prosperity is a snare for a man of his temperament. *Australia Felix*, the name Thomas Mitchell gave to the colony of Victoria in deference to its fertility, in the end is seen by Mahony as a curse, not as a blessing, and Mitchell's vision becomes Mahony's nightmare. *The Way Home* is the way to rejection and disillusionment. 'Ultima Thule', the name Mahony gives to the grand house which acknowledges his material success and at the same time assists his material failure, becomes too a sign for his own mental journey to the utmost limits of endurance. Supporting the major ironies inherent in these titles are many incidental ones. Mahony's nightmare at the end of *Ultima Thule* picks up a scene from *Australia Felix*; the conversation with Tangye in *Australia Felix* prefigures Mahony's fate, as does his angry attack on his friend Purdy as a 'crazy lunatic'. Again and again in the organization of detail such as this Richardson insists upon the inevitability of Mahony's progress towards defeat.

This aspect of the novel is given its most significant dimension, however, by the relationship between the Proem to *Australia Felix* and the last page of *Ultima Thule*. The novel opens, as it ends, with burial. The unknown digger whose grave is a mine shaft, is, to the Mahony of *Australia Felix*, one of the common herd from whom Mahony feels himself so remote. Yet he shares his fate, and like him, a grave 'indistinguishable from the common ground'. Richardson intends an ironic comparison between the men and the comparison is a just one. Mahony claims goals for himself which are not those of a materialistic society. The diggers who flocked to the Ballarat goldfields in the 1850s were, as Richardson says, driven by ambition and greed. No doubt their values helped to create those of the society that grew up around them. It was a society more notable for its pursuit of material prosperity than for its appreciation of intellectual attainment. Mahony distinguishes himself from the dominant materialistic drives of the society in which he lives. His aspirations are intellectual and imaginative. His values are intangible, and hence both difficult to define and to achieve.

In this respect there is very little point of contact between him and the unknown digger whose grave Mahony's own grave recalls. But for all his protestations Mahony himself is as addicted to materialism as are the people he despises. The diggers gamble with their lives to acquire wealth. Mahony's gambling is of a more sophisticated kind, but it too involves his own life, and the lives of his family. He is as heavily committed to a desire for prosperity and wealth, and as reckless in squandering it as any of the diggers. Indeed, the Proem as a whole establishes a connection between the feverish insecurity of life on the goldfields and Mahony's own temperamental restlessness, the effect of which is to make him a part of the world he felt to be so hostile and alien. He, too, is 'ensorcelled', and in asserting the power of the land to lead men into captivity without chains Richardson makes Mahony, individual though he is, one of the many who have no memorial in the history of Australia.

Richardson named the Proem as one of the only two places in the trilogy in which she is not speaking 'for the generation of whom the works are written'. (The other is the descriptive paragraph at the beginning of *Ultima Thule*.) It is of some significance then that this passage is rather differently constructed from those many others in *Australia Felix* in which Richardson draws heavily on source material. It is different in kind from the catalogue of the contents of Mahony's store. If the latter passage seems to have something in common with what Zola described as Balzac's 'long appraiser's enumerations', then the Proem exhibits the 'discreet equilibrium' he praises in Flaubert. The detail is accurate, and can be traced to various of the sources listed in Richardson's notebooks. But it is controlled by a strict design, and used to exemplify a point of view. It bears to the novel something of the relationship that an overture has to an opera. It establishes a particular tone, and enunciates themes which are to sound throughout the work.

It may be said then that by adapting her naturalistic method in this way, and by the ironic repetition of incidents, Richardson lends emphatic support to a notion of the inescapable destiny of Mahony, and at the same time gives him a representative role, without robbing him of his individuality. Whether she is as successful in displaying Mahony's spiritual aspirations is open to doubt. In order to depict Mahony as a 'seeker' Richardson needs to probe his intellectual life, and to enter that difficult area where a man's intellectual aspirations and spiritual doubts and hopes feed each other, and influence his emotional stability. In his moody moments, Mahony sees Mary as 'instinctively antagonistic to the imaginative and speculative sides of life'. There is truth in his accusation, as there is in the fact that were this not so, Mahony might much earlier have lost his grip on actuality, and his ability to struggle against misfortune. Richardson does not, however, really manage to enter Mahony's imaginative and speculative mental life, and give it reality. This is in part a failure of method. In a discussion of spiritualism Mahony quotes at Mary with some asperity 'Commonplace minds usually condemn everything that is beyond the scope of their understanding'. But unfortunately for the force of Mahony's argument at this point, and still more for the sense of him as a man whose 'higher needs' are crushed by the circumstances of his life, one is not always confident that his mind is superior to those he condemns.

In analysing Mahony's intellectual aspirations the reader is faced with two related problems – the quality of Mahony's thinking and the quality of his expression. Richardson stocks Mahony's mind with some of the intellectual equipment that was, in fact, current in the middle years of the nineteenth century. Her own notes on Mahony's reading include Lyell and Darwin, Huxley, Colenso, Renan and Strauss. She feeds into the novel what are virtually summaries of contemporary controversies about science and religion, and includes some of the scientific arguments that men of Mahony's time found difficult to reconcile with the orthodoxes of religious faith. The problem is, however, that these summaries are like the list of the contents of Mahony's store, and unlike the controlled and purposeful description of the goldfields with which the novel opens. Mere mention of this kind of intellectual background, and the fact that Mahony is shown from time to time reflecting on its consequences, does not in itself establish him as a man of a speculative and imaginative turn of mind. His private ponderings do not permeate the actions and occasions of his daily life. Rather he appears as a character who has been supplied by his creator with ideas which merely offer him temporary diversions, in the way that his collection of butterflies does.

Possibly as a consequence of this, the importance of Mahony's spiritual crisis, especially in the suicide scene, is diminished in relation to his financial and emotional crises. Nor does there seem any substantial ground for the strengthening of his faith, and his recognition that the world has a meaning and unity which is guaranteed by the existence of God. Mahony's scepticism has in the first instance seemed little more than an abstract possibility confined, as it were, to his hours of contemplation in his study, and not spreading outwards into his daily life. In the same way his spiritual crisis and revelation seem to have less to do with a man deeply stirred by intellectual problems, than with the more obvious, though of course no less real pressures of professional and financial anxieties leading to extreme nervous tension and physical strain. Richardson's careful diagnosis of Mahony's condition is not in question (for this, too, she made a characteristically thorough study of text books in abnormal psychology). What is in question is whether she has shown him to have that depth of intellectual life, and its accompaniment, that awareness of the complex human conditions of his life, that were necessary to her purposes.

If, in the last analysis, Mahony is to be denied the stature of a man of unusual imaginative and speculative capacity, to what can this failure be ascribed? The difficulty is no doubt partly due to Richardson's attempt to sketch in his intellectual background in summary form. This method gives the impression that the stature of a man is to be measured by the amount of knowledge he has managed to acquire, and that one measure of Mahony's frustration is his realization that he will not manage to read all the books or visit all the places he would like to acquaint himself with before his death. These frustrations are human enough, but they are not adequate reason for despair; and Richardson does not show Mahony as a man whose frustrations are more crippling than the fairly commonplace realities most people have to face.

In those scenes where Mahony tries to articulate his longings, and define his reasons for dissatisfaction with his lot, the problem is not, however, simply with the content of his mind, but the manner of his expression. Richardson does not define her notion of the 'prejudices and limitations' of a man of Mahony's time, but one limitation the novelist cannot afford to impose on a character of this kind is verbal inadequacy. Mahony's speech is characteristically pompous, stiff, and wooden, and it may be that in making it so Richardson was fulfilling her aim of allowing her characters to speak for themselves in the idiom of their time. If this is so, then one can only see it as a failure of the naturalistic method. But the evidence of the novel as a whole suggests that the problem of Mahony's language is in fact a problem of Richardson's own style, which is very uneven. Some passages of descriptive writing are well handled. Mahony's inner anxieties are often given forceful expression, especially in *Ultima Thule*, and when, in that volume, Mahony sees the actual landscape taking on almost human shapes of hostility and menace, the impact of his distorting vision is strong and compelling. (One curious fact is the very considerable difference in tone between Mahony's letters in *Ultima Thule*, and his thinking. His letters are lucid and simple, without the gaucheries and inversions which mark his train of thoughts.) But there are many passages in every section of the novel where the style is encumbered with syntactical oddities, mixed metaphors and clichés, which one cannot simply explain away as representing the idiom of Mahony's time. Nor is this simply a matter of grammatical pedantry, of finding literal errors. One of the reasons for the length of the trilogy (and this is especially true of the expansiveness of *The Way Home*) is that Richardson's style lacks penetration. A point which can be made in one sentence is often allowed to occupy several; and what follows the original statement is a series of slight variations, or near synonyms, adding bulk but not meaning.

The ponderous slowness of Mahony's reasoning, the flatness of his language and the sparse furnishing of his mind, do not allow him to appear as a man of deep spiritual perceptions or large imaginative capacity. In the important scene where he decides against suicide, he is not a man in the grip of a shattering personal crisis, who has reached into the depths of his own misery, and rediscovered his faith at the lowest point of his suffering. It is the *intention* of the scene to accomplish this, and to convey the force of Mahony's spiritual revelation; but its tone is the same as that which marks his private intellectual debates earlier in the novel. He is still the man of limited intellectual capacity grappling with not very complex ideas. He is not a character of delicate perceptions and fine insights battling spiritual despair and coming to terms with the bleakest moments of his experience. In this particular respect Richardson's achievement falls short of her intention. She has a view of Mahony which is only partly articulated in the novel, one which could perhaps not be expressed fully without some departure from the methods she has chosen, and a more powerful style than she is able to command. In the last analysis, the sense of Mahony's common humanity, upon which Richardson, through the epigraphs and the Proem, seems to be insisting, is stronger than the sense of his uniqueness.

For all his moodiness and unpredictability, his longing for change and impetuous actions to bring it about, Mahony is not a surprising character. Richardson's exhaustive treatment of him does not permit him a mystery. His inconsistencies are explicable. His character yields to explanation and does not offer the resistance of unresolvable paradoxes. Perhaps for this reason his failure is moving, but not in the end enlightening. The forces ranged against Mahony are immense – the country, its people, his temperament, his wife, his irreconcilable desires for permanence and change, his belief that ' "panta rei" is the eternal truth, "semper idem" the lie we long to see confirmed'. Against these forces Mahony cannot hope to triumph, and Richardson has demonstrated in the novel what she believed to be true of her father in real life, that the struggle was unequal. Indeed, some of the limitations in Richardson's depiction of Mahony may be explained by her adherence to the biographical facts of her father's life. Her general intention in writing the novel was, as she said, to explore the life of a man who failed in his colonial adventure. Once that intention became centred upon the figure of her own father a second motive entered the novel. Richardson's fidelity to historical fact includes fidelity to biographical fact, and it might be argued that the latter is not always advantageous to the fiction that she is creating. In *Ultima Thule* she plots accurately the last years of her father's life. This commits her to an immensely detailed account of his mental deterioration and his senile reversion to childishness. The effect is to prolong the misery of his life but not necessarily to sharpen the reader's awareness of his personal tragedy; to make his death a release, not the only possible resolution of a human conflict.

Richardson's concentration on the full explication of Mahony's progress to failure distinguishes *The Fortunes of Richard Mahony* from any Australian novel that has been written up to that time. When Richardson began work on the trilogy Australian fiction was over seventy years old. Though it is customary to begin accounts of it with *Quintus Servinton* (1830-1), the history of the Australian novel properly begins in the 1840s with Charles Rowcroft's *Tales of the Colonies*. Richardson's observation about the nature of Australian fiction was partly correct; many early novels, including *Tales of the Colonies*, were success stories. Others were full of information about the colonies, suitable for intending migrants and curious English readers. Such is William Howitt's *Tallangetta* (1857) whose object, as the author says, is 'to depict the various phases of Australian life and character more fully than could be done in my "Two Years in Victoria" '. But even the best of these early novelists were not concerned with the creation of a fictional world, but rather with the collection of information about life in the new country, strung along a loose romantic plot.

Nor were they concerned – and this generalization holds for Richardson's most distinguished predecessor Joseph Furphy – with the exploration of character. Even in Furphy's *Such is Life* (1903), densely populated though it is, character is sketched rather than examined. Richard Mahony is the first substantial character in Australian fiction. Shortly after the publication of *Ultima Thule* Richardson wrote:

. . . Interesting as the experiments are that are being made today in the novel, I never cease to believe that character-drawing is its main end and object, the conflict of personalities its drama.

She never lost sight of this belief, whatever difficulties she encountered in exercising it.

Richardson's analysis of human inadequacy, the tantalizing distance between the ideal and the achievement, and the complex web of circumstance, environment, and human frailty; her steadfast pursuit of actuality, and rejection of the comforting romantic fiction, make her one of Australia's most distinguished novelists. In *The Fortunes of Richard Mahony* she brings together knowledge of a significant period in Australian history, understanding of human weakness, and a grasp of the principles and practice of the best French, German, English and Russian writers of the nineteenth century. It is a rare combination of qualifications for the novelist, and one which had not been seen in Australian writing before. By the time *The Fortunes of Richard Mahony* was completed, fictional methods had undergone a radical transformation. The experimentalists were no longer Zola's naturalists, but Proust, Joyce and their contemporaries. Yet it is questionable whether any other approach to the historical and biographical facts of the subject Richardson chose could so well have served her purpose at the time, or made it possible for her to keep the history of a country in balance with the fate of a man. The epigraph to *Ultima Thule* '. . . and some there be which have no memorial', now takes on a meaning that Richardson can hardly have intended. For in *The Fortunes of Richard Mahony*, Mahony and the many others like him who failed, have their memorial.

LEONIE KRAMER
Professor of Australian Literature
University of Sydney

PROEM

In a shaft on the Gravel Pits, a man had been buried alive. At work in a deep wet hole, he had recklessly omitted to slab the walls of a drive; uprights and tailors yielded under the lateral pressure, and the rotten earth collapsed, bringing down the roof in its train. The digger fell forward on his face, his ribs jammed across his pick, his arms pinned to his sides, nose and mouth pressed into the sticky mud as into a mask; and over his defence-less body, with a roar that burst his ear-drums, broke stupendous masses of earth.

His mates at the windlass went staggering back from the belch of violently discharged air: it tore the wind-sail to strips, sent stones and gravel flying, loosened planks and props. Their shouts drawing no response, the younger and nimbler of the two – he was a mere boy, for all his amazing growth of beard – put his foot in the bucket and went down on the rope, kicking off the sides of the shaft with his free foot. A group of diggers, gather-ing round the pit-head, waited for the tug at the rope. It was quick in coming; and the lad was hauled to the surface. No hope: both drives had fallen in; the bottom of the shaft was blocked. The crowd melted with a 'Poor Bill – God rest his soul!' or with a silent shrug. Such accidents were not infrequent; each man might thank his stars it was not he who lay cooling down below. And so, since no more washdirt would be raised from this hole, the party that worked it made off for the nearest grog-shop, to wet their throats to the memory of the dead, and to discuss future plans.

All but one: a lean and haggard-looking man of some five and forty, who was known to his comrades as Long Jim. On hear-ing his mate's report he had sunk heavily down on a log, and there he sat, a pannikin of raw spirit in his hand, the tears cours-ing ruts down cheeks scabby with yellow mud, his eyes glassy as marbles with those that had still to fall.

He wept, not for the dead man, but for himself. This accident was the last link in a chain of ill-luck that had been forging ever since he first followed the diggings. He only needed to put his hand to a thing, and luck deserted it. In all the sinkings he had been connected with, he had not once caught his pick in a nugget or got the run of the gutter; the 'bottoms' had always proved barren, drives been exhausted without his raising the colour. At the present claim he and his mates had toiled for months, overcoming one difficulty after another. The slabbing, for instance, had cost them infinite trouble; it was roughly done, too, and, even after the pins were in, great flakes of earth would come tumbling down from between the joints, on one occasion nearly knocking silly the man who was below. Then, before they had slabbed a depth of three times nine, they had got into water, and in this they worked for the next sixty feet. They were barely rid of it, when the two adjoining claims were abandoned, and in came the flood again – this time they had to fly for their lives before it, so rapid was its rise. Not the strongest man could stand in this ice-cold water for more than three days on end – the bark slabs stank in it, too, like the skins in a tanner's yard – and they had been forced to quit work till it subsided. He and another man had gone to the hills, to hew trees for more slabs; the rest to the grog-shop. From there, when it was feasible to make a fresh start, they had to be dragged, some blind drunk, the rest blind stupid from their booze. That had been the hardest job of any: keeping the party together. They had only been eight in all – a hand-to-mouth number for a deep wet hole. Then, one had died of dysentery, contracted from working constantly in water up to his middle; another had been nabbed in a man-hunt and clapped into the 'logs'. And finally, but a day or two back, the three men who completed the night-shift had deserted for a new 'rush' to the Avoca. Now, his pal had gone, too. There was nothing left for him, Long Jim, to do, but to take his dish and turn fossicker; or even to aim no higher than washing over the tailings rejected by the fossicker.

At the thought his tears flowed anew. He cursed the day on which he had first set foot on Ballarat.

'It's 'ell for white men – 'ell, that's what it is!'

' 'Ere, 'ave another drink, matey, and fergit yer bloody troubles.'

His re-filled pannikin drained, he grew warmer round the heart; and sang the praises of his former life. He had been a lamplighter in the old country, and for many years had known no more arduous task than that of tramping round certain streets three times daily, ladder on shoulder, bitch at heel, to attend the little flames that helped to dispel the London dark. And he might have jogged on at this up to three score years and ten, had he never lent an ear to the tales that were being told of a wonderful country, where, for the mere act of stooping, and with your naked hand, you could pick up a fortune from the ground. Might the rogues who had spread these lies be damned to all eternity! Then, he had swallowed them only too willingly; and, leaving the old woman wringing her hands, had taken every farthing of his savings and set sail for Australia. That was close on three years ago. For all he knew, his wife might be dead and buried by this time; or sitting in the almshouse. She could not write, and only in the early days had an occasional newspaper reached him, on which, alongside the Queen's head, she had put the mark they had agreed on, to show that she was still alive. He would probably never see her again, but would end his days where he was. Well, they wouldn't be many; this was not a place that made old bones. And, as he sat, worked on by grief and liquor, he was seized by a desperate homesickness for the old country. Why had he ever been fool enough to leave it? He shut his eyes, and all the well-known sights and sounds of the familiar streets came back to him. He saw himself on his rounds of a winter's afternoon, when each lamp had a halo in the foggy air; heard the pit-pat of his four-footer behind him, the bump of the ladder against the prong of the lamp-post. His friend the policeman's glazed stove-pipe shone out at the corner; from the distance came the tinkle of the muffin-man's bell, the cries of the buy-a-brooms. He remembered the glowing charcoal in the stoves of the chestnut and potato sellers; the appetizing smell of the cooked-fish shops; the fragrant steam of the hot, dark coffee at the twopenny stall, when he had turned shivering out of bed; he sighed for the lights and jollity of the 'Hare and Hounds' on a Saturday night. He would never see anything of the kind again. No; here, under bare blue skies, out of which the sun frizzled you alive; here, where it couldn't rain without at once being a flood; where the very winds blew contrarily, hot from the north and bitter-chill from the south; where, no matter how great the heat by day, the night would as likely as not be nipping cold: here he was doomed to end his life, and to end it, for all the yellow sunshine, more hopelessly knotted and gnarled with rheumatism than if,

3

dawn after dawn, he had gone out in a cutting north-easter, or groped his way through the grey fog-mists sent up by grey Thames.

Thus he sat and brooded, all the hatred of the unwilling exile for the land that gives him house-room burning in his breast.

Who the man was, who now lay deep in a grave that fitted him as a glove fits the hand, careless of the pass to which he had brought his mate; who this really was, Long Jim knew no more than the rest. Young Bill had never spoken out. They had chummed together on the seventy-odd-mile tramp from Melbourne; had boiled a common billy and slept side by side in rain-soaked blankets, under the scanty hair of a she-oak. That was in the days of the first great stampede to the gold-fields, when the embryo seaports were as empty as though they were plague-ridden, and every man who had the use of his legs was on the wide bush-track, bound for the north. It was better to be two than one in this medley of bullock-teams, lorries, carts and pack-horses, of dog-teams, wheelbarrows and swagmen, where the air rang with oaths, shouts and hammering hoofs, with whip-cracking and bullock-prodding; in this hurly-burly of thieves, bushrangers and foreigners, of drunken convicts and deserting sailors, of slit-eyed Chinese and apt-handed Lascars, of expirees and ticket-of-leave men, of Jews, Turks and other infidels. Long Jim, himself stunned by it all: by the pother of landing and of finding a roof to cover him; by the ruinous price of bare necessaries; by the length of this unheard-of walk that lay before his town-bred feet: Long Jim had gladly accepted the young man's company on the road. Originally, for no more than this; at heart he distrusted Young Bill, because of his fine-gentleman airs, and intended shaking the lad off as soon as they reached the diggings. There, a man must, for safety's sake, be alone, when he stooped to pick up his fortune. But at first sight of the strange, wild scene that met his eyes he hastily changed his mind. And so the two of them had stuck together; and he had never had cause to regret it. For all his lily-white hands and finical speech Young Bill had worked like a nigger, standing by his mate through the latter's disasters; had worked till the ladyish hands were horny with warts and corns, and this, though he was doubled up with dysentery in the hot season, and racked by winter cramps. But the life had proved too hard for him, all the same. During the previous summer he had begun to drink – steadily, with the dogged persistence that was in him – and since then his work

4

had gone downhill. His sudden death had only been a hastening-on of the inevitable. Staggering home to the tent after nightfall he would have been sure, sooner or later, to fall into a dry shicer and break his neck, or into a wet one and be drowned.

On the surface of the Gravel Pits his fate was already forgotten. The rude activity of a gold-diggings in full swing had closed over the incident, swallowed it up.

Under a sky so pure and luminous that it seemed like a thinly drawn veil of blueness, which ought to have been transparent, stretched what, from a short way off, resembled a desert of pale clay. No patch of green offered rest to the eye; not a tree, hardly a stunted bush had been left standing, either on the bottom of the vast shallow basin itself, or on the several hillocks that dotted it and formed its sides. Even the most prominent of these, the Black Hill, which jutted out on the Flat like a gigantic tumulus, had been stripped of its dense timber, feverishly disembowelled, and was now become a bald protuberance strewn with gravel and clay. The whole scene had that strange, repellent ugliness that goes with breaking up and throwing into disorder what has been sanctified as final, and belongs, in particular, to the wanton disturbing of earth's gracious, green-spread crust. In the pre-golden era this wide valley, lying open to sun and wind, had been a lovely grassland, ringed by a circlet of wooded hills; beyond these, by a belt of virgin forest. A limpid river and more than one creek had meandered across its face; water was to be found there even in the driest summer. She-oaks and pepper-mints had given shade to the flocks of the early settlers; wattles had bloomed their brief delirious yellow passion against the grey-green foliage of the gums. Now, all that was left of the original 'pleasant resting-place' and its pristine beauty were the ancient volcanic cones of Warrenheip and Buninyong. These, too far off to supply wood for firing or slabbing, still stood green and timbered, and looked down upon the havoc that had been made of the fair, pastoral lands.

Seen nearer at hand, the dun-coloured desert resolved itself into uncountable pimpling clay and mud-heaps, of divers shade and varying sizes: some consisted of but a few bucketfuls of mullock, others were taller than the tallest man. There were also hundreds of rain-soaked, mud-bespattered tents, sheds and awnings; wind-sails, which fell, funnel-like, from a kind of gallows into the shafts they ventilated; flags fluttering on high posts in front of stores. The many human figures that went to and fro were hardly to be distinguished from the ground they trod. They were coated with earth, clay-clad in ochre and gamboge. Their faces were daubed with clauber; it matted great beards, and entangled the coarse hairs on chests and brawny arms. Where, here and there, a blue jumper had kept a tinge of blueness, it was so besmeared with yellow that it might have been expected to turn green. The gauze neck-veils that hung from the brims of wide-awakes or cabbage-trees were become stiff little lattices of caked clay.

There was water everywhere. From the spurs and gullies round about, the autumn rains had poured freely down on the Flat; river and creeks had been over their banks; and such narrow ground-space as remained between the thick-sown tents, the myriads of holes that abutted one on another, jealous of every inch of space, had become a trough of mud. Water meandered over this mud, or carved its soft way in channels; it lay about in puddles, thick and dark as coffee-grounds; it filled abandoned shallow holes to the brim.

From this scene rose a blurred hum of sound; rose and as it were remained stationary above it — like a smoke-cloud, which no wind comes to drive away. Gradually, though, the ear made out, in the conglomerate of noise, a host of separate noises infinitely multiplied: the sharp tick-tick of surface-picks, the dull thud of shovels, their muffled echoes from the depths below. There was also the continuous squeak and groan of windlasses; the bump of the mullock emptied from the bucket; the trundle of wheelbarrows, pushed along a plank from the shaft's mouth to the nearest pool; the dump of the dart on the heap for washing. Along the banks of a creek, hundreds of cradles rattled and grated; the noise of the spades, chopping the gravel into the puddling-tubs or the Long Toms, was like the scrunch of shingle under waves. The fierce yelping of the dogs chained to the flag-posts of stores, mongrels which yapped at friend and foe alike, supplied a note of earsplitting discord.

But except for this it was a wholly mechanical din. Human brains directed operations, human hands carried them out, but the sound of the human voice was, for the most part, lacking. The diggers were a sombre, preoccupied race, little given to lip-work. Even the 'shepherds', who, in waiting to see if their neighbours struck the lead, beguiled the time with euchre and 'lamb-skinnet', played moodily, their mouths glued to their pipe-stems; they were tail-on-end to fling down the cards for pick and shovel.

The great majority, ant-like in their indefatigable busyness, neither turned a head nor looked up: backs were bent, eyes fixed, in a hard scrutiny of cradle or tin-dish: it was the earth that held them, the familiar, homely earth, whose common fate it is to be trodden heedlessly underfoot. Here, it was the load-stone that drew all men's thoughts. And it took toll of their bodies in odd, exhausting forms of labour, which were swift to weed out the unfit.

The men at the windlasses spat into their horny palms and bent to the crank: they paused only to pass the back of a hand over a sweaty forehead, or to drain a nose between two fingers. The barrow-drivers shoved their loads, the bones of their fore-arms standing out like ribs. Beside the pools, the puddlers chop-ped with their shovels; some even stood in the tubs, and worked the earth with their feet, as wine-pressers trample grapes. The cradlers, eternally rocking with one hand, held a long stick in the other with which to break up any clods a careless puddler might have deposited in the hopper. Behind these came the great army of fossickers, washers of surface-dirt, equipped with knives and tin-dishes, and content if they could wash out half-a-penny-weight to the dish. At their heels still others, who treated the tailings they threw away. And among these last was a sprinkling of women, more than one with an infant sucking at her breast. Withdrawn into a group for themselves worked a body of Chinese, in loose blue blouses, flappy blue leg-bags and huge conical straw hats. They, too, fossicked and re-washed, using extravagant quantities of water.

Thus the pale-eyed multitude worried the surface, and, at the risk and cost of their lives, probed the depths. Now that deep sinking was in vogue, gold-digging no longer served as a play-game for the gentleman and the amateur; the greater number of those who toiled at it were work-tried, seasoned men. And yet, although it had now sunk to the level of any other arduous and uncertain occupation, and the magic prizes of the early days were seldom found, something of the old, romantic glamour still clung to this most famous gold-field, dazzling the eyes and con-founding the judgement. Elsewhere, the horse was in use at the puddling-trough, and machines for crushing quartz were under discussion. But the Ballarat digger resisted the introduction of machinery, fearing the capitalist machinery would bring in its train. He remained the dreamer, the jealous individualist; he hovered for ever on the brink of a stupendous discovery.

This dream it was, of vast wealth got without exertion, which had decoyed the strange, motley crowd, in which peers and churchmen rubbed shoulders with the scum of Norfolk Island, to exile in this outlandish region. And the intention of all alike had been: to snatch a golden fortune from the earth and then, hey, presto! for the old world again. But they were reckoning without their host: only too many of those who entered the country went out no more. They became prisoners to the soil. The fabulous riches of which they had heard tell amounted, at best, to a few thousands of pounds: what folly to depart with so little, when mother earth still teemed! Those who drew blanks nursed an unquenchable hope, and laboured all their days like navvies, for a navvy's wage. Others again, broken in health or disheartened, could only turn to an easier handiwork. There were also men who, as soon as fortune smiled on them, dropped their tools and ran to squander the work of months in a wild debauch; and they invariably returned, tail down, to prove their luck anew. And, yet again, there were those who, having once seen the metal in the raw: in dust, fine as that brushed from a butterfly's wings; in heavy, chubby nuggets; or, more exquisite still, as the daffodil-yellow veining of bluish-white quartz: these were gripped in the subtlest way of all. A passion for the gold itself awoke in them an almost sensual craving to touch and possess; and the glitter of a few specks at the bottom of pan or cradle came, in time, to mean more to them than 'home', or wife, or child.

Such were the fates of those who succumbed to the 'unholy hunger'. It was like a form of revenge taken on them, for their loveless schemes of robbing and fleeing; a revenge contrived by the ancient, barbaric country they had so lightly invaded. Now, she held them captive – without chains; ensorcelled – without witchcraft; and, lying stretched like some primeval monster in the sun, her breasts freely bared, she watched, with a malignant eye, the efforts made by these puny mortals to tear their lips away.

PART ONE

CHAPTER ONE

On the summit of one of the clay heaps, a woman shot into silhouette against the sky. An odd figure, clad in a skimpy green petticoat, with a scarlet shawl held about her shoulders, wisps of frowsy red hair standing out round her head, she balanced herself on the slippery earth, spinning her arm like the vane of a windmill, and crying at the top of her voice: 'Joe, boys! – Joe, Joe, Joey!'

It was as if, with these words, she had dropped a live shell in the diggers' midst. A general stampede ensued; in which the cry was caught up, echoed and re-echoed, till the whole Flat rang with the name of 'Joe'. Tools were dropped, cradles and tubs abandoned, windlasses left to kick their cranks backwards. Many of the workers took to their heels; others, in affright, scuttled aimlessly hither and thither, like barnyard fowls in a panic. Summoned by shouts of: 'Up with you, boys! – the traps are here!' numbers ascended from below to see the fun, while as many went hurriedly down to hiding in drive or chamber. Even those diggers who could pat the pocket in which their licence lay ceased work, and stood about with sullen faces to view the course of events. Only the group of Chinamen washing tail-heaps remained unmoved. One of them, to whom the warning woman belonged, raised his head and called a Chinese word at her; she obeyed it instantly, vanished into thin air; the rest went impassively on with their fossicking. They were not such fools as to try to cheat the Government of its righteous dues. None but had his licence safely folded in his nosecloth, and thrust inside the bosom of his blouse.

Through the labyrinth of tents and mounds, a gold-laced cap could be seen approaching; then a gold-tressed jacket came into view, the white star on the forehead of a mare. Behind the Commissioner, who rode down thus from the Camp, came the members of his staff; these again were followed by a body of mounted troopers. They drew rein on the slope, and simultaneously a line of foot police, backed by a detachment of light infantry, shot out like an arm, and walled in the Flat to the south.

On the appearance of the enemy the babel redoubled. There were groans and cat-calls. Along with the derisive 'Joeys!' the rebel diggers hurled any term of abuse that came to their lips.

'The dolly mops! The skunks! The bushrangers! – Oh, damn 'em, damn 'em! . . . damn their bloody eyes!'

'It's Rooshia – that's what it is!' said an oldish man darkly.

The Commissioner, a horse-faced, solemn man with brown side whiskers, let the reins droop on his mare's neck and sat unwinking in the tumult. His mien was copied by his staff. Only one of them, a very young boy who was new to the colony and his post, changed colour under his gaudy cap, went from white to pink and from pink to white again; while at each fresh insult he gave a perceptible start, and gazed dumbfounded at his chief's insensitive back.

The 'bloodhounds' had begun to track their prey. Rounding up, with a skill born of long practice, they drove the diggers before them towards the centre of the Flat. Here they passed from group to group and from hole to hole, calling for the production of licences with an insolence that made its object see red. They were nice of scent, too, and, nine times in ten, pounced on just those unfortunates who, through carelessness, or lack of means, or on political grounds, had failed to take out the month's licence to dig for gold. Every few minutes one or another was marched off between two constables to the Government Camp, for fine or imprisonment.

Now it was that it suddenly entered Long Jim's head to cut and run. Up till now he had stood declaring himself a free-born Briton, who might be drawn and quartered if he ever again paid the blasted tax. But, as the police came closer, a spear of fright pierced his befuddled brain, and inside a breath he was off and away. Had the abruptness of his start not given him a slight advantage, he would have been caught at once. As it was, the chase would not be a long one; the clumsy, stiff-jointed man slithered here and stuck fast there, dodging obstacles with an awkwardness that was painful to see. He could be heard sobbing and cursing as he ran.

At this point the Commissioner, half turning, signed to the troopers in his rear. Six or seven of them shook up their bridles

10

and rode off, their scabbards clinking, to prevent the fugitive's escape.

A howl of contempt went up from the crowd. The pink and white subaltern made what was almost a movement of the arm to intercept his superior's command.

It was too much for Long Jim's last mate, the youthful black-beard who had pluckily descended the shaft after the accident. He had been standing on a mound with a posse of others, following the man-hunt. At his partner's crack-brained dash for the open, his snorts of indignation found words. 'Gaw-blimy! . . . is the old fool gone dotty?' Then he drew a whistling breath. 'No, it's more than flesh and blood. . . . Stand back, boys!' And though he was as little burdened with a licence as the man under pursuit, he shouted: 'Help, help! . . . for God's sake, don't let 'em have me!' shot down the slope, and was off like the wind.

His foxly object was attained. The attention of the hunters was diverted. Long Jim, seizing the moment, vanished underground.

The younger man ran with the lightness of a hare. He had also the hare's address in doubling and turning. His pursuers never knew, did he pass from sight behind a covert of tents and mounds, where he would bob up next. He avoided shafts and pools as if by a miracle; ran along greasy planks without a slip; and, where these had been removed to balk the police, he jumped the holes, taking risks that were not for a sane man. Once he fell, but, enslimed from head to foot, wringing wet and hatless, was up again in a twinkling. His enemies were less sure-footed than he, and times without number measured their length on the oily ground. Still, one of them was gaining rapidly on him, a giant of a fellow with long thin legs; and soon the constable's foot filled the prints left by the young man's, while these were still warm. It was a fine run. The diggers trooped after in a body; the Flat rang with cheers and plaudits. Even the Commissioner and his retinue trotted in the same direction. Eventually the runaway must land in the arms of the mounted police.

But this was not his plan. Making as though he headed for the open, he suddenly dashed off at right angles, and, with a final sprint, brought up dead against a log-and-canvas store which stood on rising ground. His adversary was so close behind that a collision resulted; the digger's feet slid from under him, he fell on his face, the other on top. In their fall they struck a huge pillar of tin-dishes, ingeniously built up to the height of the store

11

itself. This toppled over with a crash, and the dishes went rolling down the slope between the legs of the police. The dog chained to the flagstaff all but strangled himself in his rage and excitement; and the owner of the store came running out.

'Purdy! . . . you? What in the name of . . .?'

The digger adroitly rolled his captor over, and there they both sat, side by side on the ground, one gripping the other's collar, both too blown to speak. A cordon of puffing constables hemmed them in.

The storekeeper frowned. 'You've no licence, you young beggar!'

And: 'Your licence, you scoundrel!' demanded the leader of the troop.

The prisoner's rejoinder was a saucy: 'Now then, out with the cuffs, Joe!'

He got on his feet as bidden; but awkwardly, for it appeared that in falling he had hurt his ankle. Behind the police were massed the diggers. These opened a narrow alley for the Camp officials to ride through, but their attitude was hostile, and there were cries of: 'Leave 'im go, yer blackguards! . . . after sich a run! None o' yer bloody quod for 'im!' along with other more threatening expressions. Sombre and taciturn, the Commissioner waved his hand. 'Take him away!'

'Well, so long, Dick!' said the culprit jauntily; and, as he offered his wrists to be handcuffed, he whistled an air.

Here the storekeeper hurriedly interposed: 'No, stop! I'll give bail.' And darting into the tent and out again, he counted five one-pound notes into the constable's palm. The lad's collar was released; and a murmur of satisfaction mounted from the crowd.

At the sound the giver made as if to retire. Then, yielding to a second thought, he stepped forward and saluted the Commissioner. 'A young hot-head, sir! He means no harm. I'll send him up in the morning, to apologize.'

('I'll be damned if you do!' muttered the digger between his teeth.)

But the Chief refused to be placated. 'Good day, doctor,' he said shortly, and with his staff at heel trotted down the slope, followed till out of earshot by a mocking fire of 'Joes'. Lingering in the rear, the youthful sympathizer turned in his saddle and waved his cap.

The raid was over for that day. The crowd dispersed; its members became orderly, hard-working men once more. The storekeeper hushed his frantic dog, and called his assistant to rebuild the pillar of tins.

The young digger sat down on the log that served for a bench, and examined his foot. He pulled and pulled, causing himself great pain, but could not get his boot off. At last, looking back over his shoulder he cried impatiently: 'Dick! . . . I say, Dick Mahony! Give us a drink, old boy! . . . I'm dead-beat.'

At this the storekeeper – a tall, slenderly built man of some seven or eight and twenty – appeared, bearing a jug and a pannikin.

'Oh, bah!' said the lad, when he found that the jug held only water. And, on his friend reminding him that he might by now have been sitting in the lock-up, he laughed and winked. 'I knew you'd go bail.'

'Well! . . . of all the confounded impudence. . . .'

'Faith, Dick, and d'ye think I didn't see how your hand itched for your pocket?'

The man he called Mahony flushed above his fair beard. It was true: he had made an involuntary movement of the hand – checked for the rest halfway, by the knowledge that the pocket was empty. He looked displeased and said nothing.

'Don't be afraid, I'll pay you back soon's ever me ship comes home,' went on the young scapegrace, who very well knew how to play his cards. At his companion's heated disclaimer, however, he changed his tone. 'I say, Dick, have a look at my foot, will you? I can't get this damned boot off.'

The elder man bent over the injury. He ceased to show displeasure. 'Purdy, you young fool, when will you learn wisdom?'

'Well, they shouldn't hunt old women, then – the swine!' gave back Purdy; and told his tale. 'Oh, lor! there go six canaries.' For, at his wincing and shrinking, his friend had taken a penknife and ripped up the jackboot. Now, practised hands explored the swollen, discoloured ankle.

When it had been washed and bandaged, its owner stretched himself on the ground, his head in the shade of a barrel, and went to sleep.

He slept till sundown, through all the traffic of a busy afternoon.

Some half-a-hundred customers came and went. The greater number of them were earth-stained diggers, who ran up for, it might be, a missing tool, or a hide bucket, or a coil of rope. They spat jets of tobacco-juice, were richly profane, paid, where coin

13

was scarce, in gold-dust from a match-box, and hurried back to work. But there also came old harridans – as often as not, diggers themselves – whose language outdid that of the males, and dirty Irish mothers; besides a couple of the white women, who inhabited the Chinese quarter. One of these was in liquor, and a great hullabaloo took place before she could be got rid of. Put out, she stood in front of the tent, her hair hanging down her back, cursing and reviling. Respectable women as well did an afternoon's shopping there. In no haste to be gone, they sat about on empty boxes or upturned barrels exchanging confidences, while weary children plucked at their skirts. A party of youngsters entered, the tallest of whom could just see over the counter, and called for shandygaffs. The assistant was for chasing them off, with hard words. But the storekeeper put, instead, a stick of barley-sugar into each dirty, outstretched hand, and the imps retired well content. On their heels came a digger and his lady-love to choose a wedding-outfit; and all the gaudy finery the store held was displayed before them. A red velvet dress flounced with satin, a pink gauze bonnet, white satin shoes and white silk stockings met their fancy. The dewy-lipped, smutty-lashed Irish girl blushed and dimpled, in consulting with the shopman upon the stays in which to lace her ample figure; the digger, whose very pores oozed gold, planked down handfuls of dust and nuggets, and brushed aside a neat Paisley shawl for one of yellow satin, the fellow to which he swore to having seen on the back of the Governor's lady herself. He showered brandy-snaps on the children, and bought a polka-jacket for a shabby old woman. Then, producing a bottle of champagne from a sack he bore, he called on those present to give him, after: ' 'Er most Gracious little Majesty, God bless 'er!' the: ' 'Oly estate of materimony!' The empty bottle smashed for luck, the couple departed arm-in-arm, carrying their purchases in the sack; and the rest of the company trooped to the door with them, to wish them joy.

Within the narrow confines of the tent, where red-herrings trailed over moleskin-shorts, and East India pickles and Hessian boots lay on the top of sugar and mess-pork; where cheeses rubbed shoulders with tallow candles, blue and red serge shirts, and captain's biscuits; where onions, and guernseys, and sardines, fine combs, cigars and bear's-grease, Windsor soap, tinned coffee and hair oil, revolvers, shovels and Oxford shoes, lay in one grand miscellany: within the crowded store, as the afternoon wore on, the air grew rank and oppressive. Precisely at six o'clock the bar was let down across the door, and the store-keeper withdrew to his living-room at the back of the tent. Here he changed his coat and meticulously washed his hands, to which clung a subtle blend of all the strong-smelling goods that had passed through them. Then, coming round to the front, he sat down on the log and took out his pipe. He made a point, no matter how brisk trade was, of not keeping open after dark. His evenings were his own.

He sat and puffed, tranquilly. It was a fine night. The first showy splendour of sunset had passed; but the upper sky was still aflush with colour. And in the centre of this frail cloud, which faded as he watched it, swam a single star.

CHAPTER TWO

With the passing of a cooler air the sleeper wakened and rubbed
his eyes. Letting his injured leg lie undisturbed, he drew up the
other knee and buckled his hands round it. In this position he
sat and talked.

He was a dark, fresh-coloured young man, of middle height,
and broadly built. He had large white teeth of a kind to crack
nuts with, and the full, wide, flexible mouth that denotes the
generous talker.

'What a wind-bag it is, to be sure!' thought his companion, as
he smoked and listened, in a gently ironic silence, to abuse of the
Government. He knew — or thought he knew — young Purdy inside out.

But behind all the froth of the boy's talk there lurked, it
seemed, a purpose. No sooner was a meal of cold chop and tea
over than Purdy declared his intention of being present at a
meeting of malcontent diggers. Nor would he even wait to wash
himself clean of mud.

His friend reluctantly agreed to lend him an arm. But he
could not refrain from taking the lad to task for getting entangled in the political imbroglio. 'When, as you know, it's
just a kind of sport to you.'

Purdy sulked for a few paces, then burst out: 'If only you
weren't so damned detached, Dick Mahony!'

'You're restless, and want excitement, my boy — that's the root
of the trouble.'

'Well, I'm jiggered! If ever I knew a restless mortal, it's yourself.'

The two men picked their steps across the Flat and up the
opposite hillside, young Purdy Smith limping and leaning heavy,
his lame foot thrust into an old slipper. He was at all times hail-
fellow-well-met with the world. Now, in addition, his plucky
exploit of the afternoon blazed its way through the settlement;

16

and blarney and bravos rained upon him. 'Golly for you, Purdy, old 'oss!' 'Showed 'em the diggers' flag, 'e did!' 'What'll you take, me buck? Come on in for a drop o' the real strip-me-down-naked!' Even a weary old strumpet, propping herself against the doorway of a dancing-saloon, waved a tipsy hand and cried: 'Arrah, an' is it yerself, Purrdy, me bhoy? Shure an' it's bussin' ye I'd be afther — if me legs would carry me!' And Purdy laughed, and relished the honey, and had an answer pat for everybody — especially the women. His companion on the other hand was greeted with a glibness that had something perfunctory in it, and no touch of familiarity.

The big canvas tent on Bakery Hill, where the meeting was to be held, was already lighted; and at the tinkle of a bell the diggers, who till then had stood cracking and hobnobbing outside, began to push for the entrance. The bulk of them belonged to the race that is quickest to resent injustice — were Irish. After them in number came the Germans, swaggering and voluble; and the inflammable French, English, Scotch and Americans formed a smaller and cooler, but very dogged group.

At the end of the tent a rough platform had been erected, on which stood a row of cane seats. In the body of the hall, the benches were formed of boards, laid from one upturned keg or tub to another. The chair was taken by a local auctioneer, a cadaverous-looking man, with never a twinkle in his eye, who, in a lengthy discourse and with the single monotonous gesture of beating the palm of one hand with the back of the other, strove to bring home to his audience the degradation of their present political status. The diggers chewed and spat, and listened to his periods with sang-froid: the shame of their state did not greatly move them. They followed, too, with composure, the rehearsal of their general grievances. As they were aware, said the speaker, the Legislative Council of Victoria was made up largely of Crown nominees; in the election of members the gold-seeking population had no voice whatsoever. This was a scandalous thing; for the digging constituent outnumbered all the rest of the population put together, thus forming what he would call the backbone and mainstay of the colony. The labour of *their* hands had raised the colony to its present pitch of prosperity. And yet these same bold and hardy pioneers were held incapable of deciding jot or tittle in the public affairs of their adopted home. Still unmoved, the diggers listened to this recital of their virtues. But when one man, growing weary of the speaker's unctuous wordiness, discharged a fierce: 'Why the hell don't yer git on to the bloody licence-tax?' the audience was fire and flame in an instant. A riotous noise ensued; rough throats rang changes on the question. Order restored, it was evident that the speech was over. Thrown violently out of his concept, the auctioneer struck and struck at his palm – in vain; nothing would come. So, making the best of a bad job, he irately sat down in favour of his successor on the programme.

This speaker did not fare much better. The assemblage, roused now, jolly and merciless, was not disposed to give quarter; and his obtuseness in dawdling over such high-flown notions as that population, not property, formed the basis of representative government, reaped him a harvest of boos and groans. This was not what the diggers had come out to hear. And they were as direct as children in their demand for the gist of the matter.

'A reg-lar ol' shicer!' was the unanimous opinion, expressed without scruple. While from the back of the hall came the curt request to him to shut his 'tater-trap'.

Next on the list was a German, a ruddy-faced man with mutton-chop whiskers and prominent, watery eyes. He could not manage the letter 'r'. In the body of a word where it was negligible, he rolled it out as though it stood three deep. Did he tackle it as an initial, on the other hand, his tongue seemed to cleave to his palate, and to yield only an 'l'. This quaint defect caused some merriment at the start, but was soon eclipsed by a more striking oddity. The speaker had the habit of, as it were, creaking with his nose. After each few sentences he paused, to give himself time to produce something between a creak and a snore – an abortive attempt to get at a mucus that was plainly out of reach.

The diggers were beside themselves with mirth.

' 'E's forgot 'is 'ankey!'

' 'Ere, boys, look slippy! – a 'ankey for ol' sausage!'

But the German was not sensitive to ridicule. He had something to say, and he was there to say it. Fixing his fish-like eyes on a spot high up the tent wall, he kept them pinned to it, while he mouthed out blood-and-thunder invectives. He was, it seemed, a red-hot revolutionist; a fierce denouncer of British rule. He declared the British monarchy to be an effete institution; the fetish of British freedom to have been 'exploded' long ago. What they needed, in this grand young country of theirs, was a 'republic'; they must rid themselves of those shackles that had been forged in the days when men were slaves. It was his sound conviction that before many weeks had passed, the Union Jack would have been hauled down for ever, and the glorious Southern Cross would wave in its stead, over a free Australia. The day on which this happened would be a never-to-be-forgotten date in the annals of the country. For what, he would like to know, had the British flag ever done for freedom, at any time in the world's history? They should read in their school-books, and there they would learn that wherever a people had risen against their tyrants, the Union Jack had waved, not over them, but over the British troops sent to stamp the rising out.

This was more than Mahony could stomach. Flashing up from his seat, he strove to assert himself above the hum of agreement that mounted from the foreign contingent, and the doubtful sort of grumble by which the Britisher signifies his disapproval.

'Mr Chairman! Gentlemen!' he cried in a loud voice. 'I call upon those loyal subjects of her Majesty who are present here, to join with me in giving three cheers for the British flag. Hip, hip, hurrah! And, again, hip, hip, hurrah! And, once more, hip, hip, hurrah!'

His compatriots followed him, though flabbily; and he continued to make himself heard above the shouts of 'Order!' and the bimming of the chairman's bell.

'Mr Chairman! I appeal to you. Are we Britons to sit still and hear our country's flag reviled? – that flag which has ensured us the very liberty we are enjoying this evening. The gentleman who has been pleased to slander it is not, I believe, a British citizen. Now, I put it to him: is there another country on the face of the earth, that would allow people of all nations to flock into a gold-bearing colony on terms of perfect equality with its own subjects? – to flock in, take all they can get, and then make off with it?' a point of view that elicited forcible grunts of assent, which held their own against hoots and hisses. Unfortunately the speaker did not stop here, but went on: 'Gentlemen! Do not, I implore you, allow yourselves to be led astray by a handful of ungrateful foreigners, who have received nothing but benefits from our Crown. What you need, gentlemen, is not revolution, but reform; not strife and bloodshed, but a liberty consistent with law and order. And this, gentlemen, –'

('You'll never get 'em like that, Dick,' muttered Purdy.)

'Not so much gentlemening, if *you* please!' said a sinister-

19

looking man, who might have been a Vandemonian in his day. '*Men's* what we are – that's good enough for us.'

Mahony was nettled. The foreigners, too, were pressing him.

'Am I then to believe, sir, what I frequently hear asserted, that there are no gentlemen left on the diggings?'

('Oh lor, Dick!' said Purdy. He was sitting with his elbows on his knees, clutching his cheeks as though he had the toothache.)

'Oh, stow yer blatherskite!'

'Believe what yer bloody well like!' retorted the Vandemonian fiercely. 'But don't come 'ere and interrupt our pleasant and h'orderly meetings with *your* blamed jaw.'

Mahony lost his temper. 'I not interrupt? – when I see you great hulks of men –'

('Oh, lor!' groaned Purdy again.)

'– who call yourselves British subjects, letting yourselves be led by the nose, like the sheep you are, by a pack of foreigners who are basely accepting this country's hospital'ty?'

'Here, let me,' said Purdy. And pushing his way along the bench he hobbled to the platform, where several arms hoisted him up.

There he stood, fronting the violent commotion that had ensued on his friend's last words; stood bedraggled, mud-stained, bandaged, his cabbage-tree hat in his hand. And Mahony, still on his feet, angrily erect, thought he understood why the boy had refused to wash himself clean, or to change his dress: he had no doubt foreseen the possibility of some such dramatic appearance.

Purdy waited for the hubbub to die down. As if by chance he had rested his hand on the bell; its provoking tinkle ceased. Now he broke into one of the frank and hearty smiles that never fail to conciliate.

'Brother diggers!'

The strongly spoken words induced an abrupt lull. The audience turned to him, still thorny and sulky it was true, but yet they turned; and one among them demanded a hearing for the youngster.

'Brother diggers! We are met here tonight with a single purpose in view. Brother diggers! We are not met here to throw mud at our dear old country's flag! Nor will we have a word said against her most gracious Majesty, the Queen. Not us! We're men first, whose business it is to stand up for a gallant little woman, and diggers with a grievance afterwards. Are you with me, boys? – Very well, then. – Now we didn't come here tonight to confab about getting votes, or having a hand in public affairs – much as we want 'em both and mean to have 'em, when the time comes. No, tonight there's only one thing that matters to us, and that's the repeal of the accursed tax!' Here, such a tempest of applause broke out that he was unable to proceed. 'Yes, I say it again,' he went on, when they would let him speak; 'the instant repeal! When that's been done, this curse taken off us, then it'll be time enough to parlez-vous about the colour of the flag we mean to have, and about going shares in the Government. But let me make one thing clear to you. We're neither traitors to the Crown, nor common rebels. We're true-blue Britons, who have been goaded to rebellion by one of the vilest pieces of tyranny that ever saw the light. Spies and informers are everywhere about us. Mr Commissioner Sleuth and his hounds may cry tally-ho every day, if 'tis their pleasure to! To put it shortly, boys, we're living under semi-martial law. To such a state have we free-born men, men who came out but to see the elephant, been reduced, by the asinine stupidity of the Government, by the impudence and knavishness of its officials. Brother diggers! When you leave the hall this evening, look over at the hill on which the Camp stands! What will you see? You will see a blaze of light, and hear the sounds of revelry by night. There, boys, hidden from our mortal view, but visible to our mind's eye, sit Charley Joe's minions, carousing at our expense, washing down each mouthful with good fizz bought with our hard-earned gold. Licence-pickings, boys, and tips from new grog-shops, and the blasted farce of the Commissariat! We're supposed –'

But here Mahony gave a loud click of the tongue – in the general howl of execration it passed unheard – and, pushing his way out of the tent, let the flap-door fall to behind him.

CHAPTER THREE

He retraced his steps by the safe-conduct of a full moon, which showed up the gaping black mouths of circular shafts and silvered the water that flooded abandoned oblong holes to their brim. Tents and huts stood white and forsaken in the moonlight: their owners were either gathered on Bakery Hill, or had repaired to one of the gambling and dancing saloons that lined the main street. Arrived at the store he set his frantic dog free, and putting a match to his pipe, began to stroll up and down.

He felt annoyed with himself for having helped to swell the crowd of malcontents; and still more for his foolishness in giving the rein to a momentary irritation. As if it mattered a doit what trash these foreigners talked! No thinking person took their bombast seriously; the authorities, with great good sense, let it pass for what it was — a noisy blowing-off of steam. At heart, the diggers were as sound as good pippins.

A graver consideration was Purdy's growing fellowship with the rebel faction. The boy was too young and still too much of a fly-by-night to have a black mark set against his name. It would be the more absurd, considering that his sincerity in espousing the diggers' cause was far from proved. He was of a nature to ride tantivy into anything that promised excitement or adventure. With, it must regretfully be admitted, an increasing relish for the limelight, for theatrical effect — see the cunning with which he had made capital out of a bandaged ankle and dirty dress! At this rate, and with his engaging ways, he would soon stand for a little god to the rough, artless crowd. No, he must leave the diggings — and Mahony rolled various schemes in his mind. He had it! In the course of the next week or two business would make a journey to Melbourne imperative. Well, he would damn the extra expense and take the boy along with him! Purdy was at a loose end, and would no doubt rise like a fish to a fly at the chance of getting to town free of cost. After all, why be hard

22

on him? He was not much over twenty, and, at that age, it was natural enough – especially in a place like this – for a lad to flit like a butterfly from every cup that took his restless fancy.

Restless? . . . h'm! It was the word Purdy had flung back at him, earlier in the evening. At the time, he had rebutted the charge, with a glance at fifteen months spent behind the counter of a store. But there was a modicum of truth in it, none the less. The life one led out here was not calculated to tone down any innate restlessness of temperament: on the contrary, it directly hindered one from becoming fixed and settled. It was on a par with the houses you lived in – these flimsy tents and draught-riddled cabins you put up with, 'for the time being' – was just as much of a makeshift affair as they. Its keynote was change. Fortunes were made, and lost, and made again, before you could say Jack Robinson; whole townships shot up over-night, to be deserted the moment the soil ceased to yield; the people you knew were here today, and gone – sold up, burnt out, or dead and buried – tomorrow. And so, whether you would or not, your whole outlook became attuned to the general unrest; you lived in a constant anticipation of what was coming next. Well, he could own to the weakness with more justification than most. If trade continued to prosper with him as it did at present, it would be no time before he could sell out and joyfully depart for the old country.

In the meantime, why complain? He had much to be thankful for. To take only a small point: was this not Saturday night? Tomorrow the store was closed, and a string of congenial occupations offered: from chopping the week's wood – a clean and wholesome task, which he gladly performed – through the pages of an engrossing book to a botanical ramble round old Bunin-yong. The thought of it cheered him. He stooped to caress his two cats, which had come out to bear him the mute and pleasant company of their kind.

What a night! The great round silver moon floated serenely through space, dimming the stars as it made them, and bathing the earth in splendour. It was so light that straight black lines of smoke could be seen mounting from chimneys and open-air fires. The grass-trees which supplied the fuel for these fires spread a pleasant balsamic odour, and the live red patches contrasted oddly with the pale ardour of the moon. Lights twinkled over all the township, but were brightest in Main Street, the course of which they followed like a rope of fireflies, and at the

23

Government Camp on the steep western slope, where no doubt, as young Purdy had impudently averred, the officials still sat over the dinner-table. It was very quiet — no grog-shops or saloons-of-entertainment in this neighbourhood, thank goodness! — and the hour was still too early for drunken roisterers to come reeling home. The only sound to be heard was that of a man's voice singing *Oft in the Stilly Night*, to the yetching accompaniment of a concertina. Mahony hummed the tune.

But it was growing cold, as the nights were apt to do on this tableland once summer was past. He whistled his dog, and Pompey hurried out with a guilty air from the back of the house, where the old shaft stood that served to hold refuse. Mahony put him on the chain, and was just about to turn in when two figures rounded the corner of a tent and came towards him, pushing their shadows before them on the milk-white ground.

' 'D evenin', doc.,' said the shorter of the two, a nuggety little man who carried his arms curved out from his sides, gorilla-fashion.

'Oh, good evening, Mr Ocock,' said Mahony, recognizing a neighbour. — 'Why, Tom, that you? Back already, my boy?' — this to a loutish, loose-limbed lad who followed behind. — 'You don't of course come from the meeting?'

'Not me, indeed!' gave back his visitor with gall, and turned his head to spit the juice from a plug. 'I've got suthin' better to do as to listen to a pack o' jabberin' furriners settin' one another by th'ears.'

'Nor you, Tom?' Mahony asked the lad, who stood sheepishly shifting his weight from one leg to the other.

'Nay, nor 'im eether,' jumped in his father, before he could speak. 'I'll 'ave none o' my boys playin' the fool up there. And that reminds me, doc., young Smith'll git 'imself inter the devil of a mess one o' these days, if you don't look after 'im a bit better'n you do. I 'eard 'im spoutin' away as I come past — usin' language about the Gover'ment fit to turn you sick.'

Mahony coughed. 'He's but young yet,' he said dryly. 'After all, youth's youth, sir, and comes but once in a lifetime. And you can't make lads into wiseacres between sundown and sunrise.'

'No, by Gawd, you can't!' affirmed his companion. 'But I think youth's just a fine name for a sort o' piggish mess. What's the good, one 'ud like to know, of gettin' old, and learnin' wisdom, and knowin' the good from the bad, when ev'ry lousy young fathead that's born inter the world starts out again to muddle

24

through it for 'imself, in 'is own way. And that things 'as got to go on like this, just the same, for ever and ever — why, it makes me fair and tired to think of it. My father didn't 'old with youth: 'e knocked it out of us by thrashin', just like lyin' and thievin'. And it's the best way, too. — Wot's that you say?' he flounced round on the unoffending Tom. 'Nothin'? You was only snifflin', was you? You keep your fly-trap shut, my fine fellow, and make no mousy sounds to me, or it'll be the worse for you, I can tell you!'

'Come, Mr Ocock, don't be too hard on the boy.'

'Not be 'ard on 'im? When I've got the nasty galoon on me 'ands again like this? — Chucks up the good post I git 'im in Kilmore, without with your leave or by your leave. Too lonely for 'is lordship it was. Missed the sound o' wimmin's petticoats, 'e did.' He turned fiercely on his son. ' 'Ere, don't you stand starin' there! You get 'ome, and fix up for the night. Now then, wot are you dawdlin' for, pig-'ead?'

The boy slunk away. When he had disappeared, his father again took up the challenge of Mahony's silent disapproval. 'I can't 'ardly bear the sight of 'im, doc. — disgracin' me as 'e 'as done. 'Im a father, and not eighteen till June! A son o' mine, who can't see a wench with 'er bodice open, but wot 'e must be arter 'er. . . . No, sir, no son o' mine! I'm a respectable man, I am!'

'Of course, of course.'

'Oh! but they're a sore trial to me, these boys, doc. 'Enry's the only one . . . if it weren't for 'Enry — Johnny, 'e can't pass the drink, and now 'ere's this young swine started to nose arter the wimmin.'

'There's good stuff in the lads, I'm sure of it. They're just sowing their wild oats.'

'They'll sow no h'oats with me.'

'I tell you what it is, Mr Ocock, you need a woman about your place, to make it a bit more homelike,' said Mahony, calling to mind the pigsty in which Ocock and his sons housed.

'Course I do!' agreed Ocock. 'And Melia, she'll come out to 'er daddy soon as ever th'ol' woman kicks the bucket. — Drat 'er! It's 'er I've got to thank for all the mischief.'

'Well, well!' said Mahony, and rising knocked out his pipe on the log. Did his old neighbour once get launched on the subject of his wife's failings, there was no stopping him. 'We all have our crosses.'

'That we 'ave. And I'm keepin' you outer your bed, doc., with me blather. – By gum! and that reminds me I come 'ere special to see you tonight. Bin gettin' a bit moonstruck, I reckon,' – and he clapped on his hat.

Drawing a sheaf of papers from an inner pocket, he selected one and offered it to Mahony. Mahony led the way indoors, and lighting a kerosene-lamp stooped to decipher the letter.

For some weeks now he had been awaiting the delivery of a load of goods, the invoice for which had long since reached him. From this communication, carried by hand, he learnt that the drayman, having got bogged just beyond Bacchus's marsh, had decamped to the Ovens, taking with him all he could cram into a spring-cart, and disposing of the remainder for what he could get. The agent in Melbourne refused to be held responsible for the loss, and threatened to prosecute, if payment for the goods were not immediately forthcoming. Mahony, who here heard the first of the affair, was highly indignant at the tone of the letter; and before he had read to the end resolved to let everything else slide, and to leave for Melbourne early next morning.

Ocock backed him up in this decision, and with the aid of a great quill pen stiffly traced the address of his eldest son, who practised as a solicitor in the capital.

'Go you straight to 'Enry, doc. 'Enry'll see you through.'

Brushing aside his dreams of a peaceful Sabbath Mahony made preparations for his journey. Waking his assistant, he gave the man – a stupid clodhopper, but honest and attached – instructions how to manage during his absence, then sent him to the township to order horses. Himself, he put on his hat and went out to look for Purdy.

His search led him through all the drunken revelry of a Saturday night. And it was close on twelve before, having followed the trace from bowling-alley to Chinese cook-shop, from the 'Adelphi' to Mother Flannigan's and haunts still less reputable, he finally succeeded in catching his bird.

CHAPTER FOUR

The two young men took to the road betimes: it still wanted
some minutes to six on the new clock in the tower of Bath's
Hotel, when they threw their legs over their saddles and rode
down the steep slope by the Camp Reserve. The hoofs of the
horses pounded the plank bridge that spanned the Yarrowee,
and striking loose stones, and smacking and sucking in the mud,
made a rude clatter in the Sunday quiet.

Having followed for a few hundred yards the wide, rut-
riddled thoroughfare of Main Street, the riders branched off to
cross rising ground. They proceeded in single file and at a foot-
pace, for the highway had been honeycombed and rendered unsafe; it also ascended steadily. Just before they entered the bush,
which was alive with the rich, strong whistling of magpies, Purdy
halted to look back and wave his hat in farewell. Mahony also
half-turned in the saddle. There it lay – the scattered, yet congested, unlovely wood and canvas settlement that was Ballarat.
At this distance, and from this height, it resembled nothing so
much as a collection of child's bricks, tossed out at random
over the ground, the low, square huts and cabins that composed
it being all of a shape and size. Some threads of smoke began
to mount towards the immense pale dome of the sky. The sun
was catching here the panes of a window, there the tin that encased a primitive chimney.

They rode on, leaving the warmth of the early sun-rays for
the cold blue shadows of the bush. Neither broke the silence.
Mahony's day had not come to an end with the finding of
Purdy. Barely stretched on his palliasse he had been routed out
to attend to Long Jim, who had missed his footing and pitched
into a shaft. The poor old tipsy idiot hauled up – luckily for him
it was a dry, shallow hole – there was a broken collar-bone to set.
Mahony had installed him in his own bed, and had spent the
remainder of the night dozing in a chair.

27

So now he was heavy-eyed, uncommunicative. As they climbed the shoulder and came to the rich, black soil that surrounded the ancient cone of Warrenheip, he mused on his personal relation to the place he had just left. And not for the first time he asked himself: what am I doing here? When he was absent from Ballarat, and could dispassionately consider the life he led there, he was so struck by the incongruity of the thing that, like the beldame in the nursery-tale, he could have pinched himself to see whether he waked or slept. Had anyone told him, three years previously, that the day was coming when he would weigh out soap and sugar, and hand them over a counter in exchange for money, he would have held the prophet ripe for Bedlam. Yet here he was, a full-blown tradesman, and as greedy of gain as any tallow-chandler. Extraordinary, aye, and distressing, too, the ease with which the human organism adapted itself; it was just a case of the green caterpillar on the green leaf. Well, he could console himself with the knowledge that his apparent submission was only an affair of the surface. He had struck no roots; and it would mean as little to his half-dozen acquaintances on Ballarat when he silently vanished from their midst, as it would to him if he never saw one of them again. Or the country either — and he let his eye roam unlovingly over the wild, sad-coloured landscape, with its skimpy, sad-coloured trees.

Meanwhile they were advancing: their nags' hoofs, beating in unison, devoured mile after mile of the road. It was a typical colonial road; it went up hill and down dale, turned aside for no obstacle. At one time it ran down a gully that was almost a ravine, to mount straight up the opposite side among boulders that reached to the belly-bands. At others, it led through a reedy swamp, or a stony watercourse; or it became a bog; or dived through a creek. Where the ground was flat and treeless, it was a rutty, well-worn track between two seas of pale, scant grass.

More than once, complaining of a mouth like sawdust, Purdy alighted and limped across the verandah of a house-of-accommodation; but they did not actually draw rein till, towards midday, they reached a knot of weatherboard verandahed stores, smithies and public-houses, arranged at the four corners of two cross-roads. Here they made a substantial luncheon; and the odour of fried onions carried far and wide. Mahony paid his three shillings for a bottle of ale; but Purdy washed down the steak with cup after cup of richly sugared tea.

In the early afternoon they set off again, revived and refreshed. Purdy caught at a bunch of aromatic leaves and burst into song; and Mahony . . . Good God! With a cloudless sky overhead, a decent bit of horseflesh between his knees, and the prospect of a three days' holiday from storekeeping, his name would not have been what it was if he had for long remained captious, downhearted. Insufficient sleep, and an empty stomach – nothing on earth besides! A fig for his black thoughts! The fact of his being obliged to spend a few years in the colony would, in the end, profit him, by widening his experience of the world and his fellow-men. It was possible to lead a sober, Godfearing life, no matter in what rude corner of the globe you were pitchforked. – And in this mood he was even willing to grant the landscape a certain charm. Since leaving Ballan the road had dipped up and down a succession of swelling rises, grass-grown and untimbered. From the top of these ridges the view was a far one: you looked straight across undulating waves of country and intervening forest-land, to where, on the horizon, a long, low sprawling range of hills lay blue – cobalt blue, and painted in with a sure brush – against the porcelain-blue of the sky. What did the washed-out tints of the foliage matter, when, wherever you turned, you could count on getting these marvellous soft distances, on always finding a range of blue-veiled hills, lovely and intangible as a dream?

There was not much traffic to the diggings on a Sunday. And having come to a level bit of ground, the riders followed a joint impulse and broke into a canter. As they began to climb again they fell naturally into one of those familiar talks, full of allusion and reminiscence, that are only possible between two of a sex who have lived through part of their green days together.

It began by Purdy referring to the satisfactory fashion in which he had disposed of his tools, his stretcher-bed, and other effects: he was not travelling to Melbourne empty-handed.

Mahony rallied him. 'You were always a good one at striking a bargain, my boy! What about: "Four mivvies for an alley!" – eh, Dickybird?'

This related to their earliest meeting, and was a standing joke between them. Mahony could recall the incident as clearly as though it had happened yesterday: how the sturdy little apple-cheeked English boy, with the comical English accent, had suddenly bobbed up at his side on the way home from school, and

29

in that laughable sing-song of his, without modulation or emphasis, had offered to 'swop' him, as above.

Purdy laughed and paid him back in kind. 'Yes, and the funk you were in for fear Spiny Tatlow 'ud see us, and peach to the rest!'

'Yes. What young idiots boys are!'

In thought he added: 'And what snobs!' For the breach of convention – he was an upper-form boy at the time – had not been his sole reason for wishing to shake off his junior. Behind him, Mahony, when he reached home, closed the door of one of the largest houses in the most exclusive square in Dublin. Whereas Purdy lived in a small, common house in a side street. Visits there had to be paid surreptitiously.

All the same these were frequent – and for the best of reasons. Mahony could still see Purdy's plump, red-cheeked English mother, who was as jolly and happy as her boy, hugging the loaf to her bosom while she cut round after round of bread and butter and jam, for two cormorant throats. And the elder boy, long-limbed and lank, all wrist and ankle, had invariably been the hungrier of the two; for, on the glossy damask of the big house, often not enough food was set to satisfy the growing appetites of himself and his sisters. – 'Dickybird, can't you see us, with our backs to the wall, in that little yard of yours, trying who could take the biggest bite? – or going round the outside: "Crust first, and though you burst, By the bones of Davy Jones!" till only a little island of jam was left?'

Purdy laughed heartily at these and other incidents fished up by his friend from the well of the years; but he did not take part in the sport himself. He had not Mahony's gift for recalling detail: to him past was past. He only became alive and eager when the talk turned, as it soon did, on his immediate prospects.

This time, to his astonishment, Mahony had had no trouble in persuading Purdy to quit the diggings. In addition, here was the boy now declaring openly that what he needed, and must have, was a fixed and steadily paying job. With this decision Mahony was in warm agreement, and promised all the help that lay in his power.

But Purdy was not done; he hummed and hawed and fidgeted; he took off his hat and looked inside it; he wiped his forehead and the nape of his neck.

Mahony knew the symptoms. 'Come, Dickybird. Spit it out, my boy!'

'Yes . . . er. . . . Well, the fact is, Dick, I begin to think it's time I settled down.'

Mahony gave a whistle. 'Whew! A lady in the case?'

'That's the chat. Just oblige yours truly by takin' a squint at this, will you?'

He handed his friend a squarely-folded sheet of thinnest blue paper, with a large purple stamp in one corner, and a red seal on the back. Opening it Mahony discovered three crossed pages, written in a delicately pointed, minute, Italian hand.

He read the letter to the end, deliberately, and with a growing sense of relief: composition, expression and penmanship, all met with his approval. 'This is the writing of a person of some refinement, my son.'

'Well, er . . . yes,' said Purdy. He seemed about to add a further word, then swallowed it, and went on: 'Though, somehow or other, Till's different to herself, on paper. But she's the best of girls, Dick. Not one o' your ethereal, die-away, bread-and-butter misses. There's something *of* Till there is, and she's always on for a lark. I never met such girls for larks as her and 'er sister. The very last time I was there, they took and hung up . . . me and some other fellers had been stoppin' up a bit late the night before, and kickin' up a bit of a shindy, and what did those girls do? They got the barman to come into my room while I was asleep, and hang a bucket o' water to one of the beams over the bed. Then I'm blamed if they didn't tie a string from it to my big toe! I gives a kick, down comes the bucket and half drowns me. – Gosh, how those girls did laugh!'

'H'm!' said Mahony dubiously; while Purdy in his turn chewed the cud of a pleasant memory. – 'Well, I for my part should be glad to see you married and settled, with a good wife always beside you.'

'That's just the rub,' said Purdy, and vigorously scratched his head. 'Till's a first-class girl as a sweetheart and all that; but when I come to think of puttin' my head in the noose, from now till doomsday – why then, somehow, I can't bring myself to pop the question.'

'There's going to be no trifling with the girl's feelings, I hope, sir?'

'Bosh! But I say, Dick, I wish you'd turn your peepers on 'er and tell me what you make of 'er. She's A1 'erself, but she's got a mother. . . . By Job, Dick, if I thought Tilly 'ud ever get like that . . . and they're exactly the same build, too.'

31

It would certainly be well for him to inspect Purdy's flame, thought Mahony. Especially since the anecdote told did not bear out the good impression left by the letter — went far, indeed, to efface it. Still, he was loath to extend his absence by spending a night at Geelong, where, as it came out, the lady lived; and he replied evasively that it must depend on the speed with which he could put through his business in Melbourne.

Purdy was silent for a time. Then, with a side-glance at his companion, he volunteered: 'I say, Dick, I know someone who'd suit you.'

'The deuce you do!' said Mahony, and burst out laughing. 'Miss Tilly's sister, no doubt?'

'No, no — not her. Jinn's all right, but she's not your sort. But they've got a girl living with 'em — a sort o' poor relation, or something — and she's a horse of quite another colour. — I say, old man, serious now, have you never thought o' gettin' spliced?'

Again Mahony laughed. At his companion's words there descended to him, once more, from some shadowy distance, some pure height, the rose-tinted vision of the wife-to-be which haunts every man's youth. And, in ludicrous juxtaposition, he saw the women, the only women he had encountered since coming to the colony: the hard-working, careworn wives of diggers; the harridans, sluts and prostitutes who made up the balance.

He declined to be drawn. 'Is it old Moll Flannigan or one of her darlints you'd be wishing me luck to, ye spalpeen?'

'Man, don't I say I've *found* the wife for you?' Purdy was not jesting, and did not join in the fresh salvo of laughter with which Mahony greeted his words. 'Oh, blow it, Dick, you're too fastidious — too damned particular! Say what you like, there's good in all of 'em — even in old Mother Flannigan 'erself — and 'specially when she's got a drop inside 'er. Fuddle old Moll a bit, and she'd give you the very shift off her back. — Don't I thank the Lord, that's all, I'm not built like you! Why, the woman isn't born I can't get on with. All's fish that comes to my net. — Oh, to be young, Dick, and to love the girls! To see their little waists, and their shoulders, and the dimples in their cheeks! See 'em put up their hands to their bonnets, and how their little feet peep out when the wind blows their petticoats against their legs!' and Purdy rose in his stirrups and stretched himself, in an excess of well-being.

'You young reprobate!'

'Bah! – you! You've got water in your veins.'

'Nothing of the sort! Set me among decent women and there's no company I enjoy more,' declared Mahony.

'Fish-blood, fish-blood! – Dick, it's my belief you were born old.'

Mahony was still young enough to be nettled by doubts cast on his vitality. Purdy laughed in his sleeve. Aloud he said: 'Well, look here, old man, I'll lay you a wager. I bet you you're not game, when you see that tulip I've been tellin' you about, to take her in your arms and kiss her. A fiver on it!'

'Done!' cried Mahony. 'And I'll have it in one note, if you please!'

'Bravo!' cried Purdy. 'Bravo, Dick!' And having gained his end, and being on a good piece of road between post-and-rail fences, he set spurs to his horse and cantered off, singing as he went:

> She wheels a wheelbarrow,
> Through streets wide and narrow,
> Crying cockles, and mussels,
> Alive, alive-oh!

But the sun was growing large in the western sky; on the ground to the left, their failing shadows slanted out lengthwise; those cast by the horses' bodies were mounted on high spindle-legs. The two men ceased their trifling, and nudged by the fall of day began to ride at a more business-like pace, pushing forward through the deep basin of Bacchus's marsh, and on for miles over wide, treeless plains, to where the road was joined by the main highway from the north, coming down from Mount Alexander and the Bendigo. Another hour, and from a gentle eminence the buildings of Melbourne were visible, the mastheads of the many vessels riding at anchor in Hobson's Bay. Here, too, the briny scent of the sea, carrying up over grassy flats, met their nostrils, and set Mahony hungrily sniffing. The brief twilight came and went, and it was already night when they urged their weary beasts over the Moonee ponds, a winding chain of brackish waterholes. The horses shambled along the broad, hilly tracks of North Melbourne; warily picked their steps through the city itself. Dingy oil-lamps, set here and there at the corners of roads so broad that you could hardly see across them, shed but a meagre light, and the further the riders advanced, the more difficult became their passage: the streets, in process of laying, were heaped with stones and intersected by trenches. Finally, dismounting, they thrust their arms through their bridles, and laboriously covered the last half-mile of the journey on foot. Having lodged the horses at a livery-stable, they repaired to a hotel in Little Collins Street. Here Purdy knew the proprietor, and they were fortunate enough to secure a small room for the use of themselves alone.

CHAPTER FIVE

Melbourne is built on two hills and the valley that lies between. It was over a year since Mahony or Purdy had been last in the capital, and next morning, on stepping out of the 'Adam and Eve', they walked up the eastern slope to look about them. From the summit of the hill their view stretched to the waters of the Bay, and its forest of masts. The nearer foreground was made up of mud flats, through which a sluggish, coffee-coloured river wound its way to the sea. On the horizon to the north, the Dandenong Ranges rose storm-blue and distinct, and seemed momently to be drawing nearer; for a cold wind was blowing, which promised rain. The friends caught their glimpses of the landscape between dense clouds of white dust, which blotted everything out for minutes at a time, and filled eyes, nose, ears with a gritty powder.

Tiring of this they turned and descended Great Collins Street – a spacious thoroughfare that dipped into the hollow and rose again, and was so long that on its western height pedestrians looked no bigger than ants. In the heart of the city men were everywhere at work, laying gas- and drain-pipes, macadamizing, paving, kerbing: no longer would the old wives' tale be credited of the infant drowned in the deeps of Swanston Street, or of the bullock which sank, inch by inch, before its owner's eyes in the Elizabeth Street bog. Massive erections of freestone were going up alongside here a primitive, canvas-fronted dwelling, there one formed wholly of galvanized iron. Fashionable shops, two storeys high, stood next tiny, dilapidated weatherboards. In the roadway, handsome chaises, landaus, four-in-hands made room for bullock-teams, eight and ten strong; for tumbrils carrying water or refuse – or worse; for droves of cattle, mobs of wild colts bound for auction, flocks of sheep on their way to be boiled down for tallow. Stock-riders and bull-punchers rubbed shoulders with elegants in skirted coats and shepherd's plaid

35

trousers, who adroitly skipped heaps of stones and mortar, or crept along the narrow edging of kerb.

The visitors from up-country paused to listen to a brass band that played outside a horse-auction mart; to watch the shooting in a rifle-gallery. The many decently attired females they met also called for notice. Not a year ago, and no reputable woman walked abroad oftener than she could help: now, even at this hour, the streets were starred with them. Purdy, open-mouthed, his eyes a-dance, turned his head this way and that, pointed and exclaimed. But then *he* had slept like a log, and felt in his own words 'as fit as a fiddle'. Whereas Mahony had sat his horse the whole night through, had never ceased to balance himself in an imaginary saddle. And when at daybreak he had fallen into a deeper sleep, he was either reviewing outrageous females on Purdy's behalf, or accepting wagers to kiss them.

Hence, diverting as were the sights of the city, he did not come to them with the naïve receptivity of Purdy. It was, besides, hard to detach his thoughts from the disagreeable affair that had brought him to Melbourne. And as soon as banks and offices began to take down their shutters, he hurried off to his interview with the carrying-agent.

The latter's place of business was behind Great Collins Street, in a lane reached by a turnpike. Found with some trouble, it proved to be a rude shanty wedged in between a Chinese laundry and a Chinese eating-house. The entrance was through a yard in which stood a collection of rabbit-hutches, while further back gaped a dirty closet. At the sound of their steps the man they sought emerged, and Mahony could not repress an exclamation of surprise. When, a little over a twelvemonth ago, he had first had dealings with him, this Bolliver had been an alert and respectable man of business. Now he was evidently on the downgrade; and the cause of the deterioration was advertised in his bloodshot eyeballs and veinous cheeks. Early as was the hour, he had already been indulging: his breath puffed sour. Mahony prepared to state the object of his visit in no uncertain terms. But his preliminaries were cut short by a volley of abuse. The man accused him point-blank of having been privy to the rascally drayman's fraud and of having hoped, by lying low, to evade his liability. Mahony lost his temper, and vowed that he would havé Bolliver up for defamation of character. To which the latter retorted that the first innings in a court of law would be his: he had already put the matter in the hands of his attorney. This was the last straw. Purdy had to intervene and get Mahony away. They left the agent shaking his fist after them and cursing the bloody day on which he'd ever been fool enough to do a deal with a bloody gentleman.

At the corner of the street the friends paused for a hasty conference. Mahony was for marching off to take the best legal advice the city had to offer. But Purdy disapproved. Why put himself to so much trouble, when he had old Ocock's recommendation to his lawyer-son in his coat pocket? What, in the name of Leary-cum-Fitz, was the sense of making an enemy for life of the old man, his next-door neighbour, and a good customer to boot?

These counsels prevailed, and they turned their steps towards Chancery Lane, where was to be found every variety of legal practitioner from barrister to scrivener. Having matched the house-number and descried the words: 'Mr Henry Ocock, Conveyancer and Attorney, Commissioner of Affidavits', painted black on two dusty windows, they climbed a wooden stair festooned with cobwebs, to a landing where an injunction to: 'Push and Enter!' was rudely inked on a sheet of paper and affixed to a door.

Obeying, they passed into a dingy little room, the entire furnishing of which consisted of a couple of deal tables, with a chair to each. These were occupied by a young man and a boy, neither of whom rose at their entrance. The lad was cutting notches in a stick and whistling tunefully; the clerk, a young fellow in the early twenties, who had a mop of flaming red hair and small-slit white-lashed eyes, looked at the strangers, but without lifting his head: his eyes performed the necessary motion.

Mahony desired to know if he had the pleasure of addressing Mr Henry Ocock. In reply the red-head gave a noiseless laugh, which he immediately quenched by clapping his hand over his mouth, and shutting one eye at his junior said: 'No – nor yet the Shar o' Persia, nor Alphybetical Foster! – What can I do for you, governor?'

'You can have the goodness to inform Mr Ocock that I wish to see him!' flashed back Mahony.

'Singin' til-ril-i-tum-tum-dee-ay! – Now then, Mike, me child, toddle!'

With patent reluctance the boy ceased his whittling, and dawdled across the room to an inner door through which he vanished, having first let his knuckles bump, as if by chance, against the wood of the panel. A second later he reappeared. 'Boss's engaged.' But Mahony surprised a lightning sign between the pair.

'No, sir, I decline to state my business to anyone but Mr Ocock himself!' he declared hotly, in response to the red-haired man's invitation to 'get it off his chest'. 'If you choose to find out when he will be at liberty, I will wait so long – no longer.'

As the office-boy had somehow failed to hit his seat on his passage to the outer door, there was nothing left for the clerk to do but himself to undertake the errand. He lounged up from his chair, and, in his case without even the semblance of a knock, squeezed through a foot wide aperture, in such a fashion that the two strangers should not catch a glimpse of what was going on inside. But his voice came to them through the thin partition. 'Oh, just a couple o' stony-broke Paddy-landers.' Mahony, who had seized the opportunity to dart an angry glance at Purdy, which should say: 'This is what one gets by coming to your second-rate pettifoggers!' now let his eyes rest on his friend and critically detailed the latter's appearance. The description fitted to a nicety. Purdy did in truth look down on his luck. Unkempt, bearded to the eyes, there he stood clutching his shapeless old cabbage-tree, in mud-stained jumper and threadbare smalls – the very spit of the unsuccessful digger. Well might they be suspected of not owning the necessary to pay their way!

'All serene, mister! The boss'ull take you on.'

The sanctum was a trifle larger than the outer room, but almost equally bare; half-a-dozen deed-boxes were piled up in one corner. Stalking in with his chin in the air, Mahony found himself in the presence of a man of his own age, who sat absorbed in the study of a document. At their entry two beady grey eyes lifted to take a brief but thorough survey, and a hand with a pencil in it pointed to the single empty chair. Mahony declined to translate the gesture and remained standing.

Under the best of circumstances, it irked him to be kept waiting. Here, following on the clerk's saucy familiarity, the wilful delay made his gorge rise. For a few seconds he fumed in silence; then, his patience exhausted, he burst out: 'My time, sir, is as precious as your own. With your permission, I will take my business elsewhere.'

At these words, and at the tone in which they were spoken, the lawyer's head shot up as if he had received a blow under the chin. Again he narrowed his eyes at the couple. And this time he laid the document from him and asked suavely: 'What can I do for you?'

The change in his manner though slight was unmistakable. Mahony had a nice ear for such refinements, and responded to the shade of difference with the promptness of one who had been on the watch for it. His irritation fell; he was ready on the instant to be propitiated. Putting his hat aside he sat down, and having introduced himself, made reference to Ballarat and his acquaintance with the lawyer's father: 'Who directed me to you, sir, for advice on a vexatious affair, in which I have had the misfortune to become involved.'

With a 'Pray be seated!' Ocock rose and cleared a chair for Purdy. Resuming his seat he joined his hands, and wound them in and out. 'I think you may take it from me that no case is so unpromising but what we shall be able to find a loophole.'

Mahony thanked him – with a touch of reserve. 'I trust you will still be of that opinion when you have heard the facts.' And went on: 'Myself, I do not doubt it. I am not a rich man, but serious though the monetary loss would be to me, I should settle the matter out of court, were I not positive that I had right on my side.' To which Ocock returned a quick: 'Oh, quite so . . . of course.'

Like his old father, he was a short, heavily built man; but there the likeness ended. He had a high, domed forehead, above a thin, hooked nose. His skin was of an almost Jewish pallor. Fringes of straight, jet-black hair grew down the walls of his cheeks and round his chin, meeting beneath it. The shaven upper lip was long and flat, with no central markings, and helped to form a mouth that had not much more shape or expression than a slit cut by a knife in a sheet of paper. The chin was bare to the size of a crown-piece; and, both while he spoke and while he listened to others speaking, the lawyer caressed this patch with his finger-tips; so that in the course of time it had arrived at a state of high polish – like the shell of an egg.

The air with which he heard his new client out was of a non-committal kind; and Mahony, having talked his first heat off, grew chilled by the wet blanket of Ocock's silence. There was nothing in this of the frank responsiveness with which your ordinary mortal lends his ear. The brain behind the dome was, one might be sure, adding, combining, comparing, and drawing its own conclusions. Why should lawyers, he wondered, treat those who came to them like children, advancing only in so far

39

as it suited them out of the darkness where they housed among strangely worded paragraphs and obscure formulas? – But these musings were cut short. Having fondled his chin for a further moment, Ocock looked up and put a question. And, while he could not but admire the lawyer's acumen, this did not lessen Mahony's discomfort. All unguided, it went straight for what he believed to be the one weak spot in his armour. It related to the drayman. Contrary to custom Mahony had, on this occasion, himself recommended the driver. And, as he admitted it, his ears rang again with the plaints of his stranded fellow-countryman, a wheedler from the South Country, off whose tongue the familiar brogue had dripped like honey. His recommendation, he explained, had been made out of charity; he had not forced the agent to engage the man; and it would surely be a gross injustice if he alone were to be held responsible.

To his relief Ocock did not seem to attach importance to the fact, but went on to ask whether any written agreement had existed between the parties. 'No writing? H'm! So . . . so!' To read his thoughts was an impossibility; but as he proceeded with his catechism it was easy to see how his interest in the case grew. He began to treat it tenderly; warmed to it, as an artist to his work; and Mahony's spirits rose in consequence.

Having selected a number of minor points that would tell in their favour, Ocock dilated upon the libellous aspersion that had been cast on Mahony's good faith. 'My experience has invariably been this, Mr Mahony: people who suggest that kind of thing, and accuse others of it, are those who are accustomed to make use of such means themselves. In this case, there may have been no goods at all – the thing may prove to have been a put-up job from beginning to end.'

But his hearer's start of surprise was too marked to be overlooked. 'Well, let us take the existence of the goods for granted. But might they not, being partly of a perishable nature, have gone bad or otherwise got spoiled on the road, and not have been in a fit condition for you to receive at your end?'

This was credible; Mahony nodded his assent. He also added, gratuitously, that he had before now been obliged to reclaim on casks of mouldy mess-pork. At which Ocock ceased coddling his chin to point a straight forefinger at him, with a triumphant: 'You see!' – But Purdy who, sick and tired of the discussion, had withdrawn to the window to watch the rain zig-zag in runlets down the dusty panes, and hiss and spatter on the sill; Purdy puckered his lips to a sly and soundless whistle.

The interview at an end, Ocock mentioned, in his frigidly urbane way, that he had recently been informed there was an excellent opening for a firm of solicitors in Ballarat: could Mr Mahony, as a resident, confirm the report? Mahony regretted his ignorance, but spoke in praise of the Golden City and its assured future. – 'This would be most welcome news to your father, sir. I can picture his satisfaction on hearing it.'

– 'Golly, Dick, that's no mopoke!' was Purdy's comment as they emerged into the rain-swept street. 'A crafty devil, if ever I see'd one.'

'Henry Ocock seems to me to be a singularly able man,' replied Mahony drily. To his thinking, Purdy had cut a poor figure during the visit: he had said no intelligent word, but had lounged lumpishly in his chair – the very picture of the country-man come up to the metropolis – and, growing tired of this, had gone like a restless child to thrum with his fingers on the panes.

'Oh, you bet! He'll slither you through.'

'What? Do you insinuate there's any need for slithering . . . as you call it?' cried Mahony.

'Why, Dick, old man. . . . And as long as he gets you through, what does it matter?'

'It matters to me, sir!'

The rain, a tropical deluge, was over by the time they reached the hollow. The sun shone again, hot and sticky, and people were venturing forth from their shelters to wade through beds of mud, or to cross, on planks, the deep, swift rivers formed by the open drains. There were several such cloud-bursts in the course of the afternoon; and each time the refuse of the city was whirled past on the flood, to be left as an edging to the footpaths when the water went down.

Mahony spent the rest of the day in getting together a fresh load of goods. For, whether he lost or won his suit, the store had to be restocked without delay.

That evening towards eight o'clock the two men turned out of the Lowther Arcade. The night was cold, dark and wet; and they had wound comforters round their bare throats. They were on their way to the Mechanics' Hall, to hear a lecture on Mesmer-ism. Mahony had looked forward to this all through the sorry job of choosing soaps and candles. The subject piqued his curiosity. It was the one drop of mental stimulant he could hope to extract from his visit. The theatre was out of the question: if none of the actors happened to be drunk, a fair proportion of the audience was sure to be.

Part of his pleasure this evening was due to Purdy having agreed to accompany him. It was always a matter of regret to Mahony that, outside the hobnob of daily life, he and his friend had so few interests in common; that Purdy should rest content with the coarse diversions of the ordinary digger.

Then, from the black shadows of the Arcade, a woman's form detached itself, and a hand was laid on Purdy's arm.

'Shout us a drink, old pal!'

Mahony made a quick, repellent movement of the shoulder. But Purdy, some vagrom fancy quickened in him, either by the voice, which was not unrefined, or by the stealthiness of the approach, Purdy turned to look.

'Come, come, my boy. We've no time to lose.'

Without raising her pleasant voice, the woman levelled a volley of abuse at Mahony, then muttered a word in Purdy's ear.

'Just half a jiff, Dick,' said Purdy. 'Or go ahead. – I'll make up on you.'

For a quarter of an hour Mahony aired his heels in front of a public-house. Then he gave it up, and went on his way. But his pleasure was damped: the inconsiderateness with which Purdy could shake him off, always had a disconcerting effect on him. To face the matter squarely: the friendship between them did not mean as much to Purdy as to him; the sudden impulse that had made the boy relinquish a promising clerkship to emigrate in his wake – into this he had read more than it would hold. – And, as he picked his muddy steps, Mahony agreed with himself that the net result, for him, of Purdy's coming to the colony, had been to saddle him with a new responsibility. It was his lot for ever to be helping the lad out of tight places. Sometimes it made him feel unnecessarily bearish. For Purdy had the knack, common to sunny, improvident natures, of taking everything that was done for him for granted. His want of delicacy in this respect was distressing. Yet, in spite of it all, it was hard to bear him a grudge for long together. A well-meaning young beggar if ever there was one! That very day how faithfully he had stuck at his side, assisting at dull discussions and duller purchasings, without once obtruding his own concerns. – And here Mahony remembered their talk on the ride to town. Purdy had expressed the wish to settle down and take a wife. A poor

42

friend that would be who did not back him up in this intention.

As he sidled into one of the front benches of a half-empty hall – the mesmerist, a corpse-like man in black, already surveyed its thinness from the platform with an air of pained surprise – Mahony decided that Purdy should have his chance. The heavy rains of the day, and the consequent probable flooding of the Ponds and the Marsh, would serve as an excuse for a change of route. He would go and have a look at Purdy's sweetheart; would ride back to the diggings by way of Geelong.

CHAPTER SIX

In a whitewashed parlour of 'Beamish's Family Hotel' some few miles north of Geelong, three young women, in voluminous skirts and with their hair looped low over their ears, sat at work. Books lay open on the table before two of them; the third was making a bookmark. Two were fair, plump, rosy, and well over twenty; the third, pale-skinned and dark, was still a very young girl. She it was who stitched magenta hieroglyphics on a strip of perforated cardboard.

'Do lemme see, Poll,' said the eldest of the trio, and laid down her pen. 'You *'ave* bin quick about it, my dear.'

Polly, the brunette, freed her needle of silk and twirled the bookmark by its ribbon ends. Spinning, the mystic characters united to form the words: 'Kiss me quick.'

Her companions tittered. 'If ma didn't know for certain 'twas meant for your brother John, she'd never 'ave let you make it,' said the second blonde, whose name was Jinny.

'Girls, what a lark it 'ud be to send it up to Purdy Smith, by Ned!' said the first speaker.

Polly blushed. 'Fy, Tilly! That wouldn't be ladylike.'

Tilly's big bosom rose and fell in a sigh. 'What's a lark never is.'

Jinny giggled, agreeably scandalized: 'What things you do say, Till! Don't let ma 'ear you, that's all.'

'Ma be blowed! — 'Ow does this look now, Polly?' And across the wax-cloth Tilly pushed a copybook, in which she had laboriously inscribed a prim maxim the requisite number of times.

Polly laid down her work and knitted her brows over the page. 'Well . . . it's better than the last one, Tilly,' she said gently, averse to hurting her pupil's feelings. 'But still not quite good enough. The f's, look, should be more like this.' And taking a steel pen she made several long-tailed f's, in a tiny, pointed hand.

44

Tilly yielded an ungrudging admiration. ' 'Ow well you do it, Poll! But I *hate* writing. If only ma weren't so set on it!'

'You'll never be able to write yourself to a certain person, 'oos name I won't mention, if you don't 'urry up and learn,' said Jinny, looking sage.

'What's the odds! We've always got Poll to write for us,' gave back Tilly, and lazily stretched out a large, plump hand to recover the copybook. 'A certain person'll never know – or not till it's too late.'

'Here, Polly dear,' said Jinny, and held out a book. 'I know it now.'

Again Polly put down her embroidery. She took the book. 'Plough!' said she.

'Plough?' echoed Jinny vaguely, and turned a pair of soft, cow-like brown eyes on the blowflies sitting sticky and sleepy round the walls of the room. 'Wait a jiff . . . lemme think! Plough? Oh, yes, I know. P-l . . .'

'P-l-o,' prompted Polly, the speller coming to a full stop.

'P-l-o-u!' shot out Jinny, in triumph.

'Not *quite* right,' said Polly. 'It's g-h, Jinny: p-l-o-u-g-h.'

'Oh, that's what I meant. I knew it right enough.'

'Well, now, trough!'

'Trough?' repeated Jinny, in the same slow, vacant way. 'Trough? Wait, lemme think a minute. T-r-o . . .'

Polly's lips all but formed the 'u', to prevent the 'f' she felt impending. 'I'm afraid you'll have to take it again, Jinny dear,' she said reluctantly, as nothing further was forthcoming.

'Oh, no, Poll. T-r-o-' began Jinny with fresh vigour. But before she could add a fourth to the three letters, a heavy foot pounded down the passage, and a stout woman, out of breath, her cap-bands flying, came bustling in and slammed the door.

'Girls, girls, now whatever d'ye think? 'Ere's Purdy Smith come ridin' inter the yard, an' another gent with 'im. Scuttle along now, an' put them books away! – Tilda, yer net's 'alf 'angin' off – you don't want yer sweet-'eart to see you all untidy like that, do you? – 'Elp 'em, Polly my dear, and be quick about it! – H'out with yer sewin', chicks!'

Sprung up from their seats the three girls darted to and fro. The telltale spelling and copybooks were flung into the drawer of the chiffonier, and the key was turned on them. Polly, her immodest sampler safely hidden at the bottom of her workbox, was the most composed of the three; and while locks were smoothed and collars adjusted in the adjoining bedroom, she remained behind to look out thimbles, needles and strips of plain sewing, and to lay them naturally about the table.

The blonde sisters reappeared, all aglow with excitement. Tilly, in particular, was in a sad flutter.

'Girls, I simply *can't* face 'im in 'ere!' she declared. 'It was 'ere, in this very room, that 'e first – you know what!'

'Nor can I,' cried Jinny, catching the fever.

'Feel my 'eart, 'ow it beats,' said her sister, pressing her hands, one over the other, to her full left breast.

'Mine's every bit as bad,' averred Jinny.

'I believe I shall 'ave the palpitations and faint away, if I stop 'ere.'

Polly was genuinely concerned. 'I'll run and call mother back.'

'No, I tell you what: let's 'ide!' cried Tilly, recovering.

Jinny wavered. 'But will they find us?'

'Duffer! Of course. Ma'll give 'em the 'int. – Come on!'

Suiting the action to the word, and imitated by her sister, she scrambled over the window sill to the verandah. Polly found herself alone. Her conscientious scrupling: 'But mother may be cross!' had passed unheeded. Now, she, too, fell into a flurry. She could not remain there, by herself, to meet two young men, one of whom was a stranger: steps and voices were already audible at the end of the passage. And so, since there was nothing else for it, she clambered after her friends – though with difficulty; for she was not very tall.

This was why, when Mrs Beamish flourished open the door, exclaiming in a hearty tone: 'An' 'ere you'll find 'em, gents – sittin' at their needles, busy as bees!' the most conspicuous object in the room was a very neat leg, clad in a white stocking and black prunella boot, which was just being drawn up over the sill. It flashed from sight, and the patter of running feet beat the floor of the verandah.

'Ha, ha, too late! The birds have flown,' laughed Purdy, and smacked his thigh.

'Well, I declare, an' so they 'ave – the *naughty* creatures!' exclaimed Mrs Beamish in mock dismay. 'But trust you, Mr Smith, for sayin' the right thing. Jus' exackly like birds they are – so shy an' scared-like. But I'll give you the 'int, gents. They'll not be far away. Jus' you show 'em two can play at that game. – Mr S., you know the h'arbour!'

'Should say I do! Many's the time I've anchored there,' cried

Purdy with a guffaw. 'Come, Dick!' And crossing to the window he straddled over the frame, and disappeared.

Reluctantly Mahony followed him.

From the verandah they went down into the vegetable-garden, where the drab and tangled growths that had outlived the summer were beaten flat by the recent rains. At the foot of the garden, behind a clump of gooseberry-bushes, stood an arbour formed of a yellow buddleia. No trace of a petticoat was visible, so thick was the leafage; but a loud whispering and tittering betrayed the fugitives.

At the apparition of the young men, who stooped to the low entrance, there was a cascade of shrieks.

'Oh, lor, 'ow you frightened me! 'Owever did you know we were 'ere?'

'You wicked fellow! Get away, will you! I 'ate the very sight of you!' – this from Tilly, as Purdy, his hands on her hips, gave her a smacking kiss.

The other girls feared a like greeting; there were more squeaks and squeals, and some ineffectual dives for the doorway. Purdy spread out his arms. 'Hi, look out, stop 'em, Dick! Now then, man, here's your chance!'

Mahony stood blinking; it was dusk inside, after the dazzle of the sun. At this reminder of the foolish bet he had taken, he hurriedly seized the young woman who was next him, and embraced her. It chanced to be Jinny. She screamed, and made a feint of feeling mortally outraged. Mahony had to dodge a box on the ears.

But Purdy burst into a horselaugh, and held his sides. Without knowing why, Tilly joined in, and Jinny, too, was infected. When Purdy could speak, he blurted out: 'Dick, you fathead! – you jackass! – you've mugged the wrong one.'

At this clownish mirth, Mahony felt the blood boil up over ears and temples. For an instant he stood irresolute. Did he admit the blunder, his victim would be hurt. Did he deny it, he would save his own face at the expense of the other young woman's feelings. So, though he could have throttled Purdy he put a bold front on the matter.

'*Carpe diem* is my motto, my boy! I intend to make both young ladies pay toll.'

His words were the signal for a fresh scream and flutter: the third young person had escaped, and was flying down the path. This called for chase and capture. She was not very agile but she knew the ground, which, outside the garden, was rocky and uneven. For a time, she had Mahony at vantage; his heart was not in the game: in cutting undignified capers among the gooseberry-bushes he felt as foolish as a performing dog. Then, however, she caught her toe in her dress and stumbled. He could not disregard the opportunity; he advanced upon her.

But two beseeching hands fended him off. 'No . . . no. Please . . . oh, *please*, don't!'

This was no catchpenny coquetry; it was a genuine dread of undue familiarity. A kindred trait in Mahony's own nature rose to meet it.

'Certainly not, if it is disagreeable to you. Shall we shake hands instead?'

Two of the blackest eyes he had ever seen were raised to his, and a flushed face dimpled. They shook hands, and he offered his arm.

Halfway to the arbour, they met the others coming to find them. The girls bore diminutive parasols; and Purdy, in rollicking spirits, Tilly on one arm, Jinny on the other, held Polly's above his head. On the appearance of the laggards, Jinny, who had put her own interpretation on the misplaced kiss, prepared to free her arm; but Purdy, winking at his friend, squeezed it to his side and held her prisoner.

Tilly buzzed a word in his ear.

'Yes, by thunder!' he ejaculated; and letting go of his companions, he spun round like a ballet-dancer. 'Ladies! Let me introduce to you my friend, Dr Richard Townshend-Mahony, F.R.C.S., M.D., Edinburgh, at present proprietor of the "Diggers' Emporium", Dead Dog Hill, Ballarat. – Dick, my hearty, Miss Tilly Beamish, world-famed for her sauce; Miss Jinny, renowned for her skill in casting the eyes of sheep; and, last but not least, pretty little Polly Perkins, alias Miss Polly Turnham, whose good deeds put those of Dorcas to the blush.'

The Misses Beamish went into fits of laughter, and Tilly hit Purdy over the back with her parasol.

But the string of letters had puzzled them, roused their curiosity.

'What'n earth do they mean? – Gracious! So clever! It makes me feel quite queer.'

'Y'ought to 'ave told us before'and, Purd, so's we could 'ave studied up.'

However, a walk to a cave was under discussion, and Purdy

urged them on. 'Phœbus is on the wane, girls. And it's going to be damn' cold tonight.'

Once more with the young person called Polly as companion, Mahony followed after. He walked in silence, listening to the rattle of the three in front. At best he was but a poor hand at the kind of repartee demanded of their swains by these young women; and today his slender talent failed him altogether, crushed by the general tone of vulgar levity. Looking over at the horizon, which swam in a kind of gold-dust haze below the sinking sun, he smiled thinly to himself at Purdy's ideas of wiving.

Reminded he was not alone by feeling the hand on his arm tremble, he glanced down at his companion; and his eye was arrested by a neatly parted head, of the glossiest black imaginable.

He pulled himself together. 'Your cousins are excellent walkers.'

'Oh, yes, very. But they are not my cousins.'

Mahony pricked up his ears. 'But you live here?'

'Yes. I help moth . . . Mrs Beamish in the house.'

But as if, with this, she had said too much, she grew tongue-tied again; and there was nothing more to be made of her. Taking pity on her timidity, Mahony tried to put her at ease by talking about himself. He described his life on the diggings and the straits to which he was at times reduced: the buttons affixed to his clothing by means of gingerbeer-bottle wire; his periodic onslaughts on sock-darning; the celebrated pudding it had taken him over four hours to make. And Polly, listening to him, forgot her desire to run away. Instead, she could not help laughing at the tales of his masculine shiftlessness. But as soon as they came in view of the others, Tilly and Purdy sitting under one parasol on a rock by the cave, Jinny standing and looking out rather aggressively after the loiterers, she withdrew her arm.

'Moth . . . Mrs Beamish will need me to help her with tea. And . . . and *would* you please walk back with Jinny?'

Before he could reply, she had turned and was hurrying away.

They got home from the cave at sundown, he with the ripe Jinny hanging a dead weight on his arm, to find tea spread in the private parlour. The table was all but invisible under its load; and their hostess looked as though she had been parboiled on her own kitchen fire. She sat and fanned herself with a sheet of newspaper while, time and again, undaunted by refusals, she

49

pressed the good things upon her guests. There were juicy beef-steaks piled high with rings of onion, and a barra-coota, and a cold leg of mutton. There were apple-pies and jam-tarts, a dish of curds-and-whey and a jug of custard. Butter and bread were fresh and new; scones and cakes had just left the oven; and the great cups of tea were tempered by pure, thick cream.

To the two men who came from diggers' fare: cold chop for breakfast, cold chop for dinner and cold chop for tea: the meal was little short of a banquet; and few words were spoken in its course. But the moment arrived when they could eat no more, and when even Mrs Beamish ceased to urge them. Pipes and pouches were produced; Polly and Jinny rose to collect the plates, Tilly and her beau to sit on the edge of the verandah: they could be seen in silhouette against the rising moon, Tilly's head drooping to Purdy's shoulder.

Mrs Beamish looked from them to Mahony with a knowing smile, and whispered behind her hand: 'I *do* wish those two 'ud 'urry up an' make up their minds, that I do! I'd like to see my Tilda settled. No offence meant to young Smith. 'E's the best o' good company. But sometimes . . . well, I cud jus' knock their 'eads together when they sit so close, an' say: come, give over yer spoonin' an' get to business! Either you want one another or you don't. – I seen you watchin' our Polly, Mr Mahony' – she made Mahony wince by stressing the second syllable of his name. 'Bless you, no – no relation whatsoever! She just 'elps a bit in the 'ouse, an' is company for the girls. We tuck 'er in a year ago – 'er own relations 'ad played 'er a dirty trick. Mustn't let 'er catch me sayin' so, though; she won't 'ear a word against 'em, and that's as it should be.'

Looking round, and finding Polly absent from the room, she went on to tell Mahony how Polly's eldest brother, a ten years' resident in Melbourne, had sent to England for the girl on her leaving school, to come out and assist in keeping his house. And how an elder sister, who was governessing in Sydney, had chosen just this moment to throw up her post and return to quarter herself upon the brother.

'An' so when Polly gets 'ere – a little bit of a thing in short frocks, in charge of the capt'n – there was no room for 'er, an' she 'ad to look about 'er for somethin' else to do. We tuck 'er in, an', I will say, I've never regretted it. Indeed I don't know now, 'ow we ever got on without 'er. – Yes, it's you I'm talkin' about,

50

miss, singin' yer praises, an' you needn't get as red as if you'd bin up to mischief! Pa'll say as much for you, too.'

'That I will!' said Mr Beamish, opening his mouth for the first time except to put food in it. 'That I will,' and he patted Polly's hand. 'The man as gits Polly'll git a treasure.'

Polly blushed, after the helpless, touching fashion of very young creatures: the blood stained her cheeks, mounted to her forehead, spread in a warm wave over neck and ears. To spare her, Mahony turned his head and looked out of the window. He would have liked to say: Run away, child, run away, and don't let them see your confusion. Polly, however, went conscientiously about her task, and only left the room when she had picked up her full complement of plates. — But she did not appear again that night.

Deserted even by Mrs Beamish, the two men pushed back their chairs from the table and drew tranquilly at their pipes.

The innkeeper proved an odd, misty sort of fellow, exceedingly backward at declaring himself; it was as though each of his heavy words had to be fetched from a distance. 'No doubt about it, it's the wife that wears the breeches,' was Mahony's inward comment. And as one after another of his well-meant remarks fell flat: 'Become almost a deaf-mute, it would seem, under the eternal female clacking.'

But for each mortal there exists at least one theme to fire him. In the case of Beamish this turned out to be the Land Question. Before the gold discovery he had been a bush shepherd, he told Mahony, and, if he had called the tune, he would have lived and died one. But the wife had had ambitions, the children were growing up, and everyone knew what it was when women got a maggot in their heads. There had been no peace for him till he had chucked his twelve-year-job and joined the rush to Mount Alexander. But at heart he had remained a bushman; and he was now all on the side of the squatters in their tussle with the Crown. He knew a bit, he'd make bold to say, about the acreage needed in certain districts per head of sheep; he could tell a tale of the risks and mischances squatting involved: 'If t'aint fire it's flood, an' if the water passes you by it's the scab or the rot.' To his thinking, the Government's attempt to restrict the areas of sheep-runs, and to give effect to the 'fourteen-year-clause' which limited the tenure, were acts of folly. The gold supply would give out as suddenly as it had begun; but sheep would graze there till the crack of doom — the land was fit for nothing else.

Mahony thought this point of view lopsided. No new country could hope to develop and prosper without a steady influx of the right kind of population; and this the colony would never have, so long as the authorities, by refusing to sell them land, made it impossible for immigrants to settle there. Why, America was but three thousand miles distant from the old country, compared with Australia's thirteen thousand, and in America land was to be had in plenty at five shillings per acre. As to Mr Beamish's idea of the gold giving out, the geological formation of the gold-fields rendered that improbable. He sympathized with the squatters, who naturally enough believed their rights to the land inalienable; but a government worthy of the name must legislate with an eye to the future, not for the present alone.

Their talk was broken by long gaps. In these, the resonant voice of Mrs Beamish could be heard rebuking and directing her two handmaidens.

'Now then, Jinny, look alive, an' don't ack like a dyin' duck in a thunderstorm, or you'll never get back to do *your* bit o' spoonin'! – Save them bones, Polly. Never waste an atom, my chuck – remember that, when you've got an 'ouse of your own! – No, girls, I always says, through their stomachs, that's the short-cut to their 'earts. The rest's on'y fal-de-lal-ing.' – On the verandah, in face of the vasty star-spangled night, Tilly's head had found its resting-place, and an arm lay round her waist.

'I shall make 'im cut off 'is beard first thing,' said Jinny that night: she was sitting half-undressed on the side of a big bed, which the three girls shared with one another.

'Um! Just you wait and see if it's as easy as you think,' retorted Tilly from her pillow. Again Purdy had let slip a golden chance to put the decisive question; and Tilly's temper was short in consequence.

'Mrs Dr Mahony . . . though I do wonder 'ow 'e ever keeps people from saying Ma-*hon*-y,' said Jinny dreamily. She, too, had spent some time in star-gazing, and believed she had ground for hope.

'Just listen to 'er, will you!' said Tilly angrily. 'Upon my word, Jinny Beamish, if one didn't know you 'ad the 'abit of marrying yourself off to every fresh cove you meet, one 'ud say you was downright bold!'

'*You* needn't talk! Everyone can see you're as mad as can be because you can't bring your old dot-and-go-one to the scratch.'

'Oh, hush, Jinny!' said Polly, grieved at this thrust into Tilly's open wound.

'Well, it's true. – Oh, look 'ere now, there's not a drop o' water in this blessed jug again. 'Oo's week is it to fill it? Tilly B., it's yours!'

'Serves you right. You can fetch it yourself.'

'Think I see myself!'

Polly intervened. 'I'll go for it, Jinny.'

'What a little duck you are, Poll! But you shan't go alone. I'll carry the candle.'

Tying on a petticoat over her bedgown, Polly took the ewer, and with Jinny as torch-bearer set forth. There was still some noise in the public part of the house, beside the bar; but the passage was bare and quiet. The girls crept mousily past the room occupied by the two young men, and after several false alarms and suppressed chirps reached the back door, and filled the jug at the tap of the galvanized-iron tank.

The return journey was not so successful. Just as they got level with the visitors' room, they heard feet crossing the floor. Polly started; the water splashed over the neck of the jug, and fell with a loud plop. At this Jinny lost her head and ran off with the candle. Polly, in a panic of fright, dived into the pantry with her burden, and crouched down behind a tub of fermenting gingerbeer. – And sure enough, a minute after, the door of the room opposite was flung open and a pair of jackboots landed in the passage.

Nor was this the worst: the door was not shut again but remained ajar. Through the chink, Polly, shrunk to her smallest – what if one of them should feel hungry, and come into the pantry and discover her? – Polly heard Purdy say with appalling loudness: 'Oh, go on, old man – don't jaw so!' He then seemed to plunge his head in the basin, for it was with a choke and a splutter that he next inquired: 'And what did you think of the little 'un? Wasn't I right?'

There was the chink of coins handled, and the other voice answered: 'Here's what I think. Take your money, my boy, and be done with it!'

'Dick! – Great Snakes! Why, damn it all, man, you don't mean to tell me . . .'

'And understand, sir, in future, that I do not make bets where a lady is concerned.'

'Oh, I know – only on the Tilly-Jinny-sort. And yet . . . good Lord, Dick!' – the rest was drowned in a bawl of laughter.

Under cover of it Polly took to her heels and fled, regardless of the open door, or the padding of her bare feet on the boards.

Without replying to the astonished Jinny's query in respect of the water, she climbed over Tilly to her place beside the wall, and shutting her eyes very tight, drew the sheet over her face: it felt as though it would never be cool again. – Hence, Jinny, agreeably wakeful, was forced to keep her thoughts to herself; for if you lie between two people, one of whom is in a bad temper, and the other fast asleep, you might just as well be alone in bed.

Next morning Polly alleged a headache and did not appear at breakfast. Only Jinny and Tilly stood on the verandah of romantic memories, and ruefully waved their handkerchiefs, keeping it up till even the forms of horses were blurred in the distance.

CHAPTER SEVEN

His tent-home had never seemed so comfortless. He ended his
solitary ride late at night and wet to the skin; his horse had cast a
shoe far from any smithy. Long Jim alone came to the door to
greet him. The shopman, on whose doltish honesty Mahony
would have staked his head, had profited by his absence to empty
the cash-box and go off on the spree. — Even one of the cats had
met its fate in an old shaft, where its corpse still swam.

The following day, as a result of exposure and hard riding,
Mahony was attacked by dysentery; and before he had recovered, the goods arrived from Melbourne. They had to be
unloaded, at some distance from the store, conveyed there, got
under cover, checked off and arranged. This was carried out in
sheets of cold rain, which soaked the canvas walls and made it
doubly hard to get about the clay tracks that served as streets.
As if this were not enough, the river in front of the house rose —
rose, and in two twos was over its banks — and he and Long Jim
spent a night in their clothes, helping neighbours less fortunately
placed to move their belongings into safety.

The lion's share of this work fell on him. Long Jim still
carried his arm in a sling, and was good for nothing but to guard
the store and summon Mahony on the appearance of customers. Since his accident, too, the fellow had suffered from
frequent fits of colic or cramp, and was for ever slipping off to
the township to find the spirits in which his employer refused
to deal. For the unloading and warehousing of the goods, it was
true, old Ocock had loaned his sons; but the strict watch
Mahony felt bound to keep over this pretty pair far outweighed
what their help was worth to him.

Now it was Sunday evening, and for the first time for more
than a week he could call his soul his own again. He stood at
the door and watched those of his neighbours who were not
Roman Catholics making for church and chapel, to which half-

a-dozen tinkly bells invited them.. The weather had finally
cleared up, and a goodly number of people waded past him
through the mire. Among them, in seemly Sabbath dress, went
Ocock, with his two black sheep at heel. The old man was a
rigid Methodist, and at a recent prayer-meeting had been moved
to bear public witness to his salvation. This was no doubt one
reason why the young scapegrace Tom's almost simultaneous
misconduct had been so bitter a pill for him to swallow: while,
through God's mercy, he was become an exemplar to the weaker
brethren, a son of his made his name to stink in the nostrils of
the reputable community. Mahony liked to believe that there
was good in everybody, and thought the intolerant harshness to
which the boy was subjected would defeat its end. Yet it was
open to question if clemency would have answered better. 'Bad
eggs, the brace of them!' had been his own verdict, after a week's
trial of the lads. One would not, the other apparently could not
work. Johnny, the elder, was dull and liverish from intemperance; and the round-faced adolescent, the news of whose father-
hood had raced the wind, was so sheep-faced, so craven, in the
presence of his elders, that he could not say bo to a battledore.
There was something unnatural about this fierce timidity – and
the doctor in Mahony caught a quick glimpse of the probable
reverse of the picture.

But it was cold, in face of all this rain-soaked clay; cold blue-
grey clouds drove across a washed-out sky; and he still felt unwell. Returning to his living-room, where a small American
stove was burning, he prepared for a quiet evening. In a corner
by the fire stood an old packing-case. He lifted the lid and thrust
his hand in: it was here he kept his books. He needed no light
to see by; he knew each volume by the feel. And after fumbling
for a little among the tumbled contents, he drew forth a work on
natural science and sat down to read. But he did not get far;
his brain was tired, intractable. Lighting his pipe, he tilted back
his chair, laid the *Vestiges* face downwards, and put his feet on
the table.

How differently bashfulness impressed one in the case of the
weaker sex! There, it was altogether pleasing. Young Ocock's
gaucherie had recalled the little maid Polly's ingenuous con-
fúsion, at finding herself the subject of conversation. He had not
once consciously thought of Polly since his return. Now, when
he did so, he found to his surprise that she had made herself
quite a warm little nest in his memory. Looked back on, she

stood out in high relief against her somewhat graceless surroundings. Small doubt she was both maidenly and refined. He
also remembered with a sensible pleasure her brisk service, her
consideration for others. What a boon it would have been,
during the past week, to have a busy, willing little woman at
work, with him and for him, behind the screen! As it was, for
want of a helping hand the place was like a pigsty. He had had
neither time nor energy to clean up. The marks of hobnailed
boots patterned the floor; loose mud, and crumbs from meals,
had been swept into corners or under the stretcher-bed; while
commodities that had overflowed the shop added to the disorder. Good Lord, no! . . . no place this for a woman.

He rose and moved restlessly about, turning things over with
his foot: these old papers should be burnt, and that heap of
straw-packing; those empty sardine- and coffee-tins be thrown
into the refuse-pit. Scrubbed and clean, it was by no means an
uncomfortable room; and the stove drew well. He was proud of
his stove; many houses had not even a chimney. He stood and
stared at it; but his thoughts were elsewhere: he found himself
trying to call to mind Polly's face. Except for a pair of big
black eyes – magnificent eyes they seemed to him in retrospect
– he had carried away with him nothing of her outward appearance. Yes, stay! – her hair: her hair was so glossy that, when
the sun caught it, highlights came out on it – so much he
remembered. From this he fell to wondering whether her brain
kept pace with her nimble hands and ways. Was she stupid or
clever? He could not tolerate stupidity. And Polly had given
him no chance to judge her; had hardly opened her lips before
him. What a timid little thing she was to be sure! He should have
made it his business to draw her out, by being kind and encour-
aging. Instead of which he had acted towards her, he felt convinced, like an ill-mannered boor.

He did not know how it was, but he couldn't detach his
thoughts from Polly this evening: to their accompaniment he
paced up and down. All of a sudden he stood still, and gave a
short, hearty laugh. He had just seen, in a kind of phantom
picture, the feet of the sisters Beamish as they sat on the
verandah edge: both young women wore flat sandal-shoes. And
so that neatest of neat ankles had been little Polly's property!
For his life he loved a well-turned ankle in a woman.

A minute later he sat down at the table again. An idea had
occurred to him: he would write Polly a letter – a letter that

called for acknowledgement – and form an opinion of the girl from her reply. Taking a sheet of thin blue paper and a magnum bonum pen he wrote:

Dear Miss Turnham,

I wonder if I might ask you to do me a favour? On getting back to Ballarat, I find that the rain has spoilt my store flag. Would you be so kind as to make me a new one? I have no lady friends here to apply to for help, and I am sure you are clever with your needle. If you consent, I will send you the old flag as a pattern, and stuff for the new one. My kind regards to all at the Hotel.

Faithfully yours,
Richard Townshend-Mahony.

P.S. I have not forgotten our pleasant walk to the cave.

He went out to the post with it himself. In one hand he carried the letter, in the other the candle-end stuck in a bottle that was known as a 'Ballarat lantern'; for it was a pitch-dark night.

Trade was slack; in consequence he found the four days that had to pass before he could hope for an answer exceptionally long. After their lapse, he twice spent an hour at the Post Office, in a fruitless attempt to get near the little window. On returning from the second of these absences, he found the letter waiting for him; it had been delivered by hand.

So far good: Polly had risen to his fly! He broke the seal.

Dear Sir,

I shall be happy to help you with your new flag if I am able. Will you kindly send the old one and the stuff down by my brother, who is coming to see me on Saturday. He is working at Rotten Gully, and his name is Ned. I do not know if I sew well enough to please you, but I will do my best.

I remain,
Yours truly,
Mary Turnham.

Mahony read, smiled and laid the letter down – only to pick it up again. It pleased him, did this prim little note: there was just the right shade of formal reserve about it. Then he began to study particulars: grammar and spelling were correct; the penmanship was in the Italian style, minute, yet flowing, the letters dowered with generous loops and tails. But surely he had seen this writing before? By Jupiter, yes! This was the hand of the letter Purdy had shown him on the road to Melbourne. The little puss! So she not only wrote her own letters, but those of her friends as well. In that case she was certainly not stupid; for she was much the youngest of the three.

Today was Thursday. Summoning Long Jim from his seat behind the counter Mahony dispatched him to Rotten Gully, with an injunction not to show himself till he had found a digger of the name of Turnham. And having watched Jim set out, at a snail's pace and murmuring to himself, Mahony went into the store, and measured and cut off material for the new flag, from two different coloured rolls of stuff.

It was ten o'clock that night before Polly's brother presented himself. Mahony met him at the door and drew him in: the stove crackled, the room was swept and garnished – he flattered himself that the report on his habitat would be a favourable one. Ned's appearance gave him a pleasant shock: it was just as if Polly herself, translated into male terms, stood before him. No need, now, to cudgel his brains for her image! In looking at Ned, he looked again at Polly. The wide-awake off, the same fine, soft, black hair came to light – here, worn rather long and curly – the same glittering black eyes, ivory-white skin, short, straight nose; and, as he gazed, an offshoot of Mahony's consciousness wondered from what quarter this middle-class English family fetched its dark, un-English strain.

In the beginning he exerted himself to set the lad at ease. He soon saw, however, that he might spare his pains. Though clearly not much more than eighteen years old, Ned Turnham had the aplomb and assurance of double that age. Lolling back in the single armchair the room boasted, he more than once stretched out his hand and helped himself from the sherry-bottle Mahony had placed on the table. And the disparity in their ages notwithstanding, there was no trace of deference in his manner. Or the sole hint of it was: he sometimes smothered a profane word, or apologized, with a winning smile, for an oath that had slipped out unawares. Mahony could not accustom himself to the foul language that formed the diggers' idiom. Here, in the case of Polly's brother, he sought to overlook the offence, or to lay the blame for it on other shoulders: at his age, and alone, the boy should never have been plunged into this Gehenna.

Ned talked mainly of himself and his doings. But other facts also transpired, of greater interest to his hearer. Thus Mahony learned that, out of a family of nine, four had found their way to the colony, and a fifth was soon to follow – a mere child this, on the under side of fifteen. He gathered, too, that the eldest brother, John by name, was regarded as a kind of Napoleon by the younger fry. At thirty, this John was a partner in the largest wholesale dry-goods warehouse in Melbourne. He had also married money, and intended in due course to stand for the Legislative Council. Behind Ned's windy bragging Mahony thought he discerned tokens of a fond, brotherly pride. If this were so, the affair had its pathetic side; for, from what the boy said, it was evident that the successful man of business held his relatives at arm's length. And as Ned talked on, Mahony conceived John to himself as a kind of electro-magnet, which, once it had drawn these lesser creatures after it, switched off the current and left them to their own devices. Ned, young as he was, had tried his hand at many trades. At present he was working as a hired digger; but this, only till he could strike a softer job. Digging was not for him, thank you; what you earned at it hardly repaid you for the sweat you dripped. His every second word, indeed, was of how he could amass most money with the minimum of bodily exertion.

This calculating, unyouthful outlook was repugnant to Mahony, and for all his goodwill, the longer he listened to Ned, the cooler he felt himself grow. Another disagreeable impression was left by the grudging, if-nothing-better-turns-up fashion in which Ned accepted an impulsive offer on his part to take him into the store. It was made on the spur of the moment, and Mahony had qualms about it while his words were still warm on the air, realizing that the overture was aimed, not at Ned in person, but at Ned as Polly's brother. But his intuition did not reconcile him to Ned's lukewarmness; he would have preferred a straight refusal. The best trait he could discover in the lad was his affection for his sister. This seemed genuine: he was going to see her again – getting a lift halfway, tramping the other twenty-odd miles – at the end of the week. Perhaps though, in the case of such a young opportunist, the thought of Mrs Beamish's lavish board played no small part; for Ned had a rather lean, underfed look. But this only occurred to Mahony afterwards. Then, his chief vexation was with himself: it would have been kinder to set a dish of solid food before the boy, in place of the naked sherry-bottle. But as usual, his hospitable leanings came too late.

One thing more. As he lighted Ned and his bundle of stuff through the shop, he was impelled to slip a coin into the boy's hand, with a murmured apology for the trouble he had put him to. And a something, the merest nuance in Ned's manner of receiving and pocketing the money, flashed the uncomfortable suspicion through the giver's mind that it had been looked for, expected. And this was the most unpleasant touch of all.

But, bless his soul! did not most large families include at least one poorish specimen? – he had got thus far, by the time he came to wind up his watch for the night. And next day he felt sure he had judged Ned over-harshly. His first impressions of people – he had had occasion to deplore the fact before now – were apt to be either dead white or black as ink; the web of his mind took on no half tints. The boy had not betrayed any actual vices; and time might be trusted to knock the bluster out of him. With this reflection Mahony dismissed Ned from his mind. He had more important things to think of, chief among which was his own state with regard to Ned's sister. And during the fortnight that followed he went about making believe to weigh this matter, to view it from every coign; for it did not suit him, even in secret, to confess to the vehemence with which, when he much desired a thing, his temperament knocked flat the hurdles of reason. The truth was, his mind was made up – and had been, all along. At the earliest possible opportunity, he was going to ask Polly to be his wife.

Doubts beset him of course. How could he suppose that a girl who knew nothing of him, who had barely seen him, would either want or consent to marry him? And even if – for 'if's' were cheap – she did say yes, would it be fair of him to take her out of a comfortable home, away from friends – such as they were! – of her own sex, to land her in these crude surroundings, where he did not know a decent woman to bear her company? Yet there was something to be said for him, too. He was very lonely. Now that Purdy had gone he was reduced, for society, to the Long Jims and Ococks of the place. What would he not give, once more to have a refined companion at his side? Certainly marriage might postpone the day on which he hoped to shake the dust of Australia off his feet. Life *à deux* would mean a larger outlay; saving not prove so easy. Still it could be done; and he would gladly submit to the delay if, by doing so, he could get Polly. Besides, if this new happiness came to him, it would help him to see the years he had spent in the colony in a truer and juster light. And then, when the hour of departure did strike, what a joy to have a wife to carry with one – a Polly to rescue, to restore to civilization!

He had to remind himself more than once, during this fortnight, that she would be able to devote only a fraction of her day to flag-making. But he was at the end of his tether by the time a parcel and a letter were left for him at the store – again by hand: little Polly had plainly no sixpences to spare. The needlework was perfect, of course; he hardly glanced at it, even when he had opened and read the letter. This was of the same decorous nature as the first. Polly returned a piece of stuff that had remained over. He had really sent material enough for two flags, she wrote; but she had not wished to keep him waiting so long. And then, in a postscript:

Mr Smith was here last Sunday. I am to say Mrs Beamish would be very pleased if you also would call again to see us.

He ran the flag up to the top of his forty-foot staff and wrote:

What I want to know, Miss Polly, is, would you be glad to see me?

But Polly was not to be drawn.

We should all be very pleased.

Some days previously Mahony had addressed a question to Henry Ocock. With this third letter from Polly, he held the lawyer's answer in his hand. It was unsatisfactory.

Yourself ats. Bolliver. We think that action will be set down for trial in about six weeks' time. In these circumstances we do not think any useful purpose will be served by you calling to see us until this is done. We should be glad if you would call after the action is entered.

Six weeks' time? The man might as well have said a year. And meanwhile Purdy was stealing a march on him, was paying clandestine visits to Geelong. Was it conceivable that anyone in

62

his five senses could prefer Tilly to Polly? It was not. In the clutch of a sudden fear Mahony went to Bath's and ordered a horse for the following morning.

This time he left his store in charge of a young consumptive, whose plight had touched his heart: the poor fellow was stranded on Ballarat without a farthing, having proved, like many another of his physique, quite unfit for work on the diggings. A strict Baptist this Hempel, and one who believed hellfire would be his portion if he so much as guessed at the 'plant' of his employer's cash-box. He also pledged his word to bear and forbear with Long Jim. The latter saw himself superseded with an extreme bad grace, and was in no hurry to find a new job.

Mahony's nag was in good condition, and he covered the distance in a trifle over six hours.

He had evidently hit on the family washing-day. The big boiler in the yard belched clouds of steam: the female inmates of the Hotel were gathered in the out-house: he saw them through the door as he rode in at the gate. All three girls stood before tubs, their sleeves rolled up, their arms in the lather. At his apparition there was a characteristic chorus of cheeps and shrills; and the door was banged to. Mrs Beamish alone came out to greet him. She was moist and blown, and smelt of soap.

Not in a mood to mince matters, he announced straightway the object of his visit. He was prepared for some expression of surprise on the part of the good woman; but the blend of sheepfaced amazement and uncivil incredulity to which he subjected him made him hot and angry; and he vouchsafed no further word of explanation.

Mrs Beamish presently so far recovered as to be able to finish wiping the suds from her fat red arms.

Thereafter, she gave way to a very feminine weakness.

'Well, and now I come to think of it, I'm blessed if I didn't suspeck somethin' of it, right from the start! Why, didn't I say to Beamish, with me own lips, 'ow you couldn't 'ardly take your eyes off 'er? Well, well, I'm sure I wish you every 'appiness — though 'ow we're h'ever goin' to get on without Polly, I reely don't know. Don't I wish it 'ad bin one o' my two as 'ad tuck your fancy — that's all! Between you an' me, I don't believe a blessed thing's goin' to come of all young Smith's danglin' round. An' Polly's still a bit young — only just turned sixteen. Not as she's any the worse o' that though; you'll get 'er h'all

63

the easier into your ways. An' now I mus' look smart, an' get you a bite o' somethin' after your ride.'

In vain did Mahony assure her that he had lunched on the road. He did not know Mrs Beamish. He was forced not only to sit down to the meal she spread, but also, under her argus eye, to eat of it.

When after a considerable delay Polly at length appeared, she had removed all traces of the tub. The hand was cold that he took in his, as he asked her if she would walk with him to the cave.

This time, she trembled openly. Like a lamb led to the slaughter, he thought, looking down at her with tender eyes. Small doubt that vulgar creature within-doors had betrayed him to Polly, and exaggerated the ordeal that lay before her. When once she was his wife he would not consent to her remaining intimate with people of the Beamishes' kidney: what a joy to get her out of their clutches! Nor should she spoil her pretty shape by stooping over a wash-tub.

In his annoyance he forgot to moderate his pace. Polly had to trip many small steps to keep up with him. When they reached the entrance to the cave, she was flushed and out of breath.

Mahony stood and looked down at her. How young she was . . . how young and innocent! Every feature of her dear little face still waited, as it were, for the strokes of time's chisel. It should be the care of his life that none but the happiest lines were graved upon its precious surface.

'Polly,' he said, fresh from his scrutiny. 'Polly, I'm not going to beat about the bush with you. I think you know I came here today only to see you.'

Polly's head drooped further forward; now, the rim of her bonnet hid her face.

'You aren't afraid of me, are you, Polly?'

Oh, no, she was not afraid.

'Nor have you forgotten me?'

Polly choked a little, in her attempt to answer. She could not tell him that she had carried his letters about with her by day, and slept with them under her pillow; that she knew every word in them by heart, and had copied and practised the bold flourish of the Dickens-like signature; that she had never let his name cross her lips; that she thought him the kindest, handsomest, cleverest man in the world, and would willingly have humbled

64

herself to the dust before him: all this boiled and bubbled in her, as she brought forth her poor little 'no'.

'Indeed, I hope not,' went on Mahony. 'Because, Polly, I've come to ask you if you will be my wife.'

Rocks, trees, hills, suddenly grown tipsy, went see-sawing round Polly, when she heard these words said. She shut her eyes, and hid her face in her hands. Such happiness seemed improbable – was not to be grasped. 'Me? . . . your wife?' she stammered through her fingers.

'Yes, Polly. Do you think you could learn to care for me a little, my dear? No, don't be in a hurry to answer. Take your own time.'

But she needed none. With what she felt to be a most unmaidenly eagerness, yet could not subdue, she blurted out: 'I know I could. I . . . I do.'

'Thank God!' said Mahony. 'Thank God for that!'

He let his arms fall to his sides; he found he had been holding them stiffly out from him. He sat down. 'And now take away your hands, Polly, and let me see your face. Don't be ashamed of showing me what you feel. This is a sacred moment for us. We are promising to take each other, you know, for richer for poorer, for better for worse – as the good old words have it. And I must warn you, my dear, you are not marrying a rich man. I live in a poor, rough place, and have only a poor home to offer you. Oh, I have had many scruples about asking you to leave your friends to come and share it with me, Polly my love!'

'I'm not afraid. I am strong. I can work.'

'And I shall take every care of you. Please God, you will never regret your choice.'

They were within sight of the house where they sat; and Mahony imagined rude, curious eyes. So he did not kiss her. Instead, he drew her arm through his, and together they paced up and down the path they had come by, while he laid his plans before her, and confessed to the dreams he had dreamt of their wedded life. It was a radiant afternoon: in the distance the sea lay deep blue, with turquoise shallows; a great white bird of a ship, her canvas spread to the breeze, was making for . . . why, today he did not care whether for port or for 'home'; the sun went down in a blaze behind a bank of emerald green. And little Polly agreed with everything he said – was all one lovely glow of acquiescence. He thought no happier mortal than himself trod the earth.

CHAPTER EIGHT

Mahony remained at the Hotel till the following afternoon, then walked to Geelong and took the steam-packet to Melbourne. The object of his journey was to ask Mr John Turnham's formal sanction to his marriage. Polly accompanied him a little way on his walk. And whenever he looked back he saw her standing fluttering her handkerchief – a small, solitary figure on the bare, red road.

He parted from her with a sense of leaving his most precious possession behind, so close had words made the tie. On the other hand, he was not sorry to be out of range for a while of the Beamish family's banter. This had set in, the evening before, as soon as he and Polly returned to the house – pacing the deck of the little steamer, he writhed anew at the remembrance. Jokes at their expense had been cracked all through supper: his want of appetite, for instance, was the subject of a dozen crude insinuations; and this, though everyone present knew that he had eaten a hearty meal not two hours previously; had been kept up till he grew stony and savage, and Polly, trying hard not to mind but red to the rims of her ears, slipped out of the room. Supper over, Mrs Beamish announced in a loud voice that the verandah was at the disposal of the 'turtle-doves'. She no doubt expected them to bill and coo in public, as Purdy and Matilda had done. On edge at the thought, he drew Polly into the comparative seclusion of the garden. Here they strolled up and down, their promenade bounded at the lower end by the dense-leaved arbour under which they had first met. In its screening shadow he took the kiss he had then been generous enough to forgo.

'I think I loved you, Polly, directly I saw you.'

In the distance a clump of hills rose steep and bare from the waste land by the sea's edge – he could see them at this moment as he leant over the taffrail: with the sun going down behind them they were the colour of smoked glass. Last night they had been white with moonlight, which lay spilled out upon them like milk. Strange old hills! Standing there unchanged, unshaken, from time immemorial, they made the troth that had been plighted under their shield seem pitifully frail. And yet . . . The vows which Polly and he had found so new, so wonderful; were not these, in truth, as ancient as the hills themselves, and as undying? Countless generations of human lovers had uttered them. The lovers passed, but the pledges remained: had put on immortality.

In the course of their talk it leaked out that Polly would not feel comfortable till her choice was ratified by brother John.

'I'm sure you will like John; he is so clever.'

'I shall like everyone belonging to you, my Polly!'

As she lost her shyness Mahony made the discovery that she laughed easily, and was fond of a jest. Thus, when he admitted to her that he found it difficult to distinguish one fair, plump, sister Beamish from the other; that they seemed to him as much alike as two firm, pink-ribbed mushrooms, the little woman was hugely tickled by his masculine want of perception. 'Why, Jinny has brown eyes and Tilly blue!'

What he did not know, and what Polly did not confess to him, was that much of her merriment arose from sheer lightness of heart. – She, silly goose that she was! who had once believed Jinny to be the picked object of his attentions.

But she grew serious again: could he tell her, please, why Mr Smith wrote so seldom to Tilly? Poor Tilly was unhappy at his long silences – fretted over them in bed at night.

Mahony made excuses for Purdy, urging his unsettled mode of life. But it pleased him to see that Polly took sides with her friend, and loyally espoused her cause.

No, there had not been a single jarring note in all their intercourse; each moment had made the dear girl dearer to him. Now, worse luck, forty-odd miles were between them again.

It had been agreed that he should call at her brother's private house, towards five o'clock in the afternoon. He had thus to kill time for the better part of the next day. His first visit was to a jeweller's in Great Collins Street. Here, he pushed aside a tray of showy diamonds – a successful digger was covering the fat, red hands of his bride with them – and chose a slender, discreetly chased setting, containing three small stones. No matter what household duties fell to Polly's share, this little ring would not be out of place on her finger.

From there he went to the last address Purdy had given him; only to find that the boy had again disappeared. Before parting from Purdy, the time before, he had lent him half the purchase-money for a horse and dray, thus enabling him to carry out an old scheme of plying for hire at the city wharf. According to the landlord of the 'Hotel Vendôme', to whom Mahony was referred for fuller information, Purdy had soon tired of this job, and selling dray and beast for what he could get had gone off on a new rush to 'Simson's Diggings' or the 'White Hills'. Small wonder Miss Tilly was left languishing for news of him.

Pricked by the nervous disquietude of those who have to do with the law, Mahony next repaired to his solicitor's office. But Henry Ocock was closeted with a more important client. This, Grindle the clerk, whom he met on the stairs, informed him, with an evident relish, and with some hidden, hinted meaning in the corners of his shifty little eyes. It was lost on Mahony, who was not the man to accept hints from a stranger.

The hour was on lunch-time; Grindle proposed that they should go together to a legal chop-house, which offered prime value for your money, and where, over the meal, he would give Mahony the latest news of his suit. At a loss how to get through the day, the latter followed him – he was resolved, too, to practise economy from now on. But when he sat down to a dirty cloth and fly-spotted cruet he regretted his compliance. Besides, the news Grindle was able to give him amounted to nothing; the case had not budged since last he heard of it. Worse still was the clerk's behaviour. For after lauding the cheapness of the establishment, Grindle disputed the price of each item on the 'meenew', and, when he came to pay his bill, chuckled over having been able to diddle the waiter of a penny.

He was plainly one of those who feel the constant need of an audience. And since there was no office-boy present, for him to dazzle with his wit, he applied himself to demonstrating to his table-companion what a sad, sad dog he was.

'Women are the deuce, sir,' he asserted, lying back in his chair and sending two trails of smoke from his nostrils. 'The very deuce! You should hear my governor on the subject! He'd tickle your ears for you. Look here, I'll give you the tip: this move, you know, to Ballarat, that he's drivin' at: what'ull you bet me there isn't a woman in the case? Fact! 'Pon my word

68

there is. And a devilish fine woman, too!' He shut one eye and laid a finger along his nose. 'You won't blow the gab? — that's why you couldn't have your parleyvoo this morning. When milady comes to town H.O.'s *non est* as long as she's here. And she with a hubby of her own, too! What 'ud our old pa say to that, eh?'

Mahony, who could draw in his feelers no further than he had done, touched the limit of his patience. 'My connection with Mr Ocock is a purely business one. I have no intention of trespassing on his private affairs, or of having them thrust upon me. Carver, my bill!'

Bowing distantly he stalked out of the eating-house and back to the 'Criterion', where he dined. 'So much for a maiden attempt at economy!'

Towards five o'clock he took his seat in an omnibus that plied between the city and the seaside suburb of St Kilda, three miles off. A cool breeze went; the hoofs of the horses beat a rataplan on the hard surface; the great road, broad enough to make three of, was alive with smart gigs and trotters.

St Kilda was a group of white houses facing the Bay. Most were of weatherboard with brick chimneys; but there were also a few of a more solid construction. Mahony's goal was one of these: a low, stone villa surrounded by verandahs, in the midst of tasteful grounds. The drive up to the door led through a shrubbery, artfully contrived of the native ti-tree; behind the house stretched kitchen and fruit-gardens. Many rare plants grew in the beds. There was a hedge of geraniums close on fifteen feet high.

His knock was answered by a groom, who made a saucy face: Mr Turnham and his lady were attending the Governor's ball this evening and did not receive. Mahony insisted on the delivery of his visiting-card. And since the servant still blocked the entrance he added: 'Inform your master, my man, that I am the bearer of a message from his sister, Miss Mary Turnham.'

The man shut him out, left him standing on the verandah. After a lengthy absence, he returned, and with a 'Well, come along in then!' opened the door of a parlour. This was a large room, well furnished in horsehair and rep. Wax-lights stood on the mantelpiece before a gilt-framed pierglass; coloured prints hung on the walls.

While Mahony was admiring the genteel comfort to which he

had long been a stranger, John Turnham entered the room. He had a quiet tread, but took determined strides at the floor. In his hand he held Mahony's card, and he looked from Mahony to it and back again.

'To what do I owe the pleasure, Mr . . . er . . . Mahony?' he asked, refreshing his memory with a glance at the pasteboard. He spoke in the brusque tone of one accustomed to run through many applicants in the course of an hour. 'I understand that you make use of my sister Mary's name.' And, as Mahony did not instantly respond, he snapped out: 'My time is short, sir!'

A tinge of colour mounted to Mahony's cheeks. He answered with equal stiffness: 'That is so. I come from Mr William Beamish's "Family Hotel", and am commissioned to bring you your sister's warm love and regards.'

John Turnham bowed; and waited.

'I have also to acquaint you with the fact,' continued Mahony, gathering hauteur as he went, 'that the day before yesterday I proposed marriage to your sister, and that she did me the honour of accepting me.'

'Ah, indeed!' said John Turnham, with a kind of ironic snort. 'And may I ask on what ground you –'

'On the ground, sir, that I have a sincere affection for Miss Turnham, and believe it lies in my power to make her happy.'

'Of that, kindly allow me to judge. My sister is a mere child – too young to know her own mind. Be seated.'

To a constraining, restraining vision of little Polly, Mahony obeyed, stifling the near retort that she was not too young to earn her living among strangers. The two men faced each other on opposite sides of the table. John Turnham had the same dark eyes and hair, the same short, straight nose as his brother and sister, but not their exotic pallor. His skin was bronzed; and his large, scarlet mouth supplied a vivid dash of colour. He wore bushy side-whiskers.

'And now, Mr Mahony, I will ask you a blunt question. I receive letters regularly from my sister, but I cannot recall her ever having mentioned your name. Who and what are you?'

'Who am I?' flared up Mahony. 'A gentleman like yourself, sir! – though a poor one. As for Miss Turnham not mentioning me in her letters, that is easily explained. I only had the pleasure of making her acquaintance five or six weeks ago.'

'You are candid,' said Polly's brother, and smiled without unclosing his lips. 'But your reply to my question tells me noth-

70

ing. May I ask what . . . er . . . under what . . . er . . . circumstances you came out to the colony, in the first instance?'

'No, sir, you may not!' cried Mahony, and flung up from his seat; he scented a deadly insult in the question.

'Come, come, Mr Mahony,' said Turnham in a more conciliatory tone. 'Nothing is gained by being tetchy. And my inquiry is not unreasonable. You are an entire stranger to me; my sister has known you but for a few weeks, and is a young and inexperienced girl into the bargain. You tell me you are a gentleman. Sir! I had as lief you said you were a blacksmith. In this grand country of ours, where progress is the watchword, effete standards and clogging traditions must go by the board. Grit is of more use to us than gentility. Each single bricklayer who unships serves the colony better than a score of gentlemen.'

'In that I am absolutely not at one with you, Mr Turnham,' said Mahony coldly. He had sat down again, feeling rather ashamed of his violence. 'Without a leaven of refinement, the very raw material of which the existing population is composed –'

But Turnham interrupted him. 'Give 'em time, sir, give 'em time. God bless my soul! Rome wasn't built in a day. But to resume. I have repeatedly had occasion to remark in what small stead the training that fits a man for a career in the old country stands him here. And that is why I am dissatisfied with your reply. Show me your muscles, sir, give me a clean bill of health, tell me if you have learnt a trade and can pay your way. See, I will be frank with you. The position I occupy today I owe entirely to my own efforts. I landed in the colony ten years ago, when this marvellous city of ours was little more than a village settlement. I had but five pounds in my pocket. Today I am a partner in my firm, and intend, if all goes well, to enter parliament. Hence I think I may, without presumption, judge what makes for success here, and of the type of man to attain it. Work, hard work, is the key to all doors. So convinced am I of this, that I have insisted on the younger members of my family learning betimes to put their shoulders to the wheel. Now, Mr Mahony, I have been open with you. Be equally frank with me. You are an Irishman?'

Candour invariably disarmed Mahony – even lay a little heavy on him, with the weight of an obligation. He retaliated with a light touch of self-depreciation. 'An Irishman, sir, in a country where the Irish have fallen, and not without reason, into general disrepute.'

Over a biscuit and a glass of sherry he gave a rough outline of the circumstances that had led to his leaving England, two years previously, and of his dismayed arrival in what he called 'the cesspool of 1852'.

'Thanks to the rose-water romance of the English press, many a young man of my day was enticed away from a modest competency, to seek his fortune here, where it was pretended that nuggets could be gathered like cabbages – I myself threw up a tidy little country practice. . . . I might mention that medicine was my profession. It would have given me intense satisfaction, Mr Turnham, to see one of those glib journalists in my shoes, or the shoes of some of my messmates on the *Ocean Queen*. There were men aboard that ship, sir, who were reduced to beggary before they could even set foot on the road to the north. Granted it is the duty of the press to encourage emigration–'

'Let the press be, Mr Mahony,' said Turnham: he had sat back, crossed his legs, and put his thumbs in his armholes. 'Let it be. What we need here is colonists – small matter how we get 'em.'

Having had his say, Mahony scamped the recital of his own sufferings: the discomforts of the month he had been forced to spend in Melbourne getting his slender outfit together; the miseries of the tramp to Ballarat on delicate unused feet, among the riff-raff of nations, under a wan December sky, against which the trunks of the gum-trees rose whiter still, and out of which blazed a copper sun with a misty rim. He scamped, too, his six months' attempt at digging – he had been no more fit for the work than a child. Worn to skin and bone, his small remaining strength sucked out by dysentery, he had in the end bartered his last pinch of gold-dust for a barrow-load of useful odds and ends; and this had formed the nucleus of his store. Here, fortune had smiled on him; his flag hardly set a-flying custom had poured in, business gone up by leaps and bounds – 'Although I have never sold so much as a pint of spirits, sir!' His profits for the past six months equalled a clear three hundred, and he had most of this to the good. With a wife to keep, expenses would naturally be heavier; but he should continue to lay by every spare penny, with a view to getting back to England.

'You have not the intention, then, of remaining permanently in the colony?'

'Not the least in the world.'

'H'm,' said John: he was standing on the hearthrug now, his legs apart. 'That, of course, puts a different complexion on the matter. Still, I may say I am entirely reassured by what you have told me – entirely so. Indeed, you must allow me to congratulate you on the good sense you displayed in striking while the iron was hot. Many a one of your medical brethren, sir, would have thought it beneath his dignity to turn shopkeeper. And now, Mr Mahony, I will wish you good day; we shall doubtless meet again before very long. Nay, one moment! There are cases, you will admit, in which a female opinion is not without value. Besides, I should be pleased for you to see my wife.'

He crossed the hall, tapped at a door and cried: 'Emma, my love, will you give us the pleasure of your company?'

In response to this a lady entered, whom Mahony thought one of the most beautiful women he had ever seen. She carried a yearling infant in her arms, and with one hand pressed its pale flaxen poll against the rich, ripe corn of her own hair, as if to dare comparison. Her cheeks were of a delicate rose pink.

'My love,' said Turnham – and one felt that the word was no mere flower of speech. 'My love, here is someone who wishes to marry our Polly.'

'To marry our Polly?' echoed the lady, and smiled a faint, amused smile – it was as though she said: to marry this infant that I bear on my arm. 'But Polly is only a little girl!'

'My very words, dearest. And too young to know her own mind.'

'But you will decide for her, John.'

John hung over his beautiful wife, wheeled up an easy chair, arranged her in it, placed a footstool. 'Pray, pray, do not over-fatigue yourself, Emma! That child is too heavy for you,' he objected, as the babe made strenuous efforts to kick itself to its feet. 'You know I do not approve of you carrying it yourself.'

'Nurse is drinking tea.'

'But why do I keep a houseful of domestics if one of the others cannot occasionally take her place?'

He made an impetuous step towards the bell. Before he could reach it there came a thumping at the door, and a fluty voice cried: 'Lemme in, puppa, lemme in!'

Turnham threw the door open, and admitted a sturdy two-year-old, whom he led forward by the hand. 'My son,' he said, not without pride.

Mahony would have coaxed the child to him; but it ran to its mother, hid its face in her lap.

Forgetting the bell John struck an attitude. 'What a picture!' he exclaimed. 'What a picture! My love, I positively must carry out my intention of having you painted in oils, with the children round you. – Mr Mahony, sir, have you ever seen anything to equal it?'

Though his mental attitude might have been expressed by a note of exclamation, set ironically, Mahony felt constrained to second Turnham's enthusiasm. And it was indeed a lovely picture: the gracious, golden-haired woman, whose figure had the amplitude, her gestures the almost sensual languor of the young nursing mother; the two children fawning at her knee, both ashblond, with vivid scarlet lips. – 'It helps one,' thought Mahony, 'to understand the mother-worship of primitive peoples.'

The nursemaid summoned and the children borne off, Mrs Emma exchanged a few amiable words with the visitor, then obeyed with an equally good grace her husband's command to rest for an hour, before dressing for the ball.

Having escorted her to another room, Turnham came back rubbing his hands. 'I am pleased to be able to tell you, Mr Mahony, that your suit has my wife's approval. You are highly favoured! Emma is not free with her liking.' Then, in a sudden burst of effusion: 'I could have wished you the pleasure, sir, of seeing my wife in evening attire. She will make a furore again; no other woman can hold a candle to her in a ballroom. Tonight is the first time since the birth of our second child that she will grace a public entertainment with her presence; and unfortunately her appearance will be a brief one, for the infant is not yet wholly weaned.' He shut the door and lowered his voice. 'You have had some experience of doctoring, you say; I should like a word with you in your medical capacity. The thing is this. My wife has persisted, contrary to my wishes, in suckling both children herself.'

'Quite right, too,' said Mahony. 'In a climate like this their natural food is invaluable to babes.'

'Exactly, quite so,' said Turnham, with a hint of impatience. 'And in the case of the first child, I made due allowance: a young mother . . . the novelty of the thing . . . you understand. But with regard to the second, I must confess I – How long, sir, in your opinion, can a mother continue to nurse her babe without injury to herself? It is surely harmful if unduly pro-

74

tracted? I have observed dark lines about my wife's eyes, and she is losing her fine complexion. – Then you confirm my fears. I shall assert my authority without delay, and insist on separation from the child. – Ah! women are strange beings, Mr Mahony, strange beings, as you are on the high road to discovering for yourself.'

Mahony returned to town on foot, the omnibus having ceased to run. As he walked – at a quick pace, and keeping a sharp lookout for the road was notoriously unsafe after dark – he revolved his impressions of the interview. He was glad it was over, and, for Polly's sake, that it had passed off satisfactorily. It had made a poor enough start: at one moment he had been within an ace of picking up his hat and stalking out. But he found it difficult at the present happy crisis to bear a grudge – even if it had not been a proved idiosyncrasy of his, always to let a successful finish erase a bad beginning. None the less, he would not have belonged to the nation he did, had he not indulged in a caustic chuckle and a pair of good-humoured pishes and pshaws, at Turnham's expense. 'Like a showman in front of his booth!'

Then he thought again of the domestic scene he had been privileged to witness, and grew grave. The beautiful young woman and her children might have served as a model for a Holy Family – some old painter's dream of a sweet benign Madonna; the trampling babe as the infant Christ; the upturned face of the little John adoring. No place this for the scoffer. Apart from the mere pleasure of the eye, there was ample justification for Turnham's transports. Were they not in the presence of one of life's sublimest mysteries – that of motherhood? Not alone the lovely Emma: no; every woman who endured the rigours of childbirth, to bring forth an immortal soul, was a holy figure.

And now for him, too, as he had been reminded, this wonder was to be worked. Little Polly as the mother of his children – what visions the words conjured up! But he was glad Polly was just Polly, and not the peerless creature he had seen. John Turnham's fears would never be his – this jealous care of a transient bodily beauty. Polly was neither too rare nor too fair for her woman's lot; and, please God, the day would come when he would see her with a whole cluster of little ones round her – little dark-eyed replicas of herself. She, bless her, should dandle and cosset them to her heart's content. Her joy in them would also be his.

CHAPTER NINE

He sawed, planed, hammered; curly shavings dropped and there was a pleasant smell of sawdust. Much had to be done to make the place fit to receive Polly. A second outhouse was necessary, to hold the surplus goods and do duty as a sleeping-room for Long Jim and Hempel: the lean-to the pair had occupied till now was being converted into a kitchen. At great cost and trouble, Mahony had some trees felled and brought in from Warrenheip. With them he put up a rude fence round his back-yard, interlacing the lopped boughs from post to post, so that they formed a thick and leafy screen. He also filled in the dis-used shaft that had served as a rubbish-hole, and chose another, farther off, which would be less malodorous in the summer heat. Finally, a substantial load of firewood carted in, and two snakes that had made the journey in hollow logs dispatched, Long Jim was set down to chop and split the wood into a neat pile. Polly would need but to walk to and from the woodstack for her firing.

Indoors he made equal revolution. That her ears should not be polluted by the language of the customers, he ran up a partition between living-room and store, thus cutting off the slab-walled portion of the house, with its roof of stringy-bark, from the log-and-canvas front. He also stopped with putty the worst gaps between the slabs. At Ocock's Auction Rooms he bought a horsehair sofa to match his armchair, a strip of carpet, a bed, a washhand-stand and a looking-glass, and tacked up a calico cur-tain before the window. His books, fetched out of the wooden case, were arranged on a brand-new set of shelves; and, when all was done and he stood back to admire his work, it was borne in on him afresh with how few creature-comforts he had hitherto existed. Plain to see now, why he had preferred to sit out-of-doors rather than within! Now, no one on the Flat had a trim-mer little place than he.

In his labours he had the help of a friendly digger – a carpenter by trade – who one evening, pipe in mouth, had stood to watch his amateurish efforts with the jack-plane. Otherwise, the Lord alone knew how the house would ever have been made shipshape. Long Jim was equal to none but the simplest jobs; and Hempel, the assistant, had his hands full with the store. Well, it was a blessing at this juncture that business could be left to him. Hempel was as straight as a die; was a real treasure – or would have been, were it not for his eternal little bark of a cough. This was proof against all remedies, and the heck-heck of it at night was quite enough to spoil a light sleeper's rest. In building the new shed, Mahony had been careful to choose a corner far from the house.

Marriages were still uncommon enough on Ballarat to make him an object of considerable curiosity. People took to dropping in of an evening – old Ocock; the postmaster; a fellow storekeeper, ex-steward to the Duke of Newcastle – to comment on his alterations and improvements. And over a pipe and a glass of sherry, he had to put up with a good deal of banter about his approaching 'change of state'.

Still, it was kindly meant. 'We'll 'ave to git up a bit o' company o' nights for yer lady when she comes,' said old Ocock, and spat under the table.

Purdy wrote from Tarrangower, where he had drifted:

Hooray, old Dick, golly for you! Old man didn't I kick up a bobbery when I heard the news. Never was so well pleased in my life. That's all you needed, Dick – now you'll turn into a first-rate colonial. How about that fiver now I'd like to know. You can tell Polly from me I shall pay it back with interest on the fatal day. Of course I'll come and see you spliced, togs or no togs – to tell the truth my kicksies are on their very last legs – and there's nothing doing here – all the loose stuff's been turned over. There's oceans of quartz, of course, and they're trying to pound it up in dollies, but you could put me to bed with a pick-axe and a shovel before I'd go in for such tomfoolery as that. – Damn it all, Dick, to think of you being cotched at last. I can't get over it, and it's a bit of a risk, too, by dad it is, for a girl of that age is a dark horse if ever there was one.

Mahony's answer to this was a couple of pound-notes: *So that my best man shall not disgrace me!* His heart went out to the

77

writer. Dear old Dickybird! pleased as Punch at the turn of events, yet quaking for fear of imaginary risks. With all Purdy's respect for his friend's opinions, he had yet an odd distrust of that friend's ability to look after himself. And now he was presuming to doubt Polly, too. Like his imperence! What the dickens did *he* know of Polly? Keenly relishing the sense of his own intimate knowledge, Mahony touched the breast-pocket in which Polly's letters lay – he often carried them out with him to a little hill, on which a single old blue-gum had been left standing; its scraggy top-knot of leaves drooped and swayed in the wind, like the few long straggling hairs on an old man's head.

The letters formed a goodly bundle; for Polly and he wrote regularly to each other, she once a week, he twice. His bore the Queen's head; hers, as befitted a needy little governess, were oftenest delivered by hand. Mahony untied the packet, drew a chance letter from it and mused as he read. Polly had still not ceded much of her early reserve – and it had taken him weeks to persuade her even to call him by his first name. She was, he thanked goodness, not of the kind who throw maidenly modesty to the winds, directly the binding word is spoken. He loved her all the better for her wariness of emotion; it tallied with a like streak in his own nature. And this, though at the moment he was going through a very debauch of frankness. To the little black-eyed girl who pored over his letters at 'Beamish's Family Hotel', he unbosomed himself as never in his life before. He enlarged on his tastes and preferences, his likes and dislikes; he gave vent to his real feelings for the country of his exile, and his longings for 'home'; told how he had come to the colony, in the first instance, with the fantastic notion of redeeming the fortunes of his family; described his collections of butterflies and plants to her, using their Latin names. And Polly drank in his words, and humbly agreed with all he wrote, or at least did not disagree; and, from this, as have done lovers from the beginning of time, he inferred a perfect harmony of mind. On one point only did he press her for a reply. Was she fond of books? If so, what evenings they would spend together, he reading aloud from some entertaining volume, she at her fancy work. And poetry? For himself he could truly say he did not care for poetry . . . except on a Saturday night or a quiet Sunday morning; and that was, because he liked it too well to approach it with any but a tranquil mind.

I think if I know you aright, as I believe I do, my Polly, you too have poetry in your soul.

He smiled at her reply, then kissed it.

I cannot write poetry myself, said Polly, *but I am very fond of it and shall indeed like very much dear Richard to listen when you read.*

But the winter ran away, one cold, wet week succeeding another, and still they were apart. Mahony urged and pleaded, but could not get Polly to name the wedding-day. He began to think pressure was being brought to bear on the girl from another side. Naturally the Beamishes were reluctant to let her go: who would be so useful to them as Polly? – who undertake, without scorn, the education of the whilom shepherd's daughters? Still, they knew they had to lose her, and he could not see that it made things any easier for them to put off the evil day. No, there was something else at the bottom of it; though he did not know what. Then one evening, pondering a letter of Polly's, he slapped his forehead and exclaimed aloud at his own stupidity. That night, into his reply he slipped four five-pound notes. *Just to buy yourself any little thing you fancy, dearest. If I chose a gift, I might send what would not be acceptable to you.* Yes, sure enough, that was it – little Polly had been in straits for money: the next news he heard was that she had bought and was stitching her wedding-gown. Taxed with her need, Polly guiltily admitted that her salary for the past three months was owing to her. But there had been great expenses in connection with the hotel; and Mr B. had had an accident to his leg. From what she wrote, though, Mahony saw that it was not the first time such remissness had occurred; and he felt grimly indignant with her employers. Keeping open house, and hospitable to the point of vulgarity, they were, it was evident, pinchfists when it came to parting with their money. Still, in the case of a little woman who had served them so faithfully! In thought he set a thick black mark against their name, for their cavalier treatment of his Polly. And extended it to John Turnham as well. John had made no move to put hand to pocket; and Polly's niceness of feeling had stood in the way of her applying to him for aid. It made Mahony yearn to snatch the girl to him, then and there; to set her free of all contact with such coarse-grained, miserly brutes.

Old Ocock negotiated the hire of a neat spring cart for him, and a stout little cob; and at last the day had actually come, when he could set out to bring Polly home. By his side was Ned Turnham. Ned, still a lean-jowled wages-man at Rotten Gully, made no secret of his glee at getting carried down thus comfortably to Polly's nuptials. They drove the eternal forty-odd miles to Geelong, each stick and stone of which was fast becoming known to Mahony; a journey that remained equally tiresome whether the red earth rose as a thick red dust, or whether as now it had turned to a mud like birdlime in which the wheels sank almost to the axles. Arrived at Geelong they put up at an hotel, where Purdy awaited them. Purdy had tramped down from Tarrangower, blanket on back, and stood in need of a new rig-out from head to foot. Otherwise his persistent ill-luck had left no mark on him.

The ceremony took place early the following morning, at the house of the Wesleyan minister, the Anglican parson having been called away. The Beamishes and Polly drove to town, a tight fit in a double buggy. On the back seat, Jinny clung to and half supported a huge clothes-basket, which contained the wedding-breakfast. Polly sat on her trunk by the splashboard; and Tilly, crowded out, rode in on one of the cart-horses, a coloured bed-quilt pinned round her waist to protect her skirts.

To Polly's disappointment neither her brother John nor his wife was present; a letter came at the eleventh hour to say that Mrs Emma was unwell, and her husband did not care to leave her. Enclosed, however, were ten pounds for the purchase of a wedding-gift; and the pleasure Polly felt at being able to announce John's generosity helped to make up to her for his absence. The only other guest present was an elder sister, Miss Sarah Turnham, who, being out of a situation at the moment, had sailed down from Melbourne. This young lady, a sprightly brunette of some three or four and twenty, without the fine, regular features of Ned and Polly, but with tenfold their vivacity and experience, caused quite a sensation; and Tilly's audible raptures at beholding her Purdy again were of short duration; for Purdy had never met the equal of Miss Sarah, and could not take his eyes off her. He and she were the life of the party. The Beamishes were overawed by the visitor's town-bred airs and the genteel elegance of her dress; Polly was a mere crumpled rose-leaf of pink confusion; Mahony too preoccupied with ring and licence to take any but his formal share in the proceedings.

'Come and see you?' echoed Miss Sarah playfully: the knot was tied; the company had demolished the good things laid out by Mrs Beamish in the private parlour of an hotel, and emptied a couple of bottles of champagne; and Polly had changed her muslin frock for a black silk travelling-gown. 'Come and *see* you? Why, of course I will, little silly!' – and, with her pretty white hands, she patted the already perfect bow of Polly's bonnet-strings. Miss Sarah had no great opinion of the match her sister was making; but she had been agreeably surprised by Mahony's person and manners, and had said so, thus filling Polly's soul with bliss. 'Provided, of course, little goosey, you have a *spare room* to offer me. – For, I confess,' she went on, turning to the rest of the party, 'I confess I feel inordinately curious to see, with my own eyes, what these famous diggings are like. From all one hears, they must be *marvellously* entertaining. – Now, I presume that *you*, Mr Smith, never touch at such *rude, out-of-the-world* places in the course of *your* travels?'

Purdy, who had discreetly concealed the fact that he was but a poverty-stricken digger himself, quibbled a light evasion, then changed the subject, and offered his escort to the steam-packet by which Miss Sarah was returning to Melbourne.

'And you, too, dear Tilly,' urged little Polly, proceeding with her farewells. 'For, mind, you promised. And *I* won't forget to . . . you know what!'

Tilly, sobbing noisily, wept on Polly's neck that she wished she was dead or at the bottom of the sea; and Polly, torn between pride and pain at Purdy's delinquency, could only kiss her several times without speaking.

The farewells buzzed and flew.

'Good-bye to you, little lass . . . beg pardon, Mrs Dr Mahony!' – 'Mind you write, Poll! I shall die to 'ear.' – 'Ta-ta, little silly goosey, and *au revoir*!' – 'Mind he don't pitch you out of the cart, Polly!' – 'Good-bye, Polly, my duck, and remember I'll come to you in a winkin', h'if and when . . .' which speech on the part of Mrs Beamish distressed Polly to the verge of tears.

But finally she was torn from their arms and hoisted into the cart; and Mahony, the reins in his hand, began to unstiffen from the wooden figure-head he had felt himself during the ceremony, and under the whirring tongues and whispered confidences of the women.

'And now, Polly, for home!' he said exultantly, when the largest pocket-handkerchief had shrunk to the size of a nit, and

Polly had ceased to twist her neck for one last, last glimpse of her friends.

And then the bush, and the loneliness of the bush, closed round them.

It was the time of flowers – of fierce young growth after the fruitful winter rains. The short-lived grass, green now as that of an English meadow, was picked out into patterns by the scarlet of the Running Postman; purple sarsaparilla festooned the stems of the scrub; there were vast natural paddocks, here of yellow everlastings, there of heaths in full bloom. Compared with the dark, spindly foliage of the she-oaks, the ti-trees' waxy flowers stood out like orange-blossoms against firs. On damp or marshy ground wattles were aflame: great quivering masses of softest gold. Wherever these trees stood, the fragrance of their yellow puff-ball blossoms saturated the air; one knew, before one saw them, that they were coming, and long after they had been left behind one carried their honeyed sweetness with one; against them, no other scent could have made itself felt. And to Mahony these waves of perfume, into which they were continually running, came, in the course of the hours, to stand for a symbol of the golden future for which he and Polly were making; and whenever in after years he met with wattles in full bloom, he was carried back to the blue spring day of this wedding-journey, and jogged on once more, in the light cart, with his girl-wife at his side.

It was necessarily a silent drive. More rain had fallen during the night; even the best bits of the road were worked into deep, glutinous ruts, and the low-lying parts were under water. Mahony, but a fairish hand with the reins, was repeatedly obliged to leave the track and take to the bush, where he steered a way as best he could through trees, stumps, boulders and crab-holes. Sometimes he rose to his feet to encourage the horse; or he alighted and pulled it by the bridle; or put a shoulder to the wheel. But today no difficulties had power to daunt him; and the farther he advanced the lighter-hearted he grew: he went back to Ballarat feeling, for the first time, that he was actually going home.

And Polly? Sitting motionless at her husband's side, her hands folded on her black silk lap, Polly obediently turned her head this way and that, when Richard pointed out a landmark to her, or called her attention to the flowers. At first, things were new and arresting, but the novelty soon wore off; and as they went on and on, and still on, it began to seem to Polly, who had never been farther afield than a couple of miles north of the 'Pivot City', as if they were driving away from all the rest of mankind, right into the very heart of nowhere. The road grew rougher, too – became scored with ridges and furrows which threw them violently from side to side. Unused to bush driving, Polly was sure at each fresh jolt that this time the cart *must* tip over; and yet she preferred the track and its dangers to Richard's adventurous attempts to carve a passage through the scrub. A little later a cold south wind sprang up, which struck through her thin silk mantle; she was very tired, having been on her feet since five o'clock that morning; and all the happy fuss and excitement of the wedding was behind her. Her heart sank. She loved Richard dearly; if he had asked her, she would have gone to the ends of the earth with him; but at this moment she felt both small and lonely, and she would have liked nothing better than Mrs Beamish's big motherly bosom, on which to lay her head. And when, in passing a swamp, a well-known noise broke on her ear – that of hundreds of bell-frogs, which were like hundreds of hissing tea-kettles just about to boil – then such a rush of homesickness took her that she would have given all she had, to know she was going back, once more, to the familiar little whitewashed room she had shared with Tilly and Jinny.

The seat of the cart was slanting and slippery. Polly was continually sliding forward, now by inches, now with a great jerk. At last Mahony noticed it. 'You are not sitting very comfortably, Polly, I fear?' he said.

Polly righted herself yet again, and reddened. 'It's my . . . my feet aren't long enough,' she replied.

'Why, my poor little love!' cried Mahony, full of quick compunction. 'Why didn't you say so?' And drawing rein and getting down, he stuffed some of Mrs Beamish's bundles – fragments of the feast, which the good woman had sent with them – under his wife's feet; stuffed too many, so that Polly drove the rest of the way with her knees raised to a hump in front of her.

All the afternoon they had been making for dim blue ranges. After leaving the flats near Geelong, the track went up and down. Grey-green forest surrounded them, out of which nobbly hills rose like islands from a sea of trees. As they approached the end of their journey, they overtook a large number of heavy vehicles labouring along through the mire. A coach with six horses dashed past them at full gallop, and left them rapidly behind. Did they have to skirt bull-punchers who were lashing or otherwise ill-treating their teams, Mahony urged on the horse and bade Polly shut her eyes.

Night had fallen and a drizzling rain set in, by the time they travelled the last couple of miles to Ballarat. This was the worst of all; and Polly held her breath while the horse picked its way among yawning pits, into which one false step would have plunged them. Her fears were not lessened by hearing that in several places the very road was undermined; and she was thankful when Richard — himself rendered uneasy by the precious cargo he bore — got out and walked at the horse's head. They drew up before a public-house. Cramped from sitting and numb with cold, Polly climbed stiffly down as bidden; and Mahony having unloaded the baggage, mounted to his seat again to drive the cart into the yard. This was a false move, as he was quick to see: he should not have left Polly standing alone. For the news of the arrival of 'Doc.' Mahony and his bride flew from mouth to mouth, and all the loafers who were in the bar turned out to stare and to quiz. Beside her tumulus of trunk, bag, bundle, little Polly stood desolate, with drooping shoulders; and cursing his want of foresight, Mahony all but drove into the gatepost, which occasioned a loud guffaw. Nor had Long Jim turned up as ordered, to shoulder the heavy luggage. These blunders made Mahony very hot and curt. Having himself stowed the things inside the bar and borrowed a lantern, he drew his wife's arm through his, and hurried her away.

It was pitch-dark, and the ground was wet and squelchy. Their feet sank in the mud. Polly clung to Richard's arm, trembling at the rude voices, the laughter, the brawling, that issued from the grog-shops; at the continual apparition of rough, bearded men. One of these, who held a candle stuck in a bottle, was accosted by Richard and soundly rated. When they turned out of the street with its few dismal oil-lamps, their way led them among dirty tents and black pits, and they had to depend for light on the lantern they carried. They crossed a rickety little bridge over a flooded river; then climbed a slope, on which in her bunchy silk skirts Polly slipped and floundered, to stop before something that was half a tent and half a log-hut. — What! this the end of the long, long journey! This the house she had to live in?

Yes, Richard was speaking. 'Welcome home, little wife! Not much of a place, you see, but the best I can give you.'

'It's . . . it's very nice, Richard,' said Polly staunchly; but her lips trembled.

Warding off the attack of a big, fierce, dirty dog, which sprang at her, dragging its paws down her dress, Polly waited while her husband undid the door, then followed him through a chaos, which smelt as she had never believed any roofed-in place could smell, to a little room at the back.

Mahony lighted the lamp that stood ready on the table, and threw a satisfied glance round. His menfolk had done well: things were in apple-pie order. The fire crackled, the kettle was on the boil, the cloth spread. He turned to Polly to kiss her welcome, to relieve her of bonnet and mantle. But before he could do this there came a noise of rowdy voices, of shouting and parleying. Picking up the lantern, he ran out to see what the matter was.

Left alone Polly remained standing by the table, on which an array of tins was set – preserved salmon, sardines, condensed milk – their tops forced back to show their contents. Her heart was heavy as lead, and she felt a dull sense of injury as well. This hut her home! – to which she had so freely invited sister and friend! She would be ashamed for them ever to set eyes on it. Not in her worst dreams had she imagined it as mean and poor as this. But perhaps. . . . With the lamp in her hand, she tip-toed guiltily to a door in the wall: it opened into a tiny bedroom with a sloping roof. No, this was all, all there was of it: just these two miserable little poky rooms! She raised her head and looked round, and the tears welled up in spite of herself. The roof was so low that you could almost touch it; the window was no larger than a pocket-handkerchief; there were chinks between the slabs of the walls. And from one of these she now saw a spider crawl out, a huge black tarantula, with horrible hairy legs. Polly was afraid of spiders; and at this the tears began to overflow and to trickle down her cheeks. Holding her skirts to her – the new dress she had made with such pride, now damp, and crushed, and soiled – she sat down and put her feet, in their soaked, mud-caked, little prunella boots, on the rung of her chair, for fear of other monsters that might be crawling the floor.

And then, while she sat thus hunched together, the voices outside were suddenly drowned in a deafening noise – in a hideous, stupefying din, that nearly split one's eardrums: it sounded as though all the tins and cans in the town were being beaten and banged before the door. Polly forgot the tarantula, forgot her bitter disappointment with her new home. Her black eyes wide with fear, her heart thudding in her chest, she sprang to her feet and stood ready, if need be, to defend herself. Where, oh where was Richard?

It was the last straw. When, some five minutes later, Mahony came bustling in: he had soothed the 'kettledrummers' and sent them off with a handsome gratuity, and he carried the trunk on his own shoulder, Long Jim following behind with bags and bundles: when he entered, he found little Polly sitting with her head huddled on her arms, crying as though her heart would break.

PART TWO

CHAPTER ONE

Over the fathomless grey seas that tossed between, dissevering the ancient and gigantic continent from the tiny motherland, unsettling rumours ran. After close on forty years' fat peace, England had armed for hostilities again, her fleet set sail for a foreign sea. Such was the news the sturdy clipper-ships brought out, in tantalizing fragments; and those who, like Richard Mahony, were mere birds-of-passage in the colony, and had friends and relatives going to the front, caught hungrily at every detail. But to the majority of the colonists what England had done, or left undone, in preparation for war, was of small account. To them the vital question was: will the wily Russian Bear take its revenge by sending men-of-war to annihilate us and plunder the gold in our banks – us, months removed from English aid? And the opinion was openly expressed that in casting off her allegiance to Great Britain, and becoming a neutral state, lay young Australia's best hope of safety.

But, even while they made it, the proposers of this scheme were knee-deep in petty, local affairs again. All Europe was depressed under the cloud of war; but they went on belabouring hackneyed themes – the unlocking of the lands, iniquitous licence-fees, official corruption. Mahony could not stand it. His heart was in England, went up and down with England's hopes and fears. He smarted under the tales told of the inefficiency of the British troops and the paucity of their numbers; under the painful disclosures made by journalists, injudiciously allowed to travel to the seat of war; he questioned, like many another of his class in the old country, the wisdom of the Duke of Newcastle's orders to lay siege to the port of Sebastopol. And of an evening, when the store was closed, he sat over stale English newspapers and a map of the Crimea, and meticulously followed the movements of the Allies.

But in this retirement he was rudely disturbed, by feeling him-

87

self touched on a vulnerable spot – that of his pocket. Before the end of the year trade had come to a standstill, and the very town he lived in was under martial law.

On both Ballarat and the Bendigo the agitation for the repeal of the licence-tax had grown more and more vehement; and spring's arrival found the digging-community worked up to a white heat. The new Governor's tour of inspection, on which great hopes had been built, served only to aggravate the trouble. Misled by the golden treasures with which the diggers, anxious as children to please, dazzled his eyes, the Governor decided that the tax was not an outrageous one; and ordered licence-raids to be undertaken twice as often as before. This defeat of the diggers' hopes, together with the murder of a comrade and the acquittal of the murderer by a corrupt magistrate, goaded even the least sensitive spirits to rebellion: the guilty man's house was fired, the police were stoned, and then, for a month or more, deputations and petitions ran to and fro between Ballarat and Melbourne. In vain: the demands of the voteless diggers went unheard. The consequence was that one day at the beginning of summer all the troops that could be spared from the capital, along with several pieces of artillery, were raising the dust on the road to Ballarat.

On the last afternoon in November work was suspended throughout the diggings, and the more cautious among the shop-keepers began to think of closing their doors. In front of the 'Diggers' Emporium', where the earth was baked as hard as a burnt crust, a little knot of people stood shading their eyes from the sun. Opposite, on Bakery Hill, a monster meeting had been held and the 'Southern Cross' hoisted – a blue bunting that bore the silver stars of the constellation after which it was named. Having sworn allegiance to it with outstretched hands, the rebels were lining up to march off to drill.

Mahony watched the thin procession through narrowed lids. In theory he condemned equally the blind obstinacy of the authorities, who went on tightening the screw, and the fool-hardiness of the men. But – well, he could not get his eye to shirk one of the screaming banners and placards: 'Down with Despotism!' 'Who so base as be a slave!' by means of which the diggers sought to inflame popular indignation. 'If only honest rebels could get on without melodramatic exaggeration. As it is, those good fellows yonder are rendering a just cause ridiculous.'

Polly tightened her clasp of his arm. She had known no peace since the evening before, when a rough-looking man had come into the store and, with revolver at full cock, had commanded Hempel to hand over all the arms and ammunition it contained. Hempel, much to Richard's wrath, had meekly complied; but it might have been Richard himself; he would for certain have refused; and then . . . Polly had hardly slept for thinking of it. She now listened in deferential silence to the men's talk; but when old Ocock – he never had a good word to say for the riotous diggers – took his pipe out of his mouth to remark: 'A pack o' Tipperary boys spoilin' for a fight – that's what I say. An' yet, blow me if I wouldn't 'a bin glad if one o' my two 'ad 'ad spunk enough to join 'em,' – at this Polly could not refrain from saying pitifully: 'Oh, Mr Ocock, do you really *mean* that?' For both Purdy and brother Ned were in the rebel band, and Polly's heart was heavy because of them.

'Can't you see my brother anywhere?' she asked Hempel, who held an old spyglass to his eyes.

'No, ma'am, sorry to say I can't,' replied Hempel. He would willingly have conjured up a dozen brothers to comfort Polly; but he could not swerve from the truth, even for her.

'Give me the glass,' said Mahony, and swept the line. – 'No, no sign of either of them. Perhaps they thought better of it after all. – Listen! now they're singing – can you hear them? The *Marseillaise* as I'm alive. – Poor fools! Many of them are armed with nothing more deadly than picks and shovels.'

'And pikes,' corrected Hempel. 'Several carry pikes, sir.'

'Ay, that's so, they've bin 'ammerin' out bits of old iron all the mornin',' agreed Ocock. 'It's said they 'aven't a quarter of a firearm apiece. And the drillin'! Lord love yer! 'Alf of 'em don't know their right 'and from their left. The troops 'ull make mincemeat of 'em, if they come to close quarters.'

'Oh, I hope not!' said Polly. 'Oh, I do hope they won't get hurt.'

Patting her hand, Mahony advised his wife to go indoors and resume her household tasks. And since his lightest wish was a command, little Polly docilely withdrew her arm and returned to her dishwashing. But though she rubbed and scoured with her usual precision, her heart was not in her work. Both on this day and the next she seemed to exist solely in her two ears. The one strained to catch any scrap of news about 'poor Ned'; the other listened, with an even sharper anxiety, to what went on in the store. Several further attempts were made to get arms and provisions from Richard; and each time an angry scene ensued. Close up beside the thin partition, her hands locked under her cooking-apron, Polly sat and trembled for her husband. He had already got himself talked about by refusing to back a Reform League; and now she heard him openly declare to someone that he disapproved of the terms of this League, from A to Z. Oh dear! If only he wouldn't. But she was careful not to add to his worries by speaking of her fears. As it was, he came to tea with a moody face.

The behaviour of the foraging parties growing more and more threatening, Mahony thought it prudent to follow the general example and put up his shutters. Wildly conflicting rumours were in the air. One report said a contingent of Creswick dare-devils had arrived to join forces with the insurgents; another that the Creswickers, disgusted at finding neither firearms nor quarters provided for them, had straightway turned and marched the twelve miles home again. For a time it was asserted that Lalor, the Irish leader, had been bought over by the Government; then, just as definitely, that his influence alone held the rebel faction together. Towards evening Long Jim was dispatched to find out how matters really stood. He brought back word that the diggers had entrenched themselves on a piece of rising ground near the Eureka lead, behind a flimsy barricade of logs, slabs, ropes and overturned carts. The Camp, for its part, was screened by a breastwork of firewood, trusses of hay and bags of corn; while the mounted police stood or lay fully armed by their horses, which were saddled ready for action at a moment's notice.

Neither Ned nor Purdy put in an appearance, and the night passed without news of them. Just before dawn, however, Mahony was wakened by a tapping at the window. Thrusting out his head he recognized young Tommy Ocock, who had been sent by his father to tell 'doctor' that the soldiers were astir. Lights could be seen moving about the Camp, a horse had neighed — father thought spies might have given them the hint that at least half the diggers from the Stockade had come down to Main Street last night, and got drunk, and never gone back. With a concerned glance at Polly Mahony struggled into his clothes. He must make another effort to reach the boys — especially Ned, for Polly's sake. When Ned had first announced his intention of siding with the insurgents, he had merely shrugged his shoulders, believing that the young vapourer would soon have had enough of it. Now he felt responsible to his wife for Ned's safety: Ned, whose chief reason for turning rebel, he suspected, was that a facetious trooper had once dubbed him 'Eytalian organ-grinder', and asked him where he kept his monkey.

But Mahony's designs of a friendly interference came too late. The troops had got away, creeping stealthily through the morning dusk; and he was still panting up Specimen Hill when he heard the crack of a rifle. Confused shouts and cries followed. Then a bugle blared, and the next instant the rattle and bang of musketry split the air.

Together with a knot of others, who like himself had run forth half dressed, Mahony stopped and waited, in extreme anxiety; and, while he stood, the stars went out, one by one, as though a finger-tip touched them. The diggers' response to the volley of the attacking party was easily distinguished: it was a dropping fire, and sounded like a thin hail-shower after a peal of thunder. Within half an hour all was over: the barricade had fallen, to cheers and laughter from the military; the rebel flag was torn down; huts and tents inside the enclosure were going up in flames.

Towards six o'clock, just as the December sun, huge and fiery, thrust the edge of its globe above the horizon, a number of onlookers ran up the slope to all that was left of the ill-fated Stockade. On the dust, bloodstains, now set hard as scabs, traced the route by which a wretched procession of prisoners had been marched to the Camp gaol. Behind the demolished barrier huts smouldered as heaps of blackened embers; and the ground was strewn with stark forms, which lay about – some twenty or thirty of them – in grotesque attitudes. Some sprawled with outstretched arms, their sightless eyes seeming to fix the pale azure of the sky; others were hunched and huddled in a last convulsion. And in the course of his fruitless search for friend and brother, an old instinct reasserted itself in Mahony: kneeling down he began swiftly and dexterously to examine the prostrate bodies. Two or three still heaved, the blood gurgling from throat and breast like water from the neck of a bottle. Here, one had a mouth plugged with shot, and a beard as stiff as though it were made of rope. Another that he turned over was a German he had once heard speak at a diggers' meeting – a windy braggart of a man, with a quaint impediment in his speech. Well, poor soul! he would never mouth invectives or tickle the ribs of an audience again. His body was a very colander of wounds. Some had not bled either. It looked as though the soldiers had viciously gone on prodding and stabbing the fallen.

Stripping a corpse of its shirt, he tore off a piece of stuff to make a bandage for a shattered leg. While he was binding the limb to a board, young Tom ran up to say that the military, returning with carts, were arresting everyone they met in the vicinity. With others who had been covering up and carrying away their friends, Mahony hastened down the back of the hill towards the bush. Here was plain evidence of a stampede. More bloodstains pointed the track, and a number of odd and clumsy weapons had been dropped or thrown away by the diggers in their flight.

He went home with the relatively good tidings that neither Ned nor Purdy was to be found. Polly was up and dressed. She had also lighted the fire and set water on to boil, 'just in case'. 'Was there ever such a sensible little woman?' said her husband with a kiss.

The day dragged by, flat and stale after the excitement of the morning. No one ventured far from cover; for the military remained under arms, and detachments of mounted troopers patrolled the streets. At the Camp the hundred-odd prisoners were being sorted out, and the maimed and wounded doctored in the rude little temporary hospital. Down in Main Street the noise of hammering went on hour after hour. The dead could not be kept, in the summer heat, must be got underground before dark.

Mahony had just secured his premises for the night, when there came a rapping at the back door. In the yard stood a stranger who, when the dog Pompey had been chidden and soothed, made mysterious signs to Mahony and murmured a well-known name. Admitted to the sitting-room he fished a scrap of dirty paper from his boot. Mahony put the candle on the table and straightened out the missive. Sure enough, it was in Purdy's hand – though sadly scrawled.

Have been hit in the pin. Come if possible and bring your tools. The bearer is square.

Polly could hear the two of them talking in low, urgent tones. But her relief that the visitor brought no bad news of her brother was dashed when she learned that Richard had to ride out into the bush, to visit a sick man. However she buttoned her bodice, and with her hair hanging down her back went into the sitting-room to help her husband; for he was turning the place upside down. He had a pair of probe-scissors somewhere, he felt sure, if he could only lay hands on them. And while he ransacked drawers and cupboards for one or other of the few poor instruments left him, his thoughts went back, inopportunely enough, to the time when he had been surgeon's dresser in the Edinburgh Royal Infirmary. *O tempora, O mores!* He wondered what old Syme, that prince of surgeons, would say, could he see his whilom student raking out a probe from among the ladles and kitchen spoons, a roll of lint from behind the saucepans.

Bag in hand, he followed his guide to where the latter had left a horse in safe-keeping; and having lengthened the stirrups and received instructions about the road, he set off for the hut in the ranges which Purdy had contrived to reach. He had an awkward cross-country ride of some four miles before him; but this did not trouble him. The chance-touched spring had opened the gates to a flood of memories; and, as he jogged along, he re-lived in thought the happy days spent as a student under the shadow of Arthur's Seat, round the College, the Infirmary and old Surgeons' Square. Once more he sat in the theatre, the breathless spectator of famous surgical operations; or as house-surgeon to the Lying-in Hospital himself assisted in daring attempts to lessen suffering and save life. It was, of course, too late now to bemoan the fact that he had broken with his profession. Yet only that very day envy had beset him. The rest of the fraternity had run to and from the tents where the wounded were housed, while he, behung with his shopman's apron, pottered about among barrels and crates. No one thought of enlisting his services; another, not he, would set (or bungle) the fracture he had temporarily splinted.

The hut – it had four slab walls and an earthen floor – was in darkness on his arrival, for Purdy had not dared to make a light. He lay tossing restlessly on a dirty old straw palliasse, and was in great pain; but greeted his friend with a dash of the old brio.

Hanging his coat over the chinks in the door, and turning back his sleeves, Mahony took up the lantern and stooped to examine the injured leg. A bullet had struck the right ankle, causing an ugly wound. He washed it out, dressed and bandaged it. He also bathed the patient's sweat-soaked head and shoulders; then sat down to await the owner of the hut's return.

As soon as the latter appeared he took his leave, promising to ride out again the night after next. In spite of the circumstances under which they met, he and Purdy parted with a slight coolness. Mahony had loudly voiced his surprise at the nature of the wound caused by the bullet: it was incredible that any of the military could have borne a weapon of this calibre. Pressed, Purdy admitted that his hurt was a piece of gross ill-luck: he had been accidentally shot by a clumsy fool of a digger, from an ancient holster-pistol.

To Mahony this seemed to cap the climax; and he did not mask his sentiments. The pitiful little forcible-feeble rebellion, all along but a futile attempt to cast straws against the wind, was now completely over and done with, and would never be heard of again. Or such at least, he added, was the earnest hope of the law-abiding community. This irritated Purdy, who was spumy with the self-importance of one who has stood in the thick of the fray. He answered hotly, and ended by rapping out with a contemptuous click of the tongue: 'Upon my word, Dick, you look at the whole thing like the tradesman you are!'

These words rankled in Mahony all the way home. – Trust Purdy for not, in anger, being able to resist giving him a flick on the raw. It made him feel thankful he was no longer so dependent on this friendship as of old. Since then he had tasted better things. Now, a woman's heart beat in sympathetic understanding; there met his, two lips which had never said an unkind word. He pushed on with a new zest, reaching home about dawn. And over his young wife's joy at his safe return, he forgot the shifting moods of his night-journey.

It had, however, this result. Next day Polly found him with his head in one of the great old shabby black books which, to her mind, spoilt the neat appearance of the bookshelves. He stood to read, the volume lying open before him on the top of the cold stove, and was so deeply engrossed that the store-bell rang twice without his hearing it. When, reminded that Hempel was absent, he whipped out to answer it, he carried the volume with him.

94

But his first treatment of Purdy's wound was also his last. Two nights later he found the hut deserted; and diligently as he prowled round it in the moonlight, he could discover no clue to the fate of its occupants. There was nothing to be done but to head his horse for home again.

Polly was more fortunate. Within three days of the fight Ned turned up, sound as a bell. He was sporting a new hat, a flashy silk neckerchief and a silver watch and chain. At sight of these kickshaws a dismal suspicion entered Mahony's mind, and refused to be dislodged. But he did not breathe his doubts – for Polly's sake. Polly was rapturously content to see her brother again. She threw her arms round his neck, and listened, with her big, black, innocent eyes – except for their fleckless candour, the counterpart of Ned's own – to the tale of his miraculous escape, and of the rich gutter he had had the good luck to strike.

Meanwhile public feeling, exasperated beyond measure by the tragedy of that summer dawn, slowly subsided. Hesitation, timidity, and a very human waiting on success had held many diggers back from joining in the final coup; but the sympathy of the community was with the rebels, and at the funerals of the fallen, hundreds of mourners, in such black coats as they could muster, marched side by side to the wild little unfenced bush cemetery. When, too, the relief-party arrived from Melbourne and martial law was proclaimed, the residents handed over their firearms as ordered; but an attempt to swear in special constables failed, not a soul stepping forward in support of the government.

There was literally nothing doing during the month the military occupied Ballarat. Mahony seized the opportunity to give his back premises a coat of paint; he also began to catalogue his collection of Lepidoptera. Hence, as far as business was concerned, it was a timely moment for the arrival of a letter from Henry Ocock, to the effect that, 'subject of course to any part-

95

heard case', 'our case' was first on the list for a date early in January.

None the less, the announcement threw Mahony into the fidgets. He had almost clean forgotten the plaguey affair: it had its roots in the dark days before his marriage. He wished now he had thought twice before letting himself be entangled in a law-suit. Now, he had a wife dependent on him, and to lose the case, and be held responsible for costs, would cripple him. And such a verdict was not at all unlikely; for Purdy, his chief witness, could not be got at: the Lord alone knew where Purdy lay hid. He at once sat down and wrote the bad news to his solicitor.

At six o'clock in the morning some few days later, he took his seat in the coach for Melbourne. By his side sat Johnny Ocock, the elder of the two brothers. Johnny had by chance been with-in earshot during the negotiations with the rascally carrier, and on learning this, Henry had straightway subpœnaed him. Mahony was none too well pleased: the boy threatened to be a handful. His old father, on delivering him up at the coach-office, had drawn Mahony aside to whisper: 'Don't let the young limb out o' yer sight, doc., or get nip or sip o' liquor. If 'e so much as wets 'is tongue, there's no holdin' 'im.' Johnny was a lean, pimply-faced youth, with cold, flabby hands.

Little Polly had to stay behind. Mahony would have liked to give her the trip and show her the sights of the capital; but the law-courts were no place for a woman; neither could he leave her sitting alone in a hotel. And a tentative letter to her brother John had not called forth an invitation; Mrs Emma was in delicate health at present, and had no mind for visitors. So he committed Polly to the care of Hempel and Long Jim, both of whom were her faithful henchmen. She herself, in proper wifely fashion, proposed to give her little house a good red-up in its master's absence.

Mahony and Johnny dismounted from the coach in the early afternoon, sore, stiff and hungry: they had broken their fast merely on half-a-dozen sandwiches, keeping their seats the while that the young toper might be spared the sight of in-toxicating liquors. Now, stopping only to brush off the top layer of dust and snatch a bite of solid food, Mahony hastened away, his witness at heel, to Chancery Lane.

It was a relief to find that Ocock was not greatly put out at Purdy having failed them. 'Leave it to us, sir. We'll make that all right.' As on the previous visit he dry-washed his hands while he spoke, and his little eyes shot flashes from one to the other, like electric sparks. He proposed just to run through the morrow's evidence with 'our young friend there'; and in the course of this rehearsal said more than once: 'Good . . . good! Why, sonny, you're quite smart.' This when Johnny succeeded in grasping his drift. But at the least hint of unreadiness or hesitation, he tut-tutted and drew his brows together. And as it went on it seemed to Mahony that Ocock was putting words into the boy's mouth; while Johnny, intimidated, said yes and amen to things he could not possibly know. Presently he interfered to this effect. Ocock brushed his remark aside. But after a second interruption from Mahony: 'I think, sir, with your permission we will ask John not to depart from what he actually heard,' the lawyer shuffled his papers into a heap and said that would do for today: they would meet at the court in the morning. Prior to shaking hands, however, he threw out a hint that he would like a word with his brother on family matters. And for half an hour Mahony paced the street below.

The remainder of the day was spent in keeping Johnny out of temptation's way, in trying to interest him in the life of the city, its monuments and curiosities. But the lad was too apathetic to look about him, and never opened his mouth. Once only in the course of the afternoon did he offer a kind of handle. In their peregrinations they passed a Book Arcade, where Mahony stopped to turn the leaves of a volume. Johnny also took up a book and began to read.

'What is it?' asked Mahony. 'Would you like to have it, my boy?'

Johnny stonily accepted the gift – it was a tale of Red Indians, the pages smudged with gaudy illustrations – and put it under his arm.

At the good supper that was set before him he picked with a meagre zest; then fell asleep. Mahony took the opportunity to write a line to Polly to tell of their safe arrival; and having sealed the letter, ran out to post it. He was not away for more than three minutes, but when he came back Johnny was gone. He hunted high and low for him, ransacked the place without success: the boy had spoken to no one, nor had he been seen to leave the coffee-room; and as the clock-hands were nearing twelve, Mahony was obliged to give up the search and go back to the hotel. It was impossible at that hour to let Ocock know of this fresh piece of ill-luck. Besides, there was just a chance the young scamp would turn up in the morning. Morning came, however, and no Johnny with it. Outwitted and chagrined, Mahony set off for the court alone.

Day had broken dim and misty, and by the time breakfast was over a north wind was raging – a furnace-like blast that bore off the sandy deserts of the interior. The sun was a yellow blotch in a copper sky; the thermometer had leapt to a hundred and ten in the shade. Blinding clouds of coarse, gritty dust swept house-high through the streets: half-suffocated, Mahony fought his way along, his veil lowered, his handkerchief at his mouth. Outside those public-houses that advertised ice, crowds stood waiting their turn of entry; while half-naked barmen, their linen trousers drenched with sweat, worked like niggers to mix drinks which should quench these bottomless thirsts. Mahony believed he was the only perfectly sober person in the lobby of the court. Even Ocock himself would seem to have been indulging.

This suspicion was confirmed by the lawyer's behaviour. No sooner did Ocock espy him than up he rushed, brandishing the note that had been got to him early that morning – and now his eyes looked like little dabs of pitch in his chalk-white face, and his manner, stripped of its veneer, let the real man show through.

'Curse it, sir, and what's the meaning of this, I'd like to know?' he cried, and struck at the sheet of notepaper with his free hand. 'A pretty fix to put us in at the last minute, upon my word! It was your business, sir, to nurse your witness . . . after all the trouble I'd been to with him! What the devil do you expect us to do now?'

Mahony's face paled under its top-dressing of dust and moisture. To Ocock's gross: 'Well, it's your own look-out, confound you! – entirely your own look-out,' he returned a cool: 'Certainly,' then moved to one side and took up his stand in a corner of the hall, out of the way of the jostle and bustle, the constant going and coming that gave the hinges of the door no rest.

When after a weary wait the time came to enter court, he continued to give Ocock, who had been deep in consultation with his clerk, a wide berth, and moved forward among a number of other people. A dark, ladder-like stair led to the upper storey. While he was mounting this, some words exchanged in a low tone behind him arrested his attention.

'Are you O.K., old man?'

'We are, if our client doesn't give us away. But he has to be handled like a hot –' Here the sentence snapped, for Mahony, bitten by a sudden doubt, faced sharply round. But it was a stranger who uncivilly accused him of treading on his toe.

The court – it was not much more than twenty feet square – was like an ill-smelling oven. Every chink and crack had been stopped against the searing wind; and the atmosphere was a brew of all the sour odours, the offensive breaths, given off by the two-score-odd people crushed within its walls. In spite of precautions the dust had got in: it lay thick on sills, desks and papers, gritted between the teeth, made the throat raspy as a file.

Mahony had given up all hope of winning his case, and looked forward to the sorry pleasure of assisting at a miscarriage of justice. During the speech for the plaintiff, however, he began to see the matter in another light. Not so much thanks to the speaker, as in spite of him. Plaintiff's counsel was a common little fellow of ungainly appearance: a double toll of fat bulged over the neck of his gown, and his wig, hastily re-donned after a breathing-space, sat askew. Nor was he anything of an orator: he stumbled over his sentences, and once or twice lost his place altogether. To his dry presentment of the case nobody seemed to pay heed. The judge, tired of wiping his spectacles dry, leant back and closed his eyes. Mahony believed he slept, as did also some of the jurors, deaf to the citation of Dawes v. Peck and Dunlop v. Lambert; to the assertion that the carrier was the agent, the goods were accepted, the property had 'passed'. This 'passing' of the property was evidently a strong point; the plaintiff's name itself was not much oftener on the speaker's lips. 'The absconding driver, me Lud, was a personal friend of the defendant's. Mr Bolliver never knew him; hence could not engage him. Had this person not been thrust upon him, Mr Bolliver would have employed the same carrier as on a previous occasion.' And so on and on.

Mahony listened hand at ear, that organ not being keyed up to the mutterings and mumblings of justice. And for all the dullness of the subject-matter and counsel's lack of eloquence his interest did not flag. It was the first time he had heard the case for the other side stated plainly; and he was dismayed to find how convincing it was. Put thus, it must surely gain over every honest, straight-thinking man. In comparison, the points Ocock was going to advance shrank to mere legal quibbles and hair-splitting evasions.

Then the plaintiff himself went into the witness-box — and Mahony's feelings became involved as well. This his adversary! — this poor old mangy greybeard, who stood blinking a pair of rheumy eyes and weakly smiling. One did not pit oneself against such human flotsam. Drunkard was stamped on every inch of the man, but this morning, in odd exception to the well-primed crew around him, he was sober — bewilderedly sober — and his shabby clothing was brushed, his frayed collar clean. Recognizing the pitiful bid for sympathy, Mahony caught himself thinking: 'Good Lord! I could have supplied him with a coat he'd have cut a better figure than that in.'

Bolliver clutched the edge of the box with his two hands. His unusual condition was a hindrance rather than a help to him; without a peg or two his woolly thoughts were not to be disentangled. He stammered forth his evidence, halting either to piece together what he was going to say, or to recollect what he had just said — it was clear he went in mortal fear of contradicting himself. The scene was painful enough while he faced his own counsel, but, when counsel for the defence rose, a half-hour followed in which Mahony wished himself far from the court.

Bolliver could not come to the point. Counsel was merciless and coarsely jocose, and brought off several laughs. His victim wound his knotty hands in and out, and swallowed oftener than he had saliva for, in a forlorn endeavour to evade the pitfalls artfully dug for him. More than once he threw a covert glance, that was like an appeal for help, at all the indifferent faces. Mahony drooped his head, that their eyes should not meet.

In high feather at the effect he was producing, counsel inserted his left arm under his gown, and held the stuff out from his back with the tips of all five fingers.

'And now you'll p'raps have the goodness to tell us whether you've ever had occasion to send goods by a carrier before, in the course of your young life?'

'Yes.' It was a humble monosyllable, returned without spirit.

'Then of course you've heard of this Murphy?'

'N . . . no, I haven't,' answered Bolliver, and let his vacillating eyes wander to the judge and back.

'You tell that to the marines!' And after half a dozen other tricky questions: 'I put it to you, it's a well-known fact that he's been a carrier hereabouts for the last couple o' years or more?'

'I don't know – I sup . . . sup-pose so.' Bolliver's tongue grew heavy and tripped up his words.

'And yet you've the cheek, you old rogue you, to insinuate that this was a put-up job?'

'I . . . I only say what I heard.'

'I don't care a button what you heard or didn't hear. What I ask, my pretty, is do you yourself say so?'

'The . . . the defendant recommended him.'

'I put it to you, this man Murphy was one of the best known carriers in Melbourne, and *that* was why the defendant recommended him – are you out to deny it?'

'N . . . n . . . no.'

'Then you can stand down!' and leaning over to Grindle, who was below him, counsel whispered with a pleased spread of the hand: 'There you are! that's our case.'

There was a painful moment just before Bolliver left the witness-box. As if become suddenly alive to the sorry figure he had cut, he turned to the judge with hands clasped, exclaimed: 'My Lord, if the case goes against me, I'm done . . . stony-broke! And the defendant's got a down on me, my Lord – 'e's made up his mind to ruin me. Look at him a-setting there – a hard man, a mean man, if ever you saw one! What would the bit of money 'ave meant to 'im? But . . .'

He was rudely silenced and hustled away, to a sharp rebuke from the judge, who woke up to give it. All eyes were turned on Mahony. Under the fire of observation – they were comparing him, he knew, with the poor old Jeremy Diddler yonder, to the latter's disadvantage – his spine stiffened and he held himself nervously erect. But, the quizzing at an end, he fumbled with his finger at his neck – his collar seemed to have grown too tight. While, without, the hot blast, dark with dust, flung itself against the corners of the house, and howled like a soul in pain.

Counsel for the defence made an excellent impression. 'Naturally! *I* can afford to pay a better-class man,' was Mahony's caustic note. He had fallen to scribbling on a sheet of paper, and was resigned to sitting through an adept presentment of Ocock's shifts and dodges. But the opening words made him prick up his ears.

'My Lord,' said counsel, 'I submit there is here no case to go to the jury. No written contract existed between the parties, to bring it within the Statute of Frauds. Therefore, the plaintiff must prove that the defendant accepted these goods. Now I submit to you, on the plaintiff's own admission, that the man Murphy was a common carrier. Your Lordship will know the cases of Hanson v. Armitage and various others, in which it has been established beyond doubt that a carrier is not an agent to accept goods.'

The judge had revived, and while counsel called the quality of the undelivered goods in question, and laid stress on the fact of no money having passed, he turned the pages of a thick red book with a moistened thumb. Having found what he sought, he pushed up his spectacles, opened his mouth, and, his eyes bent meditatively on the speaker, picked a back tooth with the nail of his first finger.

'Therefore,' concluded counsel, 'I hold that there is no question of fact to go to the jury. I do not wish to occupy your Lordship's time any further upon this submission. I have my client here, and all his witnesses are in court whom I am prepared to call, should your Lordship decide against me on the present point. But I do submit that the plaintiff, on his own showing, has made out no case; and that under the circumstances, upon his own evidence, this action must fail.'

At the reference to witnesses, Mahony dug his pencil into the paper till the point snapped. So this was their little game! And should the bluff not work . . .? He sat rigid, staring at the chipped fragment of lead, and did not look up throughout the concluding scene of the farce.

It was over; the judge had decided in his favour. He jumped to his feet, and his coat-sleeves swept the dust off the entire length of the ledge in front of him. But before he reached the foot of the stairs Grindle came flying down, to say that Ocock wished to speak to him. Very good, replied Mahony, he would call at the office in the course of the afternoon. But the clerk left the courthouse at his side. And suddenly the thought flashed through Mahony's mind: 'The fellow suspects me of trying to do a bolt – of wanting to make off without paying my bill!'

The leech-like fashion in which Grindle stuck to his heels was not to be misread. 'This is what they call nursing, I suppose – he's nursing *me* now!' said Mahony to himself. At the same time he reckoned up, with some anxiety, the money he had in his pocket. Should it prove insufficient, who knew what further affronts were in store for him.

But Ocock had recovered his oily sleekness.

'A close shave that, sir, a *ve-ry* close shave! With Warnock on the bench I thought we could manage to pull it off. Had it been Guppy now . . . Still, all's well that ends well, as the poet says. And now for a trifling matter of business.'

'How much do I owe you?'

The bill – it was already drawn up – for 'solicitor's and client's costs' came to twenty-odd pounds. Mahony paid it, and stalked out of the office.

But this was still not all. Once again Grindle ran after him, and pinned him to the floor.

'I say, Mr Mahony, a rare joke – gad, it's enough to make you burst your sides! That old thingumbob, the plaintiff, ye know, now what'n earth d'you think 'e's been an' done? Gets outer court like one o'clock – 'e'd a sorter rabbit-fancyin' business in 'is backyard. Well, 'ome 'e trots an' slits the guts of every blamed bunny, an' chucks the bloody corpses inter the street. Oh lor! What do you say to that, eh? Unfurnished in the upper storey, what? Heh, heh, heh!'

CHAPTER THREE

How truly 'home' the poor little gimcrack shanty had become to him, Mahony grasped only when he once more crossed its threshold and Polly's arms lay round his neck.

His search for Johnny Ocock had detained him in Melbourne for over a week. Under the guidance of young Grindle he had scoured the city, not omitting even the dens of infamy in the Chinese quarter; and he did not know which to be more saddened by: the revolting sights he saw, or his guide's proud familiarity with every shade of vice. But nothing could be heard of the missing lad; and at the suggestion of Henry Ocock he put an advertisement in the *Argus*, offering a substantial reward for news of Johnny alive or dead.

While waiting to see what this would bring forth, he paid a visit to John Turnham. It had not been part of his scheme to trouble his new relatives on this occasion; he bore them a grudge for the way they had met Polly's overture. But he was at his wits' end how to kill time: chafing at the delay was his main employment, if he were not worrying over the thought of having to appear before old Ocock without his son. So, one midday he called at Turnham's place of business in Flinders Lane, and was affably received by John, who carried him off to lunch at the Melbourne Club.

Turnham was a warm partisan of the diggers' cause. He had addressed a mass meeting held in Melbourne, soon after the fight on the Eureka; and he now roundly condemned the Government's policy of repression.

'I am, as you are aware, my dear Mahony, no sentimentalist. But these rioters of yours seem to me the very type of man the country needs. Could we have a better bedrock on which to build than these fearless champions of liberty?'

He set an excellent meal before his brother-in-law, and himself ate and drank heartily, unfolding his very table-napkin with

104

a kind of relish. In lunching, he inquired the object of Mahony's journey to town. At the mention of Henry Ocock's name he raised his eyebrows and pursed his lips.

'Ah, indeed! Then it is hardly necessary to ask the upshot.'

He pooh-poohed Mahony's intention of staying till the defaulting witness was found; disapproved, too, the offer of a reward. 'To be paid out of *your* pocket, of course! No, my dear Mahony, set your mind at rest and return to your wife. Lads of that sort never come to grief – more's the pity! By the bye, how *is* Polly, and how does she like life on the diggings?'

In this connection, Mahony tendered congratulations on the expected addition to Turnham's family. John embarked readily enough on the theme of his beautiful wife; but into his voice, as he talked, came a note of impatience or annoyance, which formed an odd contrast to his wonted self-possession. 'Yes . . . her third, and for some reason which I cannot fathom, it threatens to prove the most trying of any.' And here he went into medical detail on Mrs Emma's state.

Mahony urged compliance with the whims of the mother-to-be, even should they seem extravagant. 'Believe me, at a time like this such moods and caprices have their use. Nature very well knows what she is about.'

'Nature? Bah! I am no great believer in nature,' gave back John, and emptied his glass of madeira. 'Nature exists to be coerced and improved.'

They parted; and Mahony went back to twirl his thumbs in the hotel coffee-room. He could not persuade himself to take Turnham's advice and leave Johnny to his fate. And the delay was nearly over. At dawn next morning Johnny was found lying in a pitiable condition at the door of the hotel. It took Mahony the best part of the day to rouse him; to make him understand he was not to be horsewhipped; to purchase a fresh suit of clothing for him: to get him, in short, halfway ready to travel the following day – a blear-eyed, weak-witted craven, who fell into a cold sweat at every bump of the coach. Not till they reached the end of the awful journey – even a Chinaman rose to impudence about Johnny's nerves, his foul breath, his cracked lips – did Mahony learn how the wretched boy had come by the money for his debauch. At the public-house where the coach drew up, old Ocock stood grimly waiting, with a leather thong at his belt, and the news that his till had been broken open and robbed of its contents. With an involuntary recommendation to mercy, Mahony handed over the culprit and turned his steps home.

Polly stood on tip-toe to kiss him; Pompey barked till the roof rang, making leaps that fell wide of the mark; the cat hoisted its tail, and wound purring in and out between his legs. Tea was spread, on a clean cloth, with all sorts of good things to eat; an English mail had brought him a batch of letters and journals. Altogether it was a very happy home-coming.

When he had had a sponge-down and finished tea, over which he listened, with a zest that surprised him, to a hundred and one domestic details: afterwards he and Polly strolled arm-in-arm to the top of the little hill to which, before marriage, he used to carry her letters. Here they sat and talked till night fell; and, for the first time, Mahony tasted the dregless pleasure of coming back from the world outside with his toll of adventure, and being met by a woman's lively and disinterested sympathy. Agreeable incidents gained, those that were the reverse of pleasing lost their sting by being shared with Polly. Not that he told her everything; of the dark side of life he greatly preferred little Polly to remain ignorant. Still, as far as it went, it was a delightful experience. In return he confessed to her something of the uncertainty that had beset him, on hearing his opponent's counsel state the case for the other side. It was disquieting to think he might be suspected of advancing a claim that was not strictly just.

'Suspected? . . . *you?* Oh, how could anybody be so silly!'

For all the fatigues of his day Mahony could not sleep. And after tossing and tumbling for some time, he rose, threw on his clothing and went out to smoke a pipe in front of the store. Various worries were pecking at him – the hint he had given Polly of their existence seemed to have let them fairly loose upon him. Of course he would be – he was – suspected of having connived at the imposture by which his suit was won – why else have put it in the hands of such a one as Ocock? John Turnham's soundless whistle of astonishment recurred to him, and flicked him. Imagine it! He, Richard Mahony, giving his sanction to these queasy tricks!

It was bad enough to know that Ocock at any rate had believed him not averse from winning by unjust means. Yet, on the whole, he thought this mortified him less than to feel that he had been written down a Simple Simon, whom it was easy to impose on. Ah well! At best he had been but a kind of guy, set up for them to let off their verbal fireworks round. Faith and that was all these lawyer-fellows wanted – the ghost of an excuse for parading their skill. Justice played a negligible rôle in this battle of wits; else not he but the plaintiff would have come out victorious. That wretched Bolliver! . . . the memory of him wincing and flushing in the witness-box would haunt him for the rest of his days. He could see him, too, with equal clearness, broken-heartedly slitting the gizzards of his pets. A poor old derelict – the amen to a life which, like most lives, had once been flush with promise. And it had been his, Mahony's, honourable portion to give the last kick, the ultimate shove into perdition. Why, he would rather have lost the money ten times over!

To divert his mind, he began next morning to make an inventory of the goods in the store. It was high time, too: thanks to the recent disturbances he did not know where he stood. And while he was about it, he gave the place a general clean-up. A job of this kind was a powerful ally in keeping edged thoughts at bay. He and his men had their hands full for several days, Polly, who was not allowed to set foot in the store, peeping critically in at them to see how they progressed. And, after business hours, there was little Polly herself.

He loved to contemplate her.

Six months of married life had worked certain changes in his black-eyed slip of a girl; but something of the doe-like shyness that had caught his fancy still clung to her. With strangers she could even yet be touchingly bashful. Not long out of short frocks, she found it difficult to stand upon her dignity as Mrs Dr Mahony. Besides, it was second nature to Polly to efface herself, to steal mousily away. Unless, of course, someone needed help or was in distress, in which case she forgot to be shy. To her husband's habits and idiosyncrasies she had adapted herself implicitly – but this came easy; for she was sure everything Richard did was right, and that his way of looking at things was the one and only way. So there was no room for discord between them. By this time Polly could laugh over the dismay of her first home-coming: the pitch-dark night and unfamiliar road, the racket of the serenade, the apparition of the great spider: now, all this might have happened to somebody else, not Polly Mahony. Her dislike of things that creep and crawl was, it is true, inborn, and persisted; but nowadays if one of the many 'triantelopes' that infested the roof showed its hairy legs, she had only to call Hempel, and out the latter would pop with a broomstick, to do away with the creature. If a scorpion or a centipede wriggled from under a log, the cry of 'Tom!' would bring the idle lad next door double-quick over the fence. Polly had learnt not to summon her husband on these occasions; for Richard held to the maxim: 'Live and let live.' If at night a tarantula appeared on the bedroom-wall, he caught it in a covered glass and carried it outside: 'Just to come in again,' was her rueful reflection. But indeed Polly was surrounded by willing helpers. And small wonder, thought Mahony. Her young nerves were so sound that Hempel's dry cough never grated them: she doctored him and fussed over him, and was worried that she could not cure him. She met Long Jim's grumbles with a sunny face, and listened patiently to his forebodings that he would never see 'home' or his old woman again. She even brought out a clumsy goodwill in the young varmint Tom; nor did his old father's want of refinement repel her.

'But, Richard, he's such a kind old man,' she met her husband's admission of this stumbling-block. 'And it isn't his fault that he wasn't properly educated. He has had to work for his living ever since he was twelve years old.'

And Mr Ocock cried quits by remarking confidentially: 'That little lady o' yours 'as got 'er 'eadpiece screwed on the right way. It beats me, doc., why you don't take 'er inter the store and learn 'er the bizness. No offence, I'm sure,' he made haste to add, disconcerted by Mahony's cold stare.

Had anyone at this date tried to tell Polly she lived in a mean, rough home, he would have had a poor reception. Polly was long since certain that not a house on the diggings could compare with theirs. This was a trait Mahony loved in her – her sterling loyalty; a loyalty that embraced not only her dear ones themselves, but every stick and stone belonging to them. His discovery of it helped him to understand her allegiance to her own multicoloured family: in the beginning he had almost doubted its sincerity. Now, he knew her better. It was just as though a sixth sense had been implanted in Polly, enabling her to pierce straight through John's self-sufficiency or Ned's vapourings, to the real kernel of goodness that no doubt lay hid below. He himself could not get at it; but then his powers of divination were the exact opposite of Polly's. He was always struck by the weak or ridiculous side of a person, and had to dig laboriously down to the virtues. While his young wife, by a kind of genius, saw the good at a glance – and saw nothing else. And she did not stint with her gift, or hoard it up solely for use on her own kith and kin. Her splendid sympathy was the reverse of clannish; it was applied to every mortal who crossed her path.

Yes, for all her youth, Polly had quite a character of her own; and even thus early her husband sometimes ran up against a certain native sturdiness of opinion. But this did not displease him; on the contrary, he would not have thanked you for a wife who was only an echo of himself. To take the case of the animals. He had a profound respect for those creatures to which speech has been denied; and he treated the four-footers that dwelt under his roof as his fellows, humanizing them, reading his own thoughts into them, and showing more consideration for their feelings than if they had been able to speak up for themselves. Polly saw this in the light of an exquisite joke. She was always kind to Pompey and the stately Palmerston, and would as soon have forgotten to set Richard's dinner before him as to feed the pair; but they remained 'the dog' and 'the cat' to her, and, if they had enough to eat, and received neither kicks nor blows, she could not conceive of their souls asking more. It went beyond her to study the cat's dislike to being turned off its favourite chair, or to believe that the dog did not make dirty prints on her fresh scrubbed floor out of malice prepense; it was also incredible that he should have doggy fits of depression, in which up he must to stick a cold, slobbery snout into a warm human hand. And when Richard tried to conciliate Palmerston stalking sulky to the door, or to pet away the melancholy in the rejected Pompey's eyes, Polly had to lay down her sewing and laugh at her husband, so greatly did his behaviour amuse her.

Again, there was the question of literature. Books to Mahony were almost as necessary as bread; to his girl-wife, on the other hand, they seemed a somewhat needless luxury – less vital by far than the animals that walked the floor. She took great care of the precious volumes Richard had had carted up from Melbourne; but the cost of the transport was what impressed her most. It was not an overstatement, thought Mahony, to say that a stack of well-chopped, neatly piled wood meant more to Polly than all the books ever written. Not that she did not enjoy a good story: her work done, she liked few things better; and he often smiled at the ease with which she lived herself into the world of make-believe, knowing, of course, that it *was* make-believe and just a kind of humbug. But poetry, and the higher fiction! Little Polly's professed love for poetry had been merely a concession to the conventional idea of girlhood; or, at best, such a burning wish to be all her Richard desired, that, at the moment, she was convinced of the truth of what she said. But did he read to her from his favourite authors her attention *would* wander, in spite of the efforts she made to pin it down.

Mahony declaimed:

> 'Tis the sunset of life gives us mystical lore,
> And coming events cast their shadows before,

and his pleasure in the swing of the couplet was such that he repeated it.

Polly wakened with a start. Her thoughts had been miles away – had been back at the 'Family Hotel'. There Purdy, after several adventures, his poor leg a mass of suppuration, had at length betaken himself, to be looked after by his Tilly; and Polly's hopes were all alight again.

She blushed guiltily at the repetition, and asked her husband to say the lines once again. He did so.

'But they don't really, Richard, do they?' she said in an apologetic tone – she referred to the casting of shadows. 'It would be so useful if they did' – and she drew a sigh at Purdy's dilatory treatment of the girl who loved him so well.

'Oh, you prosaic little woman!' cried Mahony, and laid down his book to kiss her. It was impossible to be vexed with Polly: she was so honest, so transparent. 'Did you never hear of a certain something called poetic licence?'

No: Polly was more or less familiar with various other forms of licence, from the gold-diggers' that had caused all the fuss, down to the special licence by which she had been married; but this particular one had not come her way. And on Richard explaining to her the liberty poets allowed themselves, she shifted uncomfortably in her chair, and was sorry to think he approved. It seemed to her just a fine name for wanton exaggeration – if not something worse.

There were also those long evenings they spent over the first hundred pages of *Waverley*. Mahony, eager for her to share his enthusiasm, comforted her each night anew that they would soon reach the story proper, and then, how interested she would be! But the opening chapters were a sandy desert of words, all about people duller than any Polly had known alive; and sometimes, before the book was brought out, she would heave a secret sigh – although, of course, she enjoyed sitting cosily together with Richard, watching him and listening to his voice. But they might have put their time to a pleasanter use: by talking of themselves, or their friends, or how further to improve their home, or what the store was doing.

Mahony saw her smiling to herself one evening; and after assuring himself that there was nothing on the page before him to call that pleased look to her young face, he laid the book down and offered her a penny for her thoughts. But Polly was loath to confess to woolgathering.

'I haven't succeeded in interesting you, have I, Pollikins?'

She made haste to contradict him. Oh, it was very nice, and she loved to hear him read.

'Come, honestly now, little woman!'

She faced him squarely at that, though with pink cheeks. 'Well, not much, Richard.'

He took her on his knee. 'And what were you smiling at?'

'Me? Oh, I was just thinking of something that happened yesterday' – and Polly sat up, agog to tell.

It appeared that the day before, while he was out, the digger's wife who did Polly's rough work for her had rushed in, crying that her youngest was choking. Bonnetless, Polly had flown across to the woman's hut. There she discovered the child, a fat youngster of a year or so, purple in the face, with a button wedged in its throat. Taking it by the heels she shook the child vigorously, upside-down; and, lo and behold! this had the opposite effect to what she intended. When they straightened the child out again the button was found to have passed the danger-point and gone down. Quickly resolved, Polly cut slice on slice of thin bread-and-butter, and with this she and Mrs Hemmerde stuffed the willing babe till, full to bursting, it warded them off with its tiny hands.

Mahony laughed heartily at the tale, and applauded his wife's prompt measures. 'Short of the forceps nothing could have been better!'

Yes, Polly had a dash of native shrewdness, which he prized. And a pair of clever hands that were never idle. He had given her leave to make any changes she chose in the house, and she was for ever stitching away at white muslin, or tacking it over pink calico. These affairs made their little home very spick and span, and kept Polly from feeling dull – if one could imagine Polly dull! With the cooking alone had there been a hitch in the beginning. Like a true expert Mrs Beamish had not tolerated understudies: none but the lowliest jobs, such as raisin-stoning or potato-peeling, had fallen to the three girls' share: and in face of her first fowl Polly stood helpless and dismayed. But not for long. Sarah was applied to for the best cookery-book on sale in Melbourne, and when this arrived, Polly gave herself up to the study of it. She had many failures, both private and avowed. With the worst, she either retired behind the wood-stack, or Tom disposed of them for her, or the dog ate them up. But she persevered: and soon Mahony could with truth declare that no one raised a better loaf or had a lighter hand at pastry than his wife.

Three knocks on the wooden partition was the signal which, if he were not serving a customer, summoned him to the kitchen.

'Oh, Richard, it's risen beautifully!' And, red with heat and pride, Polly drew a great golden-crusted, blown-up sponge-cake along the oven shelf.

Richard, who had a sweet tooth, pretended to be unable to curb his impatience.

'Wait! First I must see . . .' and she plunged a knife into the cake's heart: it came out untarnished. 'Yes, it's done to a turn.'

There and then it was cut; for, said Mahony, that was the only way in which he could make sure of a piece. Afterwards chunks were dealt out to everyone Polly knew – to Long Jim, Hempel, Tommy Ocock, the little Hemmerdes. Side by side on the kitchen-table, their feet dangling in the air, husband and wife sat boy-and-girl fashion and munched hot cake, till their appetites for dinner were wrecked.

But the rains that heralded winter – and they set in early that year – had not begun to fall when more serious matters claimed Mahony's attention.

CHAPTER FOUR

It was an odd and inexplicable thing that business showed no sign of improving. Affairs on Ballarat had, for months past, run their usual prosperous course. The western township grew from day to day, and was straggling right out to the banks of the great swamp. On the Flat, the deep sinking that was at present the rule – some parties actually touched a depth of three hundred feet before bottoming – had brought a fresh host of fortune-hunters to the spot, and the results obtained bid fair to rival those of the first golden year. The diggers' grievances and their conflict with the Government were now a turned page. At a state trial all prisoners had been acquitted, and a general amnesty declared for those rebels who were still at large. Unpopular ministers had resigned or died; a new constitution for the colony awaited the Royal assent; and pending this, two of the rebel-leaders, now prominent townsmen, were chosen to sit in the Legislative Council. The future could not have looked rosier. For others, that was. For him, Mahony, it held more than one element of uncertainty.

At no time had he come near making a fortune out of store-keeping. For one thing, he had been too squeamish. From the outset he had declined to soil his hands with surreptitious grog-selling; nor would he be a party to that evasion of the law which consisted in overcharging on other goods, and throwing in drinks free. Again, he would rather have been hamstrung than stoop to the tricks in vogue with regard to the weighing of gold-dust: the greased scales, the wet sponge, false beams, and so on. Accordingly, he had a clearer conscience than the majority and a lighter till. But even at the legitimate ABC of business he had proved a duffer. He had never, for instance, learned to be a really skilled hand at stocking a shop. Was an out-of-the-way article called for, ten to one he had run short of it; and the born shopman's knack of palming off or persuading to a makeshift

113

was not his. Such goods as he had, he did not press on people; his attitude was always that of 'take it or leave it'; and he sometimes surprised a ridiculous feeling of satisfaction when he chased a drunken and insolent customer off the premises, or secured an hour's leisure unbroken by the jangle of the storebell.

Still, in spite of everything he had, till recently, done well enough. Money was loose, and the diggers, if given long credit when down on their luck, were in the main to be relied on to pay up when they struck the lead or tapped a pocket. He had had slack seasons before now, and things had always come right again. This made it hard for him to explain the present prolonged spell of dullness.

That there was something more than ordinarily wrong first dawned on him during the stock-taking in summer. Hempel and he were constantly coming upon goods that had been too long on hand, and were now fit only to be thrown away. Half-a-dozen boxes of currants showed a respectable growth of mould; a like fate had come upon some flitches of bacon; and not a bag of flour but had developed a species of minute maggot. Rats had got at his coils of rope, one of which, sold in all good faith, had gone near causing the death of the digger who used it. The remains of some smoked fish were brought back and flung at his head with a shower of curses, by a woman who had fallen ill through eating of it. And yet, in spite of the replenishing this involved, the order he sent to town that season was the smallest he had ever given. For the first time he could not fill a dray, but had to share one with a greenhorn, who, if you please, was setting up at his very door.

He and Hempel cracked their brains to account for the falling-off – or at least he did: afterwards he believed Hempel had suspected the truth and been too mealy-mouthed to speak out. It was Polly who innocently – for of course he did not draw her into confidence – Polly supplied the clue from a piece of gossip brought to the house by the woman Hemmerde. It appeared that, at the time of the rebellion, Mahony's open antagonism to the Reform League had given offence all round – to the extremists as well as to the more wary on whose behalf the League was drafted. They now got even with him by taking their custom elsewhere. He snorted with indignation on hearing of it; then laughed ironically. He was expected, was he, not only to bring his personal tastes and habits into line with those of the

114

majority, but to deny his politics as well? And if he refused, they would make it hard for him to earn a decent living in their midst. Nothing seemed easier to these unprincipled democrats than for a man to cut his coat to suit his job. Why, he might just as well turn Whig and be done with it!

He sat over his account-books. The pages were black with bad debts for 'tucker'. Here however was no mystery. The owners of these names – Purdy was among them – had without doubt been implicated in the Eureka riot, and had made off and never returned. He struck a balance, and found to his consternation that, unless business took a turn for the better, he would not be able to hold out beyond the end of the year. Afterwards, he was blessed if he knew what was going to happen. The ingenious Hempel was full of ideas for tempting back fortune – opening a branch store on a new lead was one of them, or removing bodily to Main Street – but ready money was the *sine qua non* of such schemes, and ready money he had not got. Since his marriage he had put by as good as nothing; and the enlarging and improving of his house, at that time, had made a big hole in his bachelor savings. He did not feel justified at the present pass in drawing on them anew. For one thing, before summer was out there would be, if all went well, another mouth to feed. And that meant a variety of seen and unforeseen expenses.

Such were the material anxieties he had to encounter in the course of that winter. Below the surface a subtler embarrassment worked to destroy his peace. In face of the shortage of money, he was obliged to thank his stars that he had not lost the miserable lawsuit of a few months back. Had that happened, he wouldn't at present have known where to turn. But this amounted to confessing his satisfaction at having pulled off his case, pulled it off anyhow, by no matter what crooked means. And as if this were not enough, the last words he had heard Purdy say came back to sting him anew. The boy had accused him of judging a fight for freedom from a tradesman's standpoint. Now it might be said of him that he was viewing justice from the same angle. He had scorned the idea of distorting his political opinions to fit the trade by which he gained his bread. But it was a far more serious thing if his principles, his character, his sense of equity were all to be undermined as well. If he stayed here, he would end by becoming as blunt to what was right and fair as the rest of them. As it was, he was no longer able to

115

regard the two great landmarks of man's moral development – liberty and justice – from the point of view of an honest man and a gentleman.

His self-annoyance was so great that it galvanized him to action. There and then he made up his mind: as soon as the child that was coming to them was old enough to travel, he would sell out for what he could get, and go back to the old country. Once upon a time he had hoped, when he went, to take a good round sum with him towards a first-rate English practice. Now he saw that this scheme had been a kind of Jack-o'-lantern – a marsh-light after which he might have danced for years to come. As matters stood, he must needs be content if, the passage-moneys paid, he could scrape together enough to keep him afloat till he found a modest corner to slip into.

His first impulse was to say nothing of this to his wife in the meantime. Why unsettle her? But he had reckoned without the sudden upward leap his spirits made, once his decision was taken: the winter sky was blue as violets again above him; he turned out light-heartedly of a morning. It was impossible to hide the change in his mood from Polly – even if he had felt it fair to do so. Another thing: when he came to study Polly by the light of his new plan, he saw that his scruples about unsettling her were fanciful – wraiths of his own imagining. As a matter of fact, the sooner he broke the news to her the better. Little Polly was so thoroughly happy here that she would need time to accustom herself to the prospect of life elsewhere.

He went about it very cautiously though; and with no hint of the sour and sorry incidents that had driven him to the step. As was only natural, Polly was rather easily upset at present: the very evening before, he had had occasion to blame himself for his tactless behaviour.

In her first sick young fear Polly had impulsively written off to Mother Beamish, to claim the fulfilment of that good woman's promise to stand by her when her time came. One letter gave another; Mrs Beamish not only announced that she would hold herself ready to support her 'little duck' at a moment's notice, but filled sheets with sage advice and old wives' maxims; and the correspondence, which had languished, flared up anew. Now came an ill-scrawled, misspelt epistle from Tilly – doleful, too, for Purdy had once more quitted her without speaking the binding word – in which she told that Purdy's leg, though healed,

116

was permanently shortened; the doctor in Geelong said he would never walk straight again.

Husband and wife sat and discussed the news, wondering how lameness would affect Purdy's future and what he was doing now, Tilly not having mentioned his whereabouts. 'She has probably no more idea than we have,' said Mahony.

'I'm afraid not,' said Polly with a sigh. 'Well, I hope he won't come back here, that's all'; and she considered the seam she was sewing with an absent air.

'Why, love? Don't you like old Dickybird?' asked Mahony in no small surprise.

'Oh yes, quite well. But . . .'

'Is it because he still can't make up his mind to take your Tilly – eh?'

'That, too. But chiefly because of something he said.'

'And what was that, my dear?'

'Oh, very silly,' and Polly smiled.

'Out with it, madam! Or I shall suspect the young dog of having made advances to *my* wife.'

'Richard, *dear!*' Little Polly thought he was in earnest, and grew exceedingly confused. 'Oh, no, nothing like that,' she assured him, and with red cheeks rushed into an explanation. 'He only said, in spite of you being such old friends he felt you didn't really care to have him here on Ballarat. After a time you always invented some excuse to get him away.' But now that it was out, Polly felt the need of toning down the statement, and added: 'I shouldn't wonder if he was silly enough to think you were envious of him, for having so many friends and being liked by all sorts of people.'

'Envious of him? *I?* Who on earth has been putting such ideas into your head?' cried Mahony.

'It was "mother" thought so – it was while I was still there,' stammered Polly, still more fluttered by the fact of him fastening on just these words.

Mahony tried to quell his irritation by fidgeting round the room. 'Surely, Polly, you might give up calling that woman "mother", now you belong to me – I thank you for the relationship!' he said testily. And having with much unnecessary ado knocked the ashes out of his pipe, he went on: 'It's bad enough to say things of that kind; but to repeat them, love, is in even poorer taste.'

'Yes, Richard,' said Polly meekly.

117

But her amazed inner query was: 'Not even to one's own husband?'

She hung her head, till the white thread of parting between the dark loops of her hair was almost perpendicular. She had spoken without thinking in the first place – had just blurted out a passing thought. But even when forced to explain, she had never dreamt of Richard taking offence. Rather she had imagined the two of them – two banded lovingly against one – making merry together over Purdy's nonsense. She had heard her husband laugh away much unkinder remarks than this. And perhaps if she had stopped there, and said no more, it might have been all right. By her stupid attempt to gloss things over, she had really managed to hurt him, and had made him think her gossipy into the bargain.

She went on with her sewing. But when Mahony came back from the brisk walk by means of which he got rid of his annoyance, he fancied, though Polly was as cheery as ever and had supper laid for him, that her eyelids were red.

This was why, the following evening, he promised himself to be discreet.

Winter had come in earnest; the night was wild and cold. Before the crackling stove the cat lay stretched at full length, while Pompey dozed fitfully, his nose between his paws. The red-cotton curtains that hung at the little window gave back the lamplight in a ruddy glow; the clock beat off the seconds evenly, except when drowned by the wind, which came in bouts, hurling itself against the corners of the house. And presently, laying down his book – Polly was too busy now to be read to – Mahony looked across at his wife. She was wrinkling her pretty brows over the manufacture of tiny clothes, a rather pale little woman still, none of the initial discomforts of her condition having been spared her. Feeling his eyes on her, she looked up and smiled: did ever anyone see such a ridiculous armhole? Three of one's fingers were enough to fill it – and she held the little shirt aloft for his inspection. Here was his chance: the child's coming offered the best of pretexts. Taking not only the midget garment but also the hand that held it, he told her of his resolve to go back to England and re-enter his profession.

'You know, love, I've always wished to get home again. And now there's an additional reason. I don't want my . . . our children to grow up in a place like this. Without companions – or refining influences. Who knows how they would turn out?'

118

He said it, but in his heart he knew that his children would be safe enough. And Polly, listening to him, made the same reservation: yes, but *our* children . . .

'And I propose, as soon as the youngster's old enough to travel, to haul down the flag for good and all, and book passages for the three of us in some smart clipper. We'll live in the country, love. Think of it, Polly! A little gabled, red-roofed house at the foot of some Sussex down, with fruit trees and a high hedge round it, and only the oast-houses peeping over. Doesn't it make your mouth water, my dear?'

He had risen in his eagerness, and stood with his back to the stove, his legs apart. And Polly nodded and smiled up at him — though, truth to tell, the picture he drew did not mean much to her: she had never been in Sussex, nor did she know what an oast-house was. A night such as this, with flying clouds and a shrill, piping wind, made her think of angry seas and a dark ship's cabin, in which she lay deathly sick. But it was not Polly's way to dwell on disagreeables: her mind glanced off to a pleasanter theme.

'Have you *ever* thought, Richard, how strange it will seem when there *are* three of us? You and I will never be quite alone together again. Oh, I do hope he will be a good baby and not cry much. It will worry you if he does — like Hempel's cough. And then you won't love him properly.'

'I shall love it because it is yours, my darling. And the baby of such a dear little mother is sure to be good.'

'Oh, babies will be babies, you know!' said Polly, with a new air of wisdom which sat delightfully on her.

Mahony pinched her cheek. 'Mrs Mahony, you're shirking my question. Tell me now, should you not be pleased to get back to England?'

'I'll go wherever you go, Richard,' said Polly staunchly. 'Always. And of course I should like to see mother — I mean my real mother — again. But then Ned's here . . . and John, and Sarah. I should be very sorry to leave them. I don't think any of them will ever go home now.'

'They may be here, but they don't trouble *you* often, my dear,' said Mahony, with more than a hint of impatience. 'Especially Ned the well-beloved, who lives not a mile from your door.'

'I know he doesn't often come to see us, Richard. But he's only a boy; and has to work so hard. You see it's like this. If Ned should get into any trouble, I'm here to look after him; and

I know that makes mother's mind easier – Ned was always her favourite.'

'And an extraordinary thing, too! I believe it's the boy's good looks that blind you women to his faults.'

'Oh no, indeed it isn't!' declared Polly warmly. 'It's just because Ned's Ned. The dearest fellow, if you really know him.'

'And so your heart's anchored here, little wife, and would remain here even if I carried your body off to England?'

'Oh no, Richard,' said Polly again. 'My heart would always be where you are. But I can't help wondering how Ned would get on alone. And Jerry will soon be here too, now, and he's younger still. And *how* I should like to see dear Tilly settled before I go!'

Judging that enough had been said for the time being, Mahony re-opened his book, leaving his wife to chew the cud of innocent matchmaking and sisterly cares.

In reality Polly's reflections were of quite another nature.

Her husband's abrupt resolve to leave the colony, disturbing though it was, did not take her altogether by surprise. She would have needed to be both deaf and blind not to notice that the store-bell rang much seldomer than it used to, and that Richard had more spare time on his hands. Yes, trade was dull, and that made him fidgety. Now she had always known that someday it would be her duty to follow Richard to England. But she had imagined that day to be very far off – when they were elderly people, and had saved up a good deal of money. To hear the date fixed for six months hence was something of a shock to her. And it was at this point that Polly had a sudden inspiration. As she listened to Richard talking of resuming his profession, the thought flashed through her mind: why not here? Why should he not start practice in Ballarat, instead of travelling all those thousands of miles to do it?

This was what she ruminated while she tucked and hemmed. She could imagine, of course, what his answer would be. He would say there were too many doctors on Ballarat already; not more than a dozen of them made satisfactory incomes. But this argument did not convince Polly. Richard wasn't, perhaps, a great success at storekeeping; but that was only because he was too good for it. As a doctor, he with his cleverness and gentle-manly manners would soon, she was certain, stand head and shoulders above the rest. And then there would be money galore. It was true he did not care for Ballarat – was down on both place and people. But this objection, too, Polly waived. It passed belief that anybody could really dislike this big, rich, bustling, go-ahead township, where such handsome buildings were springing up and everyone was so friendly. In her heart she ascribed her husband's want of love for it to the 'infra dig.' position he occupied. If he mixed with his equals again and got rid of the feeling that he was looked down on, it would make all the difference in the world to him. He would then be out of reach of snubs and slights, and people would understand him better – not the residents on Ballarat alone, but also John, and Sarah, and the Beamishes, none of whom really appreciated Richard. In her mind's eye Polly had a vision of him going his rounds mounted on a chestnut horse, dressed in surtout and choker, and hand in glove with the bigwigs of society – the gentlemen at the Camp, the Police Magistrate and Archdeacon Long, the rich squatters who lived at the foot of Mount Buninyong. It brought the colour to her cheeks merely to think of it.

She did not, however, breathe a word of this to Richard. She was a shade wiser than the night before, when she had vexed him by blurting out her thoughts. And the present was not the right time to speak. In these days Richard was under the impression that she needed to be humoured. He might agree with her against his better judgement, or, worse still, pretend to agree. And Polly didn't want that. She wished fairly to persuade him that, by setting up here on the diggings where he was known and respected, he would get on quicker, and make more money, than if he buried himself in some poky English village where no one had ever heard of him.

Meanwhile the unconscious centre of her ambitions wore a perplexed frown. Mahony was much exercised just now over the question of medical attendance for Polly. The thought of coming into personal contact with a member of the fraternity was distasteful to him; none of them had an inkling who or what he was. And, though piqued by their unsuspectingness, he at the same time feared lest it should not be absolute, and he have the ill-luck to hit on a practitioner who had heard of his stray spurts of doctoring and written him down a charlatan and a quack. For this reason he would call in no one in the immediate neighbourhood – even the western township seemed too near. Ultimately, his choice fell on a man named Rogers who hailed from Mount Pleasant, the rise on the opposite side of the valley and some two miles off. It was true, since he did not intend to disclose his own standing, the distance would make the fellow's fees mount up. But Rogers was at least properly qualified (half those claiming the title of physician were impudent imposters, who didn't know a diploma from the Ten Commandments), of the same *alma mater* as himself – not a contemporary, though, he took good care of that! – and, if report spoke true, a skilful and careful obstetrician.

When, however, in response to a note carried by Long Jim Rogers drew rein in front of the store, Mahony was not greatly impressed by him. He proved to be a stout, reddish man, some ten years Mahony's senior, with a hasty-pudding face and an undecided manner. There he sat, his ten spread finger-tips meeting and gently tapping one another across his paunch, and nodding: 'Just so, just so!' to all he heard. He had the trick of saying everything twice over. 'Needs to clinch his own opinion!' was Mahony's swift diagnosis. Himself, he kept in the background. And was he forced to come forward his manner was both stiff and forbidding, so on tenterhooks was he lest the other should presume to treat him as anything but the storekeeper he gave himself out to be.

A day or so later who but the wife must arrive to visit Polly! – a piece of gratuitous friendliness that could well have been dispensed with; even though Mahony felt it keenly that, at this juncture, Polly should lack companions of her own sex. But Rogers had married beneath him, and the sight of the pursy upstart – there were people on the Flat who remembered her running barefoot and slatternly – sitting there, in satin and feathers, lording it over his own little Jenny Wren, was more than Mahony could tolerate. The distance was put forward as an excuse for Polly not returning the call, and Polly was docile as usual; though for her part she had thought her visitor quite a pleasant, kindly woman. But then Polly never knew when she was being patronized!

To wipe out any little trace of disappointment, her husband suggested that she should write and ask one of the Beamish girls to stay with her: it would keep her from feeling the days long.

But Polly only laughed. 'Long? – when I have so much sewing to do?'

No, she did not want company. By now, indeed, she regretted having sent off that impulsive invitation to Mrs Beamish for the end of the year. Puzzle as she would, she could not see how she was going to put 'mother' comfortably up.

Meanwhile the rains were changing the familiar aspect of the place. Creeks – in summer dry gutters of baked clay – were now rich red rivers; and the yellow Yarrowee ran full to the brim, keeping those who lived hard by it in a twitter of anxiety. The steep slopes of Black Hill showed thinly green; the roads were ploughed troughs of sticky mire. Occasional night frosts whitened the ground, bringing cloudless days in their wake. Then down came the rain once more, and fell for a week on end. The diggers were washed out of their holes, the Flat became an untraversable bog. And now there were floods in earnest: the creeks turned to foaming torrents that swept away trees and the old roots of trees; and the dwellers on the river banks had to fly for their bare lives.

Over the top of book or newspaper Mahony watched his wife stitch, stitch, stitch, with a zeal that never flagged, at the dolly garments. Just as he could read his way, so Polly sewed hers, through the time of waiting. But whereas she, like a sensible little woman, pinned her thoughts fast to the matter in hand, he let his range freely over the future. Of the many good things this had in store for him, one in particular whetted his impatience. It took close on a twelvemonth out here to get hold of a new book. On Ballarat not even a stationer's existed; nor were there more than a couple of shops in Melbourne itself that could be relied on to carry out your order. You perforce fell behind in the race, remained ignorant of what was being said and done – in science, letters, religious controversy – in the great world overseas. To this day he didn't know whether Agassiz had or had not been appointed to the chair of Natural History in Edinburgh; or whether fresh heresies with regard to the creation of species had spoiled his chances; did not know whether Hugh Miller had actually gone crazy over the *Vestiges*; or even if those arch-combatants, Syme and Simpson, had at length sheathed their swords. Now, however, God willing, he would before very long be back in the thick of it all, in intimate touch with the doings of the most wide-awake city in Europe; and new books and pamphlets would come into his possession as they dropped hot from the press.

CHAPTER FIVE

And then one morning – it was spring now, and piping hot at noon – Long Jim brought home from the post-office a letter for Polly, addressed in her sister Sarah's sloping hand. Knowing the pleasure it would give her, Mahony carried it at once to his wife; and Polly laid aside broom and duster and sat down to read.

But he was hardly out of the room when a startled cry drew him back to her side. Polly had hidden her face, and was shaken by sobs. As he could not get her to speak, Mahony picked up the letter from the floor and read it for himself.

Sarah wrote like one distracted.

Oh, my dear sister, how can I find words to tell you of the truly 'awful' calamity that has befallen our unhappy brother.

Mahony skipped the phrases, and learnt that owing to a carriage accident Emma Turnham had been prematurely confined, and, the best medical aid notwithstanding – 'John spared absolutely "no" expense' – had died two days later.

John is like a madman. Directly I heard the 'shocking' news, I at once threw up my engagement – at 'serious' loss to myself, but that is a matter of small consequence – and came to take my place beside our poor dear brother in his great trial. But all my efforts to bring him to a proper and 'Christian' frame of mind have been fruitless. I am indeed alarmed to be alone with him, and I tremble for the children, for he is possessed of an 'insane' hatred for the sweet little loves. He has locked himself in his room, will see 'no one' nor touch a 'particle' of nourishment. Do, my dearest Polly, come at once on receipt of this, and help me in the 'truly awful' task that has been laid upon me. And pray forgive me for using this plain paper. I have had literally no time to order mourning 'of any kind'.

So that was Sarah! With a click of the tongue Mahony tossed the letter on the table, and made it clear to Polly that under no consideration would he allow her to attempt the journey to town. Her relatives seemed utterly to have forgotten her condition; if, indeed, they had ever grasped the fact that she was expecting a child.

But Polly did not heed him. 'Oh, poor, poor, Emma! Oh, poor dear John!' Her husband could only soothe her by promising to go to Sarah's assistance himself, the following day.

They had been entirely in the dark about things. For John Turnham thought proper to erect a jealous wall about his family life. What went on behind it was nobody's business but his own. You felt yourself -- were meant to feel yourself -- the alien, the outsider. And Mahony marvelled once more at the wealth of love and sympathy his little Polly had kept fresh for these two, who had wasted so few of their thoughts on her.

Polly dried her eyes; he packed his carpet-bag. He did this with a good deal of pother, pulling open the wrong drawers, tumbling up their contents and generally making havoc of his wife's arrangements. But the sight of his clumsiness acted as a kind of tonic on Polly: she liked to feel that he was dependent on her for his material comfort and well-being.

They spoke of John's brief married life.

'He loved her like a pagan, my dear,' said Mahony. 'And if what your sister Sarah writes is not exaggerated, he is bearing his punishment in a truly pagan way.'

'But you won't say that to him, dear Richard . . . will you? You'll be very gentle with him?' pleaded Polly anxiously.

'Indeed I shall, little woman. But one can't help thinking these things, all the same. You know it is written: "Thou shalt have none other gods but Me." '

'Yes, I know. But then this was *just* Emma . . . and she was so pretty and so good' – and Polly cried anew.

Mahony rose before dawn to catch the coach. Together with a packet of sandwiches, Polly brought him a small black mantle.

'For Sarah, with my dear love. You see, Richard, I know she always wears coloured dresses. And she will feel so much happier if she has *something* black to put on.' Little Polly's voice was deep with persuasion. Richard was none too well pleased, she could see, at having to unlock his bag again; she feared too, that, after the letter of the day before, his opinion of Sarah had gone down to zero.

Mahony secured a corner seat; and so, though his knees interlocked with those of his *vis-à-vis*, only one of the eight inside passengers was jammed against him. The coach started; and the long, dull hours of the journey began to wear away. Nothing broke the monotony but speculations whether the driver – a noted tippler – would be drunk before Melbourne was reached and capsize them; and the drawling voice of a Yankee prospector, who told lying tales about his exploits in California in '48 until, having talked his hearers to sleep, he dropped off himself. Then, Mahony fell to reflecting on what lay before him. He didn't like the job. He was not one of your born good Samaritans: he relished intruding as little as being intruded on. Besides, morally to sustain, to forbear with, a fellow-creature in misfortune, seemed to him as difficult and thankless a task as any required of one. Infinite tact was essential, and a skin thick enough to stand snubs and rebuffs. But here he smiled. 'Or my little wife's inability to recognize them!'

House and garden had lost their air of well-groomed smartness: the gate stood ajar, the gravel was unraked, the verandah-flooring black with footmarks. With all the blinds still down, the windows looked like so many dead eyes. Mahony's first knock brought no response; at his second, the door was opened by Sarah Turnham herself. But a very different Sarah this, from the elegant and sprightly young person who had graced his wedding. Her chignon was loose, her dress dishevelled. On recognizing Mahony, she uttered a cry and fell on his neck – he had to disengage her arms by force and speak severely to her, declaring that he would go away again, if she carried out her intention of swooning.

At last he got her round so far that she could tell her tale, which she did with a hysterical overstatement. She had, it seemed, arrived there just before her sister-in-law died. John was quarrelling furiously with all three doctors, and, before the end, insulted the only one who was left in such a fashion that he, too, marched out of the house. They had to get the dead woman measured, coffined and taken away by stealth. Whereupon John had locked himself up in his room, and had not been seen since. He had a loaded revolver with him; through the closed door he had threatened to shoot both her and the children. The servants had deserted, panic-stricken at their master's behaviour, at the sudden collapse of the well-regulated household: the last, a nurse-girl sent out on an errand some hours previously, had not returned. Sarah was at her wits' end to know what to do with the children – he might hear them screaming at this moment.

Mahony, in no hesitancy now how to deal with the situation, laid his hat aside and drew off his gloves. 'Prepare some food,' he said briefly. 'A glass of port and a sandwich or two, if you can manage nothing else – but meat of some kind.'

But there was not a morsel of meat in the house.

'Then go to the butcher's and buy some.'

Sarah gasped, and bridled. She had never in her life been inside a butcher's shop!

'Good God, woman, then the sooner you make the beginning the better!' cried Mahony. And as he strode down the passage to the door she indicated, he added: 'Now control yourself, madam! And if you have not got what I want in a quarter of an hour's time, I'll walk out of the house and leave you to your own devices!' At which Sarah, cowed and shaken, began trem-blingly to tie her bonnet-strings.

Mahony knocked three times at the door of John Turnham's room, each time more loudly. Then he took to battering with his fist on the panels, and cried: 'It is I, John, your brother-in-law! Have the goodness to unlock this door at once!'

There was still an instant of suspense; then heavy footsteps crossed the floor and the door swung back. Mahony's eyes met a haggard white face set in a dusky background.

'You!' said John in a slow, dazed way, and blinked at the light. But in the next breath he burst out: 'Where's that damned fool of a woman? Is she skulking behind you? I won't see her – won't have her near me!'

'If you mean your sister Sarah, she is not in the house at present,' said Mahony; and stepping over the threshold he shut the door. The two men faced each other in the twilight.

'What do you want?' demanded John in a hoarse voice. 'Have you, too, come to preach and sermonize? If so, you can go back where you came from! I'll have none of that cant here.'

'No, no, I leave that to those whose business it is. I'm here as your doctor'; and Mahony drew up a blind and opened a window. Instantly the level sun-rays flooded the room; and the air that came in with them smacked of the sea. Just outside the window a quince-tree in full blossom reared extravagant masses of pink snow against the blue overhead; beyond it a covered walk of vines shone golden-green. There was not a cloud in the sky. To turn back to the musty room from all this lush and lovely life was like stepping down into a vault.

John had sunk into a seat before a secretaire, and shielded his eyes from the sun. A burnt-out candle stood at his elbow; and in a line before him were ranged such images as remained to him of his dead – a dozen or more daguerreotypes, of various sizes: Emma and he before marriage and after marriage; Emma with her first babe, at different stages of its growth; Emma with the two children; Emma in ball attire; with a hat on; holding a book.

The sight gave the quietus to Mahony's scruples. Stooping, he laid his hand on John's shoulder. 'My poor fellow,' he said gently. 'Your sister was not in a fit state to travel, so I have come in her place to tell you how deeply, how truly, we feel for you in your loss. I want to try, too, to help you to bear it. For it has to be borne, John.'

At this the torrent burst. Leaping to his feet John began to fling wildly to and fro; and then, for a time, the noise of his lamentations filled the room. Mahony had assisted at scenes of this kind before, but never had he heard the like of the blasphemies that poured over John's lips. (Afterwards, when he had recovered his distance, he would refer to it as the occasion on which John took the Almighty to task, for having dared to interfere in his private life.)

At the moment he sat silent. 'Better for him to get it out,' he thought to himself, even while he winced at John's scurrility.

When, through sheer exhaustion, John came to a stop, Mahony cast about for words of consolation. All reference to the mystery of God's way was precluded; and he shrank from entering that sound plea for the working of Time, which drives a spike into the heart of the new-made mourner. He bethought himself of the children. 'Remember, she did not leave you comfortless. You have your little ones. Think of them.'

But this was a false move. Like a belated thunderclap after the storm is over, John broke out again, his haggard eyes aflame. 'Curse the children!' he cried thickly. 'Curse them, I say! If I had once caught sight of them since she . . . she went, I should have wrung their necks. I never wanted children. They came between us. They took her from me. It was a child that killed her. Now, she is gone and they are left. Keep them out of my way, Mahony! Don't let them near me. – Oh, Emma . . . wife!' and here his shoulders heaved, under dry, harsh sobs.

Mahony felt his own eyes grow moist. 'Listen to me, John. I

promise you, you shall not see your children again until you
wish to – till you're glad to recall them, as a living gift from
her you have lost. I'll look after them for you.'

'You will? . . . God bless you, Mahony!'

Judging the moment ripe, Mahony rose and went out to fetch
the tray on which Sarah had set the eatables. The meat was but
a chop, charred on one side, raw on the other; but John did not
notice its shortcomings. He fell on it like the starving man he
was, and gulped down two or three glasses of port. The colour
returned to his face, he was able to give an account of his wife's
last hours. 'And to talk is what he needs, even if he goes on till
morning.' Mahony was quick to see that there were things that
rankled in John's memory, like festers in flesh. One was that,
knowing the greys were tricky, he had not forbidden them to
Emma long ago. But he had felt proud of her skill in handling
the reins, of the attention she attracted. Far from thwarting her,
he had actually urged her on. Her fall had been a light one, and
at the outset no bad results were anticipated: a slight haemor-
rhage was soon got under control. A week later, however, it
began anew, more violently, and then all remedies were in
vain. As it became clear that the child was dead, the doctors had
recourse to serious measures. But the bleeding went on. She
complained of a roaring in the ears, her extremities grew cold,
her pulse fluttered to nothing. She passed from syncope to
coma, and from coma to death. John swore that two of the
doctors had been the worse for drink; the third was one of those
ignorant imposters with whom the place swarmed. And again
he made himself reproaches.

'I ought to have gone to look for someone else. But she was
dying . . . I could not tear myself away. – Mahony, I can still see
her. They had stretched her across the bed, so that her head
hung over the side. Her hair swept the floor – one scoundrel
trod on it . . . trod on her hair! And I had to stand by and
watch, while they butchered her – butchered my girl. – Oh, there
are things, Mahony, one cannot dwell on and live!'

'You must not look at it like that. Yet, when I recall some of
the cases I've seen contraction induced in . . .'

'Ah yes, if you had been here . . . my God, if only you had
been here!'

But Mahony did not encourage this idea; it was his duty to
unhitch John's thoughts from the past. He now suggested that,
the children and Sarah safe in his keeping, John should shut up

the house and go away. To his surprise John jumped at the proposal, was ready there and then to put it into effect. Yes, said he, he would start the very next morning, and with no more than a blanket on his back, would wander a hundred-odd miles into the bush, sleeping out under the stars at night, and day by day increasing the distance between himself and the scene of his loss. And now up he sprang, in a sudden fury to be gone. Warning Sarah into the background, Mahony helped him get together a few necessaries, and then walked him to a hotel. Here he left him sleeping under the influence of a drug, and next day saw him off on his tramp northwards, over the Great Divide.

John's farewell words were: 'Take the keys of the house with you, and don't give them up to me under a month, at least.'

That day's coach was full; they had to wait for seats till the following afternoon. The delay was not unwelcome to Mahony: it gave Polly time to get the letter he had written her the night before. After leaving John, he set about raising money for the extra fares and other unforeseen expenses: at the eleventh hour, Sarah informed him that their young brother Jerry had landed in Melbourne during Emma's illness, and had been hastily boarded out. Knowing no one else in the city, Mahony was forced, much as it went against the grain, to turn to Henry Ocock for assistance. And he was effusively received – Ocock tried to press double the sum needed on him. Fortune was no doubt smiling on the lawyer. His offices had swelled to four rooms, with appropriate clerks in each. He still, however, nursed the scheme of transferring his business to Ballarat.

'As soon, that is, as I can hear of suitable premises. I understand there's only one locality to be considered, and that's the western township.' On which Mahony, whose address was in the outer darkness, repeated his thanks and withdrew.

He found Jerry's lodging, paid the bill, and took the boy back to St Kilda – a shy slip of a lad in his early teens, with the colouring and complexion that ran in the family. John's coachman, who had shown himself not indisposed – for a substantial sum, paid in advance – to keep watch over house and grounds, was installed in an outbuilding, and next day at noon, after personally aiding Sarah, who was all a-tremble at the prospect of the bush journey, to pack her own and the children's clothes, Mahony turned the key in the door of the darkened house. But a couple of weeks ago it had been a proud and happy home.

Now it had no more virtue left in it than a crab's empty shell.

He had fumed on first learning of Jerry's superfluous presence; but before they had gone far he saw that he would have fared ill indeed, had Jerry not been there. Sarah, too agitated that morning to touch a bite of food, was seized, not an hour out, with sickness and fainting. There she sat, her eyes closed, her salts to her nose or feebly sipping brandy, unable to lift a finger to help with the children. The younger of the two slept most of the way hotly and heavily on Mahony's knee; but the boy, a regular pest, was never for a moment still. In vain did his youthful uncle pinch his leg each time he wriggled to the floor. It was not till a fierce-looking digger opposite took out a jack-knife and threatened to saw off both his feet if he stirred again, to cut out his tongue if he put another question that, scarlet with fear, little Johnny was tamed. Altogether it was a nightmare of a journey, and Mahony groaned with relief when, lamps having for some time twinkled past, the coach drew up, and Hempel and Long Jim stepped forward with their lanterns. Sarah could hardly stand. The children, wrathful at being wakened from their sleep, kicked and screamed.

CHAPTER SIX

For the first time in her young married life, Polly felt vexed
with her husband.

'Oh, he shouldn't have done that . . . no, really he shouldn't!'
she murmured; and the hand with the letter in it drooped to her
lap.

She had been doing a little surreptitious baking in Richard's
absence, and without a doubt was hot and tired. The tears rose
to her eyes. Deserting her pastry-board she retreated behind
the woodstack and sat down on the chopping-block; and then,
for some minutes, the sky was blotted out. She felt quite unequal, in her present condition, to facing Sarah, who was so
sensitive, so easily shocked; and she was deeply averse from her
fine-lady sister discovering the straitness of Richard's means
and home.

But it was hard for Polly to secure a moment's privacy.

'An' so this is w'ere you're 'idin', is it?' said Long Jim snap-
pishly – he had been opening a keg of treacle and held a sticky
plug in his hand. 'An' me runnin' my pore ol' legs off arter you!'
And Hempel met her on her entry with: 'No further bad news,
I 'ope and trust, ma'am?' – Hempel always retained his smooth
servility of manner. 'The shopman *par excellence*, my dear!'
Richard was used to say of him.

Polly reassured her attendants, blew her nose, re-read her
letter; and other feelings came uppermost. She noticed how
scribbly the writing was – Richard had evidently been hard
pushed for time. There was an apologetic tone about it, too,
which was unlike him. He was probably wondering what she
would say; he might even be making himself reproaches. It
was unkind of her to add to them. Let her think rather of the sad
state poor John had been found in, and of his two motherless
babes. As for Sarah, it would never have done to leave her out.

Wiping her eyes Polly untied her cooking-apron and set to

reviewing her resources. Sarah would have to share her bed, Richard to sleep on the sofa. The children . . . and here she knitted her brows. Then going into the yard, she called to Tom Ocock, who sat whittling a stick in front of his father's house; and Tom went down to Main Street for her, and bought a mattress which he carried home on his shoulder. This she spread on the bedroom floor, Mrs Hemmerde having already given both rooms a sound scouring, just in case a flea or a spider should be lying perdu. After which Polly fell to baking again in good earnest; for the travellers would be famished by the time they arrived.

Towards ten o'clock Tom, who was on the look-out, shouted that the coach was in, and Polly, her table spread, a good fire going, stepped to the door, outwardly very brave, inwardly all a-flutter. Directly, however, she got sight of the forlorn party that toiled up the slope: Sarah clinging to Hempel's arm, Mahony bearing one heavy child, and — could she believe her eyes? — Jerry staggering under the other: her bashfulness was gone. She ran forward to prop poor Sarah on her free side, to guide her feet to the door; and it is doubtful whether little Polly had ever spent a more satisfying hour than that which followed.

Her husband, watching her in silent amaze, believed she thoroughly enjoyed the fuss and commotion.

There was Sarah, too sick to see anything but the bed, to undress, to make fomentations for, to coax to mouthfuls of tea and toast. There was Jerry to feed and send off, with the warmest of hugs, to share Tom Ocock's palliasse. There were the children . . . well, Polly's first plan had been to put them straight to bed. But when she came to peel off their little trousers she changed her mind.

'I think, Mrs Hemmerde, if you'll get me a tub of hot water, we'll just pop them into it; they'll sleep so much better,' she said . . . not quite truthfully. Her private reflection was: 'I don't think Sarah can once have washed them properly, all that time.'

The little girl let herself be bathed in her sleep; but young John stood and bawled, digging fat fists into slits of eyes, while Polly scrubbed at his massy knees, the dimpled ups and downs of which looked as if they had been worked in by hand. She had never seen her brother's children before and was heartily lost in admiration of their plump, well-formed bodies, as her helper of the costliness of their outfit.

'Real Injun muslin, as I'm alive!' ejaculated the woman, on

133

fishing out their night-clothes. 'An' wid the sassiest lace for trimmin'! – Och, the poor little motherless angels! – Stan' quiet, you young divil you, an' lemme button you up!'

Clean as lily-bells, the pair were laid on the mattress-bed.

'At least they can't fall out,' said Polly, surveying her work with a sigh of content.

Everyone else having retired, she sat with Richard before the fire, waiting for his bath-water to reach the boil. He was anxious to know just how she had fared in his absence, she to hear the full story of his mission. He confessed to her that his offer to load himself up with the whole party had been in a momentary burst of feeling. Afterwards he had repented his impulsiveness.

'On your account, love. Though when I see how well you've managed – you dear, clever little woman!'

And Polly consoled him, being now come honestly to the stage of: 'But, Richard, what else could you do?'

'What, indeed! I knew Emma had no relatives in Melbourne, and who John's intimates might be I had no more idea than the man in the moon.'

'John hasn't any friends. He never had.'

'As for leaving the children in Sarah's charge, if you'll allow me to say so, my dear, I consider your sister Sarah the biggest goose of a female it has ever been my lot to run across.'

'Ah, but you don't really know Sarah yet,' said Polly, and smiled a little, through the tears that had risen to her eyes at the tale of John's despair.

What Mahony did not mention to her was the necessity he had been under of borrowing money; though Polly was aware he had left home with but a modest sum in his purse. He wished to spare her feelings. Polly had a curious delicacy – he might almost call it a manly delicacy – with regard to money; and the fact that John had not offered to put hand to pocket, let alone liberally flung a blank cheque at his head, would, Mahony knew, touch his wife on a tender spot. Nor did Polly herself ask questions. Richard made no allusion to John having volunteered to bear expenses, so the latter had evidently not done so. What a pity! Richard was so particular himself, in matters of this kind, that he might write her brother down close and stingy. Of course John's distressed state of mind partly served to excuse him. But she could not imagine the calamity that would cause Richard to forget his obligations.

She slid her hand into her husband's and they sat for a while in silence. Then, half to herself, and out of a very different train of thought she said: 'Just fancy them never crying once for their mother.'

*

'Talking of friends,' said Sarah, and fastidiously cleared her throat. 'Talking of friends, I wonder now what has become of one of those young gentlemen I met at your wedding. He was . . . let me see . . . why, I declare if I haven't forgotten his name!'

'Oh, I know who you mean – besides there was only one, Sarah,' Mahony heard his wife reply, and therewith fall into her sister's trap. 'You mean Purdy – Purdy Smith – who was Richard's best man.'

'Smith?' echoed Sarah. 'La, Polly! Why don't he make it Smythe?'

It was a warm evening some three weeks later. The store was closed to customers; but Mahony had ensconced himself in a corner of it with a book: since the invasion, this was the one place in which he could make sure of finding quiet. The sisters sat on the log-bench before the house; and, without seeing them, Mahony knew to a nicety how they were employed. Polly darned stockings, for John's children; Sarah was tatting, with her little finger stuck out at right angles to the rest. Mahony could hardly think of this finger without irritation: it seemed to sum up Sarah's whole outlook on life.

Meanwhile Polly's fresh voice went on, relating Purdy's fortunes. 'He took part, you know, in the dreadful affair on the Eureka last Christmas, when so many poor men were killed. We can speak of it, now they've all been pardoned; but then we had to be very careful. Well, he was shot in the ankle, and will always be lame from it.'

'What! – go hobbling on one leg for the remainder of his days? Oh, my dear!' said Sarah, and laughed.

'Yes, because the wound wasn't properly attended to – he had to hide about in the bush, for ever so long. Later on he went to the Beamishes, to be nursed. But by that time his poor leg was in a very bad state. You know he is engaged – or very nearly so – to Tilly Beamish.'

'What?' said Sarah once more. 'That handsome young fellow engaged to one of those vulgar creatures?'

'Oh, Sarah . . . not really vulgar. It isn't their fault they didn't have a better education. They lived right up-country, where there were no schools. Tilly never saw a town till she was six-teen; but she can sit any horse. – Yes, we hope very much Purdy will soon settle down now and marry her – though he left the Hotel again without proposing.' And Polly sighed.

'There he shows his good taste, my dear.'

'Oh, I'm sure he's fond of Tilly. It's only that his life is so unsettled. He's been a barman at Euroa since then; and the last we heard of him, he was shearing somewhere on the Goulburn. He doesn't seem able to stick to anything.'

'And a rolling stone gathers no moss!' gave back Sarah sen-tentiously – and in fancy Mahony saw the cut-and-dried nod with which she accompanied the words.

Here Hempel passed through the store, clad in his Sunday best, his hair plastered flat with bear's-grease.

'Going out for a stroll?' asked his master.

'That was my h'intention, sir. I don't think you'll find I've left any of my dooties undone.'

'Oh, go, by all means!' said Mahony curtly, nettled at having his harmless query misconstrued. It pointed a suspicion he had had, of late, that a change was coming over Hempel. The model employee was a shade less prompt than heretofore to fly at his word, and once or twice seemed actually to be studying his own convenience. Without knowing what the matter was, Mahony felt it politic not to be over-exacting – even mildly to conciliate his assistant. It would put him in an awkward fix, now that he was on the verge of winding up affairs, should Hempel take it in his head to leave him in the lurch.

The lean figure moved on and blocked the doorway. Now there was a sudden babble of cheepy voices, and simultaneously Sarah cried: 'Where have you been, my little cherubs? Come to your aunt, and let her kiss you!'

But the children, who had frankly no great liking for Aunt Sarah, would, Mahony knew, turn a deaf ear to this display of opportunism and make a rush for his wife. Laying down his book he ran out. 'Polly . . . cautious!'

'It's all right, Richard, I'm being careful.' Polly had let her mending fall, and with each hand held a flaxen-haired child at arm's length. 'Johnny, dirty boy! what *have* you been up to?'

'He played he was a digger and sat down in a pool – I couldn't get him to budge,' answered Jerry, and drew his sleeve over his perspiring forehead.

'Oh fy, for shame!'

'Don' care!' said John unabashed.

'Don' tare!' echoed his roly-poly sister, who existed but as his shadow.

'Don't-care was made to care, don't-care was hung!' quoted Aunt Sarah in her severest copybook tones.

Turning his head in his aunt's direction young John thrust forth a bright pink tongue. Little Emma was not behindhand.

Polly jumped up, dropping her work to the ground. 'Johnny, I shall punish you if ever I see you do that again. Now, Ellen shall put you to bed instead of Auntie.' – Ellen was Mrs Hemmerde's eldest, and Polly's first regular maidservant.

'Don' care,' repeated Johnny. 'Ellen plays pillers.'

'Edn pays pidders,' said the echo.

Seizing two hot, pudgy hands Polly dragged the pair indoors – though they held back mainly on principle. They were not affectionate children; they were too strong of will and set of purpose for that; but if they had a fondness for anyone it was for their Aunt Polly: she was ruler over a drawerful of sugar-sticks, and though she scolded she never slapped.

While this was going on Hempel stood, the picture of indecision, and eased now one foot, now the other, as if his boots pinched him.

At length he blurted out: 'I was wondering, ma'am – ahem! Miss Turnham – if, since it is an agreeable h'evening, you would care to take a walk to that 'ill I told you of?'

'Me take a walk? La, no! Whatever put such an idea as that into your head?' cried Sarah; and tatted and tatted, keeping time with a pretty little foot.

'I thought per'aps . . .' said Hempel meekly.

'*I* didn't make your thoughts, Mr *H*empel,' retorted Sarah, laying stress on the aspirate.

'Oh no, ma'am. I 'ope I didn't presume to suggest such a thing'; and with a hangdog air Hempel prepared to slink away.

'Well, well!' said Sarah double-quick; and ceasing to jerk her crochet-needle in and out, she nimbly rolled up her ball of thread. 'Since you're so insistent . . . and since, mind you, there's no society worth calling such, on these diggings. . . .' The truth was, Sarah saw that she was about to be left alone with Mahony – Jerry had sauntered off to meet Ned – and this *tête-à-tête* was by no means to her mind. She still bore her brother-in-law a grudge for his high-handed treatment of her at the time of John's bereavement. 'As if I had been one of the domestics, my dear – a paid domestic! Ordered me off to the butcher's in language that fairly shocked me.'

Mahony turned his back and strolled down to the river. He did not know which was more painful to witness: Hempel's unmanly cringing, or the air of fatuous satisfaction that succeeded it. When he returned, the pair was just setting out; he watched Sarah, on Hempel's arm, picking short steps in dainty latchet-shoes.

As soon as they were well away he called to Polly.

'The coast's clear. Come for a stroll.'

Polly emerged, tying her bonnet-strings. 'Why, where's Sarah? Oh . . . I see. Oh, Richard, I hope she didn't put on that –'

'She did, my dear!' said Mahony grimly, and tucked his wife's hand under his arm.

'Oh, how I wish she wouldn't!' said Polly in a tone of concern. 'She does get so stared at – especially of an evening, when there are so many rude men about. But I really don't think she minds. For she *has* a bonnet in her box all the time.' Miss Sarah was giving Ballarat food for talk, by appearing on her promenades in a hat: a large, flat, mushroom hat.

'I trust my little woman will never put such a ridiculous object on her head!'

'No, never . . . at least, not unless they become quite the fashion,' answered Polly. 'And I don't think they will. They look too odd.'

'Another thing, love,' continued Mahony, on whom a sudden light had dawned as he stood listening to Sarah's trumpery. 'I fear your sister is trifling with the feelings of our worthy Hempel.'

Polly, who had kept her own counsel on this matter, went crimson. 'Oh, do you really think so, Richard?' she asked evasively. 'I hope not. For of course nothing could come of it. Sarah has refused the most eligible offers.'

'Ah, but there are none here to refuse. And if you don't mind my saying so, Poll, anything in trousers seems fish to *her* net!'

On one of their pacings they found Mr Ocock come out to smoke an evening pipe. The old man had just returned from a flying visit to Melbourne. He looked glum and careworn, but livened up at the sight of Polly, and cracked one of the mouldy jokes he believed beneficial to a young woman in her condition. Still, the leading-note in his mood was melancholy; and this, although his dearest wish was on the point of being fulfilled.

'Yes, I've got the very crib for 'Enry at last, doc., Billy de la Poer's liv'ry-stable, top o' Lydiard Street. We sol' poor Billy up yesterday. The third smash in two days that makes. Lord! I dunno where it'll end.'

'Things are going a bit quick over there. There's been too much building.'

'They're at me to build, too – 'Enry is. But I says no. This place is good enough for me. If 'e's goin' to be ashamed of 'ow 'is father lives, 'e'd better stop away. I'm an ol' man now, an' a poor one. What should I want with a fine noo 'ouse? An' 'oo should I build it for, even if I 'ad the tin? For them two good-for-nothin's in there? Not if I know it!'

'Mr Ocock, you wouldn't believe how kind and clever Tom's been at helping with the children,' said Polly warmly.

'Yes, an' at bottle-washin' and sweepin' and cookin' a pasty. But a female 'ud do it just as well,' returned Tom's father with a snort of contempt.

'Pood old chap!' said Mahony, as they passed out of earshot. 'So even the great Henry's arrival is not to be without its drop of gall.'

'Surely he'll never be ashamed of his father?'

'Who knows! But it's plain he suspects the old boy has made his pile and intends him to fork out,' said Mahony carelessly; and, with this, dismissed the subject. Now that his own days in the colony were numbered, he no longer felt constrained to pump up a spurious interest in local affairs. He consigned them wholesale to that limbo in which, for him, they had always belonged.

The two brothers came striding over the slope. Ned, clad in blue serge shirt and corduroys, laid an affectionate arm round Polly's shoulder, and tossed his hat into the air on hearing that the 'Salamander', as he called Sarah, was not at home.

'For I've tons to tell you, Poll old girl. And when milady sits there turning up her nose at everything a chap says, somehow the spunk goes out of one.'

Polly had baked a large cake for her darling, and served out generous slices. Then, drawing up a chair she sat down beside him, to drink in his news.

From his place at the farther end of the table Mahony studied the trio – these three young faces which were so much alike that they might have been different readings of one and the same face. Polly, by reason of her woman's lot, looked considerably the oldest. Still, the lamplight wiped out some of the shadows, and she was never more girlishly vivacious than with Ned, entering as she did with zest into his plans and ideas — more sister now than wife. And Ned showed at his best with Polly: he laid himself out to divert her; forgot to brag or to swear; and so natural did it seem for brother to open his heart to sister that even his egoistic chatter passed muster. As for young Jerry, who in a couple of days was to begin work in the same claim as Ned, he sat round-eyed, his thoughts writ large on his forehead. Mahony translated them thus: how in the world I could ever have sat prim and proper on the school-bench, when all this — change, adventure, romance — was awaiting me? Jerry was only, Mahony knew, to push a wheelbarrow from hole to water and back again for many a week to come; but for him it would certainly be a golden barrow, and laden with gold, so greatly had Ned's tales fired his imagination.

The onlooker felt odd man out, debarred as he was by his profounder experience from sharing in the young people's light-legged dreams. He took up his book. But his reading was cut into by Ned's sprightly account of the Magpie rush; by his description of an engine at work on the Eureka, and of the wooden airpipes that were being used to ventilate deep-sinkings. There was nothing Ned did not know, and could not make entertaining. One was forced, almost against one's will, to listen to him; and on this particular evening, when he was neither sponging, nor acting the Big Gun, Mahony toned down his first sweeping judgement of his young relative. Ned was all talk; and what impressed one so unfavourably — his grumbling, his extravagant boastfulness — was the mere thistledown of the moment, puffed off into space. It mattered little that he harped continually on 'chucking up' his job. Two years had passed since he came to Ballarat, and he was still working for hire in somebody else's hole. He still groaned over the hardships of the life, and still toiled on — and all the rest was just the froth and braggadocio of aimless youth.

Not twenty-four hours later, Sarah had an accident to her *machoire* and returned post-haste to Melbourne.

'A most opportune breakage!' said Mahony, and laughed.

That day at the dinner-table he had given his sister-in-law a piece of his mind. Sarah had always resented the name bestowed on her by her parents, and was at present engaged in altering it, in giving it, so to speak, a foreign tang: henceforth she was to be not Sarah, but Sara (spoken Sahra). As often as Polly's tongue tripped over the unfamiliar syllable, Sara gently but firmly put her right; and Polly corrected herself, even begged pardon for her stupidity, till Mahony could bear it no longer. Throwing politeness to the winds, he twitted Sara with her finical affectations, her old-maidish ways, the morning sloth that expected Polly, in her delicate state of health, to carry a breakfast-tray to the bedside: cast up at her, in short, all that had made him champ and fret in silence. Sara might, after a fitting period of the huff, have overlooked the rest; but the 'old-maidish' she could not forgive. And directly dinner was over, the mishap to her mouthpiece was made known.

Too much in awe of Mahony to stand up to him – for when he was angry, he was very angry – Sara retaliated by abusing him to Polly as she packed her trunk.

'Manners, indeed! To turn and insult a visitor at his own table! And who and what is he, I should like to know, to speak to me so? Nothing but a common storekeeper. My dear, you have my deepest sympathy. It's a *dreadful* life for you. Of course you keep everything as nice as possible, under the circumstances. But the surroundings, Polly! . . . and the store . . . and the want of society. *I* couldn't put up with it, not for a week!'

Polly, sitting on the side of the tester-bed and feeling very cast down at Sara's unfriendly departure, shed a few tears at this. For part of what her sister said was true: it had been wrong of Richard to be rude to Sara while the latter was a guest in his house. But she defended him warmly. 'I couldn't be happier than I am; Richard's the best husband in the world. As for his being common, Sara, you know he comes of a much better family than we do.'

'My dear, common is as common does; and a vulgar calling ends by vulgarizing those who have the misfortune to pursue it. But there's another reason, Polly, why it is better for me to leave you. There are certain circumstances, my dear, in which, to put it mildly, it is *awkward* for two people of *opposite* sexes to go on living under the same roof.'

'Sarah! – I mean Sara – do you really mean to say Hempel has made you a proposal?' cried Polly, wide-eyed in her tears.

'I won't say, my dear, that he has so far forgotten himself as to actually offer marriage. But he has let me see only too plainly what his feelings are. Of course, I've kept him in his place – the preposterous creature! But all the same it's not *comme il faut* any longer for me to be here.'

'Did she say where she was going, or what she intended to do?' Mahony inquired of his wife that night as she bound the strings of her nightcap.

No, she hadn't, Polly admitted, rather out of countenance. But then Sara was like that – very close about her own affairs. 'I think she's perhaps gone back to her last situation. She had several letters while she was here, in that lady's hand. People are always glad to get her back. Not many finishing governesses can teach all she can' – and Polly checked off Sara's attainments on the fingers of both hands. 'She won't go anywhere under two hundred a year.'

'A most accomplished person, your sister!' said Mahony sleepily. 'Still, it's very pleasant to be by ourselves again – eh, wife?'

An even more blessed peace shortly descended on the house; for the time was now come to get rid of the children as well. Since nothing had been heard of John, they were to be boarded out over Polly's illness. Through the butcher's lady, arrangements were made with a trooper's wife, who lived outside the racket and dust of the township, and had a whole posse of little ones of her own. – 'Bless you! half-a-dozen more wouldn't make any difference to me. There's the paddock for 'em to run wild in.' This was the best that could be done for the children. Polly packed their little kit, dealt out a parting bribe of barley-sugar, and saw them hoisted into the dray that would pass the door of their destination.

Once more husband and wife sat alone together, as in the days before John's domestic catastrophe. And now Mahony said tentatively: 'Don't you think, love, we could manage to get on without that old Beamish woman? I'll guarantee to nurse you as well as any female alive.'

The question did not come as a surprise to Polly; she had already put it to herself. After the affair with Sara she awaited her new visitor in fear and trembling. Sara had at least stood in awe of Richard and held her tongue before him; Mrs Beamish prided herself on being afraid of nobody, and on always speaking her mind. And yet, even while agreeing that it would be well to put 'mother' off, Polly drooped her wings. At a time like this a woman was a woman. It seemed as if even the best of husbands did not quite understand.

'Just give her the hint we don't want her,' said Mahony airily.

But 'mother' was not the person to take a hint, no matter how broad. It was necessary to be blunt to the point of rudeness; and Polly spent a difficult hour over the composition of her letter. She might have saved her pains. Mrs Beamish replied that she knew her darling little Polly's unwillingness to give trouble; but it was not likely she would now go back on her word: she had been packed and ready to start for the past week. Polly handed the letter to her husband, and did not say what she thought she read out of it, namely that 'mother', who so seldom could be spared from home, was looking forward with pleasure to her trip to Ballarat.

'I suppose it's a case of making the best of a bad job,' sighed Mahony; and having one day drawn Mrs Beamish, at melting point, from the inside of a crowded coach, he loaded Long Jim with her bags and bundles.

His aversion was not lightened by his subsequently coming on his wife in the act of unpacking a hamper, which contained half a ham, a stone jar of butter, some home-made loaves of bread, a bag of vegetables and a plum pudding. 'Good God! does the woman think we can't give her enough to eat?' he asked testily. He had all the poor Irishman's distrust of a gift.

'She means it kindly, dear. She probably thought things were still scarce here; and she knew I wouldn't be able to do much cooking,' pleaded Polly. And going out to the kitchen she untied the last parcel, in which was a big round cheese, by stealth.

She had pulled Mrs Beamish over the threshold, had got her into the bedroom and shut the door, before any of the 'ohs' and 'ahs' she saw painted on the broad, rubicund face could be transformed into words. And hugs and kisses over, she bravely seized the bull by the horns and begged her guest not to criticize house or furnishings in front of Richard.

It took Mrs Beamish a minute or two to grasp her meaning. Then, she said heartily: 'There, there, my duck, don't you worry! I'll be as mum as mum.' And in a whisper: 'So, 'e's got a temper, Polly, 'as 'e? But this I will say: if I'd known this was all 'e 'ad to h'offer you, I'd 'a' said, stop w'ere you are, my lamb, in a comfortable, 'appy 'ome.'

'Oh, I *am* happy, mother, dear, indeed I am!' cried Polly. 'I've never regretted being married – never once!'

'There, there, now!'

'And it's only . . . I mean . . . this is the best we can afford in the meantime, and if *I* am satisfied . . .' floundered Polly, dismayed to hear her words construed into blame of her husband. 'It's only that it upsets Richard if people speak slightingly of our house, and that upsets me – and I mustn't be worried just now, you know,' she added with a somewhat shaky smile.

'Not a word will I say, ducky, make yer pore little mind easy about that. Though such a poky little 'en-coop of a place I never was in!' – and, while tying her cap-strings, Mrs Beamish swept the little bedroom and its sloping roof with a withering glance. 'I was 'orrified, girls, simply *'orrified*!' she related the incident to her daughters. 'An' I up an' told 'er so – just like me, you know. Not room enough to swing a cat in, and 'im sittin' at the 'ead of the table as 'igh an' mighty as a dook! You can thank yer stars, you two, 'e didn't take one o' you instead o' Polly.' But this was chiefly by way of a consolation-prize for Tilly and Jinny.

'An' now, my dear, tell me *everything*.' With these words, Mrs Beamish spread her skirts and settled down to a cosy chat on the subject of Polly's hopes.

But like the majority of her sex she was an adept at dividing her attention; and while making delicate inquiries of the young wife, she was also travelling her shrewd eye round the little bedchamber, spying out and appraising: not one of poor Polly's makeshifts escaped her. The result of her inspection was to cause her to feel justly indignant with Mahony. The idea! Him to rob them of Polly just to dump her down in a place like this!

144

She would never be able to resist telling him what she thought of him.

Here, however, she reckoned without Polly. Polly was sharp enough to doubt 'mother's' ability to hold her tongue; and saw to it that Richard and she were not left alone together. And of an evening when talk languished, she would beg her husband to read to them from the *Ballarat Star*, until, as often as not, Mrs Beamish fell asleep. Frequently, too, she persuaded him to go out and take a hand in a newly-formed whist club, or discuss politics with a neighbour.

Mahony went willingly enough; his home was less home than ever since the big woman's intrusion. Even his food lost its savour. Mrs Beamish had taken over the cooking, and she went about it with an air that implied he had not had a decent bite to eat since his marriage.

'There! what do you say to that now? That's something *like* a pudding!' and a great plum-duff was planked triumphantly down in the middle of the dinner-table. 'Lor, Polly! your bit of a kitchen . . . in this weather . . . I'm fair dished.' And the good woman mopped her streaming face and could herself eat nothing.

Mahony much preferred his wife's cooking, which took account of his tastes – it was done, too, without any fuss – and he persisted in upholding Polly's skill, in face of Mrs Beamish's good-natured disbelief. Polly, on edge, lest he should openly state his preference, nervously held out her plate.

'It's so good, mother, I must have a second helping,' she declared; and then, without appetite in the cruel, midday heat, did not know what to do with the solid slab of pudding. Pompey and Palmerston got into the way of sitting very close to her chair.

She confided to Richard that Mrs Beamish disapproved of his evening outings. 'Many an 'usband takes to goin' out at such a time, my dear, an' never gets back the 'abit of stoppin' at 'ome. So just you be careful, ducky!' This was a standing joke between them. Mahony would wink at Polly when he put his hat on, and wear it rakishly askew.

However, he quite enjoyed a crack with the postmaster or the town-surveyor, at this juncture. Colonial politics were more interesting than usual. The new Constitution had been proclaimed, and a valiant effort was being made to form a Cabinet; to induce, that was, a sufficient number of well-to-do men to give up time to the service of their country. It looked as if the attempt were going to fail, just as on the goldfields the Local Courts, by which since the Stockade the diggers governed themselves, were failing, because none could afford to spend his days sitting in them.

Yet however high the discussion ran, he kept one ear turned towards his home. Here, things were at a standstill. Polly's time had come and gone – but there was no end set to their suspense. It was blazing hot now in the little log house; walls and roof were black with flies; mosquitoes made the nights hideous. Even Polly lost patience with herself when, morning after morning, she got up feeling as well as ever, and knowing that she had to steer through another difficult day.

It was not the suspense alone: the strain of keeping the peace was growing too much for her.

'Oh, *don't* quarrel with her, Richard, for my sake,' she begged her husband one night. 'She means so well. And she can't help being like she is – she has always been accustomed to order Mr Beamish about. But I wish she had never, never come,' sobbed poor Polly. And Mahony, in a sudden flash of enlightenment, put his arms round her, and made humble promises. Not another word should cross his lips! 'Though I'd like nothing so well as to throw her out, and her bags and bundles after her. Come, laugh a little, my Polly. Think of the old lady flying down the slope, with her packages in a shower about her head!'

Rogers, M.D., looked in whenever he passed. At this stage he was of the jocular persuasion. 'Still an unwelcome visitor, ma'am? No little titbit of news for me today?' There he sat, twiddling his thumbs, reiterating his singsong: 'Just so!' and looking wise as an owl. Mahony knew the air – had many a time seen it donned to cloak perplexity – and covert doubts of Rogers' ability began to assail him. But then he fell mentally foul of everyone he came in touch with, at present: Ned, for the bare-faced fashion in which he left his cheerfulness on the door-mat; Mrs Beamish for the eternal 'Pore lamb!' with which she beplastered Polly, and the antiquated reckoning-table she embarrassed them by consulting.

However, this state of things could not last for ever, and at dawn, one hot January day, Polly was taken ill.

The early hours promised well. But the morning wore on, turned to midday, then to afternoon, and matters still hung fire. While towards six o'clock the patient dismayed them by sitting up in bed, saying she felt much better, and asking for a cup of tea. This drew: 'Ah, my pore lamb, you've got to feel worse yet afore you're better!' from Mrs Beamish.

It ended in Rogers taking up his quarters there, for the night.

Towards eleven o'clock Mahony and he sat, one on each side of the table, in the little sitting-room. The heat was insupportable and all three doors and the window were propped open, in the feeble hope of creating a draught. The lamp had attracted a swarm of flying things: giant moths beat their wings against the globe, or fell singed and sizzling down the chimney; winged-ants alighted with a click upon the table; blowflies and mosquitoes kept up a dizzy hum.

From time to time Mahony rose and stole into the bedroom, where Mrs Beamish sat fanning the pests off Polly, who was in a feverish doze. Leaning over his wife he let his finger lie on her wrist; and, back again in the outer room, he bit nervously at his little-finger nail – an old trick of his when in a quandary. He had curtly refused a game of bezique; so Rogers had produced a pack of cards from his own pocket – soiled, frayed cards, which had likely done service on many a similar occasion – and was whiling the time away with solitaire. To sit there watching his slow manipulation of the cards, his patent intentness on the game; to listen any longer to the accursed din of the gnats and flies passed Mahony's powers of endurance. Abruptly shoving back his chair, he went out into the yard.

This was some twenty paces across – from the row of old kerosene-tins that constituted his flower-garden, past shed and woodstack to the post-and-rail fence. How often he walked it he did not know; but when he went indoors again, his boots were heavy with mud, for a brief summer storm had come up earlier in the evening. A dense black pall of cloud had swept like a heavy curtain over the stars, to the tune of flash and bang. Now, all was clear and calm again; the white star-dust of the Milky Way powdered the sky just overhead; and though the heat was still intense, the air had a fragrant smell of saturated dust and rain-soaked earth – he could hear streamlets of water trickling down the hillside to the river below.

Out there in the dark, several things became plain to him. He saw that he had not had any real confidence in Rogers from the start; while the effect of the evening spent at close quarters had been to sink his opinion to nothing. Rogers belonged to an old school; his method was to sit by and let nature take its course – perhaps just this slowness to move had won him a name for ex-

147

treme care. His old fogyism showed up unmistakably in a short but heated argument they had had on the subject of chloroform. He cited such hoary objections to the use of the new anaesthetic in maternity cases as Mahony had never expected to hear again: the therapeutic value of pain; the moral danger the patient ran in yielding up her will ('What right have we to bid a fellow-creature sacrifice her consciousness?'); and the impious folly of interfering with the action of a creative law. It had only remained for him to quote Genesis, and the talking serpent!

Had the case been in his own hands he would have intervened before now. Rogers, on the contrary, was still satisfied with the shape of affairs – or made pretence to be. For, watching lynx-eyed, Mahony fancied each time the fat man propelled his paunch out of the sickroom it was a shade less surely: there were nuances, too, in the way he pronounced his vapid: 'As long as our strength is well maintained . . . well maintained.' Mahony doubted Polly's ability to bear much more; and he made bold to know his own wife's constitution best. Rogers was shilly-shallying: what if he delayed too long and Polly slipped through his hands? Lose Polly? Good God! the very thought turned him cold. And alive to his finger-tips with the superstition of his race, he impetuously offered up his fondest dream to those invisible powers that sat aloft, waiting to be appeased. If this was to be the price exacted of him – the price of his escape from exile – then . . . then . . .

To come back to the present, however, he was in an awkward position: he was going to be forced to take Polly's case out of the hands of the man to whom he had entrusted it. Such a step ran counter to all the stiff rules of conduct, the punctilios of decorum, laid down by the most code-ridden profession in the world.

But a fresh visit to Polly, whose pulse had grown markedly softer, put an end to his scruples.

Stalking into the sitting-room he said without preamble: 'In my opinion any further delay will mean a risk to my wife. I request you to operate immediately.'

Rogers blinked up from his cards, surprise writ across his ruddy countenance. He pushed his spectacles to his forehead. 'Eh? What? Well, well . . . yes, the time is no doubt coming when we shall have to lend Mother Nature a hand.'

'Coming? It's come . . . and gone. Are you blind, man?'

Rogers had faced many an agitated husband in his day. 'Now,

now, Mr Mahony,' he said soothingly, and laid his last two cards in line. 'You must allow me to be the judge of that. Besides,' he added, as he took off his glasses to polish them on a red bandanna; 'besides, I should have to ask you to go out and get someone to assist me.'

'I shall assist you,' returned Mahony.

Rogers smiled his broad, fat smile. 'Easier said than done, my good sir! . . . easier said than done.'

Mahony considerately turned his back; and kept it turned. Emptying a pitcher of water into a basin he began to lather his hands. 'I am a qualified medical man. Of the same university as yourself. I studied under Simpson.' It cost him an effort to get the words out. But, by speaking, he felt that he did ample penance for the fit of tetchy pride which, in the first instance, had tied his tongue.

Rogers was dumbfounded.

'Well, upon my word!' he ejaculated, letting his hands with glasses and handkerchief fall to the table. 'God bless my soul! why couldn't you say so before? And why the deuce didn't you yourself attend –'

'We can go into all that afterwards.'

But Rogers was not one of those who could deal rapidly with the unexpected: he continued to vent his surprise, and to shoot distrustful glances at his companion. He was flurried, too, at being driven forward quicker than he had a mind to go, and said sulkily that Mahony must take full responsibility for what they were about to do. Mahony hardly heard him; he was looking at the instruments laid out on the table. His fingers itched to close round them.

'I'll prepare my wife,' he said briskly. And going into the bedroom he bent over the pillow. It was damp with the sweat that had dripped from Polly's head when the pains were on her.

' 'Ere, you girl, get in quick now with your bucket and cloth, and give that place a good clean-up afore that pore lamb opens 'er eyes again. I'm cooked – that's what I am!' and sitting heavily down on the kitchen-chair, Mrs Beamish wiped her face towards the four points of the compass.

Piqued by an unholy curiosity young Ellen willingly obeyed. But a minute later she was back, having done no more than set her pail down inside the bedroom door. 'Oh, sure, Mrs

Beamish, and I can't do't!' she cried shrilly. 'It's jus' like Andy Soakes's shop . . . when they've bin quarterin' a sheep.'

'I'll *quarter* you, you lazy trollop, you!' cried Mrs Beamish, rising to her aching legs again; and her day-old anxiety found vent in a hearty burst of temper. '*I'll* teach you!' pulling, as she spoke, the floorcloth out of the girl's hand. 'Such airs and graces! Why, sooner or later, milady, you've got to go through it yourself.'

'*Me* . . .? Catch me!' said Ellen, with enormous emphasis. 'D'yer mean to say that's 'ow . . . 'ow the children always come?'

'Of course it is, you mincing Nanny-hen! – every blessed child that walks. And I jus' 'ope,' said Mrs Beamish, as she marched off herself with brush and scrubber: 'I 'ope, now you know it, you'll 'ave a little more love and gratitoode for your own mother than ever you 'ad before.'

'Oh lor!' said the girl. 'Oh, lor!' And plumping down on the chopping-block she snatched her apron to her face and began to cry.

CHAPTER EIGHT

Two months passed before Mahony could help Polly and Mrs Beamish into the coach bound for Geelong.

It had been touch and go with Polly; and for weeks her condition had kept him anxious. With the inset of the second month, however, she seemed fairly to turn the corner, and from then on made a steady recovery, thanks to her youth and an unimpaired vitality.

He had hurried the little cradle out of sight. But Polly was quick to miss it, and quite approved of its having been given to a needy expectant mother near by. Altogether she bore the thwarting of her hopes bravely.

'Poor little baby, I should have been very fond of it,' was all she said, when she was well enough to fold and pack away the tiny garments at which she had stitched with such pleasure.

It was not to Mahony's mind that she returned with Mrs Beamish – but what else could be done? After lying a prisoner through the hot summer, she was sadly in need of a change. And Mrs Beamish promised her a diet of unlimited milk and eggs, as well as the do-nothing life that befitted an invalid. Just before they left, a letter arrived from John demanding the keys of his house, and proposing that Polly should come to town to set it in order for him, and help him to engage a housekeeper. A niggardly – a truly 'John-ish' – fashion of giving an invitation, thought Mahony, and was not for his wife accepting it. But Polly was so pleased at the prospect of seeing her brother that he ended by agreeing to her going on to Melbourne as soon as she had thoroughly recuperated.

Peace between him and Mrs Beamish was dearly bought up to the last; they barely avoided a final explosion. At the beginning of her third month's absence from home the good woman grew very restive, and sighed aloud for the day on which she would be able to take her departure.

'I expec' my bein' away like this'll run clean into a fifty-poun' note,' she said one evening. 'When it comes to managin' an 'ouse, those two girls of mine 'aven't a h'ounce o' gumption between them.'

It *was* tactless of her, even Polly felt that; though she could sympathize with the worry that prompted the words. As for Mahony, had he had the money to do it, he would have flung the sum named straight at her head.

'She must never come again,' said Polly to herself, as she bent over the hair-chain she was making as a gift for John. 'It *is* a pity, but it seems as if Richard can't get on with those sort of people.'

In his relief at having his house to himself, Mahony accepted even Polly's absence with composure. To be perpetually in the company of other people irked him beyond belief. A certain amount of privacy was as vital to him as sleep.

Delighting in his new-found solitude, he put off from day to day the disagreeable job of winding up his affairs and discovering how much – or how little – ready money there would be to set sail with. Another thing, some books he had sent home for, a year or more ago, came to hand at this time, and gave him a fresh pretext for delay. There were eight or nine volumes to unpack and cut the pages of. He ran from one to another, sipping, devouring. Finally he cast anchor in a collected edition of his old chief's writings on obstetrics – slipped in, this, as a gift from the sender, a college chum – and over it, his feet on the table, his dead pipe in the corner of his mouth, Mahony sat for the better part of the night.

The effect of this master-mind on his was that of a spark on tinder. Under the flash, he cursed for the hundredth time the folly he had been guilty of in throwing up medicine. It was a vocation that had fitted him as coursing fits a hound, or housewifery a woman. The only excuse he could find for his apostasy was that he had been caught in an epidemic of unrest, which had swept through the country, upsetting the balance of men's reason. He had since wondered if the Great Exhibition of '51 had not had something to do with it, by unduly whetting people's imaginations; so that but a single cry of 'Gold!' was needed, to loose the spirit of vagrancy that lurks in every Briton's blood. His case had perhaps been peculiar in this: no one had come forward to warn or dissuade. His next relatives – mother and sisters – were, he thought, glad to know him well away. In their eyes he had lowered himself by taking up medicine; to them it was still of a piece with barber's pole and cupping-basin. Before his time no member of the family had entered any profession but the army. Oh, that infernal Irish pride! . . . and Irish poverty. It had choke-damped his youth, blighted the prospects of his sisters. He could remember, as if it were yesterday, the jibes and fleers called forth by the suit of a wealthy Dublin brewer, who had been attracted – by sheer force of contrast, no doubt – to the elder of the two swan-necked, stiff-backed Miss Townshend-Mahonys, with their long, thin noses, and the ingrained lines that ran from the curled nostrils to the corners of their super-cilious mouths, describing a sneer so deep that at a distance it was possible to mistake it for a smile. 'Beer, my dear, indeed and there are worse things in the world than beer!' he heard his mother declare in her biting way. 'By all means take him! You can wash yourself in it if water gets scarce, and I'll place my kitchen orders with you.' Lucinda, who had perhaps sniffed timidly at release, burnt crimson: thank you! she would rather eat rat-bane. – He supposed they pinched and scraped along as of old – the question of money was never broached between him and them. Prior to his marriage he had sent them what he could; but that little was in itself an admission of failure. They made no inquiries about his mode of life, preferring it to remain in shadow; enough for them that he had not amassed a fortune. Had that come to pass, they might have pardoned the rude method of its making – in fancy he listened to the witty, cutting, self-derisive words, in which they would have alluded to his success.

Lying back in his chair he thought of them thus, without un-kindliness, even with a dash of humour. That was possible, now that knocking about the world had rubbed off some of his own corners. In his young days, he, too, had been hot and bitter. What, however, to another might have formed the chief crux in their conduct – it was by squandering such money as there was, his own portion among it, on his scamp of an elder brother, that they had forced him into the calling they despised – this had not troubled him greatly. For medicine was the profession on which his choice would anyhow have fallen. And tonight the book that lay before him had infected him with the old enthusiasm. He re-lived those days when a skilfully handled case of *placenta previa*, or a successful delivery in the fourth position, had meant more to him than the Charge of the Light Brigade.

Fresh from this dip into the past, this foretaste of the future, he turned in good heart to business. An inventory had to be taken; damaged goods cleared out; a list of bad and less bad debts drawn up: he and Hempel were hard at work all next day. The result was worse even than he had expected. His outlay that summer – ever since the day on which he had set off to the aid of his bereaved relative – had been enormous. Trade had run dry, and throughout Polly's long illness he had dipped blindly into his savings. He could never have said no to Mrs Beamish when she came to him for money – rather would he have pawned the coat off his back. And she, good woman, was unused to cheeseparing. His men's wages paid, berths booked, the numerous expenses bound up with a departure defrayed, he would have but a scanty sum in hand with which to start on the other side.

For himself he was not afraid; but he shrank from the thought of Polly undergoing privations. So far, they had enjoyed a kind of frugal comfort. But should he meet with obstacles at the outset: if patients were laggardly and the practice slow to move, or if he himself fell ill, they might have a spell of real poverty to face. And it was under the goad of this fear that he hit on a new scheme. Why not leave Polly behind for a time, until he had succeeded in making a home for her? – why not leave her under the wing of brother John? John stood urgently in need of a head for his establishment, and who so well suited for the post as Polly? Surely, if it were put before him, John must jump at the offer! Parting from Polly, and were it only for a little while, would be painful; but, did he go alone, he would be free to do his utmost – and with an easy mind, knowing that she lacked none of the creature-comforts. Yes, the more he considered the plan, the better he liked it. The one flaw in his satisfaction was the thought that if their child had lived, no such smooth and simple arrangement would have been possible. He could not have foisted a family on Turnham.

Now he waited with impatience for Polly to return – his reasonable little Polly! But he did not hurry her. Polly was enjoying her holiday. Having passed to Melbourne from Geelong she wrote:

John is so very kind. He doesn't of course go out yet himself, but I was present with some friends of his at a very elegant soirée. John gave me a headdress composed of black pearls and frosted leaves. He means to go in for politics as soon as his year of mourning is up.

Mahony replied:

Enjoy yourself, my heart, and see all the sights you can.

While into more than one of his letters he slipped a banknote.

For you know I like you to pay your own way as far as possible.

And at length the day came when he could lift his wife out of the coach. She emerged powdered brown with dust and very tired, but radiantly happy: it was a great event in little Polly's life, this home-coming, and coming, too, strong and well. The house was a lively place that afternoon: Polly had so much to tell that she sat holding her bonnet for over an hour, quite unable to get as far as the bedroom; and even Long Jim's mouth went up at the corners instead of down; for Polly had contrived to bring back a little gift for everyone. And in presenting these, she found out more of what people were thinking and feeling than her husband had done in all the eight weeks of her absence.

Mahony was loath to damp her pleasure straightway; he bided his time. He could not know that Polly also had been laying plans, and that she watched anxiously for the right moment to unfold them.

The morning after her return, she got a lift in the baker's cart and drove out to inspect John's children. What she saw and heard on this visit was disquieting. The children had run wild, were grown dirty, sly, untruthful. Especially the boy. — 'A young Satan, and that's a fact, Mrs Mahony! What he needs is a man's hand over him, and a good hidin' six days outer seven.'

It was not alone little Johnny's misconduct, however, that made Polly break silence. An incident occurred that touched her still more nearly.

Husband and wife sat snug and quiet as in the early days of their marriage. Autumn had come round and a fire burnt in the stove, before which Pompey snorted in his dreams. But, for all the cosy tranquillity, Polly was not happy; and time and again she moistened and bit at the tip of her thread, before pointing it through her needle. For the book open before Richard, in which he was making notes as he read, was – the Bible. Bending over him to drop a kiss on the top of his head, Polly had been staggered by what she saw. Opposite the third verse of the first chapter of Genesis: 'And God said, Let there be light: and there was light', he had written: 'Three days before the sun!' Her heart seemed to shrivel, to grow small in her breast, at the thought of her husband being guilty of such impiety. Ceasing her pretence at sewing, she walked out of the house into the yard. Standing there under the stars she said aloud, as if someone, *the* One, could hear her: 'He doesn't mean to do wrong. . . . I *know* he doesn't!' But when she re-entered the room he was still at it. His beautiful writing, reduced to its tiniest, wound round the narrow margins.

Deeply red, Polly took her courage in both hands, and struck a blow for the soul whose salvation was more to her than her own. 'Richard, do you think that . . . is . . . is right?' she asked in a low voice.

Mahony raised his head. 'Eh? – what, Pollykin?'

'I mean, do you think you ought . . . that it is right to do what you are doing?'

The smile, half-tender, half-quizzical that she loved, broke over her husband's face. He held out his hand. 'Is my little wife troubled?'

'Richard, I only mean . . .'

'Polly, my dear, don't worry your little head over what you don't understand. And have confidence in me. You know I wouldn't do anything I believed to be wrong?'

'Yes, indeed. And you are really far more religious than I am.'

'One can be religious and yet not shut one's eyes to the truth. It's Saint Paul, you know, who says: we can do nothing against the Truth but for the Truth. And you may depend on it, Polly, the All-Wise would never have given us the brains He has, if He had not intended us to use them. Now I have long felt sure that the Bible is not wholly what it claims to be – direct inspiration.'

'Oh, Richard!' said Polly, and threw an anxious glance over her shoulder. 'If anyone should hear you!'

'We can't afford to let our lives be governed by what other people think, Polly. Nor will I give any man the right to decide for me what my share of the Truth shall be.'

On seeing the Bible closed Polly breathed again, at the same

156

time promising herself to take the traitorous volume into safe-keeping, that no third person's eye should rest on it. Perhaps, too, if it were put away Richard would forget to go on writing in it. He had probably begun in the first place only because he had nothing else to do. In the store he sat and smoked and twirled his thumbs – not half-a-dozen customers came in, in the course of the day. If he were once properly occupied again, with work that he liked, he would not be tempted to put his gifts to such a profane use. Thus she primed herself for speaking. For now was the time. Richard was declaring that trade had gone to the dogs, his takings dropped to a quarter of what they had formerly been. This headed just where she wished. But Polly would not have been Polly, had she not glanced aside for a moment, to cheer and console.

'It's the same everywhere, Richard. Everybody's complaining. And that reminds me, I forgot to tell you about the Beamishes. They're in great trouble. You see, a bog has formed in front of the Hotel, and the traffic goes round another way, so they've lost most of their custom. Mr Beamish never opens his mouth at all now, and mother is fearfully worried. That's what was the matter when she was here – only she was too kind to say so.'

'Hard lines!'

'Indeed it is. But about us; I'm not surprised to hear trade is dull. Since I was over in the western township last, no less than six new General Stores have gone up – I scarcely knew the place. They've all got big plate-glass windows; and were crowded with people.'

'Yes, there's a regular exodus up west. But that doesn't alter the fact, wife, that I've made a very poor job of storekeeping. I shall leave here with hardly a penny to my name.'

'Yes, but then, Richard,' said Polly, and bent over her strip of needlework, 'you were never cut out to be a storekeeper, were you?'

'I was not. And I verily believe, if it hadn't been for that old sobersides of a Hempel, I should have come a cropper long ago.'

'Yes, and Hempel,' said Polly softly; 'Hempel's been wanting to leave for ever so long.'

'The dickens he has!' cried Mahony in astonishment. 'And me humming and hawing about giving him notice! What's the matter with him? What's he had to complain of?'

'Oh, nothing like that. He wants to enter the ministry. A helper's needed at the Baptist Chapel, and he means to apply

157

for the post. You see, he's saved a good deal, and thinks he can study to be a minister at the same time.'

'Study for his grave, the fool! So that's it, is it? Well, well! it saves trouble in the end. I don't need to bother my head now over what's to become of him . . . him or anyone else. My chief desire is to say good-bye to this hole for ever. There's no sense, Polly, in my dawdling on. Indeed, I haven't the money to do it. So I've arranged, my dear, with our friend Ocock to come in and sell us off, as soon as you can get our personal belongings put together.'

Here Polly raised her head as if to interrupt; but Mahony, full of what he had to say, ignored the movement, and went on speaking. He did not wish to cause his wife uneasiness, by dwelling on his difficulties; but some explanation was necessary to pave the way for his proposal that she should remain behind, when he left the colony. He spent all his eloquence in making this sound natural and attractive. But it was hard, when Polly's big, astonished eyes hung on his face. 'Do you think, for my sake, you could be brave enough?' he wound up, rather unsurely. 'It wouldn't be for long, love, I'm certain of that. Just let me set foot in England once more!'

'Why . . . why, yes, dear Richard, I . . . I think I could, if you really wished it,' said Polly in a small voice. She tried to seem reasonable; though black night descended on her at the thought of parting, and though her woman's eyes saw a hundred objections to the plan, which his had overlooked. (For one thing, John had just installed Sara as housekeeper, and Sara would take it very unkindly to be shown the door.) 'I *think* I could,' she repeated. 'But before you go on, dear, I should like to ask *you* something.'

She laid down her needlework; her heart was going pit-a-pat. 'Richard, did you ever . . . I mean have you ever thought of . . . of taking up your profession again – I mean here – starting practice here? – No, wait a minute! Let me finish. I . . . I . . . oh, Richard –!' Unable to find words, Polly locked her fingers under the tablecloth and hoped she was not going to be so silly as to cry. Getting up, she knelt down before her husband, laying her hands on his knees. 'Oh, Richard, I wish you would – *how* I wish you would!'

'Why, Polly!' said Mahony, surprised at her agitation. 'Why, my dear, what's all this? – You want to know if I never thought of setting up in practice out here? Of course I did . . . in the beginning. You don't think I'd have chosen to keep a store, if there'd been any other opening for me? But there wasn't, child. The place was overrun. Never a medico came out and found digging too much for him, but he fell back in despair on his profession. I didn't see my way to join their starvation band.'

'Yes, *then*, Richard! — but now?' broke in Polly. 'Now, it's quite, quite different. Look at the size Ballarat has grown — there are more than forty thousand people settled on it; Mr Ocock told me so. And you know, dear, doctors have cleared out lately, not come fresh. There was that one, I forget his name, who drank himself to death; and the two, you remember, who were sold up just before Christmas.' But this was an unfortunate line of argument to have hit on, and Polly blushed and stumbled.

Mahony laughed at her slip, and smoothed her hair. 'Typical fates, love! They mustn't be mine. Besides, Polly, you're forgetting the main thing — how I hate the place, and how I've always longed to get away.'

'No, I'm not. But please let me go on. — You know, Richard, everyone believes some day Ballarat will be the chief city — bigger even than Geelong or Melbourne. And then to have a good practice here would mean ever such a lot of money. I'm not the only person who thinks so. There's Sara, and Mrs Beamish — I know, of course, you don't care much what they say; but still —' Polly meant: still, you see, I have public opinion on my side. As, however, once more words failed her, she hastened to add: 'John, too, is amazed to hear you think of going home to bury yourself in some little English village. He's sure there'd be a splendid opening for you here. John thinks very, very highly of you. He told me he believes you would have saved Emma's life, if you had been there.'

'I'm much obliged to your brother for his confidence,' said Mahony dryly; 'but—'

'Wait a minute, Richard! You see, dear, *I* can't help feeling myself that you ought not to be too hasty in deciding. Of course, I know I'm young, and haven't had much experience, but . . . You see, you're *known* here, Richard, and that's always something; in England you'd be a perfect stranger. And though you may say there are too many doctors on the Flat, still, if the place goes on growing as it is doing, there'll soon be room for more; and then, if it isn't you, it'll just be someone else. And that *does* seem a pity, when you are so clever — so much, much cleverer than other people! Yes, I know all about it; Mrs Beamish told me it was you I owed my life to, not Dr Rogers' – at which Mahony winced, indignant that anyone should have betrayed to Polly how near death she had been. 'Oh, I *do* want people to know you for what you really are!' said little Polly.

'Pussy, I believe she has ambitions for her husband,' said Mahony to Palmerston.

'Of course I have. You say you hate Ballarat, and all that, but have you ever thought, Richard, what a difference it would make if you were in a better position? You think people look down on you, because you're in trade. But if you were a doctor, there'd be none of that. You'd call yourself by your full name again, and write it down on the visiting list at Government House, and be as good as anybody, and be asked into society, and keep a horse. You'd live in a bigger house, and have a room to yourself and time to read and write. I'm quite sure you'd make lots of money and soon be at the top of the tree. And after all, dear Richard, *I* don't want to go home. I would much rather stay here and look after Jerry, and dear Ned, and poor John's children,' said Polly, falling back as a forlorn hope on her own preference.

'Why, what a piece of special pleading!' cried Mahony, and leaning forward, he kissed the young flushed face.

'Don't laugh at me, I'm in earnest.'

'Why, no, child. But Polly, my dear, even if I were tempted for a moment to think seriously of what you say, where would the money come from? Fees are high, it's true, if the ball's once set a-rolling. But till then? With a jewel of a wife like mine, I'd be a scoundrel to take risks.'

Polly had been waiting for this question. On hearing it, she sat back on her heels and drew a deep breath. The communication she had now to make him was the hub round which all turned. Should he refuse to consider it . . . Plucking at the fringe of the tablecloth, she brought out, piecemeal, the news that John was willing to go surety for the money they would need to borrow for the start. Not only that: he offered them a handsome sum weekly to take entire charge of his children. – 'Not here, in this little house – I know that wouldn't do,' Polly hastened to throw in, forestalling the objection she read in Richard's eyes. Now did he not think he should weigh an offer of this kind very carefully? A name like John's was not to be despised; most people in their position would jump at it. 'I understand something about it,' said the little woman, and sagely nodded her head. 'For when I was in Geelong, Mr Beamish tried his hardest to raise some money and couldn't, his sureties weren't good enough.' Mahony had not the heart to chide her for discussing his private affairs with her brother. Indeed, he rather admired the business-like way she had gone about it. And he admitted this, by ceasing to banter and by calling her attention to the various hazards and inconveniences the step would entail.

Polly heard him out in silence. Enough for her, in the beginning, that he did not decline off-hand. They had a long talk, the end of which was that he promised to sleep over John's proposal, and delay fixing the date of the auction till the morning.

Having yielded this point Mahony kissed his wife and sent her to bed, himself going out with the dog for his usual stroll.

It was a fine night – moonless, but thick with stars. So much, at least, could be said in favour of the place: there was abundant sky-room; you got a clear half of the great vault at once. How he pitied, on such a night, the dwellers in old, congested cities, whose view of the starry field was limited to a narrow strip, cut through house-tops.

Yet he walked with a springless tread. The fact was, certain of his wife's words had struck home; and in the course of the past year he had learnt to put considerable faith in Polly's practical judgement. As he wound his way up the little hill to which he had often carried his perplexities, he let his pipe go out, and forgot to whistle Pompey off butcher's garbage.

Sitting down on a log he rested his chin in his hands. Below him twinkled the sparse lights of the Flat; shouts and singing rose from the circus. – And so John would have been willing to go surety for him! Let no one say the unexpected did not happen. All said and done, they were little more than strangers to each other, and John had no notion what his money-making capacities as a doctor might be. It was true, Polly had been too delicate to mention whether the affair had come about through her persuasions or on John's own initiative. John might have some ulterior motive up his sleeve. Perhaps he did not want to lose his sister . . . or was scheming to bind a pair of desirables fast to this colony, the welfare of which he had so much at heart. Again, it might be that he wished to buy off the memory of that day on which he had stripped his soul naked. Simplest of all, why should he not be merely trying to pay back a debt? He, Mahony, might shrink from lying under an obligation to John, but, so far, the latter had not scrupled to accept favours from him. But that was always the way with your rich men; they were not troubled by paltry pride; for they knew it was possible to acquit themselves of their debts at a moment's notice, and with interest. This led him to reflect on the great help to him the loan of his wealthy relative's name would be: difficulties would melt before it. And surely no undue risk was involved in the use of it? Without boasting, he thought he was better equipped, both by aptitude and training, than the ruck of colonial practitioners. Did he enter the lists, he could hardly fail to succeed. And out here even a moderate success spelled a fortune. Gained double-quick, too. After which the lucky individual sold out and went home, to live in comfort. Yes, that was a point, and not to be overlooked. No definite surrender of one's hopes was called for; only a postponement. Ten years might do it – meaty years, of course, the best years of one's life – still. . . . It would mean very hard work; but had he not just been contemplating, with perfect equanimity, an even more arduous venture on the other side? What a capricious piece of mechanism was the human brain!

Another thought that occurred to him was that his services might prove more useful to this new country than to the old, where able men abounded. He recalled the many good lives and promising cases he had here seen lost and bungled. To take the instance nearest home – Polly's confinement. Yes, to show his mettle to such as Rogers; to earn respect where he had lived as a mere null – the idea had an insidious fascination. And as Polly sagely remarked: if it were not he, it would be someone else; another would harvest the *kudos* that might have been his. For the rough-and-ready treatment – the blue pills and black draughts – that had satisfied the early diggers had fallen into disrepute; medical skill was beginning to be appreciated. If this went on, Ballarat would soon stand on a level with any city of its size at home. But even as it was, he had never been quite fair to it; he had seen it with a jaundiced eye. And again he believed Polly hit the nail on the head, when she asserted that the poor position he had occupied was responsible for much of his dislike.

But there was something else at work in him besides. Below the surface an admission awaited him, which he shrank from making. All these pros and cons, these quibbles and hair-splittings were but a misfit attempt to cloak the truth. He might gull himself with them for a time: in his heart he knew that he would yield – if yield he did – because he was by nature only too prone to follow the line of least resistance. What he had gone through tonight was no new experience. Often enough, after fretting and fuming about a thing till it seemed as if nothing under the sun had ever mattered so much to him, it could happen that he suddenly threw up the sponge and bowed to circumstance. His vitality exhausted itself beforehand – in a passionate aversion, a torrent of words – and failed him at the critical moment. It was a weakness in his blood – in the blood of his race. – But in the present instance, he had an excuse for himself. He had not known – till Polly came out with her brother's offer – how he dreaded having to begin all over again in England, an utter stranger, without influence or recommendations, and with no money to speak of at his back.

But now he had owned up, and there was no more need of shift or subterfuge: now it was one rush and hurry to the end. He had capitulated; a thin-skinned aversion to confronting difficulties, when he saw the chance of avoiding them, had won the day. He intended – had perhaps the whole time intended – to take the hand held out to him. After all, why not? Anyone else, as Polly said, would have jumped at John's offer. He alone must argue himself blue in the face over it.

But as he sat and pondered the lengthy chain of circumstance – Polly's share in it, John's, his own, even the part played by incorporeal things – he brought up short against the word 'decision'. He might flatter himself by imagining he had been free to decide; in reality nothing was further from the truth. He had been subtly and slyly guided to his goal – led blindfold along a road that was not of his own choosing. Everything and everyone had combined to constrain him: his favours to John, the failure of his business, Polly's inclinations and persuasions, his own fastidious shrinkings. So that, in the end, all he had had to do was to brush aside a flimsy gossamer veil, which hung between him and his fate. Was it straining a point to see in the whole affair the workings of a Power outside himself – against himself, in so far as it took no count of his poor earth-blind vision?

Well, if this were so, better still: his ways were in God's hands. And after all, what did it matter where one strove to serve one's Maker – east or west or south or north – and whether the stars overhead were grouped in this constellation or in that? Their light was a pledge that one would never be overlooked or forgotten, traced by the hand of Him who had promised to note even a sparrow's fall. And here he spoke aloud into the darkness the ancient and homely formula that is man's stand-by in face of the untried, the unknown.

'If God wills. . . . God knows best.'

PART THREE

CHAPTER ONE

The house stood not far from the Great Swamp. It was of weatherboard, with a galvanized iron roof, and might have been built from a child's drawing of a house: a door in the centre, a little window on either side, a chimney at each end. Since the ground sloped downwards, the front part rested on piles some three feet high, and from the rutty clay-track that would one day be a street wooden steps led up to the door. Much as Mahony would have liked to face it with a verandah, he did not feel justified in spending more than he could help. And Polly not only agreed with him, but contrived to find an advantage in the plainer style of architecture. 'Your plate will be better seen, Richard, right on the street, than hidden under a verandah.' But then Polly was overflowing with content. Had not two of the rooms fireplaces? And was there not a wash-house, with a real copper in it, behind the detached kitchen? Not to speak of a spare room! — To the rear of the house a high paling-fence enclosed a good-sized yard. Mahony dreamed of a garden, Polly of keeping hens.

There were no two happier people on Ballarat that autumn than the Mahonys. To and fro they trudged down the hill, across the Flat, over the bridge and up the other side; first, through a Sahara of dust, then, when the rains began, ankle-deep in gluey red mud. And the building of the finest mansion never gave half so much satisfaction as did that of this flimsy little wooden house, with its thin lath-and-plaster walls. In fancy they had furnished it and lived in it, long before it was even roofed in. Mahony sat at work in his surgery — it measured ten by twelve — Polly at her Berlin-woolwork in the parlour opposite: 'And a cage with a little parrot in it, hanging at the window.'

The preliminaries to the change had gone smoothly enough — Mahony could not complain. Pleasant they had not been; but could the arranging and clinching of a complicated money-matter ever be pleasant? He had had to submit to hearing his private affairs gone into by a stranger; to make clear to strangers his capacity for earning a decent income.

With John's promissory letter in his pocket, he had betaken himself to Henry Ocock's office.

This, notwithstanding its excellent position on the brow of the western hill, could not deny its humble origin as a livery-barn. The entry was by a yard; and some of the former horse-boxes had been rudely knocked together to provide accommodation. Mahony sniffed stale dung.

In what had once been the harness-room, two young men sat at work.

'Why, Tom, my lad, you here?'

Tom Ocock raised his freckled face, from the chin of which sprouted some long fair hairs, and turned red.

'Yes, it's me. Do you want to see 'En –' at an open kick from his brother – 'Mr Ocock?'

'If you please.'

Informed by Grindle that the 'Captain' was at liberty, Mahony passed to an inner room where he was waved to a chair. In answer to his statement that he had called to see about raising some money, Ocock returned an: 'Indeed? Money is tight, sir, very tight!' his face instantly taking on the blank-wall solemnity proper to dealings with this world's main asset.

Mahony did not at once hand over John's way-smoothing letter. He thought he would first test the lawyer's attitude towards him in person – a species of self-torment men of his make are rarely able to withstand. He spoke of the decline of his business; of his idea of setting up as a doctor and building himself a house; and, as he talked, he read his answer pat and clear in the ferrety eyes before him. There was a bored tolerance of his wordiness, an utter lack of interest in the concerns of the petty tradesman.

'H'm.' Ocock, lying back in his chair, was fitting five out-stretched fingers to their fellows. 'All very well, my good sir, but may I ask if you have anyone in view as a security?'

'I have. May I trouble you to glance through this?' and triumphantly Mahony brandished John's letter.

Ocock raised his brows. 'What? Mr John Turnham? Ah, very good . . . very good indeed!' The brazen-faced change in his manner would have made a cat laugh; he sat upright, was interested, courteous, alert. 'Quite in order! And now, pray, how much do we need?'

166

Unadvised, he had not been able, said Mahony, to determine the sum. So Ocock took pencil and paper, and, prior to running off a reckoning, put him through a sharp interrogation. Under it Mahony felt as though his clothing was being stripped piece by piece off his back. At one moment he stood revealed as mean and stingy, at another as an unpractical spendthrift. More serious things came out besides. He began to see, under the limelight of the lawyer's inquiry, in what a muddle-headed fashion he had managed his business, and how unlikely it was he could ever have made a good thing of it. Still worse was his thoughtless folly in wedding and bringing home a young wife without, in this settlement where accident was rife, where fires were of nightly occurrence, insuring against either fire or death. Not that Ocock breathed a hint of censure: all was done with a twist of the eye, a purse of the lip; but it was enough for Mahony. He sat there, feeling like an eel in the skinning, and did not attempt to keep pace with the lawyer, who hunted figures into the centre of a woolly maze.

The upshot of these calculations was: he would need help to the tune of something over one thousand pounds. As matters stood at present on Ballarat, said Ocock, the plainest house he could build would cost him eight hundred; and another couple of hundred would go in furnishing; while a saddle-horse might be put down at fifty pounds. On Turnham's letter he, Ocock, would be prepared to borrow seven hundred for him – and this could probably be obtained at ten per cent on a mortgage of the house; and a further four hundred, for which he would have to pay twelve or fifteen. Current expenses must be covered by the residue of his savings, and by what he was able to make. They would include the keep of the horse, and the interest on the borrowed money, which might be reckoned roughly at a hundred and twenty per annum. In addition, he would be well advised to insure his life for five to seven hundred pounds.

The question also came up whether the land he had selected for building on should be purchased or not. He was for doing so, for settling the whole business there and then. Ocock, however, took the opposite view. Considering, said he, that the site chosen was far from the centre of the town, Mahony might safely postpone buying in the meanwhile. There had been no government land-sales of late, and all main-road frontages had still to come under the hammer. As occupier, when the time arrived, he would have first chance at the upset price; though then, it was true, he would also be liable for improvements. The one thing he must beware of was of enclosing too small a block.

Mahony agreed — agreed to everything: the affair seemed to have passed out of his hands. A sense of dismay invaded him while he listened to the lawyer tick off the obligations and responsibilities he was letting himself in for. A thousand pounds! He to run into debt for such a sum, who had never owed a farthing to anyone! He fell to doubting whether, after all, he had made choice of the easier way, and lapsed into a gloomy silence.

Ocock on the other hand warmed to geniality.

'May I say, doctor, how wise I think your decision to come over to us?' — He spoke as if Ballarat East were in the heart of the Russian steppes. 'And that reminds me. There's a friend of mine. . . . I may be able at once to put a patient in your way.'

Mahony walked home in a mood of depression which it took all Polly's arts to dispel.

Under its influence he wrote an outspoken letter to Purdy — but with no very satisfactory result. It was like projecting a feeler for sympathy into the void, so long was it since they had met, and so widely had his friend's life branched off from his.

Purdy's answer — it was headed 'The Ovens' — did not arrive till several weeks later, and was mainly about himself.

In a way I'm with you, old pill-box, he wrote. *You'll cut a jolly sight better figure as an M.D. than ever you've done behind a counter. But I don't know that I'd care to stake my last dollar on you all the same. What does Mrs Polly say? — As for me, old boy, since you're good enough to ask, why the less said the better. One of these days a poor worn old shicer'll come crawling round to your back door to see if you've any cast-off duds you can spare him. Seriously, Dick, old man, I'm stony-broke once more and the Lord only knows how I'm going to win through.*

In the course of that winter, custom died a natural death; and one day, the few oddments that remained having been sold by auction, Mahony and his assistant nailed boards horizontally across the entrance to the store. The day of weighing out pepper and salt was over; never again would the tinny jangle of the accursed bell smite his ears. The next thing was that Hempel packed his chattels and departed for his new walk in life. Mahony was not sorry to see him go. Hempel's thoughts had soared far above the counter; he was arrived at the stage of: 'I'm just as good as you!' which everyone here reached sooner or later.

'I shall always be pleased to hear how you are getting on.'

Mahony spoke kindly, but in a tone which, as Polly who stood by, very well knew, people were apt to misunderstand.

'I should think so!' she chimed in. 'I shall feel very hurt indeed, Hempel, if you don't come and see us.'

With regard to Long Jim, she had a talk with her husband one night as they went to bed.

'There really won't be anything for him to do in the new house. No heavy crates or barrels to move about. And he doesn't know a thing about horses. Why not let him go home? – he does so want to. What would you say, dear, to giving him thirty pounds for his passage-money and a trifle in his pocket? It would make him very happy, and he'd be off your hands for good. – Of course, though, just as you think best.'

'We shall need every penny we can scrape together, for ourselves, Polly. And yet, my dear, I believe you're right. In the new house, as you say, he'll be a mere encumbrance. As for me, I'd be only too thankful never to hear his cantankerous old pipe again. I don't know now what evil genius prompted me to take him in.'

'Evil genius, indeed!' retorted Polly. 'You did it because you're a dear, good, kind-hearted man.'

'Think so, wifey? I'm inclined to put it down to sheer dislike of botheration – Irish inertia . . . the curse of our race.'

'Yes, yes, I knoo you'd be wantin' to get rid o' me, now you're goin' up in the world,' was Long Jim's answer when Polly broached her scheme for his benefit. 'Well, no, I won't say anythin' against you, Mrs Mahony; you've treated me square enough. But doc., 'e's always thought 'imself a sight above one, an' when 'e does, 'e lets you feel it.'

This was more than Polly could brook. 'And sighing and groaning as you have done to get home, Jim! You're a silly, ungrateful old man, even to hint at such a thing.'

'Poor old fellow, he's grumbled so long now, that he's forgotten how to do anything else,' she afterwards made allowance for him. And added, pierced by a sudden doubt: 'I hope his wife will still be used to it, or . . . or else . . .'

And now the last day in the old house was come. The furniture, stacked in the yard, awaited the dray that was to transport it. Hardly worth carrying with one, thought Mahony, when he saw the few poor sticks exposed to the searching sunlight. Pipe in mouth he mooned about, feeling chiefly amazed that he could have put up, for so long, with the miserable little hut which his house, stripped of its trimmings, proved to be.

His reflections were cut short by old Ocock, who leaned over the fence to bid his neighbours good-bye.

'No disturbance! Come in, come in!' cried Mahony, with the rather spurious heartiness one is prone to throw into a final invitation. And Polly rose from her knees before a clothes-basket which she was filling with crockery, and bustled away to fetch the cake she had baked for such an occasion.

'I'll miss yer bright little face, that I will!' said Mr Ocock, as he munched with the relish of a Jerry or a Ned. He held his slice of cake in the hollow of one great palm, conveying with extreme care the pieces he broke off to his mouth.

'You must come and see us, as soon as ever we're settled.'

'Bless you! You'll soon find grander friends than an old chap like me.'

'Mr Ocock! And you with three sons in the law!'

'Besides, mark my words, it'll be your turn next to build,' Mahony removed his pipe to throw in. 'We'll have you over with us yet.'

'And what a lovely surprise for Miss Amelia when she arrives, to find a bran'-new house awaiting her.'

'Well, that's the end of this little roof-tree,' said Mahony. – The loaded dray had driven off, the children and Ellen perched on top of the furniture, and he was giving a last look round. 'We've spent some very happy days under it, eh, my dear?'

'Oh, very,' said Polly, shaking out her skirts. 'But we shall be just as happy in the new one.'

'God grant we may! It's not too much to hope I've now seen all the downs of my life. I've managed to pack a good many into thirty short years. – And that reminds me, Mrs Townshend-Mahony, do you know you will have been married to me two whole years, come next Friday?'

'Why, so we shall!' cried Polly, and was transfixed in the act of tying her bonnet-strings. 'How time does fly! It seems only the other day I saw this room for the first time. I peeped in, you know, while you were fetching the box. *Do* you remember how

170

I cried, Richard? I was afraid of a spider or something.' And the Polly of eighteen looked back, with a motherly amusement, at her sixteen-year-old eidolon. 'But now, dear, if you're ready . . . or else the furniture will get there before we do. We'd better take the short cut across Soldiers' Hill. That's the cat in that basket, for you to carry, and here's your microscope. I've got the decanter and the best teapot. Shall we go?'

CHAPTER TWO

And now for a month or more Mahony had been in possession of a room that was all his own. Did he retire into it and shut the door, he could make sure of not being disturbed. Polly herself tapped before entering; and he let her do so. Polly was dear; but dearer still was his long-coveted privacy.

He knew, too, that she was happily employed; the fitting-up and furnishing of the house was a job after her own heart. She had proved both skilful and economical at it: thanks to her, they had used a bare three-quarters of the sum allotted by Ocock for the purpose — and this was well; for any number of unforeseen expenses had cropped up at the last moment. Polly had a real knack for making things 'do'. Old empty boxes, for instance, underwent marvellous transformation at her hands — emerged, clad in chintz and muslin, as sofas and toilet-tables. She hung her curtains on strings, and herself sewed the seams of the parlour carpet, squatting Turk-fashion on the floor, and working away, with a great needle shaped like a scimitar, till the perspiration ran down her face. It was also she who, standing on the kitchen-table, put up the only two pictures they possessed, Ned and Jerry giving opinions on the straightness of her eye, from below: a fancy picture of the Battle of Waterloo in the parlour; a print of 'Harvey Discovering the Circulation of the Blood' on the surgery wall.

From where he sat Mahony could hear the voices of the children — John's children — at play. They frolicked with Pompey in the yard. He could endure them, now that he was not for ever tumbling over them. Yes, one and all were comfortably established under the new roof — with the exception of poor Palmerston the cat. Palmerston had declined to recognize the change, and with the immoderate homing-instinct of his kind had returned night after night to his old haunts. For some time Mahony's regular evening walk was back to the store — a road

172

he would otherwise not have taken; for it was odious to him to see Polly's neat little appointments going to rack and ruin, under the tenancy of a dirty Irish family. There he would find the animal sitting, in melancholy retrospect. Again and again he picked him up and carried him home; till that night when no puss came to his call, and Palmerston, the black and glossy, was seen no more: either he had fallen down a shaft, or been mangled by a dog, or stolen, cats still fetching a high price on Ballarat.

The window of Mahony's room faced a wide view: not a fence, hardly a bit of scrub or a tuft of grass-tree marked the bare expanse of uneven ground, now baked brown as a piecrust by the December sun. He looked across it to the cemetery. This was still wild and unfenced – just a patch of rising ground where it was permissible to bury the dead. Only the day before – the second anniversary of the Eureka Stockade – he had watched some two to three hundred men, with crêpe on their hats and sleeves, a black-draped pole at their head, march there to do homage to their fallen comrades. The dust raised by the shuffling of these many feet had accompanied the procession like a moving cloud; had lingered in its rear like the smoke from a fire. Drays and lorries crawled for ever laboriously along it, seeming glued to the earth by the monstrous sticky heat of the veiled sun. Further back rose a number of bald hills – rounded, swelling hills, shaped like a woman's breasts. And behind all, pale china-blue against the tense white sky, was the embankment of the distant ranges. Except for these, an ugly, uninviting outlook, and one to which he seldom lifted his eyes.

His room pleased him better. Polly had stretched a bright green drugget on the floor; the table had a green cloth on it; the picture showed up well against the whitewashed wall. Behind him was a large deal cupboard, which held instruments and drugs. The bookshelves with their precious burden were within reach of his hand; on the top shelf he had stacked the boxes containing his botanical and other specimens.

The first week or so there was naturally little doing: a sprained wrist to bandage, a tooth to draw, a case of fly-blight. To keep himself from growing fidgety, he overhauled his minerals and butterflies, and renewed faded labels. This done, he went on to jot down some ideas he had, with regard to the presence of auriferous veins in quartz. It was now generally agreed that quartz was the matrix; but on the question of how the gold had found its way into the rock, opinions were sharply divided. The theory of igneous injection was advanced by some; others inclined to that of sublimation. Mahony leaned to a combination of the two processes, and spent several days getting his thoughts in order; while Polly, bursting with pride, went about on tip-toe audibly hushing the children: their uncle was writing for the newspapers.

Still no patients worth the name made their appearance. To fend off the black worry that might get the better of him did he sit idle, he next drew his Bible to him, and set about doing methodically what he had so far undertaken merely by fits and starts – deciding for himself to what degree the Scriptures were inspired. Polly was neither proud nor happy while this went on, and let the children romp unchecked. At present it was not so much the welfare of her husband's soul she feared for: God must surely know by this time what a good man Richard was; he had not his equal, she thought, for honesty and uprightness; he was kind to the poor and the sick, and hadn't missed a single Sunday at church, since their marriage. But all that would not help, if once he got the reputation of being an infidel. Then, nobody would want him as a doctor at all.

Casually begun, Mahony's studies soon absorbed him to the exclusion of everything else.

Brought up in the cast-iron mould of Irish Protestantism, to which, being of a sober and devout turn of mind, he had readily submitted, he had been tossed, as a youthful student, into the freebooting Edinburgh of the forties. Edinburgh was alive in those days to her very paving-stones; town and university combined to form a hotbed of intellectual unrest, a breeding-ground for disturbing possibilities. The 'development theory' was in the air; and a book that appeared anonymously had boldly voiced, in popular fashion, Maillet's dream and the Lamarckian hypothesis of a Creation undertaken once and for all, in place of a continuous creative intervention. This book, opposing natural law to miracle, carried complete conviction to the young and eager. Audacious spirits even hazarded the conjecture that primitive life itself might have originated in a natural way: had not, but recently, an investigator who brought a powerful voltaic battery to bear on a saturated solution of silicate of potash, been startled to find, as the result of his experiment, numberless small mites of the species *Acarus horridus*? Might not the marvel electricity or galvanism, in action on albumen, turn out to be the vitalizing force? To the orthodox zoologist, phytologist and geologist, such a suggestion savoured of madness; they either took refuge in a contemptuous silence, or condescended only to reply: Had one visited the Garden of Eden during Creation, one would have found that, in the morning, man was not, while in the evening he was! – morning and evening bearing their newly established significance of geological epochs. The famous tracing of the Creator's footsteps, undertaken by a gifted compromiser, was felt by even the most bigoted to be a lame rejoinder. His *Asterolepsis*, the giant fossilfish from the Old Red Sandstone, the antiquity of which should show that the origin of life was not to be found solely in 'infusorial points', but that highly developed forms were among the earliest created – this single prop was admittedly not strong enough to carry the whole burden of proof. No, the immutability of species had been seriously impugned, and bold minds asked themselves why a single act of creation, at the outset, should not constitute as divine an origin of life as a continued series of 'creative fiats'.

Mahony was one of them. The 'development theory' did not repel him. He could see no impiety in believing that life, once established on the earth, had been left to perfect itself. Or hold that this would represent the Divine Author of all things as, after one master-stroke, dreaming away eternal ages in apathy and indifference. Why should the perfect functioning of natural law not be as convincing an expression of God's presence as a series of cataclysmic acts of creation?

None the less it was a time of crisis, for him, as for so many. For, if this were so, if science spoke true that, the miracle of life set a-going, there had been no further intervention on the part of the Creator, then the very head-and-corner stone of the Christian faith, the Bible itself, was shaken. More, much more would have to go than the Mosaic cosmogony of the first chapter of Genesis. Just as the Elohistic account of creation had been stretched to fit the changed views of geologists, so the greater part of the scriptural narratives stood in need of a wider interpretation. The fable of the Eternal's personal mediation in the affairs of man must be accepted for what it was – a beautiful allegory, the fondly dreamed fulfilment of a world-old desire. And bringing thus a sharpened critical sense to bear on the Scriptures, Mahony embarked on his voyage of discovery. Before him, but more as a warning than a beacon, shone the

175

example of a famous German savant, who, taking our Saviour's life as his theme, demolished the sacred idea of a Divine miracle, and retold the Gospel story from a rationalistic standpoint. A savagely unimaginative piece of work this, thought Mahony, and one that laid all too little weight on the deeps of poetry, the mysteries of symbols, and the power the human mind drew from these, to pierce to an ideal truth. His own modest efforts would be of quite another kind.

For he sought, not to deny God, but to discover Him anew, by freeing Him from the drift of error, superstition and dead-letterism which the centuries had accumulated about Him. Far was it from His servant's mind to wish to decry the authority of the Book of Books. This he believed to consist, in great part, of inspired utterances, and, for the rest, to be the wisest and ripest collection of moral precept and example that had come down to us from the ages. Without it, one would be rudderless indeed — a castaway in a cockleshell boat on a furious sea — and from one's lips would go up a cry like to that wrung from a famous infidel: 'I am affrighted and confounded with the forlorn solitude in which I am placed by my philosophy . . . begin to fancy myself in the most deplorable condition imaginable, environed by the deepest darkness.'

No, Mahony was not one of those who held that the Christian faith, that fine flower of man's spiritual need, would suffer detriment by the discarding of a few fabulous tales; nor did he fear lest his own faith should become undermined by his studies. For he had that in him which told him that God was; and this instinctive certainty would persist, he believed, though he had ultimately to admit the whole fabric of Christianity to be based on the Arimathean's dream. It had already survived the rejection of externals: the surrender of forms, the assurance that ceremonials were not essential to salvation belonged to his early student-days. Now, he determined to send by the board the last hampering relics of bigotry and ritual. He could no longer concede the tenets of election and damnation. God was a God of mercy, not the blind, jealous Jahveh of the Jews, or the inhuman Sabbatarian of a narrow Protestantism. And He might be worshipped anywhere or anyhow: in any temple built to His name — in the wilderness under the open sky — in silent prayer, or according to any creed.

In all this critical readjustment, the thought he had to spare for his fellow-men was of small account: his fate was not bound

176

to theirs by the altruism of a later generation. It was a time of intense individualism; and his efforts towards spiritual emancipation were made on his own behalf alone. The one link he had with his fellows – if link it could be termed – was his earnest wish to avoid giving offence: never would it have occurred to him to noise his heterodoxy abroad. Nor did he want to disturb other people's convictions. He respected those who could still draw support from the old faith, and, moreover, had not a particle of the proselytizer in him. He held that religion was either a matter of temperament, or of geographical distribution; felt tolerantly inclined towards the Jews, and the Chinese; and did not even smile at processions to the Joss-house, and the provisioning of those silent ones who needed food no more.

But just as little as he intermeddled with the convictions of others would he brook interference with his own. It was the concern of no third person what paths he followed in his journeyings after the truth – in his quest for a panacea for the ills and delusions of life. For, call it what he would – Biblical criticism, scientific inquiry – this was his aim first and last. He was trying to pierce the secret of existence – to rede the riddle that has never been solved. – What am I? Whence have I come? Whither am I going? What meaning has the pain I suffer, the evil that men do? Can evil be included in God's scheme? – And it was well, he told himself, as he pressed forward, that the flame in him burnt unwaveringly, which assured him of his kinship with the Eternal, of the kinship of all created things; so unsettling and perplexing were the conclusions at which he arrived.

Summoned to dinner, he sat at table with stupid hands and evasive eyes. Little Johnny, who was, as Polly put it, 'as sharp as mustard', was prompt to note his uncle's vacancy.

'What you staring at, Nunkey?' he demanded, his mouth full of roly-pudding, which he was stuffing down with all possible dispatch.

'Hush, Johnny. Don't tease your uncle.'

'What do you mean, my boy?'

'I mean . . .' Young John squeezed his last mouthful over his windpipe and raised his plate. 'I mean, you look just like you was seein' a emeny. – More puddin', Aunt Polly!'

'What does the child mean? An anemone?'

'*No!*' said John with the immense contempt of five years. 'I didn't say anner emeny.' Here, he began to tuck in anew, aiding the slow work of his spoon with his more habile fingers. 'A emeny's a emeny. Like on de pickshur in Aunt Polly's room. One . . . one's de English, an' one's de emeny.'

'It's the Battle of Waterloo,' explained Polly. 'He stands in front of it every day.'

'Yes. An' when I'm a big man, I'm goin' to be a sojer, an' wear a red coat, an' make "bung"!' and he shot an imaginary gun at his sister, who squealed and ducked her head.

'An ancient wish, my son,' said Mahony, when Johnny had been reproved and Trotty comforted. 'Tom-thumbs like you have voiced it since the world – or rather since war first began.'

'Don't care. Nunkey, why is de English and why is de emeny?'

But Mahony shrank from the gush of whats and whys he would let loose on himself, did he attempt to answer this question. 'Come, shall uncle make you some boats to sail in the wash-tub?'

'Wiv a mast an' sails an' everyfing?' cried John wildly; and throwing his spoon to the floor, he scrambled from his chair. 'Oh yes, Nunkey – dear Nunkey!'

'Dea Unkey!' echoed the shadow.

'Oh, you cupboard lovers, you!' said Mahony as, order restored and sticky mouths wiped, two pudgy hands were thrust with a new kindness into his.

He led the way to the yard; and having whittled out for the children some chips left by the builders, he lighted his pipe and sat down in the shade of the house. Here, through a veiling of smoke, which hung motionless in the hot, still air, he watched the two eager little mortals before him add their quota to the miracle of life.

CHAPTER THREE

Polly had no such absorbing occupation to tide her over these empty days of waiting; and sometimes – especially late in the afternoon, when her household duties were done, the children safely at play – she found it beyond her power to stitch quietly at her embroidery. Letting the canvas fall to her knee, she would listen, listen, listen till the blood sang in her ears, for the footsteps and knocks at the door that never came. And did she draw back the window-curtain and look out, there was not a soul to be seen: not a trace of the string of prosperous, paying patients she had once imagined winding their way to the door.

And meanwhile Richard was shut up in his room, making those dreadful notes in the Bible which it pinched her heart even to think of. He really did not seem to care whether he had a practice or not. All the new instruments, got from Melbourne, lay unused in their casings; and the horse was eating its head off, at over a pound a week, in the livery-barn. Polly shrank from censuring her husband, even in thought; but as she took up her work again, and went on producing in wools a green basket of yellow fruit on a magenta ground, she could not help reflecting what she would have done at this pass, had she been a man. She would have announced the beginning of her practice in big letters in the *Star*, and she would have gone down into the township and mixed with people and made herself known. With Richard, it was almost as if he felt averse from bringing himself into public notice.

Only another month now, and the second instalment of interest would fall due. Polly did not know exactly what the sum was; but she did know the date. The first time, they had had no difficulty in meeting the bill, owing to their economy in furnishing. But what about this one, and the next again? How were payments to be made, and kept up, if the patients would not come?

She wished with all her heart that she was ten years older. For what could a person who was only eighteen be supposed to understand of business? Richard's invariable answer, did she venture a word, was not to worry her little head about such things.

When, however, another week had dribbled away in the same fashion, Polly began to be afraid the date of payment had slipped his memory altogether. She would need to remind him of it, even at the risk of vexing him. And having cast about for a pretext to intrude, she decided to ask his advice on a matter that was giving her much uneasiness; though, had he been *really* busy, she would have gone on keeping it to herself.

It related to little Johnny.

Johnny was a high-spirited, passionate child, who needed most careful handling. At first she had managed him well enough. But ever since his five months' boarding-out, he had fallen into deceitful ways; and the habit of falsehood was gaining on him. Bad by nature, Polly felt sure the child was not; but she could not keep him on the straight path now he had discovered that a lie might save him a punishment. He was not to be shamed out of telling it; and the only other cure Polly knew of was whipping. She whipped him; and provoked him to fury.

A new misdeed on his part gave her the handle she sought. Johnny had surreptitiously entered her pantry and stolen a plateful of cakes. Taxed with the theft he denied it; and cornered, laid, Adam-like, the blame on his companion, asserting that Trotty had persuaded him to take the goodies; though bewildered innocence was writ all over the baby's chubby face.

Mahony had the young sinner up before him. But he was able neither to touch the child's heart, nor to make him see the gravity of what he had done: never being allowed inside the surgery, John could now not take his eyes off the wonderful display of gold and purple and red moths, which were pinned, with outstretched wings, to a sheet of cork. He stood o-mouthed and absentminded, and only once shot a blue glance at his uncle to say: 'But if dey're so baddy . . . den why did God *make* lies an' de debble?' – which intelligent query hit the nail of one of Mahony's own misgivings on the head.

No real depravity, was his verdict. Still, too much of a handful, it was plain, for Polly's inexperience. 'A problem for John himself to tackle, my dear. Why should we have to drill a nonexistent morality into his progeny? Besides, I'm not going to have you blamed for bad results, later on.' He would write to

John there and then, and request that Johnny be removed from their charge.

Polly was not prepared for this summary solution of her dilemma, and began to regret having brought it up; though she could not but agree with Richard that it would never do for the younger child to be corrupted by a bad example. However, she kept her wits about her. Did John take the boy away, said she, she was afraid she would have to ask for a larger house-keeping allowance. The withdrawal of the money for Johnny's board would make a difference to their income.

'Of course,' returned Mahony easily, and was about to dismiss the subject.

But Polly stood her ground. 'Talking of money, Richard, I don't know whether you remember . . . you've been so busy . . . that it's only about a fortnight now till the second lot of interest falls due.'

'What! – a fortnight?' exclaimed her husband, and reached out for an almanack. 'Good Lord, so it is! And nothing doing yet, Polly . . . absolutely nothing!'

'Well, dear, you can't expect to jump into a big practice all at once, can you? But you see, I think the trouble is, not nearly enough people know you've started.' And a little imploringly, and very apologetically, Polly unfolded her artless schemes for self-advertisement.

'Wife, I've a grave suspicion!' said Mahony, and took her by the chin. 'While I've sat here with my head in the clouds, you've been worrying over ways and means, and over having such an unpractical old dreamer for a husband. Now, child, that won't do. I didn't marry to have my girl puzzling her little brains where her next day's dinner was to come from. Away with you, to your stitching! Things will be all right, trust to me.'

And Polly did trust him, and was so satisfied with what she had effected that, raising her face for a kiss, she retired with an easy mind to overhaul Johnny's little wardrobe.

But the door having clicked behind her, Mahony's air of forced assurance died away. For an instant he hesitated beside the table, on which a rampart of books lay open, then vigorously clapped each volume to and moved to the window, chewing at the ends of his beard. A timely interruption! What the dickens had he been about, to forget himself in this fool's paradise, when the crassest of material anxieties – that of pounds, shillings and pence – was crouched, wolf-like, at his door?

That night he wakened with a jerk from an uneasy sleep. Though at noon the day before, the thermometer had registered over a hundred in the shade, it was now bitterly cold, and these abrupt changes of temperature always whipped up his nerves. Even after he had piled his clothes and an opossum-rug on top of the blankets, he could not drop off again. He lay staring at the moonlit square of the window, and thinking the black thoughts of night.

What if he could not manage to work up a practice? . . . found it impossible to make a living? His plate had been on the door for close on two months now, and he had barely a five-pound note to show for it. What was to be done? Here Polly's words came back to him with new stress. 'Not nearly enough people know you've started.' That was it! – Polly had laid her finger on the hitch. The genteel manners of the old country did not answer here; instead of sitting twiddling his thumbs, waiting for patients to seek him out, he ought to have adopted the screaming methods of advertisement in vogue on Ballarat. To have had 'Holloway's Pills sold here!' 'Teeth extracted painlessly!' 'Cures guaranteed!' painted man-high on his outside house-wall. To have gone up and down and round the township; to have been on the spot when accidents happened; to have hobnobbed with Tom, Dick and Harry in bars and saloons. And he saw a figure that looked like his the centre of a boisterous crowd; saw himself slapped on the back by dirty hands, shouting and shouted to drinks. He turned his pillow, to drive the image away. Whatever he had done or not done, the fact remained that a couple of weeks hence he had to make up the sum of over thirty pounds. And again he discerned a phantom self, this time a humble supplicant for an extension of term, brought up short against Ocock's stony visage, flouted by his cocksy clerk. Once more he turned his pillow. These quarterly payments, which dotted all his coming years, were like little rock-islands studding the surface of an ocean, and telling of the sunken continent below: this monstrous thousand-odd pounds he had been fool enough to borrow. Never would he be able to pay off such a sum, never again be free from the incubus of debt. Meanwhile, not the ground he stood on, not the roof over his head could actually be called his own. He had also been too pushed for money, at the time, to take Ocock's advice and insure his life.

These thoughts spun themselves to a nightmare-web, in which

he was the hapless fly. Putting a finger to his wrist, he found he had the pulse of a hundred that was not uncommon to him. He got out of bed, to dowse his head in a basin of water. Polly, only half awake, sat up and said: 'What's the matter, dear? Are you ill?' In replying to her he disturbed the children, the door of whose room stood ajar; and by the time quiet was restored, further sleep was out of the question. He dressed and quitted the house.

Day was breaking; the moon, but an hour back a globe of polished silver, had now no light left in her, and stole, a misty ghost, across the dun-coloured sky. A bank of clouds that had had their night-camp on the summit of Mount Warrenheip was beginning to disperse; and the air had lost its edge. He walked out beyond the cemetery, then sat down on a tree-stump and looked back. The houses that nestled on the slope were growing momently whiter; but the Flat was still sunk in shadow and haze, making old Warrenheip, for all its half-dozen miles of distance, seem near enough to be touched by hand. But even in full day-light this woody peak had a way of tricking the eye. From the brow of the western hill, with the Flat out of sight below, it appeared to stand at the very foot of those streets that headed east – first of one, then of another, moving with you as you changed your position, like the eyes of a portrait that follow you wherever you go. – And now the sky was streaked with crimson-madder; the last clouds scattered, drenched in orange and rose, and flames burned in the glass of every window-pane. Up came the tip of the sun's rim, grew to a fiery quarter, to a half; till, bounding free from the horizon, it began to mount and to lose its girth in the immensity of the sky.

The phantasms of the night yielded like the clouds to its power. He was still reasonably young, reasonably sound, and had the better part of a lifetime before him. Rising with a fresh alacrity, he whistled to his dog, and walked briskly home to bath and breakfast.

But that evening, at the heel of another empty day, his nervous restlessness took him anew. From her parlour Polly could hear the thud of his feet, going up and down, up and down his room. And it was she who was to blame for disturbing him!

'Yet what else could I do?'

And meditatively pricking her needle in and out of the window-curtain, Polly fell into a reverie over her husband and his ways. How strange Richard was . . . how difficult! First, to be

183

able to forget all about how things stood with him, and then to be twice as upset as other people.

John demanded the immediate delivery of his young son, undertaking soon to knock all nasty tricks out of him. On the day fixed for Johnny's departure husband and wife were astir soon after dawn. Mahony was to have taken the child down to the coach-office. But Johnny had been awake since two o'clock with excitement, and was now so fractious that Polly tied on her bonnet and accompanied them. She knew Richard's hatred of a scene.

'You just walk on, dear, and get his seat,' she said, while she dragged the cross, tired child on her hand to the public-house, where even at this hour a posse of idlers hung about.

And she did well to be there. Instantly on arriving Johnny set up a wail, because there was talk of putting him inside the vehicle; and this persisted until the coachman, a goat-bearded Yankee, came to the rescue and said he was darned if such a plucky young nipper shouldn't get his way: he'd have the child tied on beside him on the box-seat – be blowed if he wouldn't! But even this did not satisfy Johnny; and while Mahony went to procure a length of rope, he continued to prance round his aunt and to tug ceaselessly at her sleeve.

'Can I dwive, Aunt Polly, can I dwive? Ask him, can I dwive!' he roared, beating her skirts with his fists. He was only silenced by the driver threatening to throw him as a juicy morsel to the gang of bushrangers who, sure as blazes, would be waiting to stick the coach up directly it entered the bush.

Husband and wife lingered to watch the start, when the champing horses took a headlong plunge forward and, together with the coach, were swallowed up in a whirlwind of dust. A last glimpse discovered Johnny, pale and wide-eyed at the lurching speed, but sitting bravely erect.

'The spirit of your brother in that child, my dear!' said Mahony as they made to walk home.

'Poor little Johnny,' and Polly wiped her eyes. 'If only he was going back to a mother who loved him, and would understand.'

'I'm sure no mother could have done more for him than you, love.'

'Yes, but a real mother wouldn't need to give him up, however naughty he had been.'

'I think the young varmint might have shown some regret at parting from you, after all this time,' returned her husband, to whom it was offensive if even a child was lacking in good feeling. 'He never turned his head. Well, I suppose it's a fact, as they say, that the natural child is the natural barbarian.'

'Johnny never meant any harm. It was I who didn't know how to manage him,' said Polly staunchly. — 'Why, Richard, what *is* the matter?' For letting her arm fall Mahony had dashed to the other side of the road.

'Good God, Polly, look at this!'

'This' was a printed notice, nailed to a shed, which announced that a sale of frontages in Mair and Webster Streets would shortly be held.

'But it's not our road. I don't understand.'

'Good Lord, don't you see that if they're there already, they'll be out with us before we can say Jack Robinson? And then where shall I be?' gave back Mahony testily.

'Let us talk it over. But first come home and have breakfast. Then . . . yes, then, I think you should go down and see Mr Henry, and hear what he says.'

'You're right. I must see Ocock. — Confound the fellow! It's he who has let me in for this.'

'And probably he'll know some way out. What else is a lawyer for, dear?'

'Quite true, my Polly. None the less, it looks as if I were in for a run of real bad luck, all along the line.'

CHAPTER FOUR

One hot morning some few days later, Polly, with Trotty at her side, stood on the doorstep shading her eyes with her hand. She was on the look-out for her 'vegetable man', who drove in daily from the Springs with his greenstuff. He was late as usual: if Richard would only let her deal with the cheaper, more punctual Ah Sing, who was at this moment coming up the track. But Devine was a reformed character: after, as a digger, having squandered a fortune in a week, he had given up the drink and, backed by a hard-working, sober wife, was now trying to earn a living at market-gardening. So he had to be encouraged.

The Chinaman jog-trotted towards them, his baskets a-sway, his mouth stretched to a friendly grin. 'You no want cabbagee today? Me got velly good cabbagee,' he said persuasively and lowered his pole.

'No thank you, John, not today. Me wait for white man.'

'Me bling pleasant for lilly missee,' said the Chow; and un-knotting a dirty nosecloth, he drew from it an ancient lump of candied ginger. 'Lilly missee eatee him . . . oh, yum, yum! Velly good. My word!'

But Chinamen to Trotty were fearsome bogies, corresponding to the swart-faced, white-eyed chimney-sweeps of the English nursery. She hid behind her aunt, holding fast to the latter's skirts, and only stealing an occasional peep from one saucer-like blue eye.

'Thank you, John. Me takee chowchow for lilly missee,' said Polly, who had experience in disposing of such savoury morsels.

'You no buy cabbagee today?' repeated Ah Sing, with the catlike persistence of his race. And as Polly, with equal firmness and good-humour, again shook her head, he shouldered his pole and departed at a half-run, crooning as he went.

Meanwhile at the bottom of the road another figure had come into view. It was not Devine in his spring-cart; it was someone

186

on horseback, was a lady, in a holland habit. The horse, a pie-bald, advanced at a sober pace, and — 'Why, good gracious! I believe she's coming here.'

At the first of the three houses the rider had dismounted, and knocked at the door with the butt of her whip. After a word with the woman who opened, she threw her riding-skirt over one arm, put the other through the bridle, and was now making straight for them.

As she drew near she smiled, showing a row of white teeth. 'Does Dr Mahony live here?'

Misfortune of misfortunes! — Richard was out.

But almost instantly Polly grasped that this would tell in his favour. 'He won't be long, I know.'

'I wonder,' said the lady, 'if he would come out to my house when he gets back? I am Mrs Glendinning — of Dandaloo.'

Polly flushed, with sheer satisfaction: Dandaloo was one of the largest stations in the neighbourhood of Ballarat. 'Oh, I'm certain he will,' she answered quickly.

'I am so glad you think so,' said Mrs Glendinning. 'A mutual friend, Mr Henry Ocock, tells me how clever he is.'

Polly's brain leapt at the connection; on the occasion of Richard's last visit the lawyer had again repeated the promise to put a patient in his way. Ocock was one of those people, said Richard, who only remembered your existence when he saw you. — Oh, what a blessing in disguise had been that trouble-some old land-sale!

The lady had stooped to Trotty, whom she was trying to coax from her lurking-place. 'What a darling! How I envy you!'

'Have you no children?' Polly asked shyly, when Trotty's relationship had been explained.

'Yes, a boy. But I should have liked a little girl of my own. Boys are so difficult,' and she sighed.

The horse nuzzling for sugar roused Polly to a sense of her remissness. 'Won't you come in and rest a little, after your ride?' she asked; and without hesitation Mrs Glendinning said she would like to, very much indeed; and tying the horse to the fence, she followed Polly into the house.

The latter felt proud this morning of its apple-pie order. She drew up the best armchair, placed a footstool before it and herself carried in a tray with refreshments. Mrs Glendinning had taken Trotty on her lap, and given the child her long gold chains to play with. Polly thought her the most charming creature in the world. She had a slender waist, and an abundant light brown chignon, and cheeks of a beautiful pink, in which two fascinating dimples came and went. The feather from her riding-hat lay on her neck. Her eyes were the colour of forget-me-nots, her mouth was red as any rose. She had, too, so sweet and natural a manner that Polly was soon chatting frankly about herself and her life, Mrs Glendinning listening with her face pressed to the spun-glass of Trotty's hair.

When she rose, she clasped both Polly's hands in hers. 'You dear little woman . . . may I kiss you? I am ever so much older than you.'

'I am eighteen,' said Polly.

'And I on the shady side of twenty-eight!'

They laughed and kissed. 'I shall ask your husband to bring you out to see me. And take no refusal. *Au revoir!*' and riding off, she turned in the saddle and waved her hand.

For all her pleasurable excitement Polly did not let the grass grow under her feet. There being still no sign of Richard – he had gone to Soldiers' Hill to extract a rusty nail from a child's foot – Ellen was sent to summon him home; and when the girl returned with word that he was on the way, Polly dispatched her to the livery-barn, to order the horse to be got ready.

Richard took the news coolly. 'Did she say what the matter was?'

No, she hadn't; and Polly had not liked to ask her; it could surely be nothing very serious, or she would have mentioned it.

'H'm. Then it's probably as I thought. Glendinning's failing is well known. Only the other day, I heard that more than one medical man had declined to have anything further to do with the case. It's a long way out, and fees are not always forthcoming. *He* doesn't ask for a doctor, and, womanlike, she forgets to pay the bills. I suppose they think they'll try a greenhorn this time.'

Pressed by Polly, who was curious to learn everything about her new friend, he answered: 'I should be sorry to tell you, my dear, how many bottles of brandy it is Glendinning's boast he can empty in a week.'

'Drink? Oh, Richard, how terrible! And that pretty, pretty woman!' cried Polly, and drove her thoughts backwards: she had seen no hint of tragedy in her caller's lovely face. However, she did not wait to ponder, but asked, a little anxiously: 'But you'll go, dear, won't you?'

'Go? Of course I shall! Beggars can't be choosers.'

'Besides, you know, you *might* be able to do something where other people have failed.'

Mahony rode out across the Flat. For a couple of miles his route was one with the Melbourne Road, on which plied the usual motley traffic. Then, branching off at right angles, it dived into the bush – in this case a scantly wooded, uneven plain, burnt tobacco-brown and hard as iron.

Here went no one but himself. He and the mare were the sole living creatures in what, for its stillness, might have been a painted landscape. Not a breath of air stirred the weeping grey-green foliage of the gums; nor was there any bird-life to rustle the leaves, or peck, or chirrup. Did he draw rein, the silence was so intense that he could almost hear it.

On striking the outlying boundary of Dandaloo, he dismounted to slip a rail. After that he was in and out of the saddle, his way leading through numerous gateless paddocks before it brought him up to the homestead.

This, a low white wooden building, overspread by a broad verandah – from a distance it looked like an elongated mushroom – stood on a hill. At the end, the road had run alongside a well-stocked fruit and flower-garden; but the hillside itself, except for a gravelled walk in front of the house, was uncultivated – was given over to dead thistles and brown weeds.

Fastening his bridle to a post, Mahony unstrapped his bag of necessaries and stepped on to the verandah. A row of French windows stood open; but flexible green sun-blinds hid the rooms from view. The front door was a French window, too, differing from the rest only in its size. There was neither bell nor knocker. While he was rapping with the knuckles on the panel, one of the blinds was pushed aside and Mrs Glendinning came out.

She was still in hat and riding-habit; had herself, she said, reached home but half an hour ago. Summoning a station-hand to attend to the horse, she raised a blind and ushered Mahony into the dining-room, where she had been sitting at lunch, alone at the head of a large table. A Chinaman brought fresh plates, and Mahony was invited to draw up his chair. He had an appetite after his ride; the room was cool and dark; there were no flies.

Throughout the meal, the lady kept up a running fire of talk – the graceful chitchat that sits so well on pretty lips. She spoke of the coming Races; of the last Government House Ball; of the

189

untimely death of Governor Hotham. To Mahony she instinctively turned a different side out, from that which had captured Polly. With all her well-bred ease, there was a womanly deference in her manner, a readiness to be swayed, to stand corrected. The riding-dress set off her figure; and her delicate features were perfectly chiselled. ('Though she'll be florid before she's forty.')

Some juicy nectarines finished, she pushed back her chair. 'And now, doctor, will you come and see your patient?'

Mahony followed her down a broad, bare passage. A number of rooms opened off it, but instead of entering one of these she led him out to a back verandah. Here, before a small door, she listened with bent head, then turned the handle and went in.

The room was so dark that Mahony could see nothing. Gradually he made out a figure lying on a stretcher-bed. A watcher sat at the bedside. The atmosphere was more than close, smelt rank and sour. His first request was for light and air.

It was the wreck of a fine man that lay there, strapped over the chest, bound hand and foot to the framework of the bed. The forehead, on which the hair had receded to a few mean grey wisps, was high and domed, the features were straight with plenty of bone in them, the shoulders broad, the arms long. The skin of the face had gone a mahogany brown from exposure, and a score of deep wrinkles ran out fan-wise from the corners of the closed lids. Mahony untied the dirty towels that formed the bandages – they had cut ridges in the limbs they confined – and took one of the heavy wrists in his hand.

'How long has he lain like this?' he asked, as he returned the arm to its place.

'How long is it, Saunderson?' asked Mrs Glendinning. She had sat down on a chair at the foot of the bed; her skirts overflowed the floor.

The watcher guessed it would be since about the same time yesterday.

'Was he unusually violent on this occasion? – for I presume such attacks are not uncommon with him,' continued Mahony, who had meanwhile made a superficial examination of the sick man.

'I am sorry to say they are only too common, doctor,' replied the lady. – 'Was he worse than usual this time, Saunderson?' she turned again to the man; at which fresh proof of her want of knowledge Mahony mentally raised his eyebrows.

'To say trewth, I never see'd the boss so bad before,' answered Saunderson solemnly, grating the palms of the big red hands that hung down between his knees. 'And I've helped him through the jumps more'n once. It's my opinion it would ha' been a narrow squeak for him this time, if me and a mate hadn't nipped in and got these bracelets on him. There he was, ravin' and sweatin' and cursin' his head off, grey as death. Hell-gate, he called it, said he was devil's-porter at hell-gate, and kept hollerin' for napkins and his firesticks. Poor ol' boss! It *was* hell for him and no mistake!'

By dint of questioning Mahony elicited the fact that Glendinning had been unseated by a young horse, three days previously. At the time, no heed was paid to the trifling accident. Later on, however, complaining of feeling cold and unwell, he went to bed, and after lying wakeful for some hours was seized by the horrors of delirium.

Requesting the lady to leave them, Mahony made a more detailed examination. His suspicions were confirmed: there was internal trouble of old standing, rendered acute by the fall. Aided by Saunderson, he worked with restoratives for the best part of an hour. In the end he had the satisfaction of seeing the coma pass over into a natural repose.

'Well, he's through this time, but I won't answer for the next,' he said, and looked about him for a basin in which to wash his hands. 'Can't you manage to keep the drink from him? – or at least to limit him?'

'Nay, the Almighty Himself couldn't do that,' gave back Saunderson, bringing forward soap and a tin dish.

'How does it come that he lies in a place like this?' asked Mahony, as he dried his hands on a corner of the least dirty towel, and glanced curiously round. The room – in size it did not greatly exceed that of a ship's-cabin – was in a state of squalid disorder. Besides a deal table and a couple of chairs, its main contents were rows and piles of old paper-covered magazines, the thick brown dust on which showed that they had not been moved for months – or even years. The whitewashed walls were smoke-tanned and dotted with millions of fly-specks; the dried corpses of squashed spiders formed large black patches; all four corners of the ceiling were festooned with cobwebs.

Saunderson shrugged his shoulders. 'This was his den when he first was manager here, in old Morrison's time, and he's stuck to it ever since. He shuts himself up in here, and won't have a female cross the threshold – nor yet Madam G. herself.'

Having given final instructions, Mahony went out to rejoin the lady.

'I will not conceal from you that your husband is in a very precarious condition.'

'Do you mean, doctor, he won't live long?' She had evidently been lying down: one side of her face was flushed and marked. Crying, too, or he was much mistaken: her lids were red-rimmed, her shapely features swollen.

'Ah, you ask too much of me; I am only a woman; I have no influence over him,' she said sadly, and shook her head.

'What is his age?'

'He is forty-seven.'

Mahony had put him down for at least ten years older, and said so. But the lady was not listening: she fidgeted with her lace-edged handkerchief, looked uneasy, seemed to be in debate with herself. Finally she said aloud: 'Yes, I will.' And to him: 'Doctor, would you come with me a moment?'

This time she conducted him to a well-appointed bedchamber, off which gave a smaller room, containing a little four-poster draped in dimity. With a vague gesture in the direction of the bed, she sank on a chair beside the door.

Drawing the curtains Mahony discovered a fair-haired boy of some eight or nine years old. He lay with his head far back, his mouth wide open – apparently fast asleep.

But the doctor's eye was quick to see that it was no natural sleep. 'Good God! who is responsible for this?'

Mrs Glendinning held her handkerchief to her face. 'I have never told anyone before,' she wept. 'The shame of it, doctor . . . is more than I can bear.'

'Who is the blackguard? Come, answer me, if you please!'

'Oh, doctor, don't scold me . . . I am so unhappy.' The pretty face puckered and creased; the full bosom heaved. 'He is all I have. And such a bright, clever little fellow! You *will* cure him for me, won't you?'

'How often has it happened?'

'I don't know . . . about five or six times, I think . . . perhaps more. There's a place not far from here where he can get it . . . an old hut-cook my husband dismissed once, in a fit of temper – he has oh such a temper! Eddy saddles his pony and rides out there, if he's not watched; and then . . . then, they bring him back . . . like this.'

192

'But who supplies him with money?'

'Money? Oh, but doctor, he can't be kept without pocket-money! He has always had as much as he wanted. – No, it is all my husband's doing,' – and now she broke out in one of those shameless confessions, from which the medical adviser is never safe. 'He hates me; he is only happy if he can hurt me and humiliate me. I don't care what becomes of him. The sooner he dies the better!'

'Compose yourself, my dear lady. Later you may regret such hasty words. – And what has this to do with the child? Come, speak out. It will be a relief to you to tell me.'

'You are so kind, doctor,' she sobbed, and drank, with hysterical gurglings, the glass of water Mahony poured out for her. 'Yes, I will tell you everything. It began years ago – when Eddy was only a tot in jumpers. It used to amuse my husband to see him toss off a glass of wine like a grown-up person; and it *was* comical, when he sipped it, and smacked his lips. But then he grew to like it, and to ask for it, and be cross when he was refused. And then . . . then he learnt how to get it for himself. And when his father saw I was upset about it, he egged him on – gave it to him on the sly. – Oh, he is a bad man, doctor, a *bad*, cruel man! He says such wicked things, too. He doesn't believe in God, or that it is wrong to take one's own life, and he says he never wanted children. He jeers at me because I am fond of Eddy, and because I go to church when I can, and says . . . oh, I know I am not clever, but I am not quite such a fool as he makes me out to be. He speaks to me as if I were the dirt under his feet. He can't bear the sight of me. I have heard him curse the day he first saw me. And so he's only too glad to be able to come between my boy and me . . . in any way he can.'

Mahony led the weeping woman back to the dining-room. There he sat long, patiently listening and advising; sat, till Mrs Glendinning had dried her eyes and was her charming self once more.

The gist of what he said was, the boy must be removed from home at once, and placed in strict, yet kind hands.

Here, however, he ran up against a weak maternal obstinacy. 'Oh, but I couldn't part from Eddy. He is all I have. . . . And so devoted to his mammy.'

As Mahony insisted, she looked the picture of helplessness. 'But I should have no idea how to set about it. And my husband would put every possible obstacle in the way.'

'With your permission I will arrange the matter myself.'

'Oh, how kind you are!' cried Mrs Glendinning again. 'But mind, doctor, it must be somewhere where Eddy will lack none of the comforts he is accustomed to, and where his poor mammy can see him whenever she wishes. Otherwise he will fret himself ill.'

Mahony promised to do his best to satisfy her, and declining, very curtly, the wine she pressed on him, went out to mount his horse which had been brought round.

Following him on to the verandah, Mrs Glendinning became once more the pretty woman frankly concerned for her appearance. 'I don't know how I look, I'm sure,' she said apologetically, and raised both hands to her hair. 'Now I will go and rest for an hour. There is to be opossuming and a moonlight picnic tonight at Warraluen.' Catching Mahony's eye fixed on her with a meaning emphasis, she changed colour. 'I cannot sit at home and think, doctor. I *must* distract myself; or I should go mad.'

When he was in the saddle she showed him her dimples again, and her small, even teeth. 'I want you to bring your wife to see me next time you come,' she said, patting the horse's neck. 'I took a great fancy to her – a sweet little woman!'

But Mahony, jogging downhill, said to himself he would think twice before introducing Polly there. His young wife's sunny, girlish outlook should not, with his consent, be clouded by a knowledge of the sordid things this material prosperity hid from view. A whited sepulchre seemed to him now the richly appointed house, the well-stocked gardens, the acres on acres of good pasture-land: a fair outside when, within, all was foul. He called to mind what he knew by hearsay of the owner. Glendinning was one of the pioneer squatters of the district, had held the run for close on fifteen years. Nowadays, when the land round was entirely taken up, and a place like Ballarat stood within stone's-throw, it was hard to imagine the awful solitude to which the early settlers had been condemned. Then, with his next neighbour miles and miles away, Melbourne, the nearest town, a couple of days' ride through trackless bush, a man was a veritable prisoner in this desert of paddocks, with not a soul to speak to but rough station-hands, and nothing to occupy his mind but the damage done by summer droughts and winter floods. No support or comradeship in the wife either – this poor pretty foolish little woman: 'With the brains of a pigeon!' Glendinning had the name of being intelligent: was it, under

194

these circumstances, matter for wonder that he should seek to drown doubts, memories, inevitable regrets; should be led on to the bitter discovery that forgetfulness alone rendered life endurable? Yes, there was something sinister in the dead stillness of the melancholy bush; in the harsh, merciless sunlight of the late afternoon.

A couple of miles out his horse cast a shoe, and it was evening before he reached home. Polly was watching for him on the doorstep, in a twitter lest some accident had happened or he had had a brush with bushrangers.

'It never rains but it pours, dear!' was her greeting: he had been twice sent for to the Flat, to attend a woman in labour. – And with barely time to wash the worst of the ride's dust off him, he had to pick up his bag and hurry away.

CHAPTER FIVE

'A very striking-looking man! With perfect manners – and beautiful hands.'

Her head bent over her sewing, Polly repeated these words to herself with a happy little smile. They had been told her, in confidence, by Mrs Glendinning, and had been said by this lady's best friend, Mrs Urquhart of Yarangobilly: on the occasion of Richard's second call at Dandaloo, he had been requested to ride to the neighbouring station to visit Mrs Urquhart, who was in delicate health. And of course Polly had passed the flattering opinion on; for, though she was rather a good hand at keeping a secret – Richard declared he had never known a better – yet that secret did not exist – or up till now had not existed – which she could imagine herself keeping from him.

For the past few weeks these two ladies had vied with each other in singing Richard's praises, and in making much of Polly: the second time Mrs Glendinning called she came in her buggy, and carried off Polly, and Trotty, too, to Yarangobilly, where there was a nestful of little ones for the child to play with. Another day a whole brakeful of lively people drove up to the door in the early morning, and insisted on Polly accompanying them, just as she was, to the Racecourse on the road to Creswick's Creek. And everybody was so kind to her that Polly heartily enjoyed herself, in spite of her plain print dress. She won a pair of gloves and a piece of music in a philippine with Mr Urquhart, a jolly, carroty-haired man, beside whom she sat on the box-seat coming home; and she was lucky enough to have half-a-crown on one of the winners. An impromptu dance was got up that evening by the merry party, in a hall in the township; and Polly had the honour of a turn with Mr Henry Ocock, who was most affable. Richard also looked in for an hour towards the end, and valsed her and Mrs Glendinning round.

Polly had quite lost her heart to her new friend. At the outset

Richard had rather frowned on the intimacy – but then he was a person given to taking unaccountable antipathies. In this case, however, he had to yield; for not only did a deep personal liking spring up between the two women, but a wave of pity swept over Polly, blinding her to more subtle considerations. Before Mrs Glendinning had been many times at the house, she had poured out all her troubles to Polly, impelled thereto by Polly's quick sympathy and warm young eyes. Richard had purposely given his wife few details of his visits to Dandaloo; but Mrs Glendinning knew no such scruples, and cried her eyes out on Polly's shoulder.

What a dreadful man the husband must be! 'For she really is the dearest little woman, Richard. And means so well with everyone – I've never heard her say a sharp or unkind word. – Well, not *very* clever, perhaps. But everybody can't be clever, can they? And she's good – which is better. The only thing she seems a teeny-weeny bit foolish about is her boy. I'm afraid she'll never consent to part with him.' – Polly said this to prepare her husband, who was in correspondence on the subject with Archdeacon Long and with John in Melbourne. Richard was putting himself to a great deal of trouble, and would naturally be vexed if nothing came of it.

Polly paid her first visit to Dandaloo with considerable trepidation. For Mrs Urquhart, who herself was happily married – although, it was true, her merry, red-haired husband had the reputation of being a *little* too fond of the ladies, and though he certainly did not make such a paying concern of Yarango-billy as Mr Glendinning of Dandaloo – Mrs Urquhart had whispered to Polly as they sat chatting on the verandah: 'Such a *dreadful* man, my dear! . . . a perfect brute! Poor little Agnes. It is wonderful how she keeps her spirits up.'

Polly, however, was in honour bound to admit that to her the owner of Dandaloo had appeared anything but the monster report made him out to be. He was perfectly sober the day she was there, and did not touch wine at luncheon; and afterwards he had been most kind, taking her with him on a quiet little broad-backed mare to an outlying part of the station, and giving her several hints how to improve her seat. He was certainly very haggard-looking, and deeply wrinkled, and at table his hand shook so that the water in his glass ran over. But all this only made Polly feel sorry for him, and long to help him.

'My dear, you *are* favoured! I never knew James make such

an offer before,' whispered Mrs Glendinning, as she pinned her ample riding-skirt round her friend's slim hips.

The one thing about him that disturbed Polly was his manner towards his wife: he was savagely ironic with her, and trampled hobnailed on her timid opinions. But then Agnes didn't know how to treat him, Polly soon saw that: she was nervous and fluttery – evasive, too; and once during lunch even told a deliberate fib. Slight as was her acquaintance with him, Polly felt sure this want of courage must displease him; for there was something very simple and direct about his own way of speaking.

'My dear, why don't you stand up to him?' asked little Polly.

'Dearest, I dare not. If you knew him as I do, Polly . . . He *terrifies* me. – Oh, what a lucky little woman you are . . . to have a husband like yours.'

Polly had recalled these words that very morning as she stood to watch Richard ride away: never did he forget to kiss her good-bye, or to turn and wave to her at the foot of the road. Each time she admired afresh the figure he cut on horseback: he was so tall and slender, and sat so straight in his saddle. Now, too, he had yielded to her persuasions and shaved off his beard; and his moustache and side-whiskers were like his hair, of an extreme, silky blond. Ever since the day of their first meeting at Beamish's Family Hotel, Polly had thought her husband the handsomest man in the world. And the best, as well. He had his peculiarities, of course; but so had every husband; and it was part of a wife's duty to study them, to adapt herself to them, or to endeavour to tone them down. And now came these older, wiser ladies and confirmed her in her high opinion of him. Polly beamed with happiness at this juncture, and registered a silent vow always to be the best of wives.

Not like – but here she tripped and coloured, on the threshold of her thought. She had recently been the recipient of a very distressing confidence; one, too, which she was not at liberty to share, even with Richard. For, after the relief of a thorough-paced confession, Mrs Glendinning had implored her not to breathe a word to him – 'I could never look him in the face again, love!' Besides, the affair was of such a painful nature that Polly felt little desire to draw Richard into it; it was bad enough that she herself should know. The thing was this: once when Polly had stayed overnight at Dandaloo Agnes Glendinning in a sudden fit of misery had owned to her that she cared for another person more than for her own husband, and that her feelings were returned.

Shocked beyond measure, Polly tried to close her friend's lips. 'I don't think you should mention any names, Agnes,' she cried. 'Afterwards, my dear, you might regret it.'

But Mrs Glendinning was hungry for the luxury of speech – not even to Louisa Urquhart had she broken silence, she wept; and that, for the sake of Louisa's children – and she persisted in laying her heart bare. And here certain vague suspicions that had crossed Polly's mind on the night of the impromptu ball – they were gone again, in an instant, quick as thistledown on the breeze – these suddenly returned, life-size and weighty; and the name that was spoken came as no surprise to her. Yes, it was Mr Henry Ocock to whom poor Agnes was attached. There had been a mutual avowal of affection, sobbed the latter; they met as often as circumstances permitted. Polly was thunderstruck: knowing Agnes as she did, she herself could not believe any harm of her; but she shuddered at the thought of what other people – Richard, for instance – would say, did they get wind of it. She implored her friend to caution. She ought never, never to see Mr Ocock. Why did she not go away to Melbourne for a time? And why had he come to Ballarat?

'To be near me, dearest, to help me if I should need him. – Oh, you can't think what a comfort it is, Polly, to feel that he *is* here – so good, and strong, and clever! – Yes, I know what you mean . . . but this is quite, quite different. Henry does not expect me to be clever, too – does not want me to be. He prefers me as I am. He dislikes clever women . . . would never marry one. And we *shall* marry, darling, some day – when . . .'

Henry Ocock! Polly tried to focus everything she knew of him, all her fleeting impressions, in one picture – and failed. He had made himself very agreeable, the single time she had met him; but . . . There was Richard's opinion of him: Richard did not like him or trust him; he thought him unscrupulous in business, cold and self-seeking. Poor, poor little Agnes! That such a misfortune should befall just her! Stranger still that she, Polly, should be mixed up in it.

She had, of course, always known from books that such things did happen; but then they seemed quite different, and very far away. Her thoughts at this crisis were undeniably woolly; but the gist of them was, that life and books had nothing in common. For in stories the woman who forgot herself was always

199

a bad woman; whereas not the harshest critic could call poor Agnes bad. Indeed, Polly felt that even if someone proved to her that her friend had actually done wrong, she would not on that account be able to stop caring for her, or feeling sorry for her. It was all very uncomfortable and confusing.

While these thoughts came and went, she half sat, half knelt, a pair of scissors in her hand. She was busy cutting out a dress, and no table being big enough for the purpose, had stretched the material on the parlour floor. This would be the first new dress she had had since her marriage; and it was high time, considering all the visiting and going about that fell to her lot just now. Sara had sent the pattern up from Melbourne, and John, hearing what was in the wind, had most kindly and generously made her a present of the silk. Polly hoped she would not bungle it in the cutting; but skirts were growing wider and wider, and John had not reckoned with quite the newest fashion.

Steps in the passage made her note subconsciously that Ned had arrived – Jerry had been in the house for the past three weeks, with a sprained wrist. And at this moment her younger brother himself entered the room, Trotty throned on his shoulder.

Picking his steps round the sea of stuff, Jerry sat down and lowered Trotty to his knee. 'Ned's grizzling for tea.'

Polly did not reply; she was laying an odd-shaped piece of paper now this way, now that.

For a while Jerry played with the child. Then he burst out: 'I say, Poll!' And since Polly paid no heed to his apostrophe: 'Richard says I can get back to work tomorrow.'

'That's a good thing,' answered his sister with an air of abstraction: she had solved her puzzle to within half a yard.

Jerry cast a boyishly imploring glance at her back, and rubbed his chin with his hand. 'Poll, old girl – I say, wouldn't you put in a word for me with Richard? I'm hanged if I want to go back to the claim. I'm sick to death of digging.'

At this Polly did raise her head, to regard him with grave eyes. 'What! tired of work already, Jerry? I don't know what Richard will say to that, I'm sure. You had better speak to him yourself.'

Again Jerry rubbed his chin. 'That's just it – what's so beastly hard. I know he'll say I ought to stick to it.'

'So do I.'

'Well, I'd rather groom the horse than that.'

200

'But think how pleased you were at first!'

Jerry ruefully admitted it. 'One expects to dig out gold like spuds; while the real thing's enough to give you the blight. As for stopping a wages-man all my life, I won't do it. I might just as well go home and work in a Lancashire pit.'

'But Ned —'

'Oh, Ned! Ned walks about with his head in the clouds. He's always blowing of what he's *going* to do, and gets his steam off that way. I'm different.'

But Jerry's words fell on deaf ears. A noise in the next room was engaging Polly's whole attention. She heard a burr of suppressed laughter, a scuffle and what sounded like a sharp slap. Jumping up she went to the door, and was just in time to see Ellen whisk out of the dining-room.

Ned sat in an armchair, with his feet on the chimney-piece. 'I had the girl bring in a log, Poll,' he said; and looked back and up at his sister with his cheery smile. Standing behind him, Polly laid her hand on his hair. 'I'll go and see after the tea.' Ned was so unconcerned that she hesitated to put a question.

In the kitchen she had no such tender scruples; nor was she imposed on by the exaggerated energy with which Ellen bustled about. 'What was that noise I heard in the dining-room just now?' she demanded.

'Noise? I dunno,' gave back the girl crossly without facing her.

'Nonsense, Ellen! Do you think I didn't hear?'

'Oh, get along with you! It was only one of Ned's jokes.' And going on her knees, Ellen set to scrubbing the brick floor with a hiss and a scratch that rendered speech impossible. Polly took up the laden tea-tray and carried it into the dining-room. Richard had come home, and the four drew chairs to the table.

Mahony had a book with him; he propped it open against the butter-cooler, and snatched sentences as he ate. It fell to Ned to keep the ball rolling. Polly was distraite to the point of going wrong in her sugars; Jerry uneasy at the prospect of coming in conflict with his brother-in-law, whom he thought the world of.

Ned was as full of talk as an egg of meat. The theme he dwelt longest on was the new glory that lay in store for the Ballarat diggings. At present these were under a cloud. The alluvial was giving out, and the costs and difficulties of boring through the rock seemed insuperable. One might hear the opinion freely expressed that Ballarat's day as premier gold-field was done.

201

Ned set up this belief merely for the pleasure of demolishing it. He had it at first hand that great companies were being formed to carry on operations. These would reckon their areas in acres instead of feet, would sink to a depth of a quarter of a mile or more, raise washdirt in hundreds of tons per day. One such company, indeed, had already sprung into existence, out on Golden Point; and now was the time to nip in. If he, Ned, had the brass, or knew anybody who'd lend it to him, he'd buy up all the shares he could get. Those who followed his lead would make their fortunes. 'I say, Richard, it'ud be something for you.'

His words evoked no response. Sorry though I shall be, thought Polly, dear Ned had better not come to the house so often in future. I wonder if I need tell Richard why. Jerry was on pins and needles, and even put Trotty ungently from him: Richard would be so disgusted by Ned's blatherskite that he would have no patience left to listen to him.

Mahony kept his nose to his book. As a matter of principle. He made a rule of believing, on an average, about the half of what Ned said. To appear to pay attention to him would spur him on to more flagrant over-statements.

'D'ye hear, Richard? Now's your chance,' repeated Ned, not to be done. 'A very different thing this, I can tell you, from running round dosing people for the collywobbles. I know men who are raising the splosh any way they can to get in.'

'I dare say. There's never been any lack of gamblers on Ballarat,' said Mahony dryly, and passed his cup to be refilled.

Pig-headed fool! was Ned's mental retort, as he sliced a chunk of rabbit-pie. 'Well, I bet you'll feel sore some day you didn't take my advice,' he said aloud.

'We shall see, my lad, we shall see!' replied Mahony. 'In the meantime, let me inform you, I can make good use of every penny I have. So if you've come here thinking you can wheedle something out of me, you're mistaken.' He could seldom resist tearing the veil from Ned's gross hints and impostures.

'Oh no, Richard dear!' interpolated Polly, in her rôle of keeper-of-the-peace.

Ned answered huffily: ' 'Pon my word, I never met such a fellow as you for thinking the worst of people.'

The thrust went home. Mahony clapped his book to. 'You lay yourself open to it, sir! If I'm wrong, I beg your pardon. But for goodness' sake, Ned, put all these trashy ideas of making a fortune out of your mind. Digging is played out, I tell you. Decent people turned their backs on it long ago.'

'That's what I think, too,' threw in Jerry.

Mahony bit his lip. 'Come, come, now, what do you know about it?'

Jerry flushed and floundered, till Polly came to his aid. 'He's been wanting to speak to you, Richard. He hates the work as much as you did.'

'Well, he has a tongue of his own. — Speak for yourself, my boy!'

Thus encouraged, Jerry made his appeal; and fearing lest Richard should throw him, half-heard, into the same category as Ned, he worded it very tersely. Mahony, who had never given much heed to Jerry — no one did — was pleased by his straightforward air. Still, he did not know what could be done for him, and said so.

Here Polly had an inspiration. 'But I think I do. I remember Mr Ocock saying to me the other day he must take another boy into the business, it was growing so — the fourth, this will make. I don't know if he's suited yet, but even if he is, he may have heard of something else. — Only you know, Jerry, you mustn't mind *what* it is. After tea I'll put on my bonnet and go down to the Flat with you. And Ned shall come, too,' she added, with a consoling glance at her elder brother: Ned had extended his huff to his second slice of pie, which lay untouched on his plate.

'Somebody has always got something up her sleeve,' said Mahony affectionately, when Polly came to him in walking costume. 'None the less, wife, I shouldn't be surprised if those brothers of yours gave us some trouble, before we're done with them.'

CHAPTER SIX

In the weeks and months that followed, as he rode from one end of Ballarat to the other – from Yuille's Swamp in the west, as far east as the ranges and gullies of Little Bendigo – it gradually became plain to Mahony that Ned's frothy tales had some body in them after all. The character of the diggings was changing before his very eyes. Nowadays, except on an outlying muddy flat or in the hands of the retrograde Chinese, tubs, cradles, and windlasses were rarely to be met with. Engine-sheds and boiler-houses began to dot the ground; here and there a tall chimney belched smoke, beside a lofty poppet-head or an aerial trolley-line. The richest gutters were found to take their rise below the basaltic deposits; the difficulties and risks of rock-mining had now to be faced, and the capitalist, so long held at bay, at length made free of the field. Large sums of money were being subscribed; and, where these proved insufficient, the banks stepped into the breach with subsidies on mortgages. The population, in whose veins the gold-fever still burned, plunged by wholesale into the new hazard; and under the wooden verandahs of Bridge Street a motley crew of jobbers and brokers came into existence, who would demonstrate to you, *à la* Ned, how you might reap a fortune from a claim without putting in an hour's work on it – without even knowing where it was.

A temptation, indeed! . . . but one that did not affect him. Mahony let the reins droop on his horse's neck, and the animal picked its way among the impedimenta of the bush road. It concerned only those who had money to spare. Months, too, must go by before, from even the most promising of these co-operative affairs, any return was to be expected. As for him, there still came days when he had not a five-pound note to his name. It had been a delusion to suppose that, in accepting John's offer, he was leaving money troubles behind him. Despite Polly's thrift, their improved style of life cost more than he had reckoned; the patients, slow to come, were slower still to discharge their debts. Moreover, he had not guessed how heavily the quarterly payments of interest would weigh on him. With as good as no margin, with the fate of every shilling decided beforehand, the saving up of thirty-odd pounds four times a year was a veritable achievement. He was always in a quake lest he should not be able to get it together. No one suspected what near shaves he had – not even Polly. The last time hardly bore thinking about. At the eleventh hour he had unexpectedly found himself several pounds short. He did not close an eye all night, and got up in the morning as though for his own execution. Then, fortune favoured him. A well-to-do butcher, his hearty: 'What'll yours be?' at the nearest public-house waved aside, had settled his bill off-hand. Mahony could still feel the sudden lift of the black fog-cloud that had enveloped him – the sense of bodily exhaustion that had succeeded to the intolerable mental strain.

For the coming quarter-day he was better prepared – if, that was, nothing out of the way happened. Of late he had been haunted by the fear of illness. The long hours in the saddle did not suit him. He ought to have a buggy, and a second horse. But there could be no question of it in the meantime, or of a great deal else besides. He wanted to buy Polly a piano, for instance; all her friends had pianos; and she played and sang very prettily. She needed more dresses and bonnets, too, than he was able to allow her, as well as a change to the seaside in the summer heat. The first spare money he had should go towards one or the other. He loved to give Polly pleasure; never was such a contented little soul as she. And well for him that it was so. To have had a complaining, even an impatient wife at his side, just now, would have been unbearable. But Polly did not know what impatience meant; her sunny temper, her fixed resolve to make the best of everything was not to be shaken.

Well, comforts galore should be hers some day, he hoped. The practice was shaping satisfactorily. His attendance at Dandaloo had proved a key to many doors: folk of the Glendinnings' and Urquharts' standing could make a reputation or mar it as they chose. It had got abroad, he knew, that at whatever hour of the day or night he was sent for, he could be relied on to be sober; and that unfortunately was not always the case with some of his colleagues. In addition his fellow-practitioners showed signs of waking up to his existence. He had been called in lately to a couple of consultations; and the doyen of the profession on Ballarat, old Munce himself, had praised his handling of a difficult case of version.

The distances to be covered – that was what made the work stiff. And he could not afford to neglect a single summons, no matter where it led him. Still, he would not have grumbled, had only the money not been so hard to get in. But the fifty thousand-odd souls on Ballarat formed, even yet, anything but a stable population: a patient you attended one day might be gone the next, and gone where no bill could reach him. Or he had been sold off at public auction; or his wooden shanty had gone up in a flare – hardly a night passed without a fire somewhere. In these and like accidents the unfortunate doctor might whistle for his fee. It seldom happened nowadays that he was paid in cash. Money was growing as scarce here as anywhere else. Sometimes, it was true, he might have pocketed his fee on the spot, had he cared to ask for it. But the presenting of his palm professionally was a gesture that was denied him. And this stand-offishness drove from people's minds the thought that he might be in actual need of money. Afterwards he sat at home and racked his brains how to pay butcher and grocer. Others of the fraternity were by no means so nice. He knew of some who would not stir a yard unless their fee was planked down before them – old stagers these, who at one time had been badly bitten and were now grown cynically distrustful. Or tired. And indeed who could blame a man for hesitating of a pitch-dark night in the winter rains, or on a blazing summer day, whether or no he should set out on a twenty-mile ride for which he might never see the ghost of a remuneration?

Reflecting thus, Mahony caught at a couple of hard, spicy, grey-green leaves, to chew as he went: the gums, on which the old bark hung in ribbons, were in flower by now, and bore feathery yellow blossoms side by side with nutty capsules. His horse had been ambling forward unpressed. Now it laid its ears flat, and a minute later its master's slower senses caught the clop-clop of a second set of hoofs, the noise of wheels. Mahony had reached a place where two roads joined, and saw a covered buggy approaching. He drew rein and waited.

The occupant of the vehicle had wound the reins round the empty lamp-bracket, and left it to the sagacity of his horse to keep the familiar track, while he dozed, head on breast, in the corner. The animal halted of itself on coming up with its fellow, and Archdeacon Long opened his eyes.

'Ah, good day to you, doctor! – Yes, as you see, enjoying a little nap. I was out early.'

He got down from the buggy and, with bent knees and his hands in his pockets, stretched the creased cloth of his trousers, where this had cut into his flesh. He was a big, brawny, handsome man, with a massive nose, a cloven chin, and the most companionable smile in the world. As he stood, he touched here a strap, there a buckle on the harness of his chestnut – a well-known trotter, with which he often made a match – and affectionately clapped the neck of Mahony's bay. He could not keep his hands off a horse. By choice he was his own stableman, and in earlier life had been a dare-devil rider. Now, increasing weight led him to prefer buggy to saddle; but his recklessness had not diminished. With the reins in his left hand, he would run his light, two-wheeled trap up any wooded, boulder-strewn hill and down the other side, just as in his harum-scarum days he had set it at felled trees, and, if rumour spoke true, wire-fences.

Mahony admired the splendid vitality of the man, as well as the indestructible optimism that bore him triumphantly through all the hardships of a colonial ministry. No sick bed was too remote for Long, no sinner sunk too low to be helped to his feet. The leprous Chinaman doomed to an unending isolation, the drunken Paddy, the degraded white woman – each came in for a share of his benevolence. He spent the greater part of his life visiting the outcasts and outposts, beating up the unbaptized, the unconfirmed, the unwed. But his church did not suffer. He had always some fresh scheme for this on hand: either he was getting up a tea-meeting to raise money for an organ; or a series of penny-readings towards funds for a chancel; or he was training with his choir for a sacred concert. There was a boyish streak in him, too. He would enter into the joys of the annual Sunday-school picnic with a zest equal to the children's own, leading the way, in shirt-sleeves, at leap-frog and obstacle-race. In doctrine he struck a happy mean between low-church practices and ritualism, preaching short, spirited sermons to which even languid Christians could listen without tedium; and on a weekday evening he would take a hand at a rubber of whist or ecarté – and not for love – or play a sound game of chess. A man, too, who, refusing to be bound by the letter of the Thirty-nine Articles, extended his charity even to persons of the Popish faith. In short, he was one of the few to whom Mahony could speak of his own haphazard efforts at criticizing the Pentateuch.

The Archdeacon was wont to respond with his genial smile: 'Ah, it's all very well for you, doctor! – you're a freelance. I am constrained by my cloth. – And frankly, for the rest of us, that kind of thing's too – well, too disturbing. Especially when we have nothing better to put in its place.'

Doctor and parson – the latter, considerably over six feet, made Mahony, who was tall enough, look short and doubly slender – walked side by side for nearly a mile, flitting from topic to topic: the rivalry that prevailed between Ballarats East and West; the seditious uprising in India, where both had relatives; the recent rains, the prospects for grazing. The last theme brought them round to Dandaloo and its unhappy owner. The Archdeacon expressed the outsider's surprise at the strength of Glendinning's constitution, and the lively popular sympathy that was felt for his wife.

'One's heart aches for the poor little lady, struggling to bear up as though nothing were the matter. Between ourselves, doctor' – and Mr Long took off his straw hat to let the air play round his head – 'between ourselves, it's a thousand pities he doesn't just pop off the hooks in one of his bouts. Or that some of you medical gentlemen don't use your knowledge to help things on.'

He let out his great hearty laugh as he spoke, and his companion's involuntary stiffening went unnoticed. But on Mahony voicing his attitude with: 'And his immortal soul, sir? Isn't it the church's duty to hope for a miracle? . . . just as it is ours to keep the vital spark going,' he made haste to take the edge off his words. 'Now, now, doctor, only my fun! Our duty is, I trust, plain to us both.'

It was even easier to soothe than to ruffle Mahony. 'Remember me very kindly to Mrs Long, will you?' he said as the Archdeacon prepared to climb into his buggy. 'But tell her, too, I owe her a grudge just now. My wife's so lost in flannel and brown holland that I can't get a word out of her.'

'And mine doesn't know where she'd be, with this bazaar, if it weren't for Mrs Mahony.' Long was husband to a dot of a woman who, having borne him half-a-dozen children of his own feature and build, now worked as parish clerk and district visitor rolled in one; driving about in sunbonnet and gardening-gloves behind a pair of cream ponies – tiny, sharp-featured, resolute;

with little of her husband's large tolerance, but an energy that outdid his own, and made her an object of both fear and respect. 'And that reminds me: over at the cross-roads by Spring Hill, I met your young brother-in-law. And he told me, if I ran across you to ask you to hurry home. Your wife has some surprise or other in store for you. No, nothing unpleasant! Rather the reverse, I believe. But I wasn't to say more. Well, good day, doctor, good day to you!'

Mahony smiled, nodded and went on his way. Polly's surprises were usually simple and transparent things: someone would have made them a present of a sucking-pig or a bush-turkey, and Polly, knowing his relish for a savoury morsel, did not wish it to be overdone: she had sent similar chance calls out after him before now.

When, having seen his horse rubbed down, he reached home, he found her on the doorstep watching for him. She was flushed, and her eyes had those peculiar high-lights in them which led him jokingly to exhort her to caution: 'Lest the sparks should set the house on fire!'

'Well, what is it, Pussy?' he inquired as he laid his bag down and hung up his wide-awake. 'What's my little surprise-monger got up her sleeve today? Good Lord, Polly, I'm tired!'

Polly was smiling roguishly. 'Aren't you going into the surgery, Richard?' she asked, seeing him heading for the dining-room.

'Aha! So that's it,' said he, and obediently turned the handle. Polly had on occasion taken advantage of his absence to introduce some new comfort or decoration in his room.

The blind had been let down. He was still blinking in the half-dark when a figure sprang out from behind the door, barging heavily against him, and a loud voice shouted: 'Boh, you old beef-brains! Boh to a goose!'

Displeased at such horseplay, Mahony stepped sharply back – his first thought was of Ned having unexpectedly returned from Mount Ararat. Then recognizing the voice, he exclaimed incredulously: '*You*, Dickybird! You!'

'Dick, old man . . . I say, Dick! Yes, it's me right enough, and not my ghost. The old bad egg come back to roost!'

The blind was raised; and the friends, who had last met in the dingy bush hut on the night of the Stockade, stood face to face. And now ensued a babel of greeting, a quick fire of question and answer, the two voices going in and out and round each other, singly and together, like the voices in a duet. Tears rose to Polly's eyes as she listened; it made her heart glow to see Richard so glad. But when, forgetting her presence, Purdy cried: 'And I must confess, Dick . . . I took a kiss from Mrs Polly. Gad, old man, how she's come on!' Polly hastily retired to the kitchen.

At table the same high spirits prevailed: it did not often happen that Richard was brought out of his shell like this, thought Polly gratefully, and heaped her visitor's plate to the brim. His first hunger stilled, Purdy fell to giving a slapdash account of his experiences. He kept to no orderly sequence, but threw them out just as they occurred to him: a rub with bush-rangers in the Black Forest, his adventures as a long-distance drover in the Mildura, the trials of a week he had spent in a boiling-down establishment on the Murray: 'Where the stink was so foul, you two, that I vomited like a dog every day!' Under the force of this Odyssey husband and wife gradually dropped into silence, which they broke only by single words of astonishment and sympathy; while the child Trotty spooned in her pudding without seeing it, her round, solemn eyes fixed un-blinkingly on this new uncle, who was like a wonderful story-book come alive.

In Mahony's feelings for Purdy at this moment, there was none of the old intolerant superiority. He had been dependent for so long on a mere surface acquaintance with his fellows, that he now felt to the full how precious the tie was that bound him to Purdy. Here came one for whom he was not alone the re-served, struggling practitioner, the rather moody man advancing to middle-age; but also the Dick of his boyhood and early youth.

He had often imagined the satisfaction it would be to confide his troubles to Purdy. Compared, however, with the hardships the latter had undergone, these seemed of small importance; and dinner passed without any allusion to his own affairs. And now the chances of his speaking out were slight; he could have been entirely frank only under the first stimulus of meeting.

Even when they rose from the table Purdy continued to hold the stage. For he had turned up with hardly a shirt to his back, and had to be rigged out afresh from Mahony's wardrobe. It was decided that he should remain their guest in the meantime; also that Mahony should call on his behalf on the Commissioner of Police, and put in a good word for him. For Purdy had come back with the idea of seeking a job in the Ballarat Mounted Force.

When Mahony could no longer put off starting on his afternoon round, Purdy went with him to the livery-barn, limping briskly at his side. On the way, he exclaimed aloud at the marvellous changes that had taken place since he was last in the township. There were half-a-dozen gas-lamps in Sturt Street by this time, the gas being distilled from a mixture of oil and gum leaves.

'One wouldn't credit it if one didn't see it with one's own peepers!' he cried, repeatedly bringing up short before the plate-glass windows of the shops, the many handsome, verandahed hotels, the granite front of Christ Church. 'And from what I hear, Dick, now companies have jumped the claims and are deep-sinking in earnest, fortunes'll be made like one o'clock.'

But on getting home again, he sat down in front of Polly and said, with a businesslike air: 'And now tell me all about old Dick! You know, Poll, he's such an odd fish; if he himself doesn't offer to uncork, somehow one can't just pump him. And I want to know everything that concerns him – from A to Z.'

Polly could not hold out against this affectionate curiosity. Entrenching her needle in its stuff, she put her work away and complied. And soon to her own satisfaction. For the first time in her married life she was led to discuss her husband's ways and actions with another; and, to her amazement, she found that it was easier to talk to Purdy about Richard than to Richard himself. Purdy and she saw things in the same light; no rigmarole of explanation was necessary. Now with Richard, it was not so. In conversation with him, one constantly felt that he was not speaking out, or, to put it more plainly, that he was going on meanwhile with his own, very different thoughts. And behind what he did say, there was sure to lurk some imaginary scruple, some rather far-fetched delicacy of feeling which it was hard to get at, and harder still to understand.

CHAPTER SEVEN

Summer had come round again, and the motionless white heat of December lay heavy on the place. The low little houses seemed to cower beneath it; and the smoke from their chimneys drew black, perpendicular lines on the pale sky. If it was a misery at this season to traverse the blazing, dusty roads, it was almost worse to be within-doors, where the thin wooden walls were powerless to keep out the heat, and flies and mosquitoes raged in chorus. Nevertheless, determined Christmas preparations went on in dozens of tiny, zinc-roofed kitchens, the temperature of which was not much below that of the ovens themselves; and kindly, well-to-do people like Mrs Glendinning and Mrs Urquhart drove in hooded buggies, with green fly-veils dangling from their broad-brimmed hats, and dropped a goose here, a turkey there, on their less prosperous friends. They robbed their gardens, too, of the summer's last flowers, arum-lilies and brilliant geraniums, to decorate the Archdeacon's church for the festival; and many ladies spent the whole day beforehand making wreaths and crosses, and festoons to encircle the lamps.

No one was busier than Polly. She wanted to give Purdy, who had been on short commons for so long, a special Christmas treat. She had willing helpers in him and Jerry: the two of them chopped and stoned and stirred, while she, seated on the block of the woodstack, her head tied up in an old pillow-case, plucked and singed the goose that had fallen to her share. Towards four o'clock on Christmas Day they drew their chairs to the table, and with loosened collars set about enjoying the good things. Or pretending to enjoy them. This was Mahony's case; for the day was no holiday for him, and his head ached from the sun. At tea-time Hempel arrived to pay a call, looking very spruce in a long black coat and white tie; and close on his heels followed

212

old Mr Ocock. The latter, having deposited his hat under his seat and tapped several pockets, produced a letter, which he unfolded and handed to Polly with a broad grin. It was from his daughter, and contained the news of his wife's death. 'Died o' the grumbles, I lay you! An' the first good turn she ever done me.' The main point was that Miss Amelia, now at liberty, was already taking advice about the safest line of clipper-ships, and asking for a reply *by return* to a number of extraordinary questions. Could one depend on hearing God's Word preached of a Sunday? Was it customary for *females* to go armed as well as men? Were the blacks *converted*, and what amount of clothing did they wear?

'Thinks she's comin' to the back o' beyond, does Mely!' chuckled the old man, and slapped his thigh at the sudden idea that occurred to him of 'takin' a rise out of 'er'. 'Won't she stare when she gits 'ere, that's all!'

'Well, now you'll simply *have* to build,' said Polly, after threatening to write privately to Miss Amelia, to reassure her. Why not move over west, and take up a piece of ground in the same road as themselves? But from this he excused himself, with a laugh and a spit, on the score that no land-sales had yet been held in their neighbourhood: when he *did* turn out of his present four walls, which had always been plenty good enough for him, he wanted a place he could 'fit up tidy'; which it 'ud stick in his throat to do so, if he thought it might any day be sold over his head. Mahony winced at this. Then laughed, with an exaggerated carelessness. If, in a country like this, you waited for all to be fixed and sure, you would wait till Domesday. None the less, the thrust rankled. It was a fact that he himself had not spent a sou on his premises since they finished building. The thought at the back of *his* mind, too, was, why waste his hard-earned income on improvements that might benefit only the next-comer? The yard they sat in, for instance! Polly had her hens and a ramshackle hen-house; but not a spadeful of earth had been turned towards the wished-for garden. It was just the ordinary colonial backyard, fenced round with rude palings which did not match, and were mended here and there with bits of hoop-iron; its ground space littered with a medley of articles for which there was no room elsewhere: boards left lying by the builders, empty kerosene-tins, a couple of tubs, a ragged cane-chair, some old cases. Wash-lines, on which at the moment a row of stockings hung, stretched permanently from corner to corner; and the whole was dominated by the big round galvanized-iron tank.

On Boxing Day Purdy got the loan of a lorry and drove a large party, including several children, comfortably placed on straw, hassocks and low chairs, to the Races a few miles out. Half Ballarat was making in the same direction; and whoever owned a horse that was sound in the wind and anything of a stepper had entered it for some item on the programme. The Grand Stand, a bark shed open to the air on three sides, was resorted to only in the case of a sudden downpour; the occupants of the dust-laden buggies, wagonettes, brakes, carts and drays preferred to follow events standing on their seats, and on the boards that served them as seats. After the meeting, those who belonged to the Urquhart-Glendinning set went on to Yarangobilly, and danced till long past midnight on the broad verandah. It was nearly three o'clock before Purdy brought his load safely home. Under the round white moon, the lorry was strewn with the forms of sleeping children.

Early next morning while Polly, still only half awake, was pouring out coffee and giving Richard who, poor fellow, could not afford to leave his patients, an account of their doings – with certain omissions, of course: she did not mention the glaring indiscretion Agnes Glendinning had been guilty of, in disappearing with Mr Henry Ocock into a dark shrubbery – while Polly talked, the postman handed in two letters, which were of a nature to put balls and races clean out of her head. The first was in Mrs Beamish's ill-formed hand, and told a sorrowful tale. Custom had entirely gone: a new hotel had been erected on the new road; Beamish was forced to declare himself a bankrupt; and in a few days the Family Hotel, with all its contents, would be put up at public auction. What was to become of them, God alone knew. She supposed she would end her days in taking in washing, and the girls must go out as servants. But she was sure Polly, now so up in the world, with a husband doing so well, would not forget the old friends who had once been so kind to her – with much more in the same strain, which Polly skipped, in reading the letter aloud. The long and short of it was: would Polly ask her husband to lend them a couple of hundred pounds to make a fresh start with, or failing that to put his name to a bill for the same amount?

'Of course she hasn't an idea we were obliged to borrow money ourselves,' said Polly in response to Mahony's ironic laugh. 'I couldn't tell them that.'

'No . . . nor that it's a perpetual struggle to keep the wolf from the door,' answered her husband, battering in the top of an egg with the back of his spoon.

'Oh, Richard dear, things aren't quite so bad as that,' said Polly cheerfully. Then she heaved a sigh. 'I know, of course, we can't afford to help them; but I *do* feel so sorry for them' – she herself would have given the dress off her back. 'And I think, dear, if you didn't mind *very* much, we might ask one of the girls up to stay with us . . . till the worst is over.'

'Yes, I suppose that wouldn't be impossible,' said Mahony. 'If you've set your heart on it, my Polly. If, too, you can persuade Master Purdy to forgo the comfort of your good feather-bed. And I'll see if I can wring out a fiver for you to enclose in your letter.'

Polly jumped up and kissed him. 'Purdy is going anyhow. He said only last night he must look for lodgings near the Police Station.' Here, a thought struck her; she coloured and smiled. 'I'll ask Tilly first,' said she.

Mahony laughed and shook his finger at her. 'The best laid plans o' mice and men! And what's one to say to a match-maker who is still growing out of her clothes?'

At this Polly clapped a hand over his mouth, for fear Ellen should hear him. It was a sore point with her that she had more than once of late had to lengthen her dresses.

As soon as she was alone she sat down to compose a reply to Mrs Beamish. It was no easy job: she was obliged to say that Richard felt unable to come to their aid; and, at the same time, to avoid touching on his private affairs; had to disappoint as kindly as she could; to be truthful, yet tactful. Polly wrote, and re-wrote: the business cost her the forenoon.

She could not even press Tilly to pack her box and come at once; for her second letter that morning had been from Sara, who wrote that, having decided to shake the dust of the colony off her feet, she wished to pay them a flying visit before sailing, '*pour faire mes adieux*'. She signed herself 'Your affectionate sister Zara', and on her arrival explained that, tired of continually instructing people in the pronunciation of her name, she had decided to alter the spelling and be done with it. More-over, a little bird had whispered in her ear that, under its new form, it fitted her rather '*French*' air and looks a thousand times better than before.

Descending from the coach, Zara eyed Polly up and down and vowed she would never have known her; and, on the way home, Polly more than once felt her sister's gaze fixed critically on her. For her part, she was able to assure Zara that she saw no change whatever in her, since her last visit – even since the date of the wedding. And this pleased Zara mightily; for as she admitted, in removing hat and mantle, and passing the damped corner of a towel over her face, she dreaded the ageing effects of the climate on her fine complexion. Close as ever about her own concerns, she gave no reason for her abrupt determination to leave the country; but from subsequent talk Polly gathered that, for one thing, Zara had found her position at the head of John's establishment – 'Undertaken in the first place, my dear, at immense personal sacrifice!' – no sinecure. John had proved a regular martinet; he had countermanded her orders, interfered about the household bills – had even accused her of lining her own pocket. As for little Johnny – the bait originally thrown out to induce her to accept the post – he had long since been sent to boarding-school. 'A thoroughly bad, un-principled boy!' was Zara's verdict. And when Polly, big with pity, expostulated: 'But Zara, he is only six years old!' her sister retorted with a: 'My dear, I know the world, and you don't,' to which Polly could think of no reply.

Zara had announced herself for a bare fortnight's stay; but the man who carried her trunk groaned and sweated under it, and was so insolent about the size of the coin she dropped in his palm that Polly followed him by stealth into the passage, to make it up to a crown. As usual Zara was attired in the height of fashion. She brought a set of 'the hoops' with her – the first to be seen on Ballarat – and once more Polly was torn between an honest admiration of her sister's daring, and an equally honest embarrassment at the notice she attracted. Zara swam and glided about the streets, to the hilarious amazement of the population; floated feather-light, billowing here, depressing there, with all the waywardness of a child's balloon; supported – or so it seemed – by two of the tiniest feet ever bestowed on mortal woman. Aha! but that was one of the chief merits of 'the hoops', declared Zara; that, and the possibility of getting still more stuff into your skirts without materially increasing their weight. There was something in that, conceded Polly, who often felt hers drag heavy. Besides, as she reminded Richard that night, when he lay alternately chuckling and snorting at woman's folly, custom was everything. Once they had smiled at Zara appearing in a hat: 'And now we're all wearing them.'

Another practical consideration that occurred to her she expressed with some diffidence. 'But Zara, don't you . . . I mean . . . aren't they very draughty?'

Zara had to repeat her shocked but emphatic denial in the presence of Mrs Glendinning and Mrs Urquhart, both ladies having a mind to bring their wardrobes up to date. They agreed that there was much to be said in favour of the appliance, over and above its novelty. Especially would it be welcome at those times when . . . But here the speakers dropped into woman's mysterious code of nods and signs; while Zara, turning modestly away, pretended to count the stitches in a crochet-antimacassar.

Yes, nowadays, as Mrs Dr Mahony, Polly was able to introduce her sister to a society worthy of Zara's gifts; and Zara enjoyed herself so well that, had her berth not been booked, she might have contemplated extending her visit. She overflowed with gracious commendation. The house – though, of course, compared with John's splendour, a trifle plain and poky – was a decided advance on the store; Polly herself much improved: 'You *do* look robust, my dear!' And – though Zara held her peace about this – the fact of Mahony's being from home each day, for hours at a stretch, lent an additional prop to her satisfaction. Under these conditions it was possible to keep on good terms with her brother-in-law.

Zara's natty appearance and sprightly ways made her a favourite with everyone – especially the gentlemen. The episcopal bazaar came off at this time; and Zara had the brilliant idea of a bran-pie. This was the success of the entertainment. From behind the refreshment-stall where, with Mrs Long, she was pouring out cups of tea and serving cheesecakes and sausage-rolls by the hundred, Polly looked proudly across the beflagged hall, to the merry group of which her sister was the centre. Zara was holding her own, even with Mr Henry Ocock; and Mr Urquhart had constituted himself her right hand.

'Your sister is no doubt a most fascinating woman,' said Mrs Urquhart from the seat with which she had been accommodated; and heaved a gentle sigh. 'How odd that she should never have married!'

'I'm afraid Zara's too particular,' said Polly. 'It's not for want of being asked.'

Her eyes met Purdy's as she spoke – Purdy had come up laden with empty cups, a pair of infants' boots dangling round his neck – and they exchanged smiles; for Zara's latest *affaire du cœur* was a source of great amusement to them.

Polly had assisted at the first meeting between her sister and Purdy with very mixed feelings. On that occasion Purdy happened to be in plain clothes, and Zara pronounced him charming. The next day, however, he dropped in clad in the double-breasted blue jacket, the high boots and green-veiled cabbage-tree he wore when on duty; and thereupon Zara's opinion of him sank to null, and was not to be raised even by him presenting himself in full dress: white-braided trousers, red-faced shell jacket, pill-box cap, cartouche box and cavalry sword. 'La, Polly! Nothing but a common policeman!' In vain did Polly explain the difference between a member of the ordinary force and a mounted trooper of the gold-escort; in vain lay stress on Richard's pleasure at seeing Purdy buckle to steady work, no matter what. Zara's thoughts had taken wing for a land where such anomalies were not; where you were not asked to drink tea with the well-meaning constable who led you across a crowded thoroughfare or turned on his bull's eye for you in a fog, preparatory to calling up a hackney-cab.

But the chilly condescension with which, from now on, Zara treated him did not seem to trouble Purdy. When he ran in for five minutes of a morning, he eschewed the front entrance and took up his perch on the kitchen-table. From here, while Polly cooked and he nibbled half-baked pastry, the two of them followed the progress of events in the parlour.

Zara's arrival on Ballarat had been the cue for Hempel's reappearance, and now hardly a day went by on which the lay-helper did not neglect his chapel work, in order to pay what Zara called his '*devoirs*'. Slight were his pretexts for coming: a rare bit of dried seaweed for a bookmark; a religious journal with a turned-down page; a nosegay. And though Zara would not nowadays go the length of walking out with a dissenter – she preferred on her airings to occupy the box-seat of Mr Urquhart's four-in-hand – she had no objection to Hempel keeping her company during the empty hours of the forenoon when Polly was lost in domestic cares. She accepted his offerings, mimicked his faulty speech, and was continually hauling him up the precipice of self-distrust, only to let him slip back as soon as he reached the top.

One day Purdy entered the kitchen doubled up with laughter. In passing the front of the house he had thrown a look in at the parlour-window; and the sight of the prim and proper Hempel on his knees on the woolly hearthrug so tickled his sense of humour that, having spluttered out the news, back he went to the passage, where he crouched down before the parlour-door and glued his eye to the keyhole.

'Oh, Purdy, no! What if the door should suddenly fly open?'

But there was something in Purdy's pranks that a laughter-lover like Polly could never for long withstand. Here, now, in feigning to imitate the unfortunate Hempel, he was sheerly irresistible. He clapped his hands to his heart, showed the whites of his eyes, wept, gesticulated and tore his hair; and Polly, after trying in vain to keep a straight face, sat down and went off into a fit of stifled mirth – and when Polly did give way, she was apt to set everyone round her laughing, too. Ellen's shoulders shook; she held a fist to her mouth. Even little Trotty shrilled out her tinny treble, without knowing in the least what the joke was.

When the merriment was at its height, the front door opened and in walked Mahony. An instant's blank amazement, and he had grasped the whole situation – Richard was always so fearfully quick at understanding, thought Polly ruefully. Then, though Purdy jumped to his feet and the laughter died out as if by command, he drew his brows together, and without saying a word, stalked into the surgery and shut the door.

Like a schoolboy who had been caned, Purdy dug his knuckles into his eyes and rubbed his hindquarters – to the fresh delight of Trotty and the girl.

'Well, so long, Polly! I'd better be making tracks. The old man's on the warpath.' And in an undertone: 'Same old grouser! Never *could* take a joke.'

'He's tired. I'll make it all right,' gave Polly back.

– 'It was only his fun, Richard,' she pleaded, as she held out a linen jacket for her husband to slip his arms into.

'Fun of a kind I won't permit in my house. What an example to set the child! What's more, I shall let Hempel know that he is being made a butt of. And speak my mind to your sister about her heartless behaviour.'

'Oh, don't do that, Richard. I promise it shan't happen again. It was very stupid of us, I know. But Purdy didn't really mean it

unkindly; and he *is* so comical when he starts to imitate people.'
And Polly was all but off again, at the remembrance.

But Mahony, stooping to decipher the names Ellen had written on the slate, did not unbend. It was not merely the vulgar joke that had offended him. No, what really rankled was the sudden chill his unlooked-for entrance had cast over the group; they had scattered and gone scurrying about their business, like a pack of naughty children who had been up to mischief behind their master's back. He was the schoolmaster – the spoilsport. They were all afraid of him. Even Polly.

But here came Polly herself to say: 'Dinner, dear', in her kindest tone. She also put her arm round his neck and hugged him. 'Not cross any more, Richard? I know we behaved disgracefully.' Her touch put the crown on her words. Mahony drew her to him and kissed her.

But the true origin of the unpleasantness, Zara, who in her ghoulish delight at seeing Hempel grovel before her – thus Mahony worded it – behaved more kittenishly than ever at table: Zara Mahony could not so easily forgive; and for the remainder of her stay his manner to her was so forbidding that she, too, froze; and to Polly's regret the old bad relation between them came up anew.

But Zara was enjoying herself too well to cut her visit short on Mahony's account. 'Besides, poor thing,' thought Polly, 'she has really nowhere to go.' What she did do was to carry her head very high in her brother-in-law's presence; to speak at him rather than to him; and in private to insist to Polly on her powers of discernment. 'You may say what you like, my dear – I can see you have a *very great deal* to put up with!'

At last, however, the day of her departure broke, and she went off amid a babble of farewells, of requests for remembrance, a fluttering of pocket-handkerchiefs, the like of which Polly had never known; and to himself Mahony breathed the hope that they had seen the last of Zara, her fripperies and affectations. 'Your sister will certainly fit better into the conditions of English life.'

Polly cried at the parting, which might be final; then blew her nose and dried her eyes; for she had a busy day before her. Tilly Beamish had been waiting with ill-concealed impatience for Zara to vacate the spare room, and was to arrive that night.

Mahony was not at home to welcome the new-comer, nor could he be present at high tea. When he returned, towards nine o'clock, he found Polly with a very red face, and so full of fussy cares for her guest's comfort – her natural kindliness distorted to caricature – that she had not a word for him. One look at Miss Tilly explained everything, and his respects duly paid he retired to the surgery, to indulge a smile at Polly's expense. Here Polly soon joined him, Tilly, fatigued by her journey and by her bounteous meal, having betaken herself early to bed.

'Ha, ha!' laughed Mahony, not without a certain mischievous satisfaction at his young wife's discomfiture. 'And with the prospect of a second edition to follow!'

But Polly would not capitulate right off. 'I don't think it's very kind of you to talk like that, Richard,' she said warmly. 'People can't help their looks.' She moved about the room putting things straight, and avoiding his eye. 'As long as they mean well and are good. . . . But I think you would rather no one ever came to stay with us, at all.'

Fixing her with meaning insistence and still smiling, Mahony opened his arms. The next moment Polly was on his knee, her face hidden in his shoulder. There she shed a few tears. 'Oh, isn't she dreadful? I don't know *what* I shall do with her. She's been serving behind the bar, Richard, for more than a year. And she's come expecting to be taken everywhere and to have any amount of gaiety.'

At coach-time she had dragged a reluctant Purdy to the office. But as soon as he caught sight of Tilly: 'On the box, Richard, beside the driver, with her hair all towsy-wowsy in the wind – he just said: "Oh, lor, Polly!" and disappeared, and that was the last I saw of him. I don't know how I should have got on if it hadn't been for old Mr Ocock, who was down meeting a parcel. He was most kind; he helped us home with her carpet-bag, and saw after her trunk. And, oh dear, what do you think? When he was going away he said to me in the passage – so loud I'm sure Tilly must have heard him – he said: "Well! that's something like a figure of a female this time, Mrs Doc. As fine a young woman as ever I see!" '

And Polly hid her face again; and husband and wife laughed in concert.

CHAPTER EIGHT

That night a great storm rose. Mahony, sitting reading after everyone else had retired, saw it coming, and lamp in hand went round the house to secure hasps and catches; then stood at the window to watch the storm's approach. In one half of the sky the stars were still peacefully alight; the other was hidden by a dense cloud, which came racing along like a giant bat with outspread wings, devouring the stars in its flight. The storm broke; there was a sudden shrill screeching, a grinding, piping, whistling, and the wind hurled itself against the house as if to level it with the ground; failing in this, it banged and battered, making windows and doors shake like loose teeth in their sockets. Then it swept by to wreak its fury elsewhere, and there was a grateful lull out of which burst a peal of thunder. And now peal followed peal, and the face of the sky, with its masses of swirling, frothy cloud, resembled an angry sea. The lightning ripped it in fierce zigzags, darting out hundreds of spectral fangs. It was a magnificent sight.

Polly came running to see where he was, the child cried, Miss Tilly opened her door by a hand's-breadth, and thrust a red, puffy face, framed in curl-twists, through the crack. Nobody thought of sleep while the commotion lasted, for fear of fire: once alight, these exposed little wooden houses blazed like heaps of shavings. The clock-hands pointed to one before the storm showed signs of abating. Now, the rain was pouring down, making an ear-splitting din on the iron roof and leaping from every gutter and spout. It had turned very cold. Mahony shivered as he got into bed.

He seemed hardly to have closed an eye when he was wakened by a loud knocking; at the same time the wire of the nightbell was almost wrenched in two. He sat up and looked at his watch. It wanted a few minutes to three; the rain was still falling in torrents, the wind sighed and moaned. Wild horses should not drag him out on such a night! Thrusting his arms into the sleeves of his dressing-gown, he threw up the parlour window. 'Who's there?' The hiss of the rain cut his words through.

A figure on the doorstep turned at the sound. 'Is this a doctor's? I wuz sent here. Doctor! for God's sake . . .'

'What is it? Stop a minute! I'll open the door.'

He did so, letting in a blast of wind and a rush of rain that flooded the oilcloth. The intruder, off whom the water streamed, had to shout to make himself audible.

'It's me – Mat Doyle's me name! It's me wife, doctor; she's dying. I've bin all night on the road. Ah, for the love of –'

'Where is it?' Mahony put his hand to the side of his mouth, to keep his words from flying adrift in the wind.

'Paddy's Rest. You're the third I've bin to. Not one of the dirty dogs'ull stir a leg! Me girl may die like a rabbit for all they care.' – The man's voice broke, as he halloed particulars.

'Paddy's Rest? On a night like this? Why, the creek will be out.'

'Doctor! you're from th' ould country, I can hear it in your lip. Haven't you a wife, too, doctor? Then show a bit o' mercy to mine!'

'Tut, tut, man, none of that!' said Mahony curtly. 'You should have bespoken me at the proper time to attend your wife. – Besides, there'll be no getting along the road tonight.'

The other caught the note of yielding. 'Sure an' you'd go out, doctor dear, without thinkin', to save your dog if he was drownin'. I've got me buggy down there; I'll take you safe. And you shan't regret it; I'll make it worth your while, by the Lord Harry I will!'

'Pshaw!' – Mahony opened the door of the surgery and struck a match. It was a rough grizzled fellow – a 'cocky', on his own showing – who presented himself in the lamplight. His wife had fallen ill that afternoon. At first everything seemed to be going well; then she was seized with fits, had one fit after another, and all but bit her tongue in two. There was nobody with her but a young girl he had fetched from a mile away. He had meant, when her time came, to bring her to the District Hospital. But they had been taken unawares. While he waited he sat with his elbows on his knees, his face between his clenched fists.

In dressing, Mahony reassured Polly, and instructed her what to say to people who came inquiring after him; it was unlikely he would be back before afternoon. Most of the patients could wait till then. The one exception, a case of typhoid in its second week, a young Scotch surgeon, Brace, whom he had obliged in a similar emergency, would no doubt see for him – she should send Ellen down with a note. And having poured Doyle out a nobbler and put a flask in his own pocket, Mahony reopened the front door to the howl of the wind.

The lantern his guide carried shed only a tiny circle of light on the blackness; and the two men picked their steps gingerly along the flooded road. The rain ran in jets off the brim of Mahony's hat, and down the back of his neck.

Having climbed into the buggy they advanced at a funeral pace, leaving it to the sagacity of the horse to keep the track. At the creek, sure enough, the water was out, the bridge gone. To reach the next bridge, five miles off, a crazy cross-country drive would have been necessary; and Mahony was for giving up the job. But Doyle would not acknowledge defeat. He unharnessed the horse, set Mahony on its back, and himself holding to its tail, forced the beast, by dint of kicking and lashing, into the water; and not only got them safely across, but up the steep sticky clay of the opposite bank. It was six o'clock and a cloudless morning when, numb with cold, his clothing clinging to him like wet seaweed, Mahony entered the wooden hut where the real work he had come out to do began.

Later in the day, clad in an odd collection of baggy garments, he sat and warmed himself in the sun, which was fast drawing up in the form of a blankety mist the moisture from the ground. He had successfully performed, under the worst possible conditions, a ticklish operation; and was now so tired that, with his chin on his chest, he fell fast asleep.

Doyle wakened him by announcing the arrival of the buggy. The good man, who had had more than one nobbler during the morning, could not hold his tongue, but made still another wordy attempt to express his gratitude. 'Whither me girl lives or dies, it'll not be Mat Doyle who forgits what you did for him this night, doctor! An' if iver you want a bit o' work done, or someone to do your lyin' awake at night for you, just you gimme the tip. I don't mind tellin' you now, I'd me shootin'-iron here' – he touched his right hip – 'an' if you'd refused – you was the third, mind you, – I'd have drilled you where you stood, God damn me if I wouldn't!'

Mahony eyed the speaker with derision. 'Much good that would have done your wife, you fathead! Well, well, we'll say nothing to *mine*, if you please, about anything of that sort.'

'No, may all the saints bless 'er and give 'er health! An' as I say, doctor . . .' In speaking he had drawn a roll of banknotes from his pocket, and now he tried to stuff them between Mahony's fingers.

'What's this? My good man, keep your money till it's asked for!' and Mahony unclasped his hands, so that the notes fluttered to the ground.

'Then there let 'em lay!'

But when, in clothes dried stiff as cardboard, Mahony was rolling townwards – his coachman, a lad of some ten or twelve who handled the reins to the manner born – as they went he chanced to feel in his coat pocket, and there found five ten-pound notes rolled up in a neat bundle.

The main part of the road was dry and hard again; but all dips and holes were wells of liquid mud, which bespattered the two of them from top to toe as the buggy bumped carelessly in and out. Mahony diverted himself by thinking of what he could give Polly with this sum. It would serve to buy that pair of gilt cornices or the heavy gilt-framed pierglass on which she had set her heart. He could see her, pink with pleasure, expostulating: 'Richard! What *wicked* extravagance!' and hear himself reply: 'And pray may my wife not have as pretty a parlour as her neighbours?' He even cast a thought, in passing, on the pianoforte with which Polly longed to crown the furnishings of her room – though, of course, at least treble this amount would be needed to cover its cost. – But a fig for such nonsense! He knew but one legitimate use to make of the unexpected little windfall, and that was, to put it by for a rainy day. 'At my age, in my position, I *ought* to have fifty pounds in the bank!' – times without number he had said this to himself, with a growing impatience. But he had not yet managed to save a halfpenny. Thrive as the practice might, the expenses of living held even pace with it. And now, having got its cue, his brain started off again on the old treadmill, reckoning, totting up, finding totals, or more often failing to find them, till his head was as hot as his feet were cold. Today he could not think clearly at all.

Nor the next day either. By the time he reached home he was conscious of feeling very ill: he had lancinating pains in his limbs, a chill down his spine, an outrageous temperature. To set out again on a round of visits was impossible. He had just to tumble into bed.

He got between the sheets with that sense of utter well-being, of almost sensual satisfaction, which only one who is shivering with fever knows. And at first very small things were enough to fill him with content: the smoothness of the pillow's sleek linen; the shadowy light of the room after long days spent in the dusty glare outside; the possibility of resting, the knowledge that it was his duty to rest; Polly's soft, firm hands, which were always of the right temperature — warm in the cold stage, cool when the fever scorched him, and neither hot nor cold when the dripping sweats came on. But as the fever declined, these slight pleasures lost their hold. Then he was ridden to death by black thoughts. Not only was day being added to day, he meanwhile not turning over a penny; but ideas which he knew to be preposterous insinuated themselves in his brain. Thus, for hours on end he writhed under the belief that his present illness was due solely to the proximity of the Great Swamp, and lay and cursed his folly in having chosen just this neighbourhood to build in. Again, there was the case of typhoid he had been anxious about, prior to his own breakdown: under his *locum*, peritonitis had set in and carried off the patient. At the time he had accepted the news from Polly's lips with indifference — too ill to care. But a little later the knowledge of what it meant broke over him, and he suffered the tortures of the damned. Not Brace; he alone would be held responsible for the death; and perhaps not altogether unjustly. Lying there, a prey to morbid apprehensions, he rebuilt the case in memory, struggling to recall each slight variation in temperature, each swift change for better or worse; but as fast as he captured one such detail, his drowsy brain let the last but one go, and he had to beat it up anew. During the night he grew confident that the relatives of the dead woman intended to take action against him, for negligence or improper attendance.

An attempt to speak of these devilish imaginings to wife and friend was a failure. He undertook it in a fit of desperation, when it seemed as if only a strong and well grounded opposition would save his reason. But this was just what he could not get. Purdy, whom he tried first, held the crude notion that a sick person should never be gainsaid; and soothingly sympathized and agreed, till Mahony could have cried aloud at such blundering stupidity. Polly did better; she contradicted him. But not in the right way. She certainly pooh-poohed his idea of the nearness of Yuille's Swamp making the house unhealthy; but she did not argue the matter, step by step, and *convince* him that he was wrong. She just laughed at him as at a foolish child, and kissed him, and tucked him in anew. And when it came to the typhoid's fatal issue, she had not the knowledge needed to combat him with any chance of success. She heard him anxiously out, and allowed herself to be made quite nervous over a possible fault on his part, so jealous was she for his growing reputation.

So that in the end it was he who had to comfort her.

'Don't take any notice of what I say today, wife. It's this blessed fever. . . . I'm light-headed, I think.'

But he could hear her uneasily consulting with Purdy in the passage.

It was not till his pulse beat normally again that he could smile at his exaggerated fears. Now, too, reviving health brought back a wholesome interest in everyday affairs. He listened with amusement to Polly's account of the shifts Purdy was reduced to, to enter the house unseen by Miss Tilly. On his faithful daily call, the young man would creep round by the back door, and Tilly was growing more and more irate at her inability to waylay him. Yes, Polly was rather redly forced to admit, she *had* abetted him in his evasions. ('You know, Poll, I might just as well tie myself up to old Mother B. herself and be done with it!') Out of sheer pique Tilly had twice now accepted old Mr Ocock's invitation to drive with him. Once, she had returned with a huge bag of lollies; and once, with a face like a turkey-cock. Polly couldn't help thinking . . . no, really, Richard, she could not! . . . that perhaps something might *come* of it. He should not laugh; just wait and see.

Many inquiries had been made after him. People had missed their doctor, it seemed, and wanted him back. It was a real red-letter day when he could snap to the catches of his gloves again, and mount the step of a buggy.

He had instructed Purdy to arrange for the hire of this vehicle, saddle-work being out of the question for him in the meantime. And on his first long journey – it led him past Doyle's hut, now, he was sorry to see, in the hands of strangers; for the wife, on the way to making a fair recovery, had got up too soon, over-taxed her strength and died, and the broken-hearted husband was gone off no one knew where – on this drive, as mile after mile slid from under the wheels, Mahony felt how grateful was the screen of a hood between him and the sun.

While he was laid up, the eternal question of how to live on his income had left him, relatively speaking, in peace. He had

227

of late adopted the habit of doing his scraping and saving at the outset of each quarter, so as to get the money due to Ocock put by betimes. His illness had naturally made a hole in this; and now the living from hand to mouth must begin anew.

With what remained of Doyle's money he proposed to settle his account at the livery-stable. Then the unexpected happened. His reappearance – he looked very thin and washed-out – evidently jogged a couple of sleepy memories. Simultaneously two big bills were paid, one of which he had entirely given up. In consequence, he again found himself fifty pounds to the good. And driving to Ocock's office, on term day, he resolved to go on afterwards to the Bank of Australasia and there deposit this sum.

Grindle, set off by a pair of flaming 'sideboards', himself ushered Mahony into the sanctum, and the affair was disposed of in a trice. Ocock was one of the busiest of men nowadays – he no longer needed to invent sham clients and fictitious interviews – and he utilized the few odd minutes it took to procure a signature, jot down a note, open a drawer, unlock a tin box to remark abstractedly on the weather and put a polite inquiry: 'And your good lady? In the best of health, I trust?'

On emerging from the inner room, Mahony saw that the places formerly filled by Tom and Johnny were occupied by strangers; and he was wondering whether it would be indiscreet to ask what had become of the brothers, when Ocock cut across his intention. 'By the way, Jenkins, has that memorandum I spoke of been drawn up?' he turned to a clerk.

With a sheet of foolscap in his hand, he invited Mahony with a beck of the chin to re-enter his room. 'Half a moment! Now, doctor, if you happen to have a little money lying idle, I can put you on to a good thing – a very good thing indeed. I don't know, I'm sure, whether you keep an eye on the fluctuations of the share-market. If so, you'll no doubt have noticed the . . . let me say the extreme instability of "Porepunkahs". After making an excellent start, they have dropped till they are now to be had at one-twentieth of their original value.'

He did not take much interest in mining matters was Mahony's reply. However he knew something of the claim in question, if only because several of his acquaintances had abandoned their shares, in disgust at the repeated calls and the lack of dividends.

'Exactly. Well now, doctor, I'm in a position to inform you that "Porepunkahs" will very shortly be prime favourites on the market, selling at many times their original figure – their *original* figure, sir! No one with a few hundreds to spare could find a better investment. Now is the time to buy.'

A few hundreds! . . . what does he take me for? thought Mahony; and declined the transaction off-hand. It was very good of Mr Ocock to think of him; but he preferred to keep clear of that kind of thing.

'Quite so, quite so!' returned Ocock suavely, and dry-washed his hands with the smile Mahony had never learnt to fathom. 'Just as you please, of course. – I'll only ask you, doctor, to treat the matter as strictly confidential.'

'I suppose he says the same to everyone he tells,' was Mahony's comment as he flicked up his horse; and he wondered what the extent might be of the lawyer's personal interest in the 'Porepunkah Company'. Probably the number of shareholders was not large enough to take up the capital.

Still, the incident gave him food for thought, and only after closing time did he remember his intention of driving home by way of the bank.

Later in the day he came back on the incident, and pondered his abrupt refusal of Ocock's offer. There was nothing unusual in this: he never took advice well; and, was it forced upon him, nine times out of ten a certain inborn contrariness drove him to do just the opposite. Besides, he had not yet learned to look with lenience on the rage for speculation that had seized the people of Ballarat; and he held that it would be culpable for a man of his slender means to risk money in the great game.– But was there any hint of risk in the present instance? To judge from Ocock's manner, the investment was as safe as a house, and lucrative to a degree that made one's head swim. 'Many times their original figure!' An Arabian-nights fashion of growing rich, and no mistake! Very different from the laborious grind of *his* days, in which he had always to reckon with the chance of not being paid at all. That very afternoon had brought him a fresh example of this. He was returning from the Old Magpie Lead, where he had been called to a case of scarlet fever, and saw himself covering the same road daily for some time to come. But he had learned to adjudge his patients in a winking; and these, he could swear to it, would prove to be non-payers; of a kind even to cut and run, once the child was out of danger. Was he really justified, cramped for money as he was, in rejecting the straight tip Ocock had given him? And he debated this moot

229

point – argued his need against his principles – the whole way home.

As soon as he had changed and seen his suspect clothing hung out to air, he went impetuously back to Ocock's office. He had altered his mind. A small gift from a grateful patient: yes, fifty, please; they might bring him luck. – And he saw his name written down as the owner of half a hundred shares.

After this, he took a new interest in the mining sheet of the *Star*; turned to it, indeed, first of all. For a week, a fortnight, 'Porepunkahs' remained stationary; then they made a call, and, if he did not wish to forfeit, he had to pay out as many shillings as he held shares. A day or two later they sank a trifle, and Mahony's hopes with them. There even came a day when they were not mentioned; and he gave up his money for lost. But of a sudden they woke to life again, took an upward bound, and within a month were quoted at five pounds – on rumour alone. 'Very sensitive indeed,' said the *Star*. Purdy, his only confidant, went about swearing at himself for having let the few he owned lapse; and Mahony itched to sell. He could now have banked two hundred and fifty pounds.

But Ocock laughed him out of countenance – even went so far as to pat him on the shoulder. On no account was he to think of selling. 'Sit tight, doctor . . . sit tight! Till I say the word.'

And Mahony reluctantly obeyed.

CHAPTER NINE

In the course of the following winter John Turnham came to stand as one of two candidates for the newly proclaimed electoral district of Ballarat West.

The first news his relatives had of his intention was gleaned from the daily paper. Mahony lit on the paragraph by chance one morning; said: 'Hullo! Here's something that will interest you, my dear,' and read it aloud.

Polly laid down her knife and fork, pushed her plate from her, and went pink with pleasure and surprise. 'Richard! You don't mean it!' she exclaimed, and got up to look over his shoulder. Yes, there it was — John's name in all the glory of print. 'Mr John Millibank Turnham, one of the foremost citizens and most highly respected denizens of our marvellous metropolis, and a staunch supporter of democratic rights and the interests of our people.' Polly drew a deep breath. 'Do you know, Richard, I shouldn't wonder if he came to live on Ballarat — I mean if he gets in. — Does Trotty hear? This is Trotty's papa they're writing about in the papers. — Of course we must ask him to stay with us.' For this happened during an interregnum, when the spare room was temporarily out of use.

'Of course we must do nothing of the kind. Your brother will need the best rooms Bath's can give him; and when he's not actually on the hustings, he'll be hobnobbing in the bar, standing as many drinks as there are throats in the crowd,' gave back Mahony, who had the lowest possible opinion of colonial politics.

'Well, at least I can write and tell him how delighted we are,' said Polly, not to be done.

'Find out first, my dear, if there's any truth in the report. I can hardly think John would have left us in the dark to this extent.'

But John corroborated the news; and, in the letter Polly read

231

out a week later, announced the opening of his campaign for the coming month.

I shall feel much obliged to your husband if he will meanwhile exert his influence on my behalf. He is no doubt acquainted professionally with many of the leading squatters round Ballarat, whom he can induce to support my candidature.

'Umph!' said Mahony grumpily, and went on scooping out his egg. 'We're good enough to tout for him.'

'Ssh!' warned Polly, with a glance at Trotty. 'Think what it means to him, Richard, and to us, too. It will do your practice ever so much good if he gets in – to be the brother-in-law of the member! We must help all we can, dear.'

She was going driving to Yarangobilly that day with Archdeacon Long to see a new arrival Richard had recently brought into the world; and now she laid plans to kill two birds with one stone, entering into the scheme with a gusto that astonished Mahony. 'Upon my word, wife, I believe you're glad to have something to do.'

'Will my own papa gimme a dolly? . . . like Uncle Papa?' here piped Trotty.

'Perhaps. But you will have to be a *very* good girl, and not talk with your mouth full or dirty your pinnies. Oh, here's a postscript!' Polly had returned to the sheet, and was gloating over it. 'John writes:

Especially must he endeavour to win Lawyer Ocock over to my side. I lay great weight on O.'s support.

Oh, Richard, now *isn't* that unfortunate? I do hope it won't make any difference to John's chances.'

Polly's dismay had good grounds. A marked coolness had sprung up between her husband and the lawyer; and on no account, she knew, would Richard consent to approach Mr Henry. Some very hot remarks made by the latter had been passed on to her by Mrs Glendinning. She had not dared to tell Richard the worst.

The coolness dated from an afternoon when Tilly Beamish had burst into the house in a state of rampant excitement. 'Oh, Polly! oh, I say! my dear, whatever do you think? That old cove – old O. – 'as actually had the cheek to make me a proposal.'

'Tilly!' gasped Polly, and flushed to the roots of her hair. 'Oh, my dear, I *am* pleased!' For Polly's conscience was still somewhat tender about the aid she had lent Purdy in his evasions. The two women kissed, and Tilly cried a little. 'It's certainly her first offer,' thought Mrs Polly. Aloud, she asked hesitatingly: 'And do you . . . shall you . . . I mean, are you going to accept him, Tilly?'

But this was just where Tilly could not make up her mind: should she take him, or should she not? For two whole days she sat about debating the question; and Polly listened to her with all the sympathy and interest so momentous a step deserved.

'If you feel you could really learn to care for him, dear. Of course it *would* be nice for you to have a house of your own. And how happy it would make poor mother to see you settled!'

Tilly tore the last veil from her feelings, uttered gross confidences. Polly knew well enough where her real inclination lay. 'I've hoped against hope, Poll, that a *certain person* would come to the scratch at last.' Yes, it was true enough, he had nothing to offer her; but she wasn't the sort to have stuck at that. 'I'd have worked my hands to the bone for 'im, Poll, if 'e'd *only* said the word.' The one drawback to marriage with 'you know 'oo' would have been his infirmity. 'Some'ow, Polly, I can't picture myself dragging a husband with a gammy leg at my heels.' From this, Tilly's mind glanced back to the suitor who had honourably declared himself. Of course, 'old O.' hadn't a great deal of the gentleman about him; and their ages were unsuitable. ' 'E owns to fifty-eight, and as you know, Poll, I'm only just turned twenty-five,' at which Polly drooped her head a little lower over the handkerchief she was hemming, to avoid meeting her friend's eye. Poor dear Tilly! she would never see thirty again; and she need hardly have troubled, thought Polly, to be insincere with her. But in the same breath she took back the reproach. A woman herself, she understood something of the fear, and shame, and heartburning that had gone to the making of the lie. Perhaps, too, it was a gentle hint from Tilly what age she now wished to be considered. And so Polly agreed, and said tenderly: yes, certainly, the difference was very marked. Meanwhile Tilly flowed on. These were the two chief objections. On the other hand, the old boy was ludicrously smitten; and she thought one might trust her, Tilly B., to soon knock him into shape. It would also, no doubt, be possible to squeeze a few pounds out of him towards assisting 'pa and ma' in their present struggle. Again, as a married woman she would have a chance of helping Jinny to find a husband: 'Though Jinn's gone off so, Polly, I bet you'd hardly know her if you met 'er in the street.' To end all, a bird in hand, etc.; and besides, what prospects had she, if she remained a spinster?

So, when she was asked, Tilly accepted without further humming and hawing an invitation to drive out in the smart dog-cart Mr Ocock had hired for the purpose; and Polly saw her off with many a small private sign of encouragement. All went well. A couple of hours later Tilly came flying in, caught Polly up in a bear's hug, and danced her round the room. 'My dear, wish me joy! – Oh, lor, Polly, I *do* feel 'appy!' She was wearing a large half-hoop of diamonds on her ring-finger: nothing would do 'old O.' but that they should drive there and then to the finest jeweller's in Sturt Street, where she had the pick of a trayful. And now Mr Ocock, all a-smirk with sheepish pride, was fetched in to receive congratulations; and Polly produced refreshments; and healths were drunk. Afterwards the happy couple dallied in the passage and loitered on the doorstep, till evening was far advanced.

It was Polly who, in clearing away, was struck dumb by the thought: 'But now whatever is to become of Miss Amelia?'

She wondered if this consideration troubled the old man. Trouble there was, of some sort: he called at the house three days running for a word with Richard. He wore a brand-new pair of shepherd's-plaid trousers, a choker that his work-stained hands had soiled in tying, a black coat, a massive gold watch-chain. On the third visit he was lucky enough to catch Mahony, and the door of the surgery closed behind them.

Here Mr Ocock sat on the extreme edge of a chair; alternately crushed his wide-awake flat between his palms and expanded it again, as though he were playing a concertina; and coughed out a wordy preamble. He assured Mahony, to begin with, how highly he esteemed him. It was because of this, because he knew doctor was as straight as a pound of candles, that he was going to ask his advice on an awkward matter – devilish awkward! – one nobody had any idea of either – except Henry. And Henry had kicked up such a deuce of a row at his wanting to marry again, that he was damned if he'd have anything more to do with him. Besides, doctor knew what lawyers were – the whole breed of 'em! Sharp as needles – especially Henry – but with a sort of squint in their upper storey that made 'em see every mortal thing from the point of law. And that was no good to him. What he needed was a plain and honest, a . . . he hesitated for a word and repeated, 'a *honest* opinion'; for he only wanted to do the right thing, what was straight and above board. And at last out it came: did 'doc.' think it would be acting on the square, and not taking a low-down advantage of a female, if he omitted to mention to 'the future Mrs O.' that, up till six months back, he had been obliged to . . . well, he'd spit it out short and say, obliged to report himself to the authorities at fixed intervals? Women were such shy cattle, so damned odd! You never knew how they'd take a thing like this. One might raise Cain over it, another only laugh, another send him packing. He didn't want to let a fine young woman like Matilda slip if he could help it, by dad he didn't! But he felt he must either win her by fair dealing or not at all. And having got the load off his chest, the old colonist swallowed hard, and ran the back of his hand over his forehead.

He had kept his eyes glued to the table-leg in speaking, and so saw neither his hearer's involuntary start at the damaging disclosure, nor the nervous tightening of the hand that lay along the arm of the chair. Mahony sat silent, balancing a paper-knife, and fighting down a feeling of extraordinary discomfort – his very finger-tips curled under the strain. It was of little use to remind himself that, ever since he had known him, Ocock had led a decent, God-fearing life, respected both in his business relations and by his brethren of the chapel. Nor could he spare more than a glance in passing for those odd traits in the old man's character which were now explained: his itch for public approval; his unvarying harshness towards the pair of incorrigibles who weighed him down. At this moment he discounted even the integrity that had prompted the confession. His attitude of mind was one of: why the deuce couldn't the old fool have held his tongue?

Oh, these unbidden, injudicious confidences! How they complicated life! And as a doctor he was pestered with only too many; he was continually being forced to see behind the scenes. Now, outsiders, too, must needs choose him for the storehouse of their privacies. Himself he never made a confidence; but it seemed as though just this buttoned-upness on his part loosened people's tongues. Blind to the flags of warning he hoisted in looks and bearing, they innocently proceeded, as Ocock had done, to throw up insurmountable barriers. He could hear a new tone in his own voice when he replied, and was relieved to know the old man dull of perception. For now Ocock had finished speaking, and sat perspiring with anxiety to learn his fate. Mahony pulled himself together; he could, in good faith, tender the advice to let the dead past bury its dead. Whatever the original fault had been – no, no, please! . . . and he raised an arresting hand – it was, he felt sure, long since fully atoned. And Mr Ocock had said a true word: women were strange creatures. The revelation of his secret might shipwreck his late-found happiness. It also, of course, might not – and personally Mahony did not believe it would; for Ocock's business throve like the green bay-tree, and Miss Tilly had been promised a fine two-storeyed house, with bow-windows and a garden, and a carriage-drive up to the door. Again, the admission might be accepted in peace just now, and later on used as a weapon against him. In his, Mahony's, eyes, by far the wisest course would be, to let the grass grow over the whole affair.

And here he rose, abruptly terminating the interview. 'You and I, too, sir, if you please, will forget what has passed between us this morning, and never come back on it. How is Tom getting on in the drapery business? Does he like his billet?'

But none the less as he ushered his visitor out, he felt that there was a certain finality about the action. It was – as far as his private feelings were concerned – the old man's moral exit from the scene.

On the doorstep Ocock hoped that nothing that had been said would reach 'your dear little lady'. 'To 'Enry, too, doc., if you'll be so good, mum's the word! 'Enry 'ud never forgive me, nay, or you eether, if it got to 'is ears I'd bin an' let the cat outer the bag. An' 'e's got a bit of a down on you as it is, for it 'avin' bin your place I met the future Mrs O. at.'

'My good man!' broke from Mahony – and in this address, which would previously never have crossed his lips, all his sensations of the past hour were summed up. 'Has your son Henry the' – he checked himself; 'does he suppose I – *I* or my wife – had anything to do with it?'

He turned back to the surgery hot with annoyance. This, too! Not enough that he must be put out of countenance by indiscreet babblings; he must also get drawn into family squabbles, even be held responsible for them: he who, brooking no interference in his own life, demanded only that those about him should be as intolerant as he.

It all came from Polly's indiscriminate hospitality. His house was never his own. And now they had the prospect of John and his electoral campaign before them. And John's chances of success, and John's stump oratory, and the backstair-work other people were expected to do for him would form the main theme of conversation for many a day to come.

Mrs Glendinning confirmed old Ocock's words.

She came to talk over the engagement with Polly, and sitting in the parlour cried a little, and was sorry. But then 'poor little Agnes' cried so easily nowadays. Richard said her nerves had been shattered by the terrible affair just before Christmas, when Mr Glendinning had tried first to kill her, and then to cut his own throat.

Agnes said: 'But I told Henry quite plainly, darling, that I would not cease my visits to you on that account. It is both wrong and foolish to think you or Dr Mahony had anything to do with it – and after the doctor was so kind, too, so *very* kind, about getting poor Mr Glendinning into the asylum. And so you see, dear, Henry and I have had quite a disagreement'; and Agnes cried again at the remembrance. 'Of course, I can sympathize with his point of view. . . . Henry is so ambitious. All the same, dearest, it's not quite so bad – is it? – as he makes out. Matilda is certainly not very *comme il faut* – you'll forgive my saying so, love, won't you? But I think she will suit Henry's father in every way. No, the truth is, the old gentleman has made a great deal of money, and we naturally expected it to fall to Henry at his death; no one anticipated his marrying again. Not that Henry really needs the money; he is getting on so well; and I have . . . I shall have plenty, too, by and by. But you know, love, what men are.'

'Dearest Agnes! . . . don't fret about it. Mr Henry thinks too much of you, I'm sure, to be vexed with you for long. And when he looks at it calmly, he'll see how unfair it is to make us responsible. I'm like you, dear; I can't consider it a misfortune. Tilly is not a lady; but she's a dear, warm-hearted girl and will make the old man a good wife. I only hope though, Agnes, Mr Henry won't say anything to Richard. Richard is so touchy about things of that sort.'

The two women kissed, Polly with feelings of the tenderest affection: the fact that, on behalf of their friendship, Agnes had pitted her will against Mr Henry's, endeared her to Polly as nothing else could have done.

But when, vigilant as a mother-hen, she sought to prepare her husband for a possible unpleasantness, she found him already informed; and her well-meant words were like a match laid to his suppressed indignation.

'In all my born days I never heard such impudence!'

He turned embarrassingly cool to Tilly. And Tilly, innocent of offence and quite unskilled in deciphering subtleties, put this sudden change of front down to jealousy, because she was going to live in a grander house than he did. For the same reason he had begun to turn up his nose at 'Old O.', or she was very much mistaken; and in vain did Polly strive to convince her that she was in error. 'I don't know anyone Richard has a higher opinion of!'

But it was a very uncomfortable state of things; and when a message arrived over the electric telegraph announcing the dangerous illness of Mrs Beamish, distressed though she was by the news, Polly could not help heaving a tiny sigh of relief. For Tilly was summoned back to Melbourne with all speed, if she wished to see her mother alive.

They mingled their tears, Polly on her knees at the packing, Tilly weeping whole-heartedly among the pillows of the bed.

'If it 'ad only been pa now, I shouldn't have felt it half so much,' and she blew her nose for the hundredth time. 'Pa was always such a rum old stick. But poor ma . . . when I *think* how she's toiled and moiled 'er whole life long, to keep things going. She's 'ad all the pains and none of the pleasures; and now, just when I was hoping to be able to give 'er a helping hand, *this* must happen.'

The one bright spot in Tilly's grief was that the journey would be made in a private conveyance. Mr Ocock had bought a smart gig and was driving her down himself; driving past the foundations of the new house, along the seventy-odd miles of road, right up to the door of the mean lodging in a Collingwood back street, where the old Beamishes had hidden their heads. 'If only she's able to look out of the window and see me dash up in my own turn-out!' said Tilly.

Polly fitted out a substantial luncheon-basket, and was keenest sympathy to the last. But Mahony was a poor dissembler; and his sudden thaw, as he assisted in the farewell preparations, could, Polly feared, have been read aright by a child.

Tilly hugged Polly to her, and gave her kiss after kiss. 'I shall *never* forget 'ow kind you've been, Poll, and all you've done for me. I've had my disappointments 'ere, as you know; but p'raps after all it'll turn out to be for the best. One o' the good sides to it anyhow is that you and me'll be next-door neighbours, so to say, for the rest of our lives. And I'll hope to see something of you, my dear, every blessed day. But you'll not often catch me coming to this house, I can tell you that! For, if you won't mind me saying so, Poll, I think you've got one of the queerest sticks for a husband that ever walked this earth. Blows hot one day and cold the next, for all the world like the wind in spring. And without caring twopence whose corns 'e treads on.' — Which, thought Polly, was but a sorry return on Tilly's part for Richard's hospitality. After all, it was his house she had been a guest in.

Such were the wheels within wheels. And thus it came about that, when the question rose of paving the way for John Turnham's candidature, Mahony drew the line at approaching Henry Ocock.

CHAPTER TEN

John drove from Melbourne in a drag and four, accompanied by numerous friends and well-wishers. A mile or so out of Ballarat, he was met by a body of supporters headed by a brass band, and escorted in triumph to the George Hotel. Here, the horses having been led away, John at once took the field by mounting the box-seat of the coach and addressing the crowd of idlers that had gathered round to watch the arrival. He got an excellent hearing — so Jerry reported, who was an eye- and ear-witness of the scene — and was afterwards borne shoulder-high into the hotel.

With Jerry at his heels, Mahony called at the hotel that evening. He found John entertaining a large impromptu party. The table of the public dining-room was disorderly with the remains of a liberal meal; napkins lay crushed and flung down among plates piled high with empty nutshells; the cloth was wine-stained, and bestrewn with ashes and breadcrumbs, the air heady with the fumes of tobacco. Those of the guests who still lingered at the table had pushed their chairs back or askew, and sat, some a-straddle, some even with their feet on the cloth. John was confabbing with half-a-dozen black-coats in a corner. Each held a wineglass in his hand from which he sipped, while John, legs apart, did all the talking, every now and then putting out his forefinger to prod one of his hearers on the middle button of the waistcoat. It was some time before he discovered the presence of his relatives; and Mahony had leisure to admire the fashion in which, this corner-talk over, John dispersed himself among the company; drinking with this one and that; glibly answering questions; patting a glum-faced brewer on the back; and simultaneously checking over, with an oily-haired agent, his committee-meetings for the following days. His customary arrogance and pompousness of manner were laid aside. For the nonce, he was a simple man among men.

Then espying them, he hurried over, and rubbing his hands with pleasure said warmly: 'My dear Mahony, this is indeed kind! Jerry, my lad, how do, how do? Still growing, I see! We'll make a fine fellow of you yet. — Well, doctor! . . . we've every reason, I think, to feel satisfied with the lie of the land.'

But here he was snatched from them by an urgent request for a pronouncement — 'A quite informal word, sir, if you'll be so good,' — on the vexed question of vote by ballot. And this being a pet theme of John's, and a principle he was ready to defend through thick and thin, he willingly complied.

Mahony had no further talk with him. The speech over — it was a concise and spirited utterance, and, if you were prepared to admit the efficacy of the ballot, convincing enough — Mahony quietly withdrew. He had to see a patient at eleven. Polly, too, would probably be lying awake for news of her brother.

As he threw back his braces and wound up his watch, he felt it incumbent on him to warn her not to pitch her hopes too high. 'You mustn't expect, my dear, that your brother's arrival will mean much to us. He is now a public man, and will have little time for small people like ourselves. I'm bound to admit, Polly, I was very favourably impressed by the few words I heard him say,' he added.

'Oh, Richard, I'm *so* glad!' and Polly, who had been sitting on the edge of the bed, stood on tip-toe to give him a kiss.

As Mahony predicted, John's private feelings went down before the superior interests of his campaign. Three days passed before he found time to pay his sister a visit; and Polly, who had postponed a washing, baked her richest cakes and pastries, and clad Trotty in her Sunday best each day of the three: Polly was putting a good face on the matter, and consoling herself with Jerry's descriptions of John's triumphs. How she wished she could hear some of the speechifying! But Richard would never consent; and electioneering did certainly seem, from what Jerry said, a very rough-and-ready business — nothing for ladies. Hence her delight knew no bounds when John drove up unexpectedly late one afternoon, between a hard day's personal canvassing and another of the innumerable dinners he had to eat his way through. Tossing the reins to the gentleman who sat next to him, he jumped out of the wagonette — it was hung with placards of 'Vote for Turnham!' — and gave a loud rat-a-tat at the door.

Forgetting in her excitement that this was Ellen's job, Polly opened to him herself, and drew him in. 'John! How pleased I am to see you!'

'My dear girl, how are you? God bless me, how you've altered! I should never have known you.' He held her at arm's length, to consider her.

'But you haven't changed in the least, John. Except to grow younger. – Richard, here's John at last! – and Trotty, John . . . here's Trotty! – Take your thumb out of your mouth, naughty girl! – She's been watching for you all day, John, with her nose to the window.' And Polly pushed forward the scarlet, shrinking child.

John's heartiness suffered a distinct check as his eyes lit on Trotty, who stood stiff as a bit of Dresden china in her bunchy starched petticoats. 'Come here, Emma, and let me look at you.' Taking the fat little chin between thumb and first finger, he turned the child's face up and kept it so, till the red button of a mouth trembled, and the great blue eyes all but ran over. 'H'm! Yes . . . a notable resemblance to her mother. Ah, time passes, Polly my dear – time passes!' He sighed. – 'I hope you mind your aunt, Emma, and are properly grateful to her?'

Abruptly quitting his hold, he swept the parlour with a glance. 'A very snug little place you have here, upon my word!'

While Polly, with Trotty pattering after, bustled to the larder, Mahony congratulated his brother-in-law on the more favourable attitude towards his election policy which was becoming evident in the local press. John's persuasive tongue was clearly having its effect, and the hostility he had met with at the outset of his candidature was yielding to more friendly feelings on all sides. John was frankly gratified by the change, and did not hesitate to say so. When the wine arrived they drank to his success, and Polly's delicacies met with their due share of praise. Then, having wiped his mouth on a large silk handkerchief, John disclosed the business object of his call. He wanted specific information about the more influential of their friends and acquaintances; and here he drew a list of names from his pocket-book. Mahony, his chin propped on the flaxen head of the child, whom he nursed, soon fell out of the running; for Polly proved far the cleverer at grasping the nature of the information John sought, and at retailing it. And John complimented her on her shrewdness, ticked off names, took notes on what she told him; and when he was not writing sat tapping his thick, carnation-red underlip, and nodding assent. It was arranged that

Polly should drive out with him next day to Yarangobilly, by way of Dandaloo; while for the evening after they plotted a card-party, at which John might come to grips with Archdeacon Long. John expected to find the reverend gentleman a hard nut to crack, their views on the subject of a state aid to religion being diametrically opposed. Polly thought a substantial donation to the chancel-fund might smooth things over, while for John to display a personal interest in Mrs Long's charities would help still more. Then there were the Ococks. The old man could be counted on, she believed; but John might have some difficulty with Mr Henry – and here she initiated her brother into the domestic differences which had split up the Ocock family, and prevented Richard from approaching the lawyer. John, who was in his most democratic mood, was humorous at the expense of Henry, and declared the latter should rather wish his father joy of coming to such a fine, bouncing young wife in his old age. The best way of getting at Mr Henry, Polly considered, would be for Mrs Glendinning to give a luncheon or a bushing-party, with the lawyer among the guests: 'Then you and I, John, could drive out and join them – either by chance or invitation, as you think best.' Polly was heart and soul in the affair.

But business over, she put several straight questions about the boy, little Johnny – Polly still blamed herself for having meekly submitted to the child's removal from her charge – and was not to be fobbed off with evasions. The unfavourable verdict she managed to worm out of John: 'Incorrigible, my dear Polly – utterly incorrigible! His masters report him idle, disobedient, a bad influence on the other scholars,' she met staunchly with: 'Perhaps it has something to do with the school. Why not try another? Johnny had his good qualities; in many ways was quite a lovable child.'

For the first time Mahony saw his wife and her eldest brother together and he could not but be struck by Polly's attitude. Greatly as she admired and reverenced John, there was not a particle of obsequiousness in her manner, nor any truckling to his point of view; and she plainly felt nothing of the peculiar sense of discomfort that invariably attacked him, in John's presence. Either she was not conscious of her brother's grossly patronizing air, or, aware of it, did not resent it, John having always been so much her superior in age and position. Or was it indeed the truth that John did not try to patronize Polly? That his overbearing nature recognized in hers a certain springy

243

resistance, which was not to be crushed? In other words, that, in a Turnham, Turnham blood met its match.

John re-took his seat in the front of the wagonette, Trotty was lifted up to see the rosettes and streamers adorning the horses, the gentlemen waved their hats, and off they went again at a fine pace, and with a whip-cracking that brought the neighbours to their windows.

Polly had pink cheeks with it all, and even sought to excuse the meagre interest John had shown in his daughter. 'Trotty was only a baby in arms when he saw her last. Besides, I think she reminded him too much of her dear mother. For I'm sure, though he doesn't let it be seen, John still feels his loss.'

'I wonder!' said Mahony slowly and with a strong downward inflection, as he turned indoors.

On the eve of the polling Polly had the honour of accompanying her brother to a performance at the Theatre Royal. A ticket came for Richard, too; but, as usual, he was at the last moment called out. So Purdy took her on his arm and escorted her – not exactly comfortably; for, said Polly, no one who had not tried it, knew how hard it was to walk arm-in-arm with a lame person, especially if you did not want to hurt his feelings – Purdy took her to the theatre, helped her to unmuffle and to change her boots, and bore her company till her brother arrived. They had seats in the centre of the front row of the dress circle; all eyes were turned on them as they entered; and Polly's appearance was the subject of audible and embarrassing comment.

In every interval John was up and away, to shake a hand here, pass the time of day there; and watching him with affectionate pride, Polly wondered how Richard could ever have termed him 'high-handed and difficult'. John had the knack, it seemed to her, of getting on with people of every class, and of always finding the right word to say. But as the evening advanced his seat remained empty even while the curtain was up, and she was glad when, between the fourth and fifth acts, her husband at last appeared.

On his way to her Mahony ran into his brother-in-law, and John buttonholed him to discuss with him the prospects of the morrow. As they talked, their eyes rested on Polly's glossy black chignon; on the nape of her white neck; on the beautiful, rounded young shoulders which, in obedience to the fashion, stood right out of her blue silk bodice. Mahony shifted his weight uneasily from one foot to the other. He could not imagine Polly enjoying her exposed position, and disapproved strongly of John having left her. But for all answer to the hint he threw out John said slowly, and with a somewhat unctuous relish: 'My sister has turned into a remarkably handsome woman!' – words which sent the lightning-thought through Mahony that, had Polly remained the insignificant little slip of a thing of earlier days, she would not have been asked to fill the prominent place she did this evening.

John sent his adieux and excuses to Polly. He had done what was expected of him, in showing himself at a public entertainment, and a vast mass of correspondence lay unsorted on his desk. So Mahony moved forward alone.

'Oh, Richard, there you are! Oh dear, what you've missed! I never thought there could be such acting.' And Polly turned her great dark eyes on her husband; they were moist from the noble sentiments of *The True Briton*.

The day of the election broke, a gusty spring day cut up by stinging hail-showers, which beat like fusillades on the galvanized-iron roofs. Between the showers, the sun shone in a gentian-blue sky, against which the little wooden houses showed up crassly white. Ballarat made holiday. Early as Mahony left home, he met a long line of conveyances heading townwards – spring carts, dog-carts, double and single buggies, in some of which, built to seat two only, five or six persons were huddled. These and similar vehicles drew up in rows outside the public-houses, where the lean, long-legged colonial horses stood jerking at their tethers; and they were still there, still jerking, when he passed again towards evening. On a huge poster the 'Unicorn' offered to lunch free all those 'thinking men' who registered their vote for 'the one and only true democrat, the miners' friend and tyrants' foe, John Turnham'.

In the hope of avoiding a crush Mahony drove straight to the polling-booth. But already all the loafers and roughs in the place seemed to be congregated round the entrance, after the polite custom of the country to chivy, or boo, or huzza those who went in. In waiting his turn, he had to listen to comments on his dress and person, to put up with vulgar allusions to blue pills and black draughts.

Just as he was getting back into his buggy John rode up, flanked by a bodyguard of friends; John was galloping from booth to booth, to verify progress and put the thumbscrew on wobblers. He beamed – as well he might. He was certain to be one of the two members elected, and quite likely to top the poll by a respectable majority.

For once Mahony did not grumble at his outlying patients; was only too thankful to turn his back on the town. It was pandemonium. Bands of music, one shriller and more discordant than the next, marched up and down the main streets – from the fifes and drums of the Fire Brigade, to the kerosene-tins and penny-whistles of mere determined noise-makers. Straggling processions, with banners that bore the distorted features of one or other of the candidates, made driving difficult; and, to add to the confusion, the schoolchildren were let loose, to overrun the place and fly advertisement balloons round every corner. – And so it went on till far into the night, the dark hours being varied by torchlight processions, fireworks, free fights and orgies of drunkenness.

The results of the polling were promised for two o'clock the following day.

When, something after this hour Mahony reached home, he found Polly and the gentle, ox-eyed Jinny Beamish, who was the present occupant of the spare room, pacing up and down before the house. According to Jerry news might be expected now at any minute. And when he had lunched and changed his coat, Mahony, bitten by the general excitement, made his way down to the junction of Sturt Street and the Flat.

A great crowd blocked the approaches to the hustings. Here were the four candidates, who, in attending the issue, strove to look decently unconcerned. John had struck a quasi-Napoleonic attitude: his right elbow propped in the cup of his left hand, he held his drooped chin between thumb and forefinger, leaving it to his glancing black eyes to reveal how entirely alive he was to the gravity of the moment. Standing on the fringe of the crowd, Mahony listened to the piebald jokes and rude wit with which the people beguiled the interim; and tried to endure with equanimity the jostling, the profane language and offensive odours, by which he was assailed. Half an hour elapsed before the returning officer climbed the ladder at the back of the platform, and came forward to announce the result of the voting: Mr John Millibank Turnham topped the poll with a majority of four hundred and fifty-two. The crowd, which at sight of the clerk had abruptly ceased its fooling, drowned his further statements in a roar of mingled cheers and boos. The cheers had it; hats were tossed into the air, and loud cries for a speech arose.

John's advance to grip the railing led to a fresh outburst, in which the weakening opposition was quashed by the singing of: 'When Johnny comes marching home!' and 'Cheer, boys, cheer, For home and mother country!' – an incongruity of sentiment that made Mahony smile. And John, having repeatedly bowed his thanks from side to side, joined in and sang with the rest.

The opening of his speech was inaudible to Mahony. Just behind him stood one of his brother-in-law's most arrant opponents, a butcher by trade, and directly John began to hold forth this man produced a cornet-à-piston and started to blow it. In vain did Mahony expostulate: he seemed to have got into a very wasps'-nest of hostility; for the player's friends took up the cudgels and baited him in a language he would have been sorry to imitate, the butcher blaring away unmoved, with the fierce solemnity of face the cornet demands. Mahony lost his temper; his tormentors retaliated; and for a moment it looked as though there would be trouble. Then a number of John's supporters, enraged by the bellowing of the instrument, bore down and forcibly removed the musician and his clique, Mahony along with them.

Having indignantly explained, and shaken coat and collar to rights, he returned to his place on the edge of the crowd. The speaker's deep voice had gone steadily on during the disturbance. Indeed John might have been born to the hustings. Interruptions did not put him out; he was brilliant at repartee; and all the stock gestures of the public speaker came at his call: the pounding of the bowl of one hand with the closed fist of the other; the dramatic wave of the arm with which he plumbed the depths or invited defiance; the jaunty standing-at-ease, arms akimbo; the earnest bend from the waist when he took his hearers into his confidence. At this moment he was gripping the rail of the platform as though he intended to vault it, and asserting: 'Our first cry, then, is for men to people the country; our next, for independence, to work out our own salvation. Yes, my friends, the glorious future of this young and prosperous colony, which was once and most auspiciously known as Australia Felix – blest, thrice-blest Australia! – rests with ourselves alone. We who inhabit here can best judge of her requirements, and we refuse to see her hampered in her progress by the shackles of an ancient tradition. What suits our hoary mother-country – God bless and keep her and keep us loyal to her! – is but dry husks for us. England knows nothing of our most pressing needs. I ask you to consider how, previous to 1855, that pretty pair of mandarins, Lord John Russell and Earl Grey, boggled and botched the crucial question of unlocking the lands – even yet, gentlemen, the result of their muddling lies heavy on us. And the Land Question, though first in importance, is but one, as you know, of many' – and here John, playing on the tips of five wide-stretched fingers, counted them off. He wound up with a flaming plea for the creation and protection of purely national industries. 'For what, I would ask you, is the true meaning of democracy in a country such as ours? What is, for us, the democratic principle? The answer, my friends, is conservatism; yes, I repeat it – conservatism!' . . . and thus to a final peroration.

In the braying and hurrahing that followed – the din was heightened by some worthy mounting a barrel to move that 'this yere Johnny Turnham' was not a fit person to represent 'the constitooency', by the barrel being dragged from under him, and the speaker rolled in the mud; while this went on Mahony stood silent, and he was still standing meditatively pulling his whiskers when a sudden call for a doctor reached his ear. He pushed his way to the front.

How the accident happened no one knew. John had descended from the platform to a verandah, where countless hands were stretched out to shake his. A pile of shutters was leaning against the wall, and in some unexplained fashion these had fallen, striking John a blow that knocked him down. When Mahony got to him he was on his feet again, wiping a drop of blood from his left temple. He looked pale, but pooh-poohed injury or the idea of interfering with his audience's design; and Mahony saw him shouldered and borne off.

That evening there was a lengthy banquet, in which all the notables of the place took part. Mahony's seat was some way off John's; he had to lean forward, did he wish to see his brother-in-law.

Towards eleven o'clock, just as he was wondering if he could slip out unobserved, a hand was laid on his arm. John stood behind him, white to the lips. 'Can I have a word with you upstairs?'

Here he confessed to a knife-like pain in his left side; the brunt of the blow, it seemed, had met him slantways between rib and hip. A cursory examination made Mahony look grave.

'You must come back with me, John, and let me see to you properly.'

Having expressed the chief guest's regrets to the company, he ordered a horse and trap, and helping John into it drove him home. And that night John lay in their bed, letting out the groans he had suppressed during the evening; while Polly snatched forty winks beside Jinny Beamish, and Mahony got what sleep he could on the parlour sofa.

CHAPTER ELEVEN

There for some weeks John was a prisoner, with a fractured rib encased in strips of plaster. 'In your element again, old girl!' Mahony chaffed his wife, when he met her bearing invalid trays.

'Oh, it doesn't all fall on me, Richard. Jinny's a great help – sitting with John and keeping him company.'

Mahony could see it for himself. Oftenest when he entered the room it was Jinny's black-robed figure – she was in mourning for her parents; for Mrs Beamish had sunk under the two-fold strain of failure and disgrace, and the day after her death it had been necessary to cut old Beamish down from a nail – oftenest it was Jinny he found sitting behind a curtain of the tester-bed, watching while John slept, ready to read to him or to listen to his talk when he awoke. This service set Polly free to devote herself to the extra cooking; and John was content. 'A most modest and unassuming young woman,' ran his verdict on Jinny.

Polly reported it to her husband in high glee. 'Who could ever have believed two sisters would turn out so differently? Tilly to get so . . . so . . . well, you know what I mean . . . and Jinny to improve as she has done. Have you noticed, Richard, she hardly ever – really quite seldom now – drops an h? It must all have been due to Tilly serving in that low bar.'

By the time John was so far recovered as to exchange bed for sofa, it had come to be exclusively Jinny who carried in to him the dainties Polly prepared – the wife as usual was content to do the dirty work! John declared Miss Jinny had the foot of a fay; also that his meals tasted best at her hands. Jinny even succeeded in making Trotty fond of her; and the love of the fat, shy child was not readily won. Entering the parlour one evening Mahony surprised quite a family scene: John, stretched on the sofa, was stringing cats'-cradles, Jinny sat beside him with Trotty on her knee.

On the whole, though, the child did not warm to her father.

'Aunty, kin dat man take me away f'om you?'

'That man? Why, Trotty darling, he's your father!' said Polly, shocked.

'Kin 'e take me away f'om you and Uncle Papa?'

'He could if he wanted to. But I'm sure he doesn't,' answered her aunt, deftly turning a well-rolled sheet of pastry.

And righting her dolly, which she had been dragging upside down, Trotty let slip her fears with the sovereign ease of childhood.

From the kitchen Polly could hear the boom of John's deep bass: it made nothing of the lath-and-plaster walls. Of course, shut up as he was, he had to talk to somebody, poor fellow; and Richard was too busy to spare him more than half an hour of an evening. Jinny was a good listener. Through the crack of the door, Polly could see her sitting humbly drinking in John's words, and even looking rather pretty, in her fair, full womanliness.

'Oh, Polly!' she burst out one day, after being held thus spellbound. 'Oh, my dear, what a splendid man your brother is! I feel sometimes I could sink through the floor with shame at my ignorance, when 'e talks to me so.'

But as time went on Mahony noticed that his wife grew decidedly thoughtful; and if John continued to sing Jinny's praises, he heard nothing more of it. He had an acute suspicion what troubled Polly; but did not try to force her confidence.

Then one afternoon, on his getting home, she came into the surgery looking very perturbed, and could hardly find words to break a certain piece of news to him. It appeared that not an hour previously, Jinny, flushed and tearful, had lain on her neck, confessing her feelings for John and hinting at the belief that they were returned.

'Well, I think you might have been prepared for something of this sort, Polly,' he said with a shrug, when he had heard her out. 'Convalescence is notoriously dangerous for fanning the affections.'

'Oh, but I never *dreamt* of such a thing, Richard! Jinny is a dear good girl and all that, but she is *not* John's equal. And that he can even *think* of putting her in poor Emma's place! — What shall I say to him?'

'Say nothing at all. Your brother John is not the man to put up with interference.'

251

'He longs so for a real home again, Polly darling,' said Jinny, wiping her eyes. 'And *how* 'appy it will make me to fulfil 'is wish! Don't let me feel unwelcome and an intruder, dear. I know I'm not nearly good enough for 'im, and 'e could 'ave had the choice of ever such handsome women. But 'e 'as promised to be patient with me, and to teach me everything I ought to know.'

Polly's dismay at the turn of events yielded to a womanly sympathy with her friend. 'It's just like poor little Agnes and Mr Henry over again,' was her private thought. For she could not picture John stooping to guide and instruct.

But she had been touched on a tender spot – that of ambitious pride for those related to her – and she made what Mahony called 'a real Turnham attempt' to stand up to John. Against her husband's express advice.

'For if your brother chooses to contract a mésalliance of this kind, it's nobody's business but his own. Upon my word though, Polly, if you don't take care, this house will get a bad name over the matches that are made in it. You had better have your spare room boarded up, my dear.'

Mahony was feeling particularly rasped by John's hoity-toity behaviour in this connection. Having been nursed back to health, John went about with his chin in the air, and hardly condescended to allude to his engagement – let alone talk it over with his relatives. So Mahony retired into himself – after all, the world of John's mind was so dissimilar to his own that he did not even care to know what went on in it. 'The fellow has been caught on the hop by a buxom form and a languishing eye,' was how he dismissed the matter in thought.

'I raise my wife to my own station, Mary. And you will greatly oblige me by showing Jane every possible attention,' was the only satisfaction Polly could get from John, made in his driest tone.

Before the engagement was a week old Tilly reappeared – she was to be married from their house on the hither side of Christmas. At first she was too full of herself and her own affairs to let either Polly or Jinny get a word in. Just to think of it! That old cabbage-grower, Devine, had gone and bought the block of land next the one Mr O. was building on. She'd lay a bet he would put up a house the dead spit of theirs. Did ever anyone hear such cheek?

At the news that was broken to her, the first time she paused for breath, she let herself heavily down on a chair.

'Well, I'm blowed!' was all she could ejaculate. 'Blowed! . . . that's what I am.'

But afterwards, when Jinny had left the room, she gave free play to a very real envy and regret. 'In all my life I never did! Jinn to be Mrs John! . . . and, as like as not, the *H*onourable Mrs John before she's done. Oh, Polly, my dear, why *ever* didn't I wait!'

On being presented to John, however, she became more reconciled to her lot. ' 'E's got a temper, your brother has, or I'm very much mistaken. It won't be all beer and skittles for 'er ladyship. For Jinn hasn't a scrap of spunk *in* 'er, Polly. She got so mopey the last year or two, there was no doing anything with 'er. Now it was just the other way round with me. No matter how black things looked, I always kept my pecker up. Poor ma used to say I grew more like her every day.'

And at a still later date: 'No, Polly, my dear, I wouldn't change places with the future Mrs T. after all, thank you – not for Joseph! I *say*! she'll need to mind her p's and q's.' For Tilly had listened to John explaining to Jinny what he expected of her, what she might and might not do; and had watched Jinny sitting meekly by and saying yes to everything.

There was nothing in the way of the marriage; indeed, did it not take place immediately, Jinny would have to look about her for a situation of some kind; and, said John, that was nothing for *his* wife. His house stood empty; he was very much in love; and pressed for the naming of the day. So it was decided that Polly should accompany Jinny to lodgings in Melbourne, help her choose her trousseau and engage servants. Afterwards there would be a quiet wedding – by reason of Jinny's mourning – at which Richard, if he could possibly contrive to leave his patients, would give the bride away. Polly was to remain in John's house while the happy couple were on honeymoon, to look after the servants. This arrangement would also make the break less hard for the child. Trotty was still blissfully unconscious of what had befallen her. She had learnt to say 'new mama' parrot-wise, without understanding what the words meant. And meanwhile, the fact that she was to go with her aunt for a long, exciting coach-ride filled her childish cup with happiness.

As Polly packed the little clothes, she thought of the night, six years before, when the fat, sleeping babe had been laid in her arms.

'Of course it's only natural John should want his family round him again. But I *shall* miss the dear little soul,' she said to her husband who stood watching her.

'What you need is a little one of your own, wife.'

'Ah, don't I wish I had!' said Polly, and drew a sigh. 'That would make up for everything. Still if it can't be, it can't.'

A few days before the set time John received an urgent summons to Melbourne, and went on ahead, leaving Mahony suspecting him of a dodge to avoid travelling *en famille*. In order that his bride-elect should not be put to inconvenience, John hired four seats for the three of them; but: 'He might just as well have saved his money,' thought Polly, when she saw the coach. Despite their protests they were packed like herrings in a barrel – had hardly room enough to use their hands. Altogether it was a trying journey. Jinny, worked on by excitement and fatigue, took a fit of hysterics; Trotty, frightened by the many rough strangers, cried and had to be nursed; and the whole burden of the undertaking lay on Polly's shoulders. She had felt rather timid about it, before starting; but was obliged to confess she got on better than she expected. A kind old man sitting opposite, for instance – a splitter he said he was – actually undid Jinny's bonnet-strings, and fetched water for her at the first stoppage.

Polly had not been in Melbourne since the year after her marriage, and was looking forward intensely to the visit. She went laden with commissions; her lady-friends gave her a list as long as her arm. Richard, too, had entrusted her to get him second-hand editions of various medical works, as well as a new stethoscope. Thirdly, she had promised old Mr Ocock to go to William's Town to meet Miss Amelia, who even now was tossing somewhere on the Indian Ocean, and to escort the poor young lady up to Ballarat.

Having seen them start, Mahony went home to drink his coffee and read his paper in a quiet that was new to him. John's departure had already eased the strain. Then Tilly had been boarded out at the Methodist minister's. Now, with the exit of Polly and her charges, a great peace descended on the little house. The rooms lay white and still in the sun, and though all doors stood open, there was not a sound to be heard but the buzzing of the blowflies round the sweets of the flytraps. He was free to look as glum as he chose of a morning if he had neuralgia; or to be silent when worried over a troublesome case. No longer would Miss Tilly's bulky presence and loud-voiced reiterations of her prospects grate his nerves; or John's full-blooded absorption in himself, and poor foolish Jinny's quavering doubts whether she would ever be able to live up to so magnificent a husband, offend his sense of decorum.

Another reason he was glad to see the last of them was that, in the long run, he had rebelled at the barefaced way they made use of Polly, and took advantage of her good nature. She had not only cooked for them and waited on them; he had even caught her stitching garments for the helpless Jinny. This was too much: such extreme obligingness on his wife's part seemed to detract from her personal dignity. He could never though have got Polly to see it. Undignified to do a kindness? What a funny, selfish idea! The fact was, there was a certain streak in Polly's nature that made her more akin to all these good people than to him – him with his unsociable leanings towards a hermit's cell; his genuine need of an occasional hour's privacy and silence, in which to think a few thoughts through to the end.

On coming in from his rounds he turned out an old linen jacket that belonged to his bachelor days, and raked up some books he had not opened for an almost equally long time. He also steered clear of friends and acquaintances, went nowhere, saw no one but his patients. And Ellen, to whose cookery Polly had left him with many misgivings, took things easy. 'He's so busy reading, he never knows what he puts in his mouth. I believe he'd eat his boot-soles, if I fried 'em up neat wid a bit of parsley,' she reported over the back fence on Doctor's odd ways.

During the winter months the practice had as usual fallen off. By now it was generally beginning to look up again; but this year, for some reason, the slackness persisted. He saw how lean his purse was, whenever he had to take a banknote from it to enclose to Polly; there was literally nothing doing, no money coming in. Then, he would restlessly lay his book aside, and drawing a slip of paper to him set to reckoning and dividing. Not for the first time he found himself in the doctor's awkward quandary: how to be decently and humanly glad of a rise in the health-rate.

He had often regretted having held to the half-hundred shares he had bought at Henry Ocock's suggestion; had often spent in fancy the sum they would have brought in, had he sold when they touched their highest figure. Such a chance would hardly come his way again. After the one fictitious flare-up, 'Porepunkahs' had fallen heavily – the first main prospect-drive, at a depth of three hundred and fifty feet, had failed to strike the gutter – and nowadays they were not even quoted. Thus had ended his single attempt to take a hand in the great game.

One morning he sat at breakfast, and thought over his weekly epistle to Polly. In general, this chronicled items of merely personal interest. The house had not yet been burnt down – her constant fear, when absent; another doctor had got the Asylum; he himself stood a chance of being elected to the Committee of the District Hospital. Today, however, there was more to tell. The English mail had come in, and the table was strewn with foreign envelopes and journals. Besides the usual letters from relatives, one in a queer, illiterate hand had reached him, the address scrawled in purple ink on the cheapest note-paper. Opening it with some curiosity, Mahony found that it was from his former assistant, Long Jim.

The old man wrote in a dismal strain. Everything had gone against him. His wife had died, he was out of work and penniless, and racked with rheumatism – oh, it was 'a crewl climat'! Did he stop in England, only 'the house' remained to him; he'd end in a pauper's grave. But he believed if he could get back to a scrap of warmth and the sun, he'd be good for some years yet. Now he'd always known Dr Mahony for the kindest, most liberal of gentlemen; the happiest days of his life had been spent under him, on the Flat; and if he'd only give him a lift now, there was nothing he wouldn't do to show his gratitude. Doctor knew a bit about him, too. Here, he couldn't seem to get on with folk at all. They looked crooked at him, and just because he'd once been spunky enough to try his luck overseas. Mahony pshawed and smiled; then wondered what Polly would say to this letter. She it was who had been responsible for packing the old man off.

Unfolding the *Star*, he ran his eye over its columns. He had garnered the chief local news and was skimming the mining intelligence, when he suddenly stopped short with an exclamation of surprise; and his grip on the paper tightened. There it stood, black on white. 'Porepunkahs' had jumped to three pounds per share! What the dickens did that mean? He turned back to the front sheet, to find if any clue to the claim's renewed activity had escaped him; but sought in vain. So bolting the rest of his breakfast, he hurried down to the town, to see if, on the spot, he could pick up information with regard to the mysterious rise.

The next few days kept him in a twitter of excitement. 'Porepunkahs' went on advancing – not by leaps and bounds as before, but slowly and steadily – and threw off a dividend. He got into bed at night with a hot head, from wondering whether he ought to hold on or sell out; and inside a week he was off to consult the one person who was in a position to advise him. Henry Ocock's greeting resembled an embrace – 'It evidently means a fortune for him' – and all trifling personal differences were forgotten in the wider common bond. The lawyer virtually ordered Mahony to 'sit in', till he gave the word. By this time 'Porepunkahs' had passed their previous limit, and even paid a bonus: it was now an open secret that a drive undertaken in an opposite direction to the first had proved successful; the lead was scored and seamed with gold. Ocock spoke of the stone, specimens of which he had held in his hand – declared he had never seen its equal.

But when the shares stood at fifty-three pounds each, Mahony could restrain himself no longer; and, in spite of Ocock's belief that another ten days would see a *coup*, he parted with forty-five of the half-hundred he held. Leaving the odd money with the lawyer for re-investment, he walked out of the office the possessor of two thousand pounds.

It was only a very ordinary late spring day; the season brought its like by the score: a pale azure sky, against which the distant hills looked purple; above these a narrow belt of cloud, touched, in its curves, to the same hue. But to Mahony it seemed as if such a perfect day had never dawned since he first set foot in Australia. His back was eased of its burden; and, like Christian on having passed the wall known as Salvation, he could have wept tears of joy. After all these years of pinching and sparing he was out of poverty's grip. The suddenness of the thing was what staggered him. He might have drudged till his hair was grey; it was unlikely he would ever, at one stroke, have come into possession of a sum like this. – And that whole day he went about feeling a little more than human, and seeing people, places, things, through a kind of beatific mist. Now, thank God, he could stand on his own legs again; could relieve John of his bond, pay off the mortgage on the house, insure his life before it was too late. And, everything done, he would still have over a thousand pounds to his credit. A thousand pounds! No longer need he thankfully accept any and every call; or reckon sourly that, if the leakage on the roof was to be mended, he must go without a new surtout. Best of all, he could now begin in earnest to save.

First, though, he allowed himself two very special pleasures. He sent Polly a message on the electric telegraph to say that he would come down himself to fetch her home. In secret he planned a little trip to Schnapper Point. At the time of John's wedding he had been unable to get free; this would be the first holiday he and Polly had ever had together.

The second thing he did was: to indulge the love of giving that was innate in him; and of giving in a somewhat lordly way. He enjoyed the broad grin that illumined Ellen's face at his unlooked-for generosity; Jerry's red stammered thanks for the gift of the cob the boy had long coveted. It did him good to put two ten-pound notes in an envelope and inscribe Ned's name on it; he had never yet been able to do anything for these poor lads. He also, without waiting to consult Polly – fearing, indeed, that she might advise against it – sent off the money to Long Jim for the outward voyage, and a few pounds over. For there were superstitious depths in him; and, at this turn in his fortunes, it would surely be of ill omen to refuse the first appeal for help that reached him.

Polly was so much a part of himself that he thought of her last of all. But then it was with moist eyes. She, who had never complained, should of a surety not come short! And he dropped asleep that night to the happy refrain: 'Now she shall have her piano, God bless her! . . . the best that money can buy.'

258

PART FOUR

CHAPTER ONE

The new house stood in Webster Street. It was twice as large as the old one, had a garden back and front, a verandah round three sides. When Mahony bought it, and the piece of ground it stood on, it was an unpretentious weatherboard in a rather dilapidated condition. The situation was good though – without being too far from his former address – and there was stabling for a pair of horses. And by the time he had finished with it, it was one of those characteristically Australian houses which, added to wherever feasible, without a thought for symmetry or design – a room built on here, a covered passage there, a bathroom thrown out in an unexpected corner, with odd steps up and down – have yet a spacious, straggling comfort all their own.

How glad he was to leave the tiny, sunbaked box that till now had been his home. It had had neither blind nor shutter; and, on his entering it of a summer midday, it had sometimes struck hotter than outside. The windows of his new room were fitted with green venetians; round the verandah-posts twined respectively a banksia and a Japanese honeysuckle, which further damped the glare; while on the patch of buffalo-grass in front stood a spreading fig-tree, that leafed well and threw a fine shade. He had also added a sofa to his equipment. Now, when he came in tired or with a headache, he could stretch himself at full length. He was lying on it at this moment.

Polly, too, had reason to feel satisfied with the change. A handsome little Broadwood, with a ruby-silk and carved-wood front, stood against the wall of her drawing-room; gilt cornices surmounted the windows; and from the centre of the ceiling hung a lustre-chandelier that was the envy of everyone who saw it: Mrs Henry Ocock's was not a patch on it, and yet had cost more. This time Mahony had virtually been able to give his wife a free hand in her furnishing. And in her new spare room she could put up no less than three guests!

Of course, these luxuries had not all rained on them at once. Several months passed before Polly, on the threshold of her parlour, could exclaim, with an artlessness that touched her husband deeply: 'Never in my life did I think I should have such a beautiful room!' Still, as regarded money, the whole year had been a steady ascent. The nest-egg he had left with the lawyer had served its purpose of chaining that old hen, Fortune, to the spot. Ocock had invested and re-invested on his behalf – now it was twenty 'Koh-i-noors', now thirty 'Consolidated Beehives' – and Mahony was continually being agreeably surprised by the margins it threw off in its metamorphoses. That came of his having placed the matter in such competent hands. By now he had learned to put blind faith in Ocock's judgement. The lawyer had, for instance, got him finally out of 'Porepunkahs' in the nick of time – the reef had not proved as open to the day as was expected – and pulled him off, in the process, another three hundred odd. Compared with Ocock's own takings, of course, his was a modest spoil; the lawyer had made a fortune, and was now one of the wealthiest men in Ballarat. He had built not only new and handsome offices on the crest of the hill, but also, prior to his marriage, a fine dwelling-house standing in extensive grounds on the farther side of Yuille's Swamp. Altogether it had been a year of great and sweeping changes. People had gone up, gone down – had changed places like children at a game of General Post. More than one of Mahony's acquaintances had burnt his fingers. On the other hand, old Devine, Polly's one-time market-gardener, had made his thousands. There was actually talk of his standing for Parliament, in which case his wife bid fair to be received at Government House. And the pair of them with hardly an 'h' between them!

From the sofa where he lay, Mahony could hear the murmur of his wife's even voice. Polly sat the further end of the verandah talking to Jinny, who dandled her babe in a rocking-chair that made a light tip-tap as it went to and fro. Jinny said nothing: she was no doubt sunk in adoration of her – or rather John's – infant; and Mahony all but dozed off, under the full, round tones he knew so well.

In his case the saying had once more been verified: to him that hath shall be given. Whether it was due to the better position of the new house; or to the fact that easier circumstances gave people more leisure to think of their ailments; or merely that money attracted money: whatever the cause, his practice had of late made giant strides. He was in demand for consultations; sat on several committees; while a couple of lodges had come his way as good as unsought.

Against this he had one piece of ill-luck to set. At the close of the summer, when the hot winds were in blast, he had gone down under the worst attack of dysentery he had had since the early days. He really thought this time all was over with him. For six weeks, in spite of the tenderest nursing, he had lain prostrate, and as soon as he could bear the journey had to prescribe himself a change to the seaside. The bracing air of Queenscliff soon picked him up; he had, thank God, a marvellous faculty of recuperation: while others were still not done pitying him, he was himself again, and well enough to take the daily plunge in the sea that was one of his dearest pleasures. — To feel the warm, stinging fluid lap him round, after all these drewthy years of dust and heat! He could not have enough of it, and stayed so long in the water that his wife, sitting at a decent distance from the Bathing Enclosure, grew anxious, and agitated her little white parasol.

'There's nothing to equal it, Mary, this side Heaven!' he declared as he rejoined her, his towel about his neck. 'I wish I could persuade you to try a dip, my dear.'

But Mary preferred to sit quietly on the beach. 'The dressing and undressing is such a trouble,' said she. As it was, one of her elastic-sides was full of sand.

Yes, Polly was Mary now, and had been, since the day Ned turned up again on Ballarat, accompanied by a wife and child. Mary was in Melbourne at the time, at John's nuptials; Mahony had opened the door himself to Ned's knock; and there, in a spring-cart, sat the frowsy, red-haired woman who was come to steal his wife's name from her. This invasion was the direct result of his impulsive generosity. Had he only kept his money in his pocket!

He had been forced to take the trio in and give them houseroom. But he bore the storming of his hard-won privacy with a bad grace, and Mary had much to gloss over on her return.

She had been greatly distressed by her favourite brother's ill-considered marriage. For, if they had not held Jinny to be John's equal, what *was* to be said of Ned's choice? Mrs Ned had lived among the mining population of Castlemaine, where her father kept a public-house; and, said Richard, her manners were accordingly: loud, slap-dash, familiar – before she had been twenty-four hours under his roof she was bluntly addressing him as 'Mahony'. There was also a peculiar streak of touchiness in her nature ('Goes with hair of that colour, my dear!') which rendered her extremely hard to deal with. She had, it seemed, opposed the idea of moving to Ballarat – that was all in her favour, said Mary – and came primed to detect a snub or a slight at every turn. This morbid suspiciousness it was that led Mary to yield her rights in the matter of the name: the confusion between them was never-ending; and, at the first hint that the change would come gracefully from her, Mrs Ned had flown into a passion.

'It's all the same to me, Richard, what I'm called,' Mary soothed him. 'And don't you think Polly was beginning to sound *rather* childish, now I'm nearly twenty-four?'

But: 'Oh, what *could* Ned have seen in her?' she sighed to herself dismayed. For Mrs Ned was at least ten years older than her husband; and whatever affection might originally have existed between them was now a thing of the past. She tyrannized mercilessly over him, nagging at him till Ned, who was nothing if not good-natured, turned sullen and left off tossing his child in the air.

'We must just make the best of it, Richard,' said Mary. 'After all, she's really fond of the baby. And when the second comes ... you'll attend her yourself, won't you, dear? I think somehow her temper may improve when that's over.'

For this was another thing: Mrs Ned had arrived there in a condition that raised distressing doubts in Mary as to the dates of Ned's marriage and the birth of his first child. She did not breathe them to Richard; for it seemed to her only to make matters of this kind worse, openly to speak of them. She devoted herself to getting the little family under a roof of its own. Through Richard's influence Ned obtained a clerkship in a carrying-agency, which would just keep his head above water; and she found a tiny, three-roomed house that was near enough to let her be daily with her sister-in-law when the latter's time came. Meanwhile, she cut out and helped to sew a complete little outfit ('What she had before was no better than rags!'); and Mrs Ned soon learned to know on whom she could lean and to whom she might turn, not only for practical aid, but also for a never failing sympathy in what she called her 'troubles'.

'I vow your Mary's the kindest-hearted little soul it's ever been me luck to run across,' she averred one day to Mahony, who was visiting her professionally. 'So common-sense, too – no nonsense about *her*! I shouldn't have thought a gaby like Ned could have sported such a trump of a sister.'

'Another pensioner for your *caritas*, dear,' said Mahony, in passing on the verdict. What he did not grieve his wife by repeating were certain bad reports of Ned lately brought him by Jerry. According to Jerry – and the boy's word was to be relied on – Ned had kept loose company in Castlemaine, and had acquired the habit of taking more than was good for him. Did he not speedily amend his ways, there would be small chance of him remaining in his present post.

Here, Mahony was effectually roused by a stir on the verandah. Jinny had entered the house to lay down her sleeping babe, and a third voice, Purdy's, became audible. The wife had evidently brought out a bottle of her famous home-brewed gingerbeer: he heard the cork pop, the drip of the overflow on the boards, the clink of the empty glass; and Purdy's warm words of appreciation.

Then there was silence. Rising from the sofa, Mahony inserted himself between blind and window, and peeped out.

His first thought was: what a picture! Mary wore a pale pink cotton gown which, over the light swellings of her crinoline, bulged and billowed round her, and generously swept the ground. Collar and cuffs of spotless lawn outlined neck and wrists. She bent low over her stitching, and the straight white parting of her hair intensified the ebony of the glossy bands. Her broad pure forehead had neither line nor stain. On the trellis behind her a vine hung laden with massy bunches of muscatels.

Purdy sat on the edge of the verandah, with his back to Mahony. Between thumb and forefinger he idly swung a pair of scissors.

Urged by some occult sympathy, Mary at once glanced up and discovered her husband. Her face was lightly flushed from stooping – and the least touch of colour was enough to give its delicate ivory an appearance of vivid health. She had grown fuller of late – quite fat, said Richard, when he wished to tease her: a luxuriant young womanliness lay over and about her. Now, above the pale wild-rose of her cheeks her black eyes danced with a mischievous glee; for she believed her husband intended swinging his leg noiselessly over the sill and creeping up to startle Purdy – and this appealed to her sense of humour.

But, as he remained standing at the window, she just smiled slyly, satisfied to be in communion with him over their unsuspecting friend's head.

Here, however, Purdy brought his eyes back from the garden, and she abruptly dropped hers to her needlework.

The scissors were shut with a snap, and thrown, rather than laid, to the other implements in the workbox. 'One 'ud think you were paid to finish that wretched sewing in a fixed time, Polly,' said Purdy cantankerously. 'Haven't you got a word to say?'

'It's for the Dorcas Society. They're having a sale of work.'

'Oh, damn Dorcases! You're always slaving for somebody. You'll ruin your eyes. I wonder Dick allows it. I shouldn't – I know that.'

The peal of laughter that greeted these words came equally from husband and wife. Then: 'What the dickens does it matter to you, sir, how much sewing my wife chooses to do?' cried Mahony, and, still laughing, stepped out of the window.

'Hello! – you there?' said Purdy and rose to his feet. 'What a beastly fright to give one!' He looked red and sulky.

'I scored that time, my boy!' and linking his arm in Mary's, Mahony confronted his friend. 'Afraid I'm neglecting my duties, are you? Letting this young woman spoil her eyes? – Turn 'em on him, my love, in all their splendour, that he may judge for himself.'

'Nonsense, Richard,' said Mary softly, but with an affectionate squeeze of his arm.

'Well, ta-ta, I'm off!' said Purdy. And as Mahony still continued to quiz him, he added in a downright surly tone: 'Just the same old Dick as ever! Blinder than any bat to all that doesn't concern yourself! I'll eat my hat if it's ever entered your noddle that Polly's quite the prettiest woman on Ballarat.'

'Don't listen to him, Richard, please!' and: 'Don't let your head be turned by such fulsome flattery, my dear!' were wife and husband's simultaneous exclamations.

'I shouldn't think so,' said Mary sturdily, and would have added more, but just at this minute Jinny came out of the house, with the peculiar noiseless tread she had acquired in moving round an infant's crib; and Purdy vanished.

Jinny gazed at her sister-in-law with such meaning – with such a radiant, superior, yet wistful mother-look – that Mary could not but respond.

'Did you get her safely laid down, dear?'

'Perfectly, Mary! Without even the quiver of an eyelash. You recollect, I told you yesterday when her little head touched the pillow, she opened her eyes and looked at me. Today there was nothing of that sort. It was quite perfect'; and Jinny's voice thrilled at the remembrance: it was as if, in continuing to sleep during the transit, her – or rather John's – tiny daughter had proved herself a marvellous sagacity.

Mahony gave an impatient shrug in Jinny's direction. But he, too, had to stand fire: she had been waiting all day for a word with him. The babe, who was teething, was plagued by various disorders; and Jinny knew each fresh pin's-head of a spot that joined the rash.

Mahony made light of her fears; then turning to his wife asked her to hurry on the six-o'clock dinner: he had to see a patient between that meal and tea. Mary went to make arrangements – Richard always forgot to mention such things till the last moment – and also to please Jinny by paying a visit to the baby.

'The angels can't look very different when they sleep, I think,' murmured its mother, hanging over the couch.

When Mary returned, she found her husband picking caterpillars off the vine: Long Jim, odd man now about house and garden, was not industrious enough to keep the pests under. In this brief spell of leisure – such moments grew ever rarer in Richard's life – husband and wife locked their arms and paced slowly up and down the verandah. It was late afternoon on a breathless, pale-skied February day; and the boards of the flooring gritted with sandy dust beneath their feet.

'He *was* grumpy this afternoon, wasn't he?' said Mary, without preamble. 'But I've noticed once or twice lately that he can't take a joke any more. He's grown queer altogether. Do you know he's the only person who still persists in calling me by my old name? He was quite rude about it when I asked him why. Perhaps he's liverish, from the heat. It might be a good thing, dear, if you went round and overhauled him. Somehow, it seems unnatural for Purdy to be bad-tempered.'

'It's true he may be a bit out of sorts. But I fear the evil's deeper-seated. It's my opinion the boy is tiring of regular work. Now that he hasn't even the excitement of the gold-escort to look forward to. . . . And he's been a rolling stone from the beginning, you know.'

265

'If only he would marry and settle down! I do wish I could find a wife for him. The right woman could make anything of Purdy'; and yet once more Mary fruitlessly scanned, in thought, the lists of her acquaintance.

'What if it's a case of sour grapes, love? Since the prettiest woman on Ballarat is no longer free. . . .'

'Oh, Richard, hush! Such foolish talk!'

'But is it? . . . let me look at her. Well, if not the prettiest, at least a very pretty person indeed. It certainly becomes you to be stouter, wife.'

But Mary had not an atom of vanity in her. 'Speaking of prettiness reminds me of something that happened at the Races last week – I forgot to tell you, at the time. There were two gentlemen there from Melbourne; and as Agnes Ocock went past, one of them said out loud: "Gad! That's a lovely woman." Agnes heard it herself, and was most distressed. And the whole day, wherever she went, they kept their field-glasses on her. Mr Henry was furious.'

'If you'll allow me to say so, my dear, Mrs Henry cannot hold a candle to someone I know – to my mind, at least.'

'If I suit you, Richard, that's all I care about.'

'Well, to come back to what we were saying. My advice is, give Master Purdy a taste of the cold shoulder the next time he comes hanging about the house. Let him see his ill-temper didn't pass unnoticed. There's no excuse for it. God bless me! doesn't he sleep the whole night through in his bed?' – and Mahony's tone took on an edge. The broken nights that were nowadays the rule with himself were the main drawbacks to his prosperity. He had never been a really good sleeper; and, in consequence, was one of those people who feel an intense need for sleep, and suffer under its curtailment. As things stood at present his rest was wholly at the mercy of the night-bell – a remorseless instrument, given chiefly to pealing just as he had managed to drop off. Its gentlest tinkle was enough to rouse him – long before it had succeeded in penetrating the ears of the groom, who was supposed to open. And when it remained silent for a night, some trifling noise in the road would simulate its jangle in his dreams. 'It's a wonder I have any nerves left,' he grumbled, as the hot, red dawns crept in at the sides of the bedroom-window. For the shortening of his sleep at one end did not mean that he could make it up at the other. All that summer he had fallen into the

266

habit of waking at five o'clock, and not being able to doze off again. The narrowest bar of light on the ceiling, the earliest twitter of the sparrows was enough to strike him into full consciousness; and Mary was hard put to it to darken the room and ensure silence; and would be till the day came when he could knock off work and take a thorough holiday. This he promised himself to do, before he was very much older.

CHAPTER TWO

Mary sat with pencil and paper and wrinkled her brows. She was composing a list, and every now and then, after an inward calculation, she lowered the pencil to note such items as: three tipsy-cakes, four trifles, eight jam-sandwiches. John Turnham had run up from Melbourne to fetch home wife and child; and his relatives were giving a musical card-party in his honour. By the window Jinny sat on a low ottoman suckling her babe, and paying but scant heed to her sister-in-law's deliberations: to her it seemed a much more important matter that the milk should flow smoothly down the precious little throat, than that Mary's supper should be a complete success. With her free hand she imprisoned the two little feet, working one against the other in slow enjoyment; or followed the warm little limbs up inside the swaddling, after the fashion of nursing mothers.

The two women were in the spare bedroom, which was dusk and cool and dimity-white; and they exchanged remarks in a whisper; for the lids had come down more than once on the big black eyes, and now only lifted automatically from time to time, to send a last look of utter satiation at the mother-face. Mary always said: 'She'll drop off sooner indoors, dear.' But this was not the whole truth. Richard had hinted that he considered the seclusion of the house better suited to the business of nursing than the comparative publicity of the verandah; for Jinny was too absorbed in her task to take thought for the proprieties. Here now she sat – she had grown very big and full since her marriage – in the generous, wide-lapped pose of some old Madonna.

Mary, thrown entirely on her own judgement, was just saying with decision: 'Well, better to err on the right side and have too much than too little,' and altering a four into a five, when steps came down the passage and John entered the room. Jinny made him a sign, and John, now Commissioner of Trade and Customs, advanced as lightly as could be expected of a heavy, well-grown man.

'Does she sleep?' he asked.

His eyes had flown to the child; only in the second place did they rest on his wife. At the sight of her free and easy bearing his face changed, and he said stiffly: 'I think, Jane, a little less exposure of your person, my dear . . .'

Flushing to her hair-roots, Jinny began as hastily as she dared to re-arrange her dress.

Mary broke a lance on her behalf. 'We were quite alone, John, ' she reminded her brother. 'Not expecting a visit from you.' And added: 'Richard says it is high time Baby was weaned. Jinny is feeling the strain.'

'As long as this rash continues I shall not permit it,' answered John, riding rough-shod over even Richard's opinion. ('I shouldn't agree to it either, John dear,' murmured Jinny.) 'And now, Mary, a word with you about the elder children. I understand that you are prepared to take Emma back – is that so?'

Yes, Mary was pleased to say Richard had consented to Trotty's return; but he would not hear of her undertaking Johnny. At eleven years of age the proper place for a boy, he said, was a Grammar School. With Trotty, of course, it was different. 'I always found her easy to manage, and should be more than glad to have her'; and Mary meant what she said. Her heart ached for John's motherless children. Jinny's interest in them had lasted only so long as she had none of her own; and Mary, who being childless had kept a large heart for all little ones, marvelled at the firm determination to get rid of her step-children which her sister-in-law, otherwise so pliable, displayed.

Brother and sister talked things over, intuitively meeting half-way, understanding each other with a word, as only blood relations can. Jinny, the chief person concerned, sat meekly by, or chimed in merely to echo her husband's views.

'By the way, I ran into Richard on Specimen Hill,' said John as he turned to leave the room. 'And he asked me to let you know that he would not be home to lunch.'

'There . . . if that isn't always the way!' exclaimed Mary. 'As sure as I cook something he specially likes, he doesn't come in. Tilly sent me over the loveliest little sucking-pig this morning. Richard would have enjoyed it.'

'You should be proud, my dear Mary, that his services are in such demand.'

'I am, John – no one could be prouder. But all the same I wish he could manage to be a little more regular with his meals. It makes cooking so difficult. Tomorrow, because I shan't have a minute to spare, he'll be home punctually, demanding something nice. But I warn you, tomorrow you'll all have to picnic!'

However, when the day came, she was better than her word, and looked to it that neither guests nor husband went short. Since a couple of tables on trestles took up the dining-room, John and Mahony lunched together in the surgery; while Jinny's meal was spread on a tray and sent to her in the bedroom. Mary herself had time only to snatch a bite standing. From early morning on, tied up in a voluminous apron, she was cooking in the kitchen, very hot and floury and preoccupied, drawing grating shelves out of the oven, greasing tins and patty-pans, dredging flour. The click-clack of egg-beating resounded continuously; and mountains of sponge-cakes of all shapes and sizes rose under her hands. This would be the largest, most ambitious party she had ever given – the guests expected numbered between twenty and thirty, and had, besides, carte blanche to bring with them anyone who happened to be staying with them – and it would be a disgrace under which Mary, reared in Mrs Beamish's school, could never again have held up her head, had a single article on her supper-table run short.

In all this she had only such help as her one maidservant could give her – John had expressly forbidden Jinny the kitchen. True, during the morning Miss Amelia Ocock, a gentle little elderly body with a harmless smile and a prominent jaw, who was now an inmate of her father's house, together with Zara, returned from England and a visitor at the Ococks' – these two walked over to offer their aid in setting the tables. But Miss Amelia, fluttery and undecided as a bird, was far too timid to do herself justice; and Zara spent so long arranging the flowers in the central epergnes that before she had finished with one of them it was lunch time.

'I could have done it myself while she was cutting the stalks,' Mary told her husband. 'But Zara hasn't really been any good at flowers since her "mixed bouquet" took first prize at the Flower Show. Of course, though, it looks lovely now it's done.'

Purdy dropped in during the afternoon and was more useful; he sliced the crusts off loaf-high mounds of sandwiches, and tested the strength and flavour of the claret-cup. Mary could not make up her mind, when it came to the point, to follow

270

Richard's advice and treat him coldly. She did, however, tell him that his help would be worth a great deal more to her if he talked less and did not always look for an answer to what he said. But Purdy was not to be quashed. He had taken it into his head that she was badly treated, in being left 'to slave' alone, within the oven's radius; and he was very hard on Jinny, whom he had espied comfortably dandling her child on the front verandah. 'I'd like to wring the bloomin' kid's neck!'

'Purdy, for shame!' cried Mary outraged. 'It's easy to see you're still a bachelor. Just wait, sir, till you have children of your own!'

Under her guidance he bore stacks of plates across the yard to the dining-room — where the blinds were lowered to keep the room cool — and strewed these, and corresponding knives and forks, up and down the tables. He also carried over the heavy soup-tureen in which was the claret-cup. But he had a man's slippery fingers, and, between these and his limp, Mary trembled for the fate of her crockery. He made her laugh, too, and distracted her attention; and she was glad when it was time for him to return to barracks.

'Now come early tonight,' she admonished him. 'And mind you bring your music. Miss Amelia's been practising up that duet all the week. She'll be most disappointed if you don't ask her to sing with you.'

On the threshold of the kitchen Purdy set his fingers to his nose in the probable direction of Miss Amelia; then performed some skittish female twists and turns about the yard. 'So hoarse, love . . . a bad cold . . . not in voice!' Mary laughed afresh, and ordered him off.

But when he had gone she looked grave, and out of an oddly disquieting feeling said to herself: 'I do hope he'll be on his best behaviour tonight, and not tread on Richard's toes.'

As it was, she had to inform her husband of something that she knew would displease him. John had come back in the course of the afternoon and announced, without ceremony, that he had extended an invitation to the Devines for the evening.

'It's quite true what's being said, dear,' Mary strove to soothe Richard, as she helped him make a hasty toilet in the bathroom. 'Mr Devine *is* going to stand for Parliament; and he has promised his support, if he gets in, to some measure John has at heart. John wants to have a long talk with him tonight.'

But Richard was exceedingly put out. 'Well, I hope, my dear, that as it's your brother who has taken such a liberty, *you'll* explain the situation to your guests. I certainly shall not. But I do know there was no need to exclude Ned and Polly from such an omnium-gatherum as this party of yours will be.'

Even while he spoke there came a rat-a-tat at the front door, and Mary had to hurry off. And now knock succeeded knock with the briefest of intervals, the noise carrying far in the quiet street. Mysteriously bunched-up figures, their heads veiled in the fleeciest of clouds, were piloted along the passage; and: 'I *hope* we are not the first!' was murmured by each new-comer in turn. The gentlemen went to change their boots on the back verandah; the ladies to lay off their wraps in Mary's bedroom. And soon this room was filled to overflowing with the large soft abundance of crinoline; hoops swaying from this side to that, as the guests gave place to one another before the looking-glass, where bands of hair were smoothed and the catches of bracelets snapped. Music-cases lay strewn over the counterpane; the husbands who lined up in the passage, to wait for their wives, also bearing rolls of music. Mary, in black silk with a large cameo brooch at her throat, and only a delicate pink on her cheeks to tell of all her labours, moved helpfully to and fro, offering a shoe-horn, a hand-mirror, pins and hairpins. She was caught, as she passed Mrs Henry Ocock, a modishly late arrival, by that lady's plump white hand, and a whispered request to be allowed to retain her mantle. 'Henry was really against my coming, dearest. So anxious . . . so absurdly anxious!'

'And pray where's the *H*onourable Mrs T. tonight?' inquired 'old Mrs Ocock', rustling up to them: Tilly was the biggest and most handsomely dressed woman in the room. 'On her knees worshipping, I bet you, up to the last minute! Or else not allowed to show her nose till the *H*onourable John's got his studs in. – Now then, girls, how much longer are you going to stand preening and prinking?'

The 'girls' were Zara, at this present a trifle *passée*, and Miss Amelia, who was still further from her prime; and gathering the two into her train, as a hen does its chickens, Tilly swept them off to face the ordeal of the gentlemen and the drawing-room.

Mary and Agnes brought up the rear. Mr Henry was on the watch, and directly his wife appeared wheeled forward the best armchair and placed her in it, with a footstool under her feet. Mary planted Jinny next her and left them to their talk of nurseries: for Richard's sake she wished to screen Agnes from the vulgarities of Mrs Devine. Herself she saw with dismay, on entering, that Richard had already been pounced on by the husband: there he stood, listening to his ex-greengrocer's words – they were interlarded with many an awkward and familiar gesture – on his face an expression his wife knew well, while one small, impatient hand tugged at his whiskers.

But 'old Mrs Ocock' came to his rescue, bearing down upon him with an outstretched hand, and a howdee-do that could be heard all over the room: Tilly had long forgotten that she had ever borne him a grudge; she it was who could now afford to patronize. 'I hope I see you well, doctor? – Oh, not a bit of it. . . . I left him at 'ome. Mr O. has something wrong, if you please, with his leg or his big toe – gout or rheumatiz or something of that sort – and 'e's been so crabby with it for the last day or so that tonight I said to 'im: "No, my dear, you'll just take a glass of hot toddy, and go early and comfortable to your bed." Musical parties aren't in his line anyhow.'

A lively clatter of tongues filled the room, the space of which was taxed to its utmost: there were present, besides the friends and intimates of the house, several of Mahony's colleagues, a couple of Bank Managers, the Police Magistrate, the Post-master, the Town Clerk, all with their ladies. Before long, however, ominous pauses began to break up the conversation, and Mary was accomplished hostess enough to know what these meant. At a sign from her, Jerry lighted the candles on the piano, and thereupon a fugue-like chorus went up: 'Mrs Mahony, won't you play something? – Oh, do! – Yes, please, do. . . . I should enjoy it so much.'

Mary did not wait to be pressed; it was her business to set the ball rolling; and she stood up and went to the piano as uncon-cernedly as she would have gone to sweep a room or make a bed.

Placing a piece of music on the rack, she turned down the corners of the leaves. But here Archdeacon Long's handsome, weatherbeaten face looked over her shoulder. 'I hope you're going to give us the cannons, Mrs Mahony?' he said genially. And so Mary obliged him by laying aside the *morceau* she had chosen, and setting up instead a 'battle-piece', that was a general favourite.

'Aha! that's the ticket,' said Henry Ocock, and rubbed his

hands as Mary struck up, pianissimo, the march that told of the enemy's approach.

And: 'Boompity-boomp-boomp-boomp!' Archdeacon Long could not refrain from underlining each fresh salvo of artillery; while: 'That's a breach in their walls for 'em!' was Chinnery of the London Chartered's contribution to the stock of fun.

Mahony stood on the hearthrug and surveyed the assembly. His eyes fled Mrs Devine, most unfortunately perched on an ottoman in the middle of the room, where she sat, purple, shiny and beaming, two hot, fat, red hands clasped over her stomach ('Like a heathen idol! Confound the woman! I shall have to go and do the polite to her'), and sought Mary at the piano, hanging with pleasure on the slim form in the rich silk dress. This caught numberless lights from the candles, as did also the wings of her glossy hair. He watched, with a kind of amused tenderness, how at each forte passage head and shoulders took their share of lending force to the tones. He never greatly enjoyed Mary's playing. She did well enough at it, God bless her! – it would not have been Mary if she hadn't – but he came of a musical family; his mother had sung Handel faultlessly in her day, besides having a mastery of several instruments: and he was apt to be critical. Mary's firm, capable hands looked out of place on a piano; seemed to stand in a sheerly business relation to the keys. Nor was it otherwise with her singing: she had a fair contralto, but her ear was at fault; and he sometimes found himself swallowing nervously when she attacked high notes.

'Oh, doctor! your wife *do* play the pianner lovely,' said Mrs Devine, and her fat front rose and fell in an ecstatic sigh.

'Richard dear, will you come?' Mary laid her hands on his shoulder: their guests were clamouring for a *duo*. Her touch was a caress: here he was, making himself as pleasant as he knew how, to this old woman. When it came to doing a kindness, you could rely on Richard; he was all bark and no bite.

Husband and wife blended their voices – Mary had been at considerable pains to get up her part – and then Richard went on to a solo. He had a clear, true tenor that was very agreeable to hear; and Mary felt quite proud of his attainments. Later in the evening he might be persuaded to give them a reading from Boz, or a recitation. At that kind of thing, he had not his equal.

But first there was a cry for his flute; and in vain did Mahony protest that weeks had elapsed since he last screwed the instrument together. He got no quarter, even from Mary – but then

274

Mary was one of those inconvenient people to whom it mattered not a jot what a fool you made of yourself, as long as you did what was asked of you. And so, from memory and unaccompanied, he played them the old familiar air of *The Minstrel Boy*. The theme, in his rendering, was overlaid by florid variations and cumbered with senseless repetitions; but, none the less, the wild, wistful melody went home, touching even those who were not musical to thoughtfulness and retrospect. The most obstinate chatterers, whom neither sham battles nor Balfe and Blockley had silenced, held their tongues; and Mrs Devine openly wiped her eyes.

> O, the minstrel boy to the wars has gone!
> In the ranks of death you'll find him.

While it was proceeding, Mary found herself seated next John. John tapped his foot in time to the tune; and under cover of the applause at its close remarked abruptly: 'You should fatten Richard up a bit, Mary. He could stand it.'

From where they sat they had Richard in profile, and Mary studied her husband critically, her head a little on one side. 'Yes, he *is* rather thin. But I don't think he was ever meant to be fat.'

'Ah well! we are none of us as young as we used to be,' was John's tribute to the power of music. And throwing out his stomach, he leaned back in his chair and plugged the armholes of his vest with his thumbs.

And now, after due pressing on the part of host and hostess, the other members of the company advanced upon the piano, either singly or in couples, to bear a hand in the burden of entertainment. Their seeming reluctance had no basis in fact; for it was an unwritten law that everyone who could must add his mite; and only those who literally had 'not a note of music in them' were exempt. Tilly took a mischievous pleasure in announcing bluntly: 'So sorry, my dear, not to be able to do you a tool-de-rool! But when the *H*onourable Mrs T. and I were nippers we'd no time to loll round pianos, nor any pianos to loll round!' – this, just to see her brother-in-law's dark scowl; for no love – not even a liking – was lost between her and John. But with this handful of exceptions all nobly toed the line. Ladies with the tiniest reeds of voices, which shook like reeds, warbled of Last Roses and Prairie Flowers; others, with more force but due decorum, cried to Willie that they had Missed

275

Him, or coyly confessed to the presence of Silver Threads Among the Gold; and Mrs Chinnery, an old-young woman with a long, lean neck, which she twisted this way and that in the exertion of producing her notes, declared her love for an Old Armchair. The gentlemen, in baritones and profundos, told the amorous adventures of Ben Bolt; or desired to know what Home would be Without a Mother. Purdy spiced the hour with a comic song, and in the character of an outraged wife tickled the risibility of the ladies.

> Well, well, sir, so you've come at last!
> I thought you'd come no more.
> I've waited, with my bonnet on,
> From one till half-past four!

Zara and Mrs Long both produced *Home They brought her Warrior Dead!* from their portfolios; so Zara good-naturedly gave way and struck up *Robert, toi que j'aime!* which she had added to her repertory while in England. No one could understand a word of what she sang; but the mere fitting of the foreign syllables to the appropriate notes was considered a feat in itself, and corroborative of the high gifts Zara possessed.

Strenuous efforts were needed to get Miss Amelia to her feet. She was dying, as Mary knew, to perform her duet with Purdy; but when the moment came she put forward so many reasons for not complying that most people retired in despair. It took Mary to persevere. And finally the little woman was persuaded to the piano, where, red with gratification, she sat down, spread her skirts and unclasped her bracelets.

'Poor little Amelia!' said Mary to herself, as she listened to a romantic ballad in which Purdy, in the character of a high-minded nobleman, sought the hand of a virtuous gipsy-maid. 'And he doesn't give her a second thought. If one could just tell her not to be so silly!'

Not only had Purdy never once looked near Amelia – for the most part he had sat rather mum-chance, halfway in and out of a French window, even Zara's attempts to enliven him falling flat – but, during an extra loud performance, Tilly had confided to Mary the family's plans for their spinster relative. And: 'The poor little woman!' thought Mary again as she listened. For, after having been tied for years to the sick bed of a querulous mother; after braving the long sea-voyage, which for such a timid soul was full of ambushes and terrors, Miss Amelia had reached her journey's end only to find both father and brother comfortably wived, and with no use for her. Neither of them wanted her. She had been given house-room first by her father, then by the Henrys, and once more had had to go back to the paternal roof.

'It was nothing for Mossieu Henry in the long run,' was his stepmother's comment. But she laughed good-humouredly as she said it; for, his first wrath at her intrusion over, Henry had more or less become her friend; and now maintained that it was not a bad thing for his old father to have a sensible, managing woman behind him. Tilly had developed in many ways since her marriage; and Henry and she mutually respected each other's practical qualities.

The upshot of the affair was, she now told Mary, that Miss Amelia's male relatives had subscribed a dowry for her. 'It was me that insisted Henry should pay his share – him getting all the money 'e did with Agnes.' And Amelia was to be married off to 'Well, if you turn your head, my dear, you'll see who. Back there, helping to hold up the doorpost.'

Under cover of Zara's roulades Mary cautiously looked round. It was Henry's partner – young Grindle, now on the threshold of the thirties. His side-whiskers a shade less flamboyant than of old, a heavy watch-chain draped across his front, Grindle stood and lounged with his hands in his pockets.

Mary made round eyes. 'Oh, but Tilly! . . . isn't it very risky? He's so much younger than she is. Suppose she shouldn't be happy?'

'That'll be all right, Mary, trust me. Only give 'er a handle to 'er name, and Amelia 'ud be happy with anyone. She hasn't *that* much backbone in 'er. Besides, my dear, you think, she's over forty! Let her take 'er chance and be thankful. It isn't every old maid 'ud get such an offer.'

'And is . . . is *he* agreeable?' asked Mary, still unconvinced.

Tilly half closed her right eye and protruded the tip of her tongue. 'You could stake your last fiver on it, he is!'

But now that portion of the entertainment devoted to art was at an end, and the serious business of the evening began. Card-tables had been set out – for loo, as for less hazardous games. In principle, Mahony objected to the high play that was the order of the day; but if you invited people to your house you could not ask them to screw their points down from crowns to

277

halfpence. They would have thanked you kindly and have stayed at home. Here, at the loo-table places were eagerly snapped up, Henry Ocock and his stepmother being among the first to secure seats; both were keen, hard players, who invariably re-lined their well-filled pockets.

It would not have been the thing for either Mahony or his wife to take a hand; several of the guests held aloof. John had buttonholed old Devine; Jinny and Agnes were still lost in domesticities. Dear little Agnes had grown so retiring of late, thought Mary; she quite avoided the society of gentlemen, in which she had formerly taken such pleasure. Richard and Archdeacon Long sat on the verandah, and in moving to and fro, Mary caught a fragment of their talk: they were at the debatable question of table-turning, and her mental comment was a motherly and amused: 'That Richard, who is so clever, can interest himself in such nonsense!' Further on, Zara was giving Grindle an account of her voyage 'home', and ticking off the reasons that had led her to return. She sat across a hammock, and daintily exposed a very neat ankle. 'It was much too sleepy and dull for *me*! No, I've *quite* decided to spend the rest of my days in the colony.'

Mrs Devine was still perched on her ottoman. She beamed at her hostess. 'No, I dunno one card from another, dearie, and don' want to. Oh, my dear, what a *lovely* party it 'as been, and 'ow well you've carried it h'off!'

Mary nodded and smiled; but with an air of abstraction. The climax of her evening was fast approaching. Excusing herself, she slipped away and went to cast a last eye over her supper-tables, up and down which benches were ranged, borrowed from the Sunday School. To her surprise she found herself followed by Mrs Devine.

'*Do* let me 'elp you, my dear, do, now! I feel that stiff and silly sittin' stuck up there with me 'ands before me. And jes' send that young feller about 'is business.'

So Purdy and his offers of assistance were returned with thanks to the card-room, and Mrs Devine pinned up her black silk front. But not till she had freely vented her astonishment at the profusion of Mary's good things. ' 'Ow *do* you git 'em to rise so? — No, I never did! Fit for Buckin'am Palace and Queen Victoria! And all by your little self, too. — My dear, I must give you a good '*ug*!'

Hence, when at twelve o'clock the company began to stream

in, they found Mrs Devine installed behind the barricade of cups, saucers and glasses; and she it was who dispensed tea and coffee and ladled out the claret-cup; thus leaving Mary free to keep an argus eye on her visitors' plates. At his entry Richard had raised expostulating eyebrows; but his tongue of course was tied. And Mary made a lifelong friend.

And now for the best part of an hour Mary's sandwiches, sausage-rolls and meat-pies; her jam-rolls, pastries and lemon-sponges; her jellies, custards and creams; her blanc and jaune-manges and whipped syllabubs; her trifles, tipsy-cakes and char-lotte-russes formed the theme of talk and objects of attention. And though the ladies picked with becoming daintiness, the gentlemen made up for their partners' deficiencies; and there was none present who did not, in the shape of a hearty and well-turned compliment, add yet another laurel to Mary's crown.

CHAPTER THREE

It had struck two before the party began to break up. The first move made, however, the guests left in batches, escorting one another to their respective house-doors. The Henry Ococks' buggy had been in waiting for some time, and Mrs Henry's pretty head was drooping with fatigue before Henry, who was in the vein, could tear himself from the card-table. Mahony went to the front gate with them; then strolled with the Longs to the corner of the road.

He was in no hurry to retrace his steps. The air was balmy, after that of the overcrowded rooms, and it was a fabulously beautiful night. The earth lay steeped in moonshine, as in the light of a silver sun. Trees and shrubs were patterned to their last leaf on the ground before them. What odd mental twist made mortals choose rather to huddle indoors, by puny candle-light, than to be abroad laving themselves in a splendour such as this?

Leaning his arms on the top rail of a fence, he looked across the slope at the Flat, now hushed and still as the encampment of a sleeping army. Beyond, the bush shimmered palely grey — in his younger years he had been used, on a night like this when the moon sailed full and free, to take his gun and go opossuming. Those two old woody gods, Warrenheip and Buninyong, stood out more imposingly than by day; but the ranges seemed to have retreated. The light lay upon them like a visible burden, flattening their contours, filling up clefts and fissures with a milky haze.

'Good evening, doctor!'

Spoken in his very ear, the words made him jump. He had been lost in contemplation; and the address had a ghostly sud-denness. But it was no ghost that stood beside him — nor indeed was it a night for those presences to be abroad whose element is the dark.

Ill-pleased at the intrusion, he returned but a stiff nod: then, since he could not in decency greet and leave-take in a breath, feigned to go on for a minute with his study of the landscape. After which he said: 'Well, I must be moving. Good night to you.'

'So you're off your sleep, too, are you?' As often happens, the impulse to speak was a joint one. The words collided.

Instinctively Mahony shrank into himself; this familiar bracketing of his person with another's was distasteful to him. Besides, the man who had sprung up at his elbow bore a reputation that was none of the best. The owner of a small chemist's shop on the Flat, he contrived to give offence in sundry ways: he was irreligious – an infidel, his neighbours had it – and of a Sabbath would scour his premises or hoe potatoes rather than attend church or chapel. Though not a confirmed drunkard, he had been seen to stagger in the street, and be unable to answer when spoken to. Also, the woman with whom he lived was not generally believed to be his lawful wife. Hence the public fought shy of his nostrums; and it was a standing riddle how he managed to avoid putting up his shutters. More nefarious practices no doubt, said the relentless *vox populi*. – Seen near at hand, he was a tall, haggard-looking fellow of some forty years of age, the muscles on his neck standing out like those of a skinny old horse.

Here, his gratuitous assumption of a common bond drew a cold: 'Pray what reason have you to think that?' from Mahony. And without waiting for a reply he again said good night and turned to go.

The man accepted the rebuff with a meekness that was painful to see. 'Thought, comin' on you like this, you were a case like my own. No offence, I'm sure,' he said humbly. It was evident he was well used to getting the cold shoulder. Mahony stayed his steps. 'What's the matter with you?' he asked. 'Aren't you well? There's a remedy to be found for most ills under the sun.'

'Not for mine! The doctor isn't born or the drug discovered that could cure me.'

The tone of bragging bitterness grated anew. Himself given to the vice of overstatement, Mahony had small mercy on it in others. 'Tut, tut!' he deprecated.

There was a brief silence before the speaker went on more quietly: 'You're a young man, doctor, I'm an old one.' And he

281

looked old as he spoke; Mahony saw that he had erred in putting him down as merely elderly. He was old and grey and down-at-heel – fifty, if a day – and his clothes hung loose on his bony frame. 'You'll excuse me if I say I know better'n you. When a man's done, he's done. And that's me. Yes,' – he grew inflated again in reciting his woes – 'I'm one o' your hopeless cases, just as surely as if I was being eaten up by a cancer or a consumption. To mend me, you doctors 'ud need to start me afresh – from the mother-egg.'

'You exaggerate, I'm sure.'

'It's that – knowin' one's played out, with by rights still a good third of one's life to run – that's what puts the sleep away. In the daylight it's none so hard to keep the black thoughts under; themselves they're not so daresome; and there's one's pipe, and the haver o' the young fry. But night's the time! Then they come tramplin' along, a whole army of 'em, carryin' banners with letters a dozen feet high, so's you shan't miss rememberin' what you'd give your soul to forget. And so it'll go on, et cetera and ad lib., till it pleases the old Joker who sits grinnin' up aloft to put His heel down – as you or me would squash a bull-ant or a scorpion.'

'You speak bitterly, Mr Tangye. Does a night like this not bring you calmer, clearer thoughts?' and Mahony waved his arm in a large, loose gesture at the sky.

His words passed unheeded. The man he addressed spun round and faced him, with a rusty laugh. 'Hark at that!' he cried. 'Just hark at it! Why, in all the years I've been in this God-forsaken place – long as I've been here – I've never yet heard my own name properly spoken. You're the first, doctor. You shall have the medal.'

'But, man alive, you surely don't let that worry you? Why, I've the same thing to put up with every day of my life. I smile at it.' And Mahony believed what he said, forgetting, in the antagonism such spleen roused in him, the annoyance the false stressing of his own name could sometimes cause him.

'So did I, once,' said Tangye, and wagged his head. 'But the day came when it seemed the last straw; a bit o' mean spite on the part o' this hell of a country itself.'

'You dislike the colony, it appears, intensely?'

'You like it?' The counter question came tip for tap.

'I can be fair to it, I hope, and appreciate its good sides.' As always, the mere hint of an injustice made Mahony passionately just.

'Came 'ere of your own free will, did you? Weren't crowded out at home? Or bamboozled by a pack o' lying tales?' Tangye's voice was husky with eagerness.

'That I won't say either. But it is entirely my own choice that I remain here.'

'Well, I say to you, think twice of it! If you have the chance of gettin' away, take it. It's no place this, doctor, for the likes of you and me. Haven't you never turned and asked yourself what the devil you were doin' here? And that reminds me. . . . There was a line we used to have drummed into us at school – it's often come back to me since. *Coelum, non animum, mutant, qui trans mare currunt.* In our green days we gabbled that off by rote; then, it seemed just one more o' the eel-sleek phrases the classics are full of. Now, I take off my hat to the man who wrote it. He knew what he was talkin' about – by the Lord Harry, he did!'

The Latin had come out tentatively, with an odd, unused intonation. Mahony's retort: 'How on earth do you know what suits me and what doesn't?' died on his lips. He was surprised into silence. There had been nothing in the other's speech to show that he was a man of any education – rather the reverse.

Meanwhile Tangye went on: 'I grant you it's an antiquated point o' view; but doesn't that go to prove what I've been sayin'; that you and me are old-fashioned, too – out-o'-place here, out-o'-date? The modern sort, the sort that gets on in this country, is a prime hand at cuttin' his coat to suit his cloth; for all that the stop-at-homes, like the writer o' that line and other ancients, prate about the Ethiopian's hide or the leopard and his spots. They didn't buy their experience dear, like we did; didn't guess that if a man *don't* learn to fit himself in, when he gets set down in such a land as this, he's a goner; any more'n they knew that most o' those who hold out here – all of 'em at any rate who've climbed the ladder, nabbed the plunder – have found no more difficulty in changin' their spots than they have their trousers. Yes, doctor, there's only one breed that flourishes, and you don't need me to tell you which it is. Here they lie' – and he nodded to right and left of him – 'dreamin' o' their money-bags, and their dividends, and their profits, and how they'll diddle and swindle one another afresh, soon as the sun gets up tomorrow. Harder 'n nails they are, and sharp as needles. You ask me why I do my walkin' out in the night-time? It's so's to

283

avoid the sight o' their mean little eyes, and their greedy, graspin' faces.'

Mahony's murmured disclaimer fell on deaf ears. Like one who had been bottled up for months, Tangye flowed on. 'What a life! What a set! What a place to end one's days in! Remember, if you can, the yarns that were spun round it for our benefit, from twenty thousand safe miles away. It was the Land o' Promise and Plenty, topful o' gold, strewn over with nuggets that only waited for hands to pick 'em up. – Lies! – lies from beginnin' to end! I say to you this is the hardest and cruellest country ever created, and a man like me's no more good here than the muck – the parin's and stale fishguts and other leavin's – that knocks about a harbour and washes against the walls. I'll tell you the only use I'll have been here, doctor, when my end comes: I'll dung some bit o' land for 'em with my moulder and rot. That's all. They'd do better with my sort if they knocked us on the head betimes, and boiled us down for our fat and marrow.'

Not much in that line to be got from *your* carcase, my friend, thought Mahony, with an inward smile.

But Tangye had paused merely to draw breath. 'What I say is, instead o' layin' snares for us, it ought to be forbid by law to give men o' my make ship room. At home in the old country we'd find our little nook, and jog along decently to the end of our days. But just the staid, respectable, orderly sort I belonged to's neither needed nor wanted here. I fall to thinkin' sometimes on the fates of the hundreds of honest, steady-goin' lads, who at one time or another have chucked up their jobs over there – for this. The drink no doubt's took most: they never knew before that one *could* sweat as you sweat here. And the rest? Well, just accident . . . or the sun . . . or dysentery . . . or the bloody toil that goes by the name o' work in these parts – you know the list, doctor, better'n me. They say the waste o' life in a new country can't be helped; doesn't matter; has to be. But that's cold comfort to the wasted. No! I say to you, there ought to be an Act of Parliament to prevent young fellows squanderin' themselves, throwin' away their lives as I did mine. For when we're young, we're not sane. Youth's a fever o' the brain. And I *was* young once, though you mightn't believe it; I had straight joints, and no pouch under my chin, and my full share o' windy hopes. Senseless truck these! To be spilled overboard bit by bit – like on a hundred-mile tramp a new-chum finishes by pitchin' from

284

his swag all the needless rubbish he's started with. What's wanted to get on here's somethin' quite else. Horny palms and costive bowels; more'n a dash o' the sharper; and no sickly squeamishness about knockin' out other men and steppin' into their shoes. And I was only an ordinary young chap; not over-strong nor over-shrewd, but honest – honest, by God I was! That didn't count. It even stood in my way. For I was too good for this and too mealy-mouthed for that; and while I stuck, con-siderin' the fairness of a job, someone who didn't care a damn whether it was fair or not, walked in over my head and took it from me. There isn't anything I haven't tried my luck at, and with everything it's been the same. Nothin's prospered; the money wouldn't come – or stick if it did. And so here I am – all that's left of me. It isn't much; and by and by a few rank weeds 'ull spring from it, and old Joey there, who's paid to grub round the graves, old Joey 'ull curse and say: a weedy fellow that, a rotten, weedy blackguard; and spit on his hands and hoe, till the weeds lie bleedin' their juices – the last heirs of me – the last issue of my loins!'

'Pray, does it never occur to you, you fool, that *flowers* may spring from you?'

He had listened to Tangye's diatribe in a white heat of im-patience. But when he spoke he struck an easy tone – nor was he in any hesitation how to reply: for that, he had played devil's advocate all too often with himself in private. An unlovely country, yes, as Englishmen understood beauty; and yet not without a charm of its own. An arduous life, certainly, and one full of pitfalls for the weak or the unwary; yet he believed it was no more impossible to win through here, and with clean hands, than anywhere else. To generalize as his companion had done was absurd. Preposterous, too, the notion that those of their fellow-townsmen who had carried off the prizes owed their success to some superiority in bodily strength . . . or sharp dealing . . . or thickness of skin. With Mr Tangye's permission he would cite himself as an example. He was neither a very robust man, nor, he ventured to say, one of any marked ability in the other two directions. Yet he had managed to succeed without, in the process, sacrificing jot or tittle of his principles; and today he held a position that any member of his profession across the seas might envy him.

'Yes, but till you got there!' cried Tangye. 'Hasn't every superfluous bit of you – every thought of interest that wasn't essential to the daily grind – been pared off?'

'If,' said Mahony stiffening, 'if what you mean by that is, have I allowed my mind to grow narrow and sluggish, I can honestly answer no.'

In his heart he denied the charge even more warmly; for, as he spoke, he saw the great cork-slabs on which hundreds of moths and butterflies made dazzling spots of colour; saw the sheets of pink blotting-paper between which his collection of native plants lay pressed; the glass case filled with geological specimens; his Bible, the margins of which round Genesis were black with his handwriting; a pile of books on the new marvel Spiritualism; Colenso's *Pentateuch*; the big black volumes of the *Arcana Coelestia*; Locke on Miracles: he saw all these things and more. 'No, I'm glad to say I have retained many interests outside my work.'

Tangye had taken off his spectacles and was polishing them on a crumpled handkerchief. He seemed about to reply, even made a quick half-turn towards Mahony; then thought better of it, and went on rubbing. A smile played round his lips.

'And in conclusion let me say this,' went on Mahony, not unnettled by his companion's expression. 'It's sheer folly to talk about what life makes of us. Life is not an active force. It's we who make what *we* will, of life. And in order to shape it to the best of our powers, Mr Tangye, to put our brief span to the best possible use, we must never lose faith in God or our fellow-men; never forget that, whatever happens, there *is* a sky, with stars in it, above us.

'Ah, there's a lot of bunkum talked about life,' returned Tangye dryly, and settled his glasses on his nose. 'And as a man gets near the end of it, he sees just *what* bunkum it is. Life's only got one meanin', doctor; seen plain, there's only one object in everything we do; and that's to keep a sound roof over our heads and a bite in our mouths – and in those of the helpless creatures who depend on us. The rest has no more sense or significance than a nigger's hammerin' on the tamtam. The lucky ones o' this world don't grasp it; but we others do; and after all p'raps, it's worth while havin' gone through it to have got at *one* bit of the truth, however small. Good night.'

He turned on his heel, and before his words were cold on the air had vanished, leaving Mahony blankly staring.

The moonshine still bathed the earth, gloriously untroubled

by the bitterness of human words and thoughts. But the night seemed to have grown chilly; and Mahony gave an involuntary shiver. 'Someone walking over my . . . now what would that specimen have called it? Over the four by eight my remains will one day manure!'

'An odd, abusive, wrong-headed fellow,' he mused, as he made his way home. 'Who would ever have thought, though, that the queer little chemist had so much in him? A failure? . . . yes, he was right there; and as unlovely as failures always are – at close quarters.' But as he laid his hands on the gate, he jerked up his head and exclaimed half aloud: 'God bless my soul! What he wanted was not argument or reason but a little human sympathy.' As usual, however, the flash of intuition came too late. 'For such a touchy nature I'm certainly extraordinarily obtuse where the feelings of others are concerned,' he told himself as he hooked in the latch.

'Why, Richard, where *have* you been?' came Mary's clear voice – muted so as not to disturb John and Jinny, who had retired to rest. Purdy and she sat waiting on the verandah. 'Were you called out? We've had time to clear everything away. Here, dear, I saved you some sandwiches and a glass of claret. I'm sure you didn't get any supper yourself, with looking after other people.'

Long after Mary had fallen asleep he lay wakeful. His foolish blunder in response to Tangye's appeal rankled in his mind. He could not get over his insensitiveness. How he had boasted of his prosperity, his moral nicety, his saving pursuits – he to boast! – when all that was asked of him was a kindly: 'My poor fellow-soul, you have indeed fought a hard fight; but there *is* a God above us who will recompense you at His own time, take the word for it of one who has also been through the Slough of Despond.' And then just these . . . these hobbies of his, of which he had made so much. Now that he was alone with himself he saw them in a very different light. Lepidoptera collected years since were still unregistered, plants and stones unclassified; his poor efforts at elucidating the Bible waited to be brought into line with the Higher Criticism; Home's levitations and fire-tests called for investigation; while the leaves of some of the books he had cited had never even been cut. The mere thought of these things was provocative, rest-destroying. To induce drowsiness he went methodically through the list of his acquaintances, and sought to range them under one or other of Tangye's headings. And over this there came moments when he lapsed into depths . . . fetched himself up again – but with an effort . . . only to fall back. . . .

But he seemed barely to have closed his eyes when the night-bell rang. In an instant he was on his feet in the middle of the room, applying force to his sleep-cogged wits.

He threw open the sash. 'Who's there? What is it?'

Henry Ocock's groom. 'I was to fetch you out to our place at once, governor.'

'But – Is Mrs Henry taken ill?'

'Not as I know of,' said the man dryly. 'But her and the boss had a bit of a tiff on the way home, and Madam's excited-like.'

'And am I to pay for their tiffs?' muttered Mahony hotly.

'Hush, Richard! He'll hear you,' warned Mary, and sat up. 'I shall decline to go. Henry's a regular old woman.'

Mary shook her head. 'You can't afford to offend the Henrys. And you know what he is – so hasty. He'd call in someone else on the spot, and you'd never get back. If only you hadn't stayed out so long, dear, looking at the moon!'

'Good God! Mary, is one never to have a moment to oneself? Never a particle of pleasure or relaxation?'

'Why, Richard!' expostulated his wife, and even felt a trifle ashamed of his petulance. 'What would you call tonight, I wonder? Wasn't the whole evening one of pleasure and relaxation?'

And Mahony, struggling into shirt and trousers, had to admit that he would be hard put to it to give it another name.

288

CHAPTER FOUR

'Hush, dolly! Mustn't cry, and make a noise. Uncle Richard's cross.'

Trotty sat on a hassock and rocked a china babe, with all the appurtenant mother-fuss she had picked up from the tending of her tiny stepsister. The present Trotty was a demure little maid of some seven summers, who gave the impression of having been rather rudely elongated. Her flaxen hair was stiffly imprisoned behind a round black comb; and her big blue eyes alone remained to her from a lovely infancy. ('Poor Emma's eyes,' said Mary.)

Imitative as a monkey she went on – with a child's perfect knowledge that it is all make-believe, yet with an entire credence in the power of make-believe: 'Naughty child – *will* you be quiet? There! You've frown your counterpane off now. Wonder what next you'll do. I declare I'll slap you soon – you make me so cross.'

Through the surgery-window the words floated out: 'For goodness' sake, don't bother me now with such trifles, Mary! It's not the moment – with a whole string of people waiting in the other room.'

'Well, if only you'll be satisfied with what I do, dear, and not blame me afterwards.'

'Get Purdy to give you a hand with Ned's affair. He has time and to spare.' And wetting his finger-tip Mahony nervously flipped over a dozen pages of the book that lay open before him.

'Well . . . if you think I should,' said Mary, with a spice of doubt.

'I do. And now go, wife, and remember to shut the door after you. Oh, and tell that woman in the kitchen to stop singing. Her false notes drive me crazy. – How many are there, this morning?'

'Eight – no, nine, if that's another,' replied Mary, with an ear to the front door.

'Tch! I'll have to stop then,' and Mahony clapped to the work he had been consulting. 'Never a minute to keep abreast of the times.' But: 'That's a good, helpful wife,' as Mary stooped to kiss him. 'Do the best you can, maavourneen, and never mind me.'

'Take me with you, Auntie!' Trotty sprang up from her stool, overturning babe and cradle.

'Not today, darling. Besides, why are you here? You know I've forbidden you to be on the front verandah when the patients come. Run away to the back and play there.'

Mary donned hat and shawl, opened her parasol and went out into the sun. With the years she had developed into rather a stately young woman: she held her head high and walked with a firm, free step.

Her first visit was to the stable to find Long Jim – or Old Jim as they now called him; for he was nearing the sixties. The notice to leave, which he had given the day before, was one of the 'trifles' it fell to her to consider. Personally Mary thought his going would be no great loss: he knew nothing about a garden, yet resented instruction; and it had always been necessary to get outside help in for the horses. If he went they could engage someone who would combine the posts. But Richard had taken umbrage at the old man's tone; had even been nervously upset over it. It behoved her to find out what the matter was.

'I want a change,' said Old Jim dourly in response to her inquiry; and went on polishing wheel-spokes, and making the wheel fly. 'I've bin 'ere too long. An' now I've got a bit o' brass together, an' am thinkin' I'd like to be me own master for a spell.'

'But at your age, Jim, is it wise? – to throw up a comfortable home, just because you've laid a little past?'

'It's enough to keep me. I turned over between four and five 'undred last week in "Piecrusts".'

'Oh!' said Mary, taken by surprise. 'Then that – that's your only reason for wishing to leave?' And as he did not reply, but went on swishing: 'Come, Jim, if you've anything on your mind, say it out. The doctor didn't like the way you spoke to him last night.'

At this the old man straightened his back, took a straw from between his teeth, spat and said: 'Well, if you must know, Mrs Mahony, the doctor's not the boss it pleases me to be h'under any more – and that's the trewth. I'm tired of it – dog-tired. You can slave yer 'ead off for 'im, and 'e never notices a thing you do, h'or if 'e does, it's on'y to find fault. It h'ain't 'uman, I say, and I'll be danged if I stand it h'any longer.'

But people who came to Mary with criticism of Richard got no mercy. 'You're far too touchy, Jim. *You* know, if anyone does, how rushed and busy the doctor is, and you ought to be the first to make allowance for him – after all he's done for you. You wouldn't be here now, if it hadn't been for him. And then to expect him to notice and praise you for every little job you do!'

But Jim was stubborn. 'E didn't want to deny anything. But 'e'd rather go. An' this day a week if it suited her.

'It's really dreadful how uppish the lower classes get as soon as they have a little money in their pocket,' she said to herself, as she walked the shadeless, sandy road. But this thought was like a shadow cast by her husband's mind on hers, and was ousted by the more indigenous: 'But after all who can blame him, poor old fellow, for wanting to take life easy if he has the chance.' She even added: 'He might have gone off, as most of them do, without a word.'

Then her mind reverted to what he had said of Richard, and she pondered the antagonism that had shown through his words. It was not the first time she had run up against this spirit, but, as usual, she was at a loss to explain it. Why should people of Old Jim's class dislike Richard as they did? – find him so hard to get on with? He was invariably considerate of them, and treated them very generously with regard to money. And yet . . . for some reason or other they felt injured by him; and thought and spoke of him with a kind of churlish resentment. She was not clever enough to find the key to the riddle – it was no such simple explanation as that he felt himself too good for them. That was not the case: he was proud, certainly, but she had never known anyone who – under, it was true, a rather sarcastic manner – was more broadly tolerant of his fellow-men. And she wound up her soliloquy with the lame admission: 'Yes, in spite of all his kindness, I suppose he *is* queer . . . decidedly queer,' and then she heaved a sigh. What a pity it was! When you knew him to be, at heart, such a dear, good, well-meaning man.

A short walk brought her to the four-roomed cottage where Ned lived with wife and children. Or had lived, till lately. He had been missing from his home now for over a week. On the last occasion of his being in Melbourne with the carrying-van, he had decamped, leaving the boy who was with him to make the return-journey alone. Since then, nothing could be heard of him; and his billet in the Agency had been snapped up.

'Or so they say!' said his wife, with an angry sniff. 'I don't believe a word of it, Mary. Since the railway's come, biz has gone to the dogs; and they're only too glad to get the chance of sacking another man.'

Polly looked untidier than ever; she wore a slatternly wrapper, and her hair was thrust unbrushed into its net. But she suffered, no doubt, in her own way; she was red-eyed, and very hasty-handed with her nestful of babes. Sitting in the cheerless parlour, Ned's dark-eyed eldest on her knee, Mary strove to soothe and encourage. But: it has never been much of a home for the poor boy was her private opinion; and she pressed her cheek affectionately against the little black curly head that was a replica of Ned's own.

'What's goin' to become of us all, the Lord only knows,' said Polly, after having had the good cry the sympathetic presence of her sister-in-law justified. 'I'm not a brown cent troubled about Ned – only boiling with 'im. 'E's off on the booze, sure enough – and 'e'll turn up again, safe and sound, like loose fish always do. Wait till I catch 'im though! He'll get it hot.

'We never ought to have come here,' she went on drying her eyes. 'Drat the place and all that's in it, that's what I say! He did better'n this in Castlemaine; and I'd pa behind me there. But once Richard had sent 'im that twenty quid, he'd no rest till he got away. And I thought, when he was so set on it, maybe it'd have a good effect on 'im, to be near you both. But that was just another shoot into the brown. You've been A1, Mary; you've done your level best. But Richard's never treated Ned fair. I don't want to take Ned's part; he's nothing in the world but a pretty-faced noodle. But Richard's treated 'im as if he was the dirt under 'is feet. And Ned's felt it. Oh, I know whose doing it was, we were never asked up to the house when you'd company. It wasn't *yours*, my dear! But we can't all have hyphens to our names, and go driving round with kid gloves on our hands and our noses in the air.'

Mary felt quite depressed by this fresh attack on her husband. Reminding herself, however, that Polly was excited and over-wrought, she did not speak out the defence that leapt to her tongue. She said staunchly: 'As you put it, Polly, it does seem as if we haven't acted rightly towards Ned. But it wasn't Richard's doing alone. I've been just as much to blame as he has.'

She sat on, petting the fractious children and giving kindly assurances: as long as she and Richard had anything themselves, Ned's wife and Ned's children should not want: and as she spoke, she slipped a substantial proof of her words into Polly's unproud hand. Besides, she believed there was every chance now of Ned soon being restored to them; and she told how they were going, that very morning, to invoke Mr Smith's aid. Mr Smith was in the Police, as Polly knew, and had influential friends among the Force in Melbourne. By tomorrow there might be good news to bring her.

Almost an hour had passed when she rose to leave. Mrs Ned was so grateful for the visit and the help that, out in the narrow little passage, she threw her arms round Mary's neck and drew her to her bosom. Holding her thus, after several hearty kisses, she said in a mysterious whisper, with her lips close to Mary's ear: 'Mary, love, may I say something to you?' and the permission granted, went on: 'That is, give you a bit of a hint, dearie?'

'Why, of course you may, Polly.'

'Sure you won't feel hurt, dear?'

'Quite sure. What is it?' and Mary disengaged herself, that she might look the speaker in the face.

'Well, it's just this – you mentioned the name yourself, or I wouldn't have dared. It's young Mr Smith, Mary. My dear, in future don't you have 'im quite so much about the house as you do at present. It ain't the thing. People *will* talk, you know, if you give 'em a handle.' ('Oh, but Polly!' in a blank voice from Mary.) 'Now, now, I'm not blaming you – not the least tiddly-wink. But there's no harm in being careful, is there, love, if you don't want your name in people's mouths? I'm that fond of you, Mary – you don't mind me speaking, dearie?'

'No, Polly, I don't. But it's the greatest nonsense – I never heard such a thing!' said Mary hotly. 'Why, Purdy is Richard's oldest friend. They were schoolboys together.'

'Maybe they were. But I hear 'e's mostly up at your place when Richard's out. And you're a young and pretty woman, my dear; it's Richard who ought to think of it, and he so much older than you. Well, just take the hint, love. It comes best, don't it, from one of the family?'

But Mary left the house in a sad flurry; and even forgot for a street-length to open her parasol.

Her first impulse was to go straight to Richard. But she had not covered half-a-dozen yards before she saw that this would never do. At the best of times Richard abominated gossip; and the fact of it having, in the present case, dared to fasten its fangs in someone belonging to him would make him doubly wroth. He might even try to find out who had started the talk; and get himself into hot water over it. Or he might want to lay all the blame on his own shoulders — make himself the reproaches Ned's Polly had not spared him. Worse still, he would perhaps accuse Purdy of inconsiderateness towards her, and fly into a rage with him; and then the two of them would quarrel, which would be a thousand pities. For though he often railed at Purdy, yet that was only Richard's way: he was genuinely fond of him, and unbent to him as to nobody else.

But these were just so many pretexts put forward to herself by Mary for keeping silence; the real reason lay deeper. Eight years of married life had left her, where certain subjects were concerned, with all the modesty of her girlhood intact. There were things, indelicate things, which *could* not be spoken out, even between husband and wife. For her to have to step before Richard and say: someone else feels for me in the same way as you, my husband, do, would make her ever after unable frankly to meet his eyes. Besides giving the vague, cobwebby stuff a body it did not deserve.

But yet again this was not the whole truth: she had another, more uncomfortable side of it to face; and the flies buzzed unheeded round her head. The astonishment she had shown at her sister-in-law's warning had not been altogether sincere. Far down in her heart Mary found a faint, faint trace of complicity. For months past — she could admit it now — she had not felt easy about Purdy. Something disagreeable, disturbing, had crept into their relations. The jolly, brotherly manner she liked so well had deserted him; besides short-tempered he had grown deadly serious, and not the stupidest woman could fail altogether to see what the matter was. But she had wilfully bandaged her eyes. And if, now and then, some word or look had pierced her guard and disquieted her in spite of herself, she had left it at an incredulous: 'Oh, but then . . . But even if . . . In that case . . .' She now saw her fervent hope had been that the affair would blow over without coming to anything; prove to be just another passing fancy on the part of the unstable Purdy. How many had she not assisted at! This very summer, for instance, a charming young lady from Sydney had stayed with the Urquharts; and, as long as her visit lasted, they had seen little or nothing of

294

Purdy. Whenever he got off duty he was at Yarangobilly. As it happened, however, Mr Urquhart himself had been so assiduous in taking his guest about that Purdy had had small chance of making an impression. And, in looking back on the incident, what now rose most clearly before Mary's mind was the way in which Mrs Urquhart – poor thing, she was never able to go anywhere with her husband: either she had a child in arms or another coming; the row of toddlers mounted up in steps – the way in which she had said, with her pathetic smile: 'Ah, my dear! Willie needs someone gayer and stronger than I am, for company.' Mary's heart had been full of pity at the time, for her friend's lot; and it swelled again now at the remembrance.

But oh dear! this was straying from the point. Impatiently she jerked her thoughts back to herself and her own dilemma. What ought she to do? She was not a person who could sit still with folded hands and await events. How would it be if she spoke to Purdy herself? . . . talked seriously to him about his work? . . . tried to persuade him to leave Ballarat. Did he mean to hang on here for ever, she would say – never intend to seek promotion? But then again, the mere questioning would cause a certain awkwardness. While, at the slightest trip or blunder on her part, what was unsaid might suddenly find itself said; and the whole thing cease to be the vague, cloudy affair it was at present. And though she would actually rather this happened with regard to Purdy than Richard, yet . . . yet . . .

Worried and perplexed, unable to see before her the straight plain path she loved, Mary once more sighed from the bottom of her heart.

'Oh if *only* men wouldn't be so foolish!'

Left to himself Mahony put away his books, washed his hands and summoned one by one to his presence the people who waited in the adjoining room. He drew a tooth, dressed a wounded wrist, prescribed for divers internal disorders – all told, a baker's dozen of odd jobs.

When the last patient had gone he propped open the door, wiped his forehead and read the thermometer that hung on the wall: it marked 102°. Dejectedly he drove, in fancy, along the glaring, treeless roads, inches deep in cinnamon-coloured dust. How one learnt to hate the sun out here. What wouldn't he give for a cool, grey-green Irish day, with a wet wind blowing in from the sea? – a day such as he had heedlessly squandered hundreds of, in his youth. Now it made his mouth water only to think of them.

It still wanted ten minutes to ten o'clock and the buggy had not yet come round. He would lie down and have five minutes' rest before starting: he had been up most of the night, and on getting home had been kept awake by neuralgia.

When an hour later Mary reached home, she was amazed to find groom and buggy still drawn up in front of the house.

'Why, Molyneux, what's the matter? Where's the doctor?'

'I'm sure I don't know, Mrs Mahony. I've hollered to Biddy half-a-dozen times, but she doesn't take any notice. And the mare's that restless. . . . There, there, steady old girl, steady now! It's these damn' flies.'

Mary hurried indoors. 'Why, Biddy. . . .'

'Sure and it's yourself,' said the big Irishwoman who now filled the kitchen-billet. 'Faith and though you scold me, Mrs Mahony, I couldn't bring it over me heart to wake him. The pore man's sleeping like a saint.'

'Biddy, you ought to know better!' cried Mary peeling off her gloves.

'It's pale as the dead he is.'

'Rubbish. It's only the reflection of the green blind. *Richard!* Do you know what the time is?'

But the first syllable of his name was enough. 'Good Lord, Mary, I must have dropped off. What the dickens . . . Come, help me, wife. Why on earth didn't those fools wake me?'

Mary held his driving-coat, fetched hat and gloves, while he flung the necessaries into his bag. 'Have you much to do this morning? Oh, that post-mortem's at twelve, isn't it?'

'Yes; and a consultation with Munce at eleven – I'll just manage it and no more,' muttered Mahony with an eye on his watch. 'I can't let the mare take it easy this morning. Yes, a full day. And Henry Ocock's fidgeting for a second opinion; thinks his wife's not making enough progress. Well, ta-ta, sweetheart! Don't expect me back to lunch.' And taking a short cut across the lawn, he jumped into the buggy and off they flew.

Mary's thoughts were all for him in this moment. 'How proud we ought to feel!' she said to herself. 'That makes the second time in a week old Munce has sent for him. But how like Henry Ocock,' she went on with puckered brow. 'It's quite insulting – after the trouble Richard has put himself to. If Agnes's case puzzles him, I should like to know who will understand it better. I think I'll go and see her myself this afternoon. It can't be *her* wish to call in a stranger.'

Not till some time after did she remember her own private embarrassment. And, by then, the incident had taken its proper place in her mind – had sunk to the level of insignificance to which it belonged.

'Such a piece of nonsense!' was her final verdict. 'As if I could worry Richard with it, when he has so many really important things to occupy him.'

CHAPTER FIVE

Yes, those were palmy days; the rate at which the practice spread astonished even himself. No slack seasons for him now; winter saw him as busy as summer; and his chief ground for complaint was that he was unable to devote the meticulous attention he would have wished to each individual case. 'It would need the strength of an elephant to do that.' But it was impossible not to feel gratified by the many marks of confidence he received. And if his work had but left him some leisure for study and an occasional holiday, he would have been content. But in these years he was never able to get his neck out of the yoke; and Mary took her annual jaunts to Melbourne and sea-breezes alone.

In a long talk they had with each other, it was agreed that, except in an emergency, he was to be chary of entering into fresh engagements – this referred in the first place to confinements, of which his book was always full; and secondly, to outlying bush-cases, the journey to and from which wasted many a precious hour. And where it would have been impolitic to refuse a new and influential patient, someone on his list – a doubtful payer or a valetudinarian – was gently to be let drop. And it was Mary who arranged who this should be. Some umbrage was bound to be given in the process; but with her help it was reduced to a minimum. For Mary knew by heart all the links and ramifications of the houses at which he visited; knew precisely who was related to whom, by blood or marriage or business; knew where offence might with safety be risked, and where it would do him harm. She had also a woman's tact in smoothing things over. A born doctor's wife, declared Mahony in grateful acknowledgement. For himself he could not keep such fiddling details in his head for two minutes on end.

But though he thus succeeded in setting bounds to his activity, he still had a great deal too much to do; and, in tired moments, or when tic plagued him, thought the sole way out of the impasse would be to associate someone with him as partner or assistant. And once he was within an ace of doing so, chance throwing what he considered a likely person across his path. In attending a coroner's inquest, he made the acquaintance of a member of the profession who was on his way from the Ovens district – a coach journey of well over two hundred miles – to a place called Walwala, a day's ride to the west of Ballarat. And since this was a pleasant-spoken man and intelligent – though with a some-what down-at-heel look – besides being a stranger to the town, Mahony impulsively took him home to dinner. In the evening they sat and talked. The visitor, whose name was Wakefield, was considerably Mahony's senior. By his own account he had had but a rough time of it for the past couple of years. A good practice which he had worked up in the seaport of Warrnambool had come to an untimely end. He did not enter into the reasons for this. 'I was unfortunate . . . had a piece of ill-luck,' was how he referred to it. And knowing how fatally easy was a trip in diagnosis, a slip of the scalpel, Mahony tactfully helped him over the allusion. From Warrnambool Wakefield had gone to the extreme north of the colony; but the eighteen months spent there had nearly been his undoing. Money had not come in badly; but his wife and family had suffered from the great heat, and the scattered nature of the work had worn him to skin and bone. He was now casting about him for a more suitable place. He could not afford to buy a practice, must just creep in where he found a vacancy. And Walwala, where he understood there had never been a resident practitioner, seemed to offer an opening.

Mahony felt genuinely sorry for the man; and after he had gone sat and revolved the idea, in the event of Walwala proving unsuitable, of taking Wakefield on as his assistant. He went to bed full of the scheme and broached it to Mary before they slept. Mary made big eyes to herself as she listened. Like a wise wife, however, she did not press her own views that night, while the idea bubbled hot in him; for, at such times, when some new project seemed to promise the millennium, he stood opposition badly. But she lay awake telling off the reasons she would put before him in the morning; and in the dark allowed herself a tender, tickled little smile at his expense.

'What a man he is for loading himself up with the wrong sort of people!' she reflected. 'And then afterwards, he gets tired of them, and impatient with them – as is only natural.'

At breakfast she came back on the subject herself. In her opinion, he ought to think the matter over very carefully. Not another doctor on Ballarat had an assistant; and his patients would be sure to resent the novelty. Those who sent for Dr Mahony would not thank you to be handed over to 'goodness knows who'.

'Besides, Richard, as things are now, the money wouldn't really be enough, would it? And just as we have begun to be a little easy ourselves — I'm afraid you'd miss many comforts you have got used to again, dear,' she wound up, with a mental glance at the fine linen and smooth service Richard loved.

Yes, that was true, admitted Mahony with a sigh; and being this morning in a stale mood, he forthwith knocked flat the card-house it had amused him to build. Himself he had only half believed in it; or believed so long as he refrained from going into prosaic details. There was work for two and money for one — that was the crux of the matter. Successful as the practice was, it still did not throw off a thousand a year. Bad debts ran to a couple of hundred annually; and their improved style of living — the expenses of house and garden, of horses and vehicles, the men-servants, the open house they had to keep — swallowed every penny of the rest. Saving was actually harder than when his income had been but a third of what it was at present. New obligations beset him. For one thing, he had to keep pace with his colleagues; make a show of being just as well-to-do as they. Retrenching was out of the question. His patients would at once imagine that something was wrong — the practice on the downgrade, his skill deserting him — and take their ailments and their fees elsewhere. No, the more one had, the more one was forced to spend; and the few odd hundreds for which Henry Ocock could yearly be counted on came in very handy. As a rule he laid these by for Mary's benefit; for her visits to Melbourne, her bonnets and gowns. It also let her satisfy the needs of her generous little heart in matters of hospitality — well, it was perhaps not fair to lay the whole blame of their incessant and lavish entertaining at her door. He himself knew that it would not do for them to lag a foot behind other people.

Hence the day on which he would be free to dismiss the subject of money from his mind seemed as far off as ever. He might indulge wild schemes of taking assistant or partner; the plain truth was, he could not afford even the sum needed to settle in a *locum tenens* for three months, while he recuperated. — Another and equally valid reason was that the right man for a *locum* was far to seek. As time went on, he found himself pushed more and more into a single branch of medicine — one, too, he had never meant to let grow over his head in this fashion. For it was common medical knowledge out here that, given the distances and the general lack of conveniences, thirty to forty maternity cases per year were as much as a practitioner could with comfort take in hand. *His* books for the past year stood at over a hundred! The nightwork this meant was unbearable, infants showing a perverse disinclination to enter the world except under cover of the dark.

His popularity — if such it could be called — with the other sex was something of a mystery to him. For he had not one manner for the bedside and another for daily life. He never sought to ingratiate himself with people, or to wheedle them; still less would he stoop to bully or intimidate; was always by preference the adviser rather than the dictator. And men did not greatly care for this arm's-length attitude; they wrote him down haughty and indifferent, and pinned their faith to a blunter, homelier manner. But with women it was otherwise; and these also appreciated the fact that, no matter what their rank in life, their age or their looks, he met them with the deference he believed due to their sex. Exceptions there were, of course. Affectation or insincerity angered him — with the 'Zaras' of this world he had scant patience — while among the women themselves, some few — Ned's wife, for example — felt resentment at his very appearance, his gestures, his tricks of speech. But the majority were his staunch partisans; and it was becoming more and more the custom to engage Dr Mahony months ahead, thus binding him fast. And though he would sometimes give Mary a fright by vowing that he was going to 'throw up mid. and be done with it', yet her ambition — and what an ambitious wife she was, no one but himself knew — that he should some day become one of the leading specialists on Ballarat, seemed not unlikely of fulfilment. If his health kept good. And . . . and if he could possibly hold out!

For there still came times when he believed that to turn his back for ever, on place and people, would make him the happiest of mortals. For a time this idea had left him in peace. Now it haunted him again. Perhaps, because he had at last grasped the unpalatable truth that it would never be his luck to save: if saving were the only key to freedom, he would still be there, still chained fast, and though he lived to be a hundred. Certain it was, he did not become a better colonist as the years went on. He had learnt to hate the famous climate – the dust and drought and brazen skies; the drenching rains and bottomless mud – to rebel against the interminable hours he was doomed to spend in his buggy. By nature he was a recluse – not an outdoor-man at all. He was tired, too, of the general rampage, the promiscuous connections and slap-dash familiarity of colonial life; sick to death of the all-absorbing struggle to grow richer than his neighbours. He didn't give a straw for money in itself – only for what it brought him. And what was the good of that, if he had no leisure to enjoy it? Or was it the truth that he feared being dragged into the vortex? . . . of learning to care, he, too, whether or no his name topped subscription-lists; whether his entertainments were the most sumptuous, his wife the best-dressed woman in her set? Perish the thought!

He did not disquiet Mary by speaking of these things. Still less did he try to explain to her another, more elusive side of the matter. It was this. Did he dig into himself, he saw that his uncongenial surroundings were not alone to blame for his restless state of mind. There was in him a gnawing desire for change as change; a distinct fear of being pinned for too long to the same spot; or, to put it another way, a conviction that to live on without change meant decay. For him, at least. Of course, it was absurd to yield to feelings of this kind; at his age, in his position, with a wife dependent on him. And so he fought them – even while he indulged them. For this was the year in which, casting the question of expense to the winds, he pulled down and rebuilt his house. It came over him one morning on waking that he could not go on in the old one for another day, so cramped was he, so tortured by its lath-and-plaster thinness. He had difficulty in winning Mary over; she was against the outlay, the trouble and confusion involved; and was only reconciled by the more solid comforts and greater conveniences offered her. For the new house was of brick, the first brick house to be built on Ballarat (and oh the joy! said Richard, of walls so thick that you could not hear through them), had an extra-wide verandah which might be curtained in for parties and dances, and a side-entrance for patients, such as Mary had often sighed for.

As a result of the new grandeur, more and more flocked to

his door. The present promised to be a record year even in the annals of the Golden City. The completion of the railway-line to Melbourne was the outstanding event. Virtually halving the distance to the metropolis in count of time, it brought a host of fresh people — capitalists, speculators, politicians — about the town, and money grew perceptibly easier. Letters came more quickly, too; Melbourne newspapers could be handled almost moist from the press. One no longer had the sense of lying shut off from the world, behind the wall of a tedious coach-journey. And the merry Ballaratians, who had never feared or shrunk from the discomforts of this journey, now travelled constantly up and down: attending the Melbourne race-meetings; the Government House balls and lawn-parties; bringing back the gossip of Melbourne, together with its fashions in dress, music and social life.

Mary, in particular, profited by the change; for in one of those 'general posts' so frequently played by the colonial cabinet, John Turnham had come out Minister of Railways; and she could have a 'free pass' for the asking. John paid numerous visits to his constituency; but he was now such an important personage that his relatives hardly saw him. As likely as not he was the guest the Henry Ococks in their new mansion, or of the mayor of the borough. In the past two years Mahony had only twice exchanged a word with his brother-in-law.

And then they met again.

In Melbourne, at six o'clock one January morning, the Honourable John, about to enter a saloon-compartment of the Ballarat train, paused, with one foot on the step, and disregarding the polite remarks of the station-master at his heels, screwed up his prominent black eyes against the sun. At the farther end of the train, a tall, thin, fair-whiskered man was peering disconsolately along a row of crowded carriages. 'God bless me! isn't that . . . Why, so it is!' And leaving the official standing, John walked smartly down the platform.

'My dear Mahony! — this is indeed a surprise. I had no idea you were in town.'

'Why not have let me know you proposed coming?' he inquired as they made their way, the train meanwhile held up on their account, towards John's spacious, reserved saloon.

('What he means is, why I didn't beg a pass of him.') And Mahony, who detested asking favours, laid exaggerated emphasis on his want of knowledge. He had not contemplated the journey till an hour beforehand. Then, the proposed delegate having been suddenly taken ill, he had been urgently requested to represent the Masonic Lodge to which he belonged, at the Installation of a new Grand Master.

'Ah, so you found it possible to get out of harness for once?' said John affably, as they took their seats.

'Yes, by a lucky chance I had no case on hand that could not do without me for twenty-four hours. And my engagement-book I can leave with perfect confidence to my wife.'

'Mary is no doubt a very capable woman; I noticed that afresh, when last she was with us,' returned John; and went on to tick off Mary's qualities like a connoisseur appraising the points of a horse. 'A misfortune that she is not blessed with any family,' he added.

Mahony stiffened; and responded dryly: 'I'm not sure that I agree with you. With all her energy and spirit Mary is none too strong.'

'Well, well! these things are in the hands of Providence; we must take what is sent us.' And caressing his bare chin John gave a hearty yawn.

The words flicked Mahony's memory: John had had an addition to his family that winter, in the shape – to the disappointment of all concerned – of a second daughter. He offered belated congratulations. 'A regular Turnham this time, according to Mary. But I am sorry to hear Jane has not recovered her strength.'

'Oh, Jane is doing very well. But it has been a real disadvantage that she could not nurse. The infant is . . . well, ah . . . perfectly formed, of course, but small – small.'

'You must send them both to Mary, to be looked after.'

The talk then passed to John's son, now a schoolboy in Geelong; and John admitted that the reports he received of the lad continued as unsatisfactory as ever. 'The young rascal has ability, they tell me, but no application.' John propounded various theories to account for the boy having turned out poorly, chief among which was that he had been left too long in the hands of women. They had over-indulged him. 'Mary no more than the rest, my dear fellow,' he hastened to smooth Mahony's rising plumes. 'It began with his mother in the first place. Yes, poor Emma was weak with the boy – lamentably weak!'

Here, with a disconcerting abruptness, he drew to him a blue linen bag that lay on the seat, and loosening its string took out a sheaf of official papers, in which he was soon engrossed. He had had enough of Mahony's conversation in the meantime, or so it seemed; had thought of something better to do, and did it.

His brother-in-law eyed him as he read. 'He's a bad colour. Been living too high, no doubt.'

A couple of new books were on the seat by Mahony; but he did not open them. He had a tiring day behind him, and the briefest of nights. Besides attending the masonic ceremony, which had lasted into the small hours, he had undertaken to make various purchases, not the least difficult of which was the buying of a present for Mary – all the little fal-lals that went to finish a lady's ball-dress. Railway-travelling was, too, something of a novelty to him nowadays; and he sat idly watching the landscape unroll, and thinking of nothing in particular. The train was running through mile after mile of flat, treeless country, liberally sprinkled with trapstones and clumps of tussock grass, which at a distance could be mistaken for couched sheep. Here and there stood a solitary she-oak, most doleful of trees, its scraggy, pine-needle foliage bleached to grey. From the several little stations along the line: mere three-sided sheds, which bore a printed invitation to intending passengers to wave a flag or light a lamp, did they wish to board the train: from these shelters long, bare, red roads, straight as ruled lines, ran back into the heart of the burnt-up, faded country. Now and then a moving ruddy cloud on one of them told of some vehicle crawling its laborious way.

When John, his memoranda digested, looked up ready to resume their talk, he found that Mahony was fast asleep; and, since his first words, loudly uttered, did not rouse him, he took out his case, chose a cigar, beheaded it and puffed it alight.

While he smoked, he studied his insensible relative. Mahony was sitting uncomfortably hunched up; his head had fallen forward and to the side, his mouth was open, his gloved hands lay limp on his knee.

'H'm!' said John to himself as he gazed. And: 'H'm,' he repeated after an interval. – Then pulling down his waistcoat and generally giving himself a shake to rights, he reflected that, for his own two-and-forty years, he was a very well preserved man indeed.

'Oh, Richard! . . . and my dress is blue,' said Mary distractedly, and sitting back on her heels let her arms fall to her sides. She was on her knees, and before her lay a cardboard box from which she had withdrawn a pink fan, pink satin boots with stockings to match, and a pink head-dress.

'Well, why the dickens didn't you say so?' burst out the giver.

'I did, dear. As plainly as I could speak.'

'Never heard a word!'

'Because you weren't listening. I told you so at the time. Now what *am* I to do?' and, in her worry over the contretemps, Mary quite forgot to thank her husband for the trouble he had been to on her behalf.

'Get another gown to go with them.'

'Oh, Richard . . . how like a man! After all the time and money this one has cost me. No, I couldn't do that. Besides, Agnes Ocock is wearing pink and wouldn't like it.' And with a forehead full of wrinkles she slowly began to replace the articles in their sheaths. 'Of course they're very nice,' she added, as her fingers touched the delicate textures.

'They would need to be, considering what I paid for them. I wish now I'd kept my money in my pocket.'

'Well, your mistake is hardly my fault, is it, dear?' But Richard had gone off in a mood midway between self-annoyance and the huff.

Mary's first thought was to send the articles to Jinny with a request to exchange them for their counterparts in the proper colour. Then she dismissed the idea. Blind slave to her nursery that Jinny was, she would hardly be likely to give the matter her personal supervision: the box would just be returned to the shop, and the transfer left to the shop-people's discretion. They might even want to charge more. No, another plan now occurred to Mary. Agnes Ocock might not yet have secured the various small extras to go with her ball-dress; and, if not, how nice it would be to make her a present of these. They were finer, in better taste, than anything to be had on Ballarat; and she had long owed Agnes some return for her many kindnesses. Herself she would just make do with the simpler things she could buy in town. And so, without saying anything to Richard, who would probably have objected that Henry Ocock was well able to afford to pay for his own wife's finery, Mary tied up the box and drove to Plevna House, on the outer edge of Yuille's Swamp.

'Oh, no, I could never have got myself such beautiful things as these, Mary,' and Mrs Henry let her hands play lovingly with the silk stockings, her pretty face a-glow with pleasure. 'Henry has no understanding, dear, for the etceteras of a costume. He thinks, if he pays for a dress or a mantle, that that is enough; and when the *little* bills come in, he grumbles at what he calls my extravagance. I sometimes wish, Mary, I had kept back just a teeny-weeny bit of my own money. Henry would never have missed it, and I should have been able to settle a small bill for myself now and then. But you know how it is at first, love. Our one idea is to hand over all we possess to our lord and master.'

She tried on the satin boots; they were a little long, but she would stuff the toes with wadding. 'If I am *really* not robbing you, Mary?'

Mary reassured her, and thereupon a visit was paid to the nursery, where Mr Henry's son and heir lay sprawling in his cradle. Afterwards they sat and chatted on the verandah, while a basket was being filled with peaches for Mary to take home.

Not even the kindly drapery of a morning-wrapper could conceal the fact that Agnes was growing very stout – quite losing her fine figure. That came of her having given up riding-exercise. And all to please Mr Henry. He did not ride himself, and felt nervous or perhaps a little jealous when his wife was on horseback.

She was still very pretty of course – though by daylight the fine bloom of her cheeks began to break up into a network of tiny veins – and her fair, smooth brow bore no trace of the tragedy she had gone through. The double tragedy; for, soon after the master of Dandaloo's death in a Melbourne lunatic asylum, the little son of the house had died, not yet fourteen years of age, in an Inebriates' Home. Far was it from Mary to wish her friend to brood or repine; but to have ceased to remember as utterly as Agnes had done had something callous about it; and, in her own heart, Mary devoted a fresh regret to the memory of the poor little stepchild of fate.

The ball for which all these silken niceties were destined had been organized to raise funds for a public monument to the two explorers, Burke and Wills, and was to be one of the grandest ever given in Ballarat. His Excellency the Governor would, it was hoped, be present in person; the ladies had taken extra-ordinary pains with their toilettes, and there had been the usual grumblings at expense on the part of the husbands – though not a man but wished and privately expected *his* wife 'to take the shine out of all the rest'.

Mary had besought Richard to keep that evening free – it was her lot always to go out to entertainments under someone else's wing – and he had promised to do his utmost. But, a burnt child in this respect, Mary said she would believe it when she saw it; and the trend of events justified her scepticism. The night arrived; she was on the point of adjusting her wreath of forget-me-nots before her candle-lit mirror, when the dreaded summons came. Mahony had to change and hurry off, without a moment's delay.

'Send for Purdy. He'll see you across,' he said as he banged the front door.

But Mary dispatched the gardener at a run with a note to Tilly Ocock, who, she knew, would make room for her in her double-seated buggy.

Grindle got out, and Mary, her bunchy skirts held to her, took his place at the back beside Mrs Amelia. Tilly sat next the driver, and talked to them over her shoulder – a great big jolly rattle of a woman, who ruled her surroundings autocratically.

'Lor, no – we left 'im counting eggs,' she answered an inquiry on Mary's part. 'Pa's got a brood of Cochin Chinas that's the pride and glory of 'is heart. And 'e's built 'imself the neatest little place for 'em you could meet on a summer's day: you *must* come over and admire it, my dear – that'll please 'im, no end. It was a condition I made for 'is going on keeping fowls. They were a perfect nuisance, all over the garden and round the kitchen and the back, till it wasn't safe to put your foot down anywhere – fowls *are* such messy things! At last I up and said I wouldn't have it any longer. So then 'e and Tom set to work and built themselves a fowl-house and a run. And there they spend their days thinking out improvements.'

Here Tilly gave the driver a cautionary dig with her elbow; as she did this, an under-pocket chinked ominously. 'Look out now, Davy, what you're doing with us! – Yes, that's splosh, Mary. I always bring a bag of change with me, my dear, so that those who lose shan't have an excuse for not paying up.' Tilly was going to pass her evening, as usual, at the card-table. 'Well, I hope you two'll enjoy yourselves. Remember now, Mrs Grindle, if you please, that you're a married woman and must behave yourself, and not go in for any high jinks,' she teased her prim little stepdaughter, as they dismounted from the conveyance and stood straightening their petticoats at the entrance to the hall.

'You know, Matilda, I do not intend to dance tonight,' said Mrs Amelia in her sedate fashion: it was as if she sampled each word before parting with it.

'Oh, I know, bless you! and know why, too. If only it's not another false alarm! Poor old pa'd so like to have a grandchild 'e was allowed to carry round. 'E mustn't go near Henry's, of course, for fear the kid 'ud swallow one of 'is dropped aitches and choke over it.' And Tilly threw back her head and laughed. 'But you must hurry up, Mely, you know, if you want to oblige 'im.'

'Really, Tilly!' expostulated Mary. ('She sometimes *does* go too far,' she thought to herself. 'The poor little woman!') 'Let us two keep together,' she said as she took Amelia's arm. 'I don't intend to dance much either, as my husband isn't here.'

But once inside the gaily decorated hall, she found it impossible to keep her word. Even on her way to a seat beside Agnes Ocock she was repeatedly stopped, and, when she sat down, up came first one, then another, to 'request the pleasure'. She could not go on refusing everybody: if she did, it would look as if she deliberately set out to be peculiar – a horrible thought to Mary. Besides, many of those who made their bow were important, influential gentlemen; for Richard's sake she must treat them politely.

For his sake, again, she felt pleased; rightly or wrongly she put the many attentions shown her down to the fact of her being his wife. So she turned and offered apologies to Agnes and Amelia, feeling at the same time thankful that Richard had not Mr Henry's jealous disposition. There sat Agnes, looking as pretty as a picture, and was afraid to dance with anyone but her own husband. And he preferred to play at cards!

309

'I think, dear, you might have ventured to accept the Archdeacon for a quadrille,' she whispered behind her fan, as Agnes regretfully declined Mr Long.

But Agnes shook her head. 'It's better not, Mary. It saves trouble afterwards. Henry *doesn't* care to see it.' Perhaps Agnes herself, once a passionate dancer, was growing a little too comfortable, thought Mary, as her own programme wandered from hand to hand.

Among the last to arrive was Purdy, red with haste, and making a great thump with his lame leg as he crossed the floor.

'I'm beastly late, Polly. What have you got left for me?'

'Why, really nothing, Purdy. I thought you weren't coming. But you may put your name down here if you like,' and Mary handed him her programme with her thumb on an empty space: she generally made a point of sitting out a dance with Purdy that he might not feel neglected; and of late she had been especially careful not to let him notice any difference in her treatment of him. But when he gave back the card she found that he had scribbled his initials in all three blank lines. 'Oh, you mustn't do that. I'm saving those for Richard.'

'Our dance, I believe, Mrs Mahony?' said a deep voice as the band struck up 'The Rats Quadrilles'. And, swaying this way and that in her flounced blue tarletan, Mary rose, put her hand within the proffered crook, and went off with the Police Magistrate, an elderly greybeard; went to walk or be teetotumed through the figures of the dance, with the supremely sane unconcern that she displayed towards all the arts.

'What odd behaviour!' murmured Mrs Henry, following Purdy's retreating form with her eyes. 'He took no notice of us whatever. And did you see, Amelia, how he stood and stared after Mary? Quite rudely, I thought.'

Here Mrs Grindle was forced to express an opinion of her own − always a trial for the nervous little woman. 'I think it's because dear Mary looks so charming tonight, Agnes,' she ventured in her mouse-like way. Then moved up to make room for Archdeacon Long, who laid himself out to entertain the ladies.

*

It was after midnight when Mahony reached home. He would rather have gone to bed, but having promised Mary to put in an appearance, he changed and walked down to the town.

310

The ball was at its height. He skirted the rotating couples, seeking Mary. Friends hailed him.

'Ah, well done, doctor!'

'Still in time for a spin, sir.'

'Have you seen my wife?'

'Indeed and I have. Mrs Mahony's the belle o' the ball.'

'Pleased to hear it. Where is she now?'

'Look here, Mahony, we've had a reg'lar dispute,' cried Willie Urquhart pressing up; he was flushed and decidedly garrulous. 'Almost came to blows we did, over whose was the finest pair o' shoulders – your wife's or Henry O.'s. I plumped for Mrs M., and I b'lieve she topped the poll. By jove! that blue gown makes 'em look just like . . . what shall I say? . . . like marble.'

'Does fortune smile?' asked Mahony of Henry Ocock as he passed the card-players: he had cut Urquhart short with a nod. 'So his Excellency didn't turn up, after all?'

'Sent a telegraphic communication at the last moment. No, I haven't seen her. But stay, there's Matilda wanting to speak to you, I believe.'

Tilly was making all manner of signs to attract his attention.

'Good evening, doctor. Yes, I've a message. You'll find 'er in the cloakroom. She's been in there for the last half-'our or so. I think she's got the headache or something of that sort, and is waiting for you to take 'er home.'

'Oh, thank goodness, there you are, Richard!' cried Mary as he opened the door of the cloakroom; and she rose from the bench on which she had been sitting with her shawl wrapped round her. 'I thought you'd never come.' She was pale, and looked distressed.

'Why, what's wrong, my dear? . . . feeling faint?' asked Mahony incredulously. 'If so, you had better wait for the buggy. It won't be long now; you ordered it for two o'clock.'

'No, no, I'm not ill, I'd rather walk,' said Mary breathlessly. 'Only please let us get away. And without making a fuss.'

'But what's the matter?'

'I'll tell you as we go. No, these boots won't hurt. And I can walk in them quite well. Fetch your own things, Richard.' Her one wish was to get her husband out of the building.

They stepped into the street; it was a hot night and very dark. In her thin satin dancing-boots, Mary leaned heavily on Richard's arm, as they turned off the street-pavements into the unpaved roads.

311

Mahony let the lights of the main street go past; then said: 'And now, Madam Wife, you'll perhaps be good enough to enlighten me as to what all this means?'

'Yes, dear, I will,' answered Mary obediently. But her voice trembled; and Mahony was sharp of hearing.

'Why, Polly sweetheart . . . surely nothing serious?'

'Yes, it is. I've had a very unpleasant experience this evening, Richard – very unpleasant indeed. I hardly know how to tell you. I feel so upset.'

'Come – out with it!'

In a low voice, with downcast eyes, Mary told her story. All had gone well till about twelve o'clock: she had danced with this partner and that, and thoroughly enjoyed herself. Then came Purdy's turn. She was with Mrs Long when he claimed her, and she at once suggested that they should sit out the dance on one of the settees placed round the hall, where they could amuse themselves by watching the dancers. But Purdy took no notice – 'He was strange in his manner from the very beginning' – and led her into one of the little rooms that opened off the main body of the hall.

'And I didn't like to object. We were conspicuous enough as it was, his foot made such a bumping noise; it was worse than ever tonight, I thought.'

For the same reason, though she had felt uncomfortable at being hidden away in there, she had not cared to refuse to stay: it seemed to make too much of the thing. Besides, she hoped some other couple would join them. But –

'But Mary . . .!' broke from Mahony; he was blank and bewildered.

Purdy, however, had got up after a moment or two and shut the door. And then – 'Oh, it's no use, Richard, I can't tell you!' said poor Mary. 'I don't know how to get the words over my lips. I think I've never felt so ashamed in all my life.' And, worn out by the worry and excitement she had gone through, and afraid, in advance, of what she had still to face, Mary began to cry.

Mahony stood still; let her arm drop. 'Do you mean me to understand,' he demanded, as if unable to believe his ears: 'to understand that Purdy . . . dared to . . . that he dared to behave to you in any but a –' And since Mary was using her pocket-handkerchief and could not reply: 'Good God! Has the fellow taken leave of his senses? Is he mad? Was he drunk? Answer me!

What does it all mean?' And Mary still continuing silent, he threw off the hand she had replaced on his arm. 'Then you must walk home alone. I'm going back to get at the truth of this.'

But Mary clung to him. 'No, no, you must hear the whole story first.' Anything rather than let him return to the hall. Yes, at first she thought he really had gone mad. 'I can't tell you what I felt, Richard . . . knowing it was Purdy – just Purdy. To see him like that – looking so horrible – and to have to listen to the dreadful things he said! Yes, I'm sure he had had too much to drink. His breath smelt so.' She had tried to pull away her hands; but he had held her, had put his arms round her.

At the anger she felt racing through her husband she tightened her grip, stringing meanwhile phrase to phrase with the sole idea of getting him safely indoors. Not till they were shut in the bedroom did she give the most humiliating detail of any: how, while she was still struggling to free herself from Purdy's embrace, the door had opened and Mr Grindle looked in. 'He drew back at once, of course. But it was awful, Richard! I turned cold. It seemed to give me more strength, though. I pulled myself away and got out of the room, I don't know how. My wreath was falling off. My dress was crumpled. Nothing would have made me go back to the ballroom. I couldn't have faced Amelia's husband – I think I shall never be able to face him again,' and Mary's tears flowed anew.

Richard was stamping about the room, aimlessly moving things from their places. 'God Almighty! he shall answer to me for this. I'll go back and take a horsewhip with me.'

'For my sake, don't have a scene with him. It would only make matters worse,' she pleaded.

But Richard strode up and down, treading heedlessly on the flouncings of her dress. 'What? – and let him believe such behaviour can go unpunished? That whenever it pleases him, he can insult my wife – insult *my* wife? Make her the talk of the place? Brand her before the whole town as a light woman?'

'Oh, not the whole town, Richard. I shall have to explain to Amelia . . . and Tilly . . . and Agnes – that's all,' sobbed Mary in parenthesis.

'Yes, and I ask if it's a dignified or decent thing for you to have to do? – to go running round assuring your friends of your virtue!' cried Richard furiously. 'Let me tell you this, my dear: at whatever door you knock, you'll be met by disbelief. Fate played you a shabby trick when it allowed just that low cad to put his head in. What do you think would be left of any woman's reputation after Grindle Esquire had pawed it over? No, Mary, you've been rendered impossible; and you'll be made to feel it for the rest of your days. People will point to you as the wife who takes advantage of her husband's absence to throw herself into another man's arms; and to me as the convenient husband who provides the opportunity' – and Mahony groaned. In an impetuous flight of fancy he saw his good name smirched, his practice laid waste.

Mary lifted her head at this, and wiped her eyes. 'Oh, you always paint everything so black. People know me – know I would never, never do such a thing.'

'Unfortunately we live among human beings, my dear, not in a community of saints! But what does a good woman know of how a slander of this kind clings?'

'But if I have a perfectly clear conscience?' Mary's tone was incredulous, even a trifle aggrieved.

'It spells ruin all the same in a hole like this, if it once gets about.'

'But it shan't. I'll put my pride in my pocket and go to Amelia the first thing in the morning. I'll make it right somehow. – But I must say, Richard, in the whole affair I don't think you feel a bit sorry for me. Or at least only for me as your wife. The horridest part of what happened was mine, not yours – and I think you might show a little sympathy.'

'I'm too furious to feel sorry,' replied Richard with gaunt truthfulness, still marching up and down.

'Well, I do,' said Mary with a spice of defiance. 'In spite of everything, I feel sorry that anyone could so far forget himself as Purdy did tonight.'

'You'll be telling me next you have warmer feelings still for him!' burst out Mahony. 'Sorry for the crazy lunatic who, after all these years, after all I've done for him and the trust I've put in him, suddenly falls to making love to the woman who bears my name? Why, a madhouse is the only place he's fit for.'

'There you're unjust. And wrong, too. It . . . it wasn't as sudden as you think. Purdy has been queer in his behaviour for quite a long time now.'

'What in Heaven's name do you mean by that?'

'I mean what I say,' said Mary staunchly, though she turned a still deeper red. 'Oh, you might just as well be angry with yourself for being so blind and stupid.'

314

'Do you mean to tell me you were aware of something?' Mahony stopped short in his perambulations and fixed her, open-mouthed.

'I couldn't help it. – Not that there was much to know, Richard. And I thought of coming to you about it – indeed I did. I tried to, more than once. But you were always so busy; I hadn't the heart to worry you. For I knew very well how upset you would be.'

'So it comes to this, does it?' said Mahony with biting emphasis. 'My wife consents to another man paying her illicit attentions behind her husband's back!'

'Oh, no, no, no! But I knew how fond you were of Purdy. And I always hoped it would blow over without . . . without coming to anything.'

'God forgive me!' cried Mahony passionately. 'It takes a woman's brain to house such a preposterous idea.'

'Oh, I'm not quite the fool you make me out to be, Richard. I've got some sense in me. But it's always the same. I think of you, and you think of no one but yourself. I only wanted to spare you. And this is the thanks I get for it.' And sitting down on the side of the bed she wept bitterly.

'Will you assure me, madam, that till tonight nothing I could have objected to has ever passed between you?'

'No, Richard, I won't! I won't tell you anything else. You get so angry you don't know what you're saying. And if you can't trust me better than that – Purdy said tonight you didn't understand me . . . and never had.'

'Oh, he did, did he? There we have it! Now I'll know every word the scoundrel has ever said to you – and if I have to drag it from you by force.'

But Mary set her lips, with an obstinacy that was something quite new in her. It first amazed Mahony, then made him doubly angry. One word gave another; for the first time in their married lives they quarrelled – quarrelled hotly. And, as always at such times, many a covert criticism, a secret disapproval which neither had ever meant to breathe to the other, slipped out and added fuel to the fire. It was appalling to both to find on how many points they stood at variance.

Some half hour later, leaving Mary still on the edge of the bed, still crying, Mahony stalked grimly into the surgery, and taking pen and paper scrawled, without even sitting down to do it:

315

You damned scoundrel! If ever you show your face here again, I'll thrash you to within an inch of your life.

Then he stepped on to the verandah and crossed the lawn, carrying the letter in his hand.

But already his mood was on the turn: it seemed as if, in the physical effort of putting the words to paper, his rage had spent itself. He was conscious now of a certain limpness, both of mind and body; his fit of passion over, he felt dulled, almost indifferent to what had happened. Now, too, another feeling was taking possession of him, opening up vistas of a desert emptiness that he hardly dared to face.

But stay! . . . was that not a movement in the patch of blackness under the fig-tree? Had not something stirred there? He stopped, and strained his eyes. No, it was only a bough that swayed in the night air. He went out of the garden to the corner of the road and came back empty handed. But at the same spot he hesitated, and peered. 'Who's there?' he asked sharply. And again: 'Is there anyone there?' But the silence remained unbroken; and once more he saw that the shifting of a branch had misled him.

Mary was moving about the bedroom. He ought to go to her and ask pardon for his violence. But he was not yet come to a stage when he felt equal to a reconciliation; he would rest for a while, let his troubled balance right itself. And so he lay down on the surgery sofa, and drew a rug over him.

He closed his eyes, but could not sleep. His thoughts raced and flew; his brain hunted clues and connections. He found himself trying to piece things together; to fit them in, to recollect. And every now and then some sound outside would make him start up and listen . . . and listen. Was that not a footstep? . . . the step of one who might come feeling his way . . . dim-eyed with regret? There were such things in life as momentary lapses, as ungovernable impulses – as fiery contrition . . . the anguish of remorse. And yet, once more, he sat up and listened till his ears rang.

Then, not the ghostly footsteps of a delusive hope, but a hard, human crunching that made the boards of the verandah shake. Tossing off the opossum-rug, which had grown unbearably heavy, he sprang to his feet; was wide awake and at the window, staring sleep-charged into the dawn, before a human hand had found the night-bell and a distracted voice cried:

'Does a doctor live here? A doctor, I say . . .?'

The hot airless night had become the hot airless day: in the garden the leaves on trees and shrubs drooped as under an invisible weight. All the stale smells of the day before persisted – that of the medicaments on the shelves, of the unwetted dust on the roads, the sickly odour of malt from a neighbouring brewery. The blowflies buzzed about the ceiling; on the table under the lamp a dozen or more moths lay singed and dead. Now it was nearing six o'clock; clad in his thinnest driving-coat, Mahony sat and watched the man who had come to fetch him beat his horse to a lather.

'Mercy! . . . have a little mercy on the poor brute,' he said more than once.

He had stood out for some time against obeying the summons, which meant, at lowest, a ten-mile drive. Not if he were offered a hundred pounds down, was his first impetuous refusal; for he had not seen the inside of a bed that night. But at this he trapped an odd look in the other's eyes, and suddenly became aware that he was still dressed as for the ball. Besides, an equally impetuous answer was flung back at him: he promised no hundred pounds, said the man – hadn't got it to offer. He appealed solely to the doctor's humanity: it was a question of saving a life – that of his only son. So here they were.

'We doctors have no business with troubles of our own,' thought Mahony, as he listened to the detailed account of an ugly accident. On the roof of a shed the boy had missed his foot, slipped and fallen some twenty feet, landing astride a piece of quartering. Picking himself up, he had managed to crawl home, and at first they thought he would be able to get through the night without medical aid. But towards two o'clock his sufferings had grown unbearable. God only knew if, by this time, he had not succumbed to them.

'My good man, one does not die of pain alone.'

They followed a flat, treeless road, the grass on either side of which was burnt to hay. Buggy and harness – the latter eked out with bits of string and an old bootlace – were coated with the dust of months; and the gaunt, long-backed horse shuffled through a reddish flour, which accompanied them as a choking cloud. A swarm of small black flies kept pace with the vehicle, settling on nose, eyes, neck and hands of its occupants, crawling over the horse's belly and in and out of its nostrils. The animal made no effort to shake itself free, seemed indifferent to the pests: they were only to be disturbed by the hail of blows which the driver occasionally stood up to deliver. At such moments Mahony, too, started out of the light doze he was continually dropping into.

Arrived at their destination – a miserable wooden shanty on a sheep-run at the foot of the ranges – he found his patient tossing on a dirty bed, with a small pulse of 120, while the right thigh was darkly bruised and swollen. The symptoms pointed to serious internal injuries. He performed the necessary operation.

There was evidently no woman about the place; the coffee the father brought him was thick as mud. On leaving, he promised to return next day and to bring someone with him to attend to the lad.

For the home-journey, he got a mount on a young and fidgety mare, whom he suspected of not long having worn the saddle. In the beginning he had his hands full with her. Then, however, she ceased her antics and consented to advance at an easy trot.

How tired he felt! He would have liked to go to bed and sleep for a week on end. As it was, he could not reckon on even an hour's rest. By the time he reached home the usual string of patients would await him; and these disposed of, and a bite of breakfast snatched, out he must set anew on his morning round. He did not feel well either: the coffee seemed to have disagreed with him. He had a slight sense of nausea and was giddy; the road swam before his eyes. Possibly the weather had something to do with it; though a dull, sunless morning it was hot as he had never known it. He took out a stud, letting the ends of his collar fly.

Poor little Mary, he thought inconsequently: he had hurt and frightened her by his violence. He felt ashamed of himself now. By daylight he could see her point of view. Mary was so tactful and resourceful that she might safely be trusted to hush up the affair, to explain away the equivocal position in which she had

318

been found. After all, both of them were known to be decent, God-fearing people. And one had only to look at Mary to see that here was no light woman. Nobody in his senses — not even Grindle — could think evil of that broad, transparent brow, of those straight, kind, merry eyes.

No, this morning his hurt was a purely personal one. That it should just be Purdy who did him this wrong! Purdy, playmate and henchman, ally in how many a boyish enterprise, in the hardships and adventures of later life. 'Mine own familiar friend, in whom I trusted, which did eat of my bread!' Never had he turned a deaf ear to Purdy's needs; he had fed him and clothed him, caring for him as for a well-loved brother. Surely few things were harder to bear than a blow in the dark from one who stood thus deeply in your debt, on whose gratitude you would have staked your head. It was, of course, conceivable that he had been swept off his feet by Mary's vivid young beauty, by over-indulgence, by the glamour of the moment. But if a man could not restrain his impulses where the wife of his most intimate friend was concerned . . . Another thing: as long as Mary had remained an immature slip of a girl, Purdy had not given her a thought. When, however, under her husband's wing she had blossomed out into a lovely womanhood, of which any man might be proud, then she had found favour in his eyes. And the slight this put on Mary's sterling moral qualities, on all but her physical charms, left the worst taste of any in the mouth.

Then, not content with trying to steal her love, Purdy had also sought to poison her mind against him. How that rankled! For until now he had hugged the belief that Purdy's opinion of him was coloured by affection and respect, by the tradition of years. Whereas, from what Mary had let fall, he saw that the boy must have been sitting in judgement on him, regarding his peculiarities with an unloving eye, picking his motives to pieces: it was like seeing the child of your loins, of your hopes, your unsleeping care, turn and rend you with black ingratitude. Yes, everything went to prove Purdy's unworthiness. Only *he* had not seen it, only he had been blind to the truth. And wrapped in this smug blindness he had given his false friend the run of his home, setting, after the custom of the country, no veto on his eternal presence. Disloyalty was certainly abetted by just the extravagant, exaggerated hospitality of colonial life. Never must the doors of your house be shut; all you had you were expected to share with any sundowner of fortune who chanced to stop at your gate.

The mare shied with a suddenness that almost unseated him: the next moment she had the bit between her teeth and was galloping down the road. Clomp-clomp-clomp went her hoofs on the baked clay; the dust smothered and stung, and he was holding for all he was worth to reins spanned stiff as iron. On they flew; his body hammered the saddle; his breath came sobbingly. But he kept his seat; and a couple of miles farther on he was down, soothing the wild-eyed, quivering, sweating beast, whose nostrils worked like a pair of bellows. There he stood, glancing now back along the road, now up at the sky. His hat had gone flying at the first unexpected plunge; he ought to return and look for it. But he shrank from the additional fatigue, the delay in reaching home this would mean. The sky was still overcast: he decided to risk it. Knotting his handkerchief he spread it cap-wise over his head and got back into the saddle.

Mine own familiar friend! And more than that: he could add to David's plaint and say, my only friend. In Purdy the one person he had been intimate with passed out of his life. There was nobody to take the vacant place. He had been far too busy of late years to form new friendships: what was left of him after the day's work was done was but a kind of shell: the work was the meaty contents. As you neared the forties, too, it grew even harder to fit yourself to other people: your outlook had become too set, your ideas too unfluid. Hence you clung the faster to ties formed in the old, golden days, worn though these might be to the thinness of a hair. And then, there was one's wife, of course – one's dear, good wife. But just her very dearness and goodness served to hold possible intimates at arm's length. The knowledge that you had such a confidante, that all your thoughts were shared with her, struck disastrously at a free exchange of privacies. No, he was alone. He had not so much as a dog now, to follow at heel and look up at him with the melancholy eyes of its race. Old Pompey had come at poison, and Mary had not wished to have a strange dog in the new house. She did not care for animals, and the main charge of it would have fallen on her. He had no time – no time even for a dog!

Better it would assuredly be to have someone to fall back on: it was not good for a man to stand so alone. Did troubles come, they would strike doubly hard because of it; then was the time to rejoice in a warm, human handclasp. And moodily pondering the reasons for his solitariness, he was once more inclined to lay a share of the blame on the conditions of the life. The population of the place was still in a state of flux: he and a mere handful of others would soon, he believed, be the oldest residents in Ballarat. People came and went, tried their luck, failed, and flitted off again, much as in the early days. What was the use of troubling to become better acquainted with a person, when, just as you began really to know him, he was up and away? At home, in the old country, a man as often as not died in the place where he was born; and the slow, eventless years, spent shoulder to shoulder, automatically brought about a kind of intimacy. But this was only a surface reason: there was another that went deeper. He had no talent for friendship, and he knew it; indeed, he would even invert the thing, and say bluntly that his nature had a twist in it which directly hindered friendship; and this, though there came moments when he longed, as your popular mortal never did, for close companionship. Sometimes he felt like a hungry man looking on at a banquet, of which no one invited him to partake, because he had already given it to be understood that he would decline. But such lapses were few. On nine days out of ten, he did not feel the need of either making or receiving confidences; he shrank rather, with a peculiar shy dread, from personal unbosomings. Some imp housed in him — some wayward, wilful, mocking Irish devil — bidding him hold back, remain cool, dry-eyed, in face of others' joys and pains. Hence the break with Purdy was a real calamity. The associations of some five-and-twenty years were bound up in it; measured by it, one's marriage seemed a thing of yesterday. And even more than the friend, he would miss the friendship and all it stood for: this solid base of joint experience; this past of common memories into which one could dip as into a well; this handle of 'Do you remember?' which opened the door to such a wealth of anecdote. From now on, the better part of his life would be a closed book to any but himself; there were allusions, jests without number, homely turns of speech, which not a soul but himself would understand. The thought of it made him feel old and empty; affected him like the news of a death. — But *must* it be? Was there no other way out? Slow to take hold, he was a hundred times slower to let go. Before now he had seen himself sticking by a person through misunderstandings, ingratitude, deception, to the blank wonder of the onlookers. Would he not be ready here, too, to forgive . . . to forget?

But he felt hot, hot to suffocation, and his heart was pounding in uncomfortable fashion. The idea of stripping and plunging into ice-cold water began to make a delicious appeal to him. Nothing surpassed such a plunge after a broken night. But of late he had had to be wary of indulging: a bath of this kind, taken when he was over-tired, was apt to set the accursed tic a-going; and then he could pace the floor in agony. And yet . . . Good God, how hot it was! His head ached distractedly; an iron band of pain seemed to encircle it. With a sudden start of alarm he noticed that he had ceased to perspire – now he came to think of it, not even the wild gallop had induced perspiration. Pulling up short, he fingered his pulse. It was abnormal, even for him . . . and feeble. Was it fancy, or did he really find a difficulty in breathing? He tore off his collar, threw open the neck of his shirt. He had a sensation as if all the blood in his body was flying to his head: his face must certainly be crimson. He put both hands to this top-heavy head, to support it; and in a blind fit of vertigo all but lost his balance in the saddle: the trees spun round, the distance went black. For a second still he kept upright; then he flopped to the ground, falling face downwards, his arms huddled under him.

The mare, all her spirit gone, stood lamb-like and waited. As he did not stir she turned and sniffed at him, curiously. Still he lay prone, and, having stretched her tired jaws, she raised her head and uttered a whinny – an almost human cry of distress. This, too, failing in its effect, she nosed the ground for a few yards, then set out at a gentle, mane-shaking trot for home.

*

Found, a dark conspicuous heap on the long bare road, and carted back to town by a passing bullock-wagon, Mahony lay, once the death-like coma had yielded, and tossed in fever and delirium. By piecing his broken utterances together Mary learned all she needed to know about the case he had gone out to attend, and his desperate ride home. But it was Purdy's name that was oftenest on his lips; it was Purdy he reviled and implored; and when he sprang up with the idea of calling his false friend to account, it was as much as she could do to restrain him.

She had the best of advice. Old Dr Munce himself came two and three times a day. Mary had always thought him a dear old man; and she felt surer than ever of it when he stood patting her hand and bidding her keep a good heart; for they would certainly pull her husband through.

'There aren't so many of his kind here, Mrs Mahony, that we can afford to lose him.'

But altogether she had never known till now how many and how faithful their friends were. Hardly, for instance, had Richard been carried in, stiff as a log and grey as death, when good Mrs Devine was fumbling with the latch of the gate, an old sunbonnet perched crooked on her head: she had run down just as she was, in the midst of shelling peas for dinner. She begged to be allowed to help with the nursing. But Mary felt bound to refuse. She knew how the thought of what he might have said in his delirium would worry Richard, when he recovered his senses: few men laid such weight as he on keeping their private thoughts private.

Not to be done, Mrs Devine installed herself in the kitchen to superintend the cooking. Less for the patient, into whom at first only liquid nourishment could be injected, than: 'To see as your own strength is kep' up, dearie.' Tilly swooped down and bore off Trotty. Delicate fruits, new-laid eggs, jellies and wines came from Agnes Ocock; while Amelia Grindle, who had no such dainties to offer, arrived every day at three o'clock, to mind the house while Mary slept. Archdeacon Long was also a frequent visitor, bringing not so much spiritual as physical aid; for, as the frenzy reached its height and Richard was maddened by the idea that a plot was brewing against his life, a pair of strong arms were needed to hold him down. Over and above this, letters of sympathy flowed in; grateful patients called to ask with tears in their eyes how the doctor did; virtual strangers stopped the servant in the street with the same query. Mary was sometimes quite overwhelmed by the kindness people showed her.

The days that preceded the crisis were days of keenest anxiety. But Mary never allowed her heart to fail her. For if, in the small things of life, she was given to building on a mortal's good sense, how much more could she rely at such a pass on the sense of the One above all others. What she said to herself as she moved tirelessly about the sick room, damping cloths, filling the ice-bag, infiltering drops of nourishment, was: 'God is good!' and these words, far from breathing a pious resignation, voiced a confidence so bold that it bordered on irreverence. Their real meaning was: Richard has still ever so much work to do in the world, curing sick people and saving their lives. God must know this, and cannot now mean to be so foolish as to *waste* him, by letting him die.

And her reliance on the Almighty's far-sighted wisdom was justified. Richard weathered the crisis, slowly revived to life and health; and the day came when, laying a thin white hand on hers, he could whisper: 'My poor little wife, what a fright I must have given you!' And added: 'I think an illness of some kind was due – overdue – with me.'

When he was well enough to bear the journey they left home for a watering-place on the Bay. There, on an open beach facing the Heads, Mahony lay with his hat pulled forward to shade his eyes, and with nothing to do but to scoop up handfuls of the fine coral sand and let it flow again, like liquid silk, through his fingers. From beneath the brim he watched the water churn and froth on the brown reefs; followed the sailing-ships which, beginning as mere dots on the horizon, swelled to stately white waterbirds, and shrivelled again to dots; drank in, with greedy nostrils, the mixed spice of warm sea, hot seaweed and aromatic tea-scrub.

And his strength came back as rapidly as usual. He soon felt well enough, leaning on Mary's arm, to stroll up and down the sandy roads of the township; to open book and newspaper; and finally to descend the cliffs for a dip in the transparent, turquoise sea. At the end of a month he was at home again, sunburnt and hearty, eager to pick up the threads he had let fall. And soon Mary was able to make the comfortable reflection that everything was going on just as before.

In this, however, she was wrong; never, in their united lives, would things be quite the same again. Outwardly, the changes might pass unnoticed – though even here, it was true, a certain name had now to be avoided, with which they had formerly made free. But this was not exactly hard to do, Purdy having promptly disappeared: they heard at second-hand that he had at last accepted promotion and gone to Melbourne. And since Mary had suffered no inconvenience from his thoughtless conduct, they tacitly agreed to let the matter rest. That was on the surface. Inwardly, the differences were more marked. Even in the mental attitude they adopted towards what had happened, husband and wife were thoroughly dissimilar. Mary did not refer to it because she thought it would be foolish to re-open so disagreeable a subject. In her own mind, however, she faced it frankly, dating back to it as the night when Purdy had been so odious and Richard so angry. Mahony, on the other hand, gave the affair a wide berth even in thought. For him it was a kind of Pandora's box, of which, having once caught a glimpse of the contents, he did not again dare to raise the lid. Things might escape from it that would alter his whole life. But he, too, dated from it in the sense of suddenly becoming aware, with a throb of regret, that he had left his youth behind him. And such phrases as: 'When I was young', 'In my younger days', now fell instinctively from his lips.

Nor was this all. Deep down in Mary's soul there slumbered a slight embarrassment; one she could not get the better of: it spread and grew. This was a faint, ever so faint a doubt of Richard's wisdom. Odd she had long known him to be, different in many small and some great ways from those they lived amongst; but hitherto this very oddness of his had seemed to her an outgrowth on the side of superiority — fairer judgement, higher motives. Just as she had always looked up to him as rectitude in person, so she had thought him the embodiment of a fine, though somewhat unworldly wisdom. Now her faith in his discernment was shaken. His treatment of her on the night of the ball had shocked, confused her. She was ready to make allowance for him: she had told her story clumsily, and had afterwards been both cross and obstinate; while part of his violence was certainly to be ascribed to his coming breakdown. But this did not cover everything; and the ungenerous spirit in which he had met her frankness, his doubt of her word, of her good faith — his utter unreasonableness in short — had left a cold patch of astonishment in her, which would not yield. She lit on it at unexpected moments. Meanwhile, she groped for an epithet that would fit his behaviour. Beginning with some rather vague and high-flown terms she gradually came down, until with the sense of having found the right thing at last, she fixed on the adjective 'silly' — a word which, for the rest, was in common use with Mary, had she to describe anything that struck her as queer or extravagant. And sitting over her fancywork, into which, being what Richard called 'safe as the grave', she sewed more thoughts than most women: sitting thus, she would say to herself with a half smile and an incredulous shake of the head: 'So silly!'

But hers was one of those inconvenient natures which trust blindly or not at all: once worked on by a doubt or a suspicion, they are never able to shake themselves free of it again. As time went on, she suffered strange uncertainties where some of Richard's decisions were concerned. In his good intentions she retained an implicit belief; but she was not always satisfied that he acted in the wisest way. Occasionally it struck her that he did not see as clearly as she did; at other times, that he let a passing whim run away with him and override his common sense. And, her eyes thus opened, it was not in Mary to stand dumbly by and watch him make what she held to be mistakes. Openly to interfere, however, would also have gone against the grain in her; she had bowed for too long to his greater age and experience. So, seeing no other way out, she fell back on indirect methods. To her regret. For, in watching other women 'manage' their husbands, she had felt proud to think that nothing of this kind was necessary between Richard and her. Now she, too, began to lay little schemes by which, without his being aware of it, she might influence his judgement, divert or modify his plans.

Her enforced use of such tactics did not lessen the admiring affection she bore him: that was framed to withstand harder tests. Indeed, she was even aware of an added tenderness towards him, now she saw that it behoved her to have forethought for them both. But into the wife's love for her husband there crept something of a mother's love for her child; for a wayward and impulsive, yet gifted creature, whose welfare and happiness depended on her alone. And it is open to question whether the mother dormant in Mary did not fall with a kind of hungry joy on this late-found task. The work of her hands done, she had known empty hours. That was over now. With quickened faculties, all her senses on the alert, she watched, guided, hindered, foresaw.

CHAPTER EIGHT

Old Ocock failed in health that winter. He was really old now, was two or three and sixty; and, with the oncoming of the rains and cold, gusty winds, various infirmities began to plague him.

'He's done himself rather too well since his marriage,' said Mahony in private. 'After being a worker for the greater part of his life, it would have been better for him to work on to the end.'

Yes, that, Mary could understand and agree with. But Richard continued: 'All it means, of course, is that the poor fellow is beginning to prepare for his last long journey. These aches and pains of his represent the packing and the strapping without which not even a short earthly journey can be undertaken. And his is into eternity.'

Mary, making lace over a pillow, looked up at this, a trifle apprehensively. 'What things you do say! If anyone heard you, they'd think you weren't very . . . very religious.' Her fear lest Richard's outspokenness should be mistaken for impiety never left her.

Tilly was plain and to the point. 'Like a bear with a sore back that's what 'e is, since 'e can't get down among his blessed birds. He leads Tom the life of the condemned, over the feeding of those bantams. As if the boy could help 'em not laying when they ought!'

At thirty-six Tilly was the image of her mother. Entirely gone was the slight crust of acerbity that had threatened her in her maiden days, when, thanks to her misplaced affections, it had seemed for a time as if the purple prizes of life – love, offers of marriage, a home of her own – were going to pass her by. She was now a stout, high-coloured woman with a roar of a laugh, full, yet firm lips, and the whitest of teeth. Mary thought her decidedly toned down and improved since her marriage; but Mahony put it that the means Tilly now had at her disposal were such as to make people shut an eye to her want of refinement. However that might be, 'old Mrs Ocock' was welcomed everywhere – even by those on whom her bouncing manners grated. She was invariably clad in a thick and handsome black silk gown, over which she wore all the jewellery she could crowd on her person – huge cameo brooches, ear-drops, rings and bracelets, lockets and chains. Her name topped subscription-lists, and, having early weaned her old husband of his dissenting habits, she was a real prop to Archdeacon Long and his church, taking the chief and most expensive table at tea-meetings, the most thankless stall at bazaars. She kept open house, too, and gave delightful parties, where, while some sat at loo, others were free to turn the rooms upside-down for a dance, or to ransack wardrobes and presses for costumes for charades. She drove herself and her friends about in various vehicles, briskly and well, and indulged besides in many secret charities. Her husband thought no such woman had ever trodden the earth, and publicly blessed the day on which he first set eyes on her.

'After the dose I'd 'ad with me first, 'twas a bit of a risk, that I knew. And it put me off me sleep for a night or two before'and. But my Tilly's the queen o' women – I say the queen, sir! I've never 'ad a wrong word from 'er, an' when I go she gits every penny I've got. Why, I'm jiggered if she didn't stop at 'ome from the Races t'other day, an' all on my account!'

'Now then, pa, drop it. Or the doctor'll think you've been mixing your liquors. Give your old pin here and let me poultice it.'

He had another sound reason for gratitude. Somewhere in the background of his house dwelt his two ne'er-do-well sons; Tilly had accepted their presence uncomplainingly. Indeed she sometimes stood up for Tom, against his father. 'Now, pa, stop nagging at the boy will you? You'll never get anything out of 'im that way. Tom's right enough if you know how to take him. He'll never set the Thames on fire, if that's what you mean. But I'm thankful, I can tell you, to have a handy chap like him at my back. If I 'ad to depend on your silly old paws, I'd never get anything done at all.'

And so Tom, a flaxen-haired, sheepish-looking man of something over thirty, led a kind of go-as-you-please existence about the place, a jack-of-all-trades – in turn carpenter, whitewasher, paper-hanger – an expert fetcher and carrier, bullied by his father, sheltered under his stepmother's capacious wing. 'It isn't his fault 'e's never come to anything. 'E hadn't half a chance. The truth is, Mary, for all they say to the opposite, men are harder than women – so unforgiving-like. Just because Tom

328

made a slip once, they've never let 'im forget it, but tied it to 'is coat-tails for 'im to drag with 'im through life. Little-minded I call it. — Besides, if you ask me, my dear, it must have been a case of six of one and half-a-dozen of the other. Tom as sedoocer! — can you picture it, Mary? It's enough to make one split.' And with a meaning glance at her friend, Tilly broke out in a contagious peal of laughter.

As for Johnny — well . . . and she shrugged her shoulders. 'A bad egg's bad, Mary, and no amount o' cooking and doctoring 'll sweeten it. But he didn't make 'imself, did 'e? — and my opinion is, parents should look to themselves a bit more than they do.'

As she spoke, she threw open the door of the little room where Johnny housed. It was an odd place. The walls were plastered over with newspaper-cuttings, with old prints from illustrated journals, with snippets torn off valentines and keepsakes. Stuck one on another, these formed a kind of loose wallpaper, which stirred in the draught. Tilly went on: 'I see myself to it being kept cleanish; 'e hates the girl to come bothering round. Oh, just Johnny's rubbish!' For Mary had stooped curiously to the table which was littered with a queer collection of objects: match-boxes on wheels; empty reels of cotton threaded on strings; bits of wood shaped in rounds and squares; boxes made of paper; dried seaweed glued in patterns on strips of cardboard. 'He's forever pottering about with 'em. What amusement 'e gets out of it, only the Lord can tell.'

She did not mention the fact, known to Mary, that when Johnny had a drinking-bout it was she who looked after him, got him comfortably to bed, and made shift to keep the noise from his father's ears. Yes, Tilly's charity seemed sheerly inexhaustible.

Again, there was the case of Jinny's children.

For in this particular winter Tilly had exchanged her black silk for a stuff gown, heavily trimmed with crepe. She was in mourning for poor Jinny, who had died not long after giving birth to a third daughter.

'Died *of* the daughter, in more senses than one,' was Tilly's verdict.

John had certainly been extremely put out at the advent of yet another girl; and the probability was that Jinny had taken his reproaches too much to heart. However it was, she could not rally; and one day Mary received a telegram saying that if she wished to see Jinny alive, she must come at once. No mention was made of Tilly, but Mary ran to her with the news, and Tilly declared her intention of going, too. 'I suppose I may be allowed to say good-bye to my own sister, even though I'm not a *H*onourable?

'Not that Jinn and I ever really drew together,' she continued as the train bore them over the ranges. 'She'd too much of poor pa in 'er. And I was all ma. Hard luck that it must just be her who managed to get such a domineering brute for a husband. You'll excuse me, Mary, won't you? – a domineering brute!

'And to think I once envied her the match!' she went on meditatively, removing her bonnet and substituting a kind of nightcap intended to keep her hair free from dust. 'Lauks, Mary, it's a good thing fate doesn't always take us at our word. We don't know which side our bread's buttered on, and that's the truth. Why, my dear, I wouldn't exchange my old boy for all the *H*onourables in creation!'

They were in time to take leave of Jinny lying white as her pillows behind the red rep hangings of the bed. The bony parts of her face had sprung into prominence, her large soft eyes fallen in. John, stalking solemnly and noiselessly in a long black coat, himself led the two women to the bedroom, where he left them; they sat down one on each side of the great fourposter. Jinny hardly glanced at her sister: it was Mary she wanted, Mary's hand she fumbled for while she told her trouble. 'It's the children, Mary,' she whispered. 'I can't die happy because of the children. John doesn't understand them.' Jinny's whole existence was bound up in the three little ones she had brought into the world.

'Dearest Jinny, don't fret. I'll look after them for you, and take care of them,' promised Mary wiping away her tears.

'I thought so,' said the dying woman, relieved, but without gratitude: it seemed but natural to her, who was called upon to give up everything, that those remaining should make sacrifices. Her fingers plucked at the sheet. 'John's been good to me,' she went on, with closed eyes. 'But . . . if it 'adn't been for the children . . . yes, the children . . . I think I'd 'a' done better –' her speech lapsed oddly, after her years of patient practice – 'to 'ave taken . . . to 'a' taken' – the name remained unspoken.

Tilly raised astonished eyebrows at Mary. 'Wandering!' she telegraphed in lip-language, forming the word very largely and distinctly; for neither knew of Jinny having had any but her one glorious chance.

Tilly's big heart yearned over her sister's forlorn little ones; they could be heard bleating like lambs for the mother to whom till now they had never cried in vain. Her instant idea was to gather all three up in her arms and carry them off to her own roomy, childless home, where she would have given them a delightful, though not maybe a particularly discriminating upbringing. But the funeral over, the blinds raised, the two ladies and the elder babes clad in the stiff, expensive mourning that befitted the widower's social position, John put his foot down: and to Mary was extremely explicit: 'Under no circumstances will I permit Matilda to have anything to do with the rearing of my children – excellent creature though she be!'

On the other hand, he would not have been unwilling for Mary to mother them. This, of course, was out of the question: Richard had accustomed himself to Trotty, but would not thank you, she knew, for any fresh encroachment on his privacy. Before leaving, however, she promised to sound him on the plan of placing Trotty as a weekly boarder at a Young Ladies' Seminary, and taking the infant in her place. For it came out that John intended to set Zara – Zara, but newly returned from a second voyage to England and still sipping like a bee at the sweets of various situations – at the head of his house once more. And Mary could not imagine Zara rearing a baby.

Equally hard was it to understand John not having learnt wisdom from his two previous failures to live with his sister. But, in seeking tactfully to revive his memory, she ran up against such an ingrained belief in the superiority of his own kith and kin that she was baffled, and could only fold her hands and hope for the best.

'Besides, Jane's children are infinitely more tractable than poor Emma's,' was John's parting shot. – Strange, thought Mary, how attached John was to his second family.

He had still another request to make of her. The reports he received of the boy Johnny, now a pupil at the Geelong Grammar School, grew worse from term to term. It had become clear to him that he was unfortunate enough to possess an out-and-out dullard for a son. Regretfully giving up, therefore, the design he had cherished of educating Johnny for the law, he had resolved to waste no more good money on the boy, but to take him, once he was turned fifteen, into his own business. Young John, however, had proved refractory, expressing a violent antipathy to the idea of office-life. 'It is here that I should be glad of another opinion – and I turn to you, Mary, my dear. Jane was of no use whatever in such matters, none whatever, being, and very properly so, entirely wrapped up in her own children.' So Mary arranged to break her homeward journey at Geelong, for the purpose of seeing and summing up her nephew.

Johnny – he was Jack at school, but that, of course, his tomfools of relations couldn't be expected to remember – Johnny was waiting on the platform when the train steamed in. 'Oh, what a bonny boy!' said Mary to herself. 'All poor Emma's good looks.'

Johnny had been kicking his heels disconsolately: another of these wretched old women coming down to jaw him! He wished every one of them at the bottom of the sea. However, he pulled himself together and went forward to greet his aunt: he was not in the least bashful. And as they left the station he took stock of her, out of the tail of his eye. With a growing approval: this one at any rate he needn't feel ashamed of; and she was not so dreadfully old after all. Perhaps she mightn't turn out quite such a wet blanket as the rest; though, from experience, he couldn't connect any pleasure with relatives' visits: they were nasty pills that had to be swallowed. He feared and disliked his father; Aunt Zara had been sheerly ridiculous, with her frills and simpers – the boys had imitated her for weeks after – and once, most shameful of all, his stepmother had come down and publicly wept over him. His cheeks still burnt at the remembrance; and he had been glad to hear that she was dead: served her jolly well right! But this Aunt Mary seemed a horse of another colour; and he did not sneak her into town by a back way, as he had planned to do before seeing her.

Greatly as Mary might admire the tall fair lad by her side, she found herself at a loss how to deal with him, the mind of a schoolboy of thirteen being a closed book to her. Johnny looked demure and answered 'Yes, Aunt Mary', to everything she said; but this was of small assistance in getting at the real boy inside.

Johnny had no intention, in the beginning, of taking her into his often-betrayed and badly bruised confidence. However, a happy instinct led her to suggest a visit to a shop that sold brandy-snaps and ginger-beer; and this was too much for his strength of mind. Golly, didn't he have a tuck-in! And a whole pound of bull's-eyes to take back with him to school!

It was over the snaps, with an earth-brown moustache drawn round his fresh young mouth, the underlip of which swelled like

332

a ripe cherry, that he blurted out: 'I say, Aunt Mary, *don't* let the pater stick me in that beastly old office of his. I . . . I want to go to sea.'

'Oh, but Johnny! Your father would never consent to that, I'm sure.'

'I don't see why not,' returned the boy in an aggrieved voice. 'I hate figures and father knows it. I tell you I mean to go to sea!' And as he said it his lip shot out, and suddenly, for all his limpid blue eyes and flaxen hair, it was his father's face that confronted Mary.

'He wouldn't think it respectable enough, dear. He wants you to rise higher in the world, and to make money. You must remember who he is.'

'Bosh!' said Johnny. 'Look at Uncle Ned . . . and Uncle Jerry . . . and the governor himself. He didn't have to sit in a beastly old hole of an office when he was my age.'

'That was quite different,' said Mary weakly. 'And as for your Uncle Jerry, Johnny – why, afterwards he was as glad as could be to get into an office at all.'

'Well, I'd sooner be hanged!' retorted young John. But the next minute flinging away dull care, he inquired briskly: 'Can you play tipcat, Aunt Mary?' And vanquished by her air of kindly interest, he gave her his supreme confidence. 'I say, don't peach, will you, but I've got a white rat. I keep it in a locker under my bed.'

A nice frank handsome boy, wrote Mary. *Don't be too hard on him, John. His great wish is to travel and see the world – or as he puts it, to go to sea. Mightn't it be a good thing to humour him in this? A taste of the hardships of life would soon cure him of any such fancies.*

'Stuff and nonsense!' said John the father, and threw the letter from him. 'I didn't send Mary there to let the young devil get round her like that.' And thereupon he wrote to the Headmaster that the screw was to be applied to Johnny as never before. This was his last chance. If it failed, and his next report showed no improvement, he would be taken away without further ado and planked down under his father's nose. No son of his should go to sea, he was damned if they should! For, like many another who has yielded to the wandering passion in his youth, John had small mercy on it when it reared its head in his descendants.

333

CHAPTER NINE

Henry Ocock was pressing for a second opinion; his wife had been in poor health since the birth of her last child. Mahony drove to Plevna House one morning between nine and ten o'clock.

A thankless task lay before him. Mrs Henry's case had been a fruitful source of worry to him; and he now saw nothing for it but a straight talk with Henry himself.

He drove past what had once been the Great Swamp. From a bed of cattle-ploughed mud interspersed with reedy waterholes; in summer a dry and dust-swept hollow: from this, the vast natural depression had been transformed into a graceful lake, some three hundred acres in extent. On its surface pleasure boats lay at their moorings by jetties and boatsheds; groups of stiff-necked swans sailed or ducked and straddled; while shady walks followed the banks, where the whiplike branches of the willows, showing shoots of tenderest green, trailed in the water or swayed like loose harp-strings to the breeze.

All the houses that had sprung up round Lake Wendouree had well-stocked spreading grounds; but Ocock's outdid the rest. The groom opening a pair of decorative iron gates which were the showpiece of the neighbourhood, Mahony turned in and drove past exotic firs, Moreton Bay fig-trees and araucarias; past cherished English hollies growing side by side with giant cacti. In one corner stood a rockery, where a fountain played and goldfish swam in a basin. The house itself, of brick and two-storeyed, with massive bay-windows, had an ornamental veran-dah on one side. The drawing-room was a medley of gilt and lustres, mirrors and glass shades; the finest objects from Danda-loo had been brought here, only to be outdone by Henry's own additions. Yes, Ocock lived in grand style nowadays, as befitted one of the most important men in the town. His old father once gone – and Mahony alone knew why the latter's existence acted as a drag – he would no doubt stand for Parliament.

334

Invited to walk into the breakfast-room, Mahony there found the family seated at table. It was a charming scene. Behind the urn Mrs Henry, in be-ribboned cap and morning wrapper, dandled her infant; while Henry, in oriental gown and Turkish fez, had laid his newspaper by to ride his young son on his foot. Mahony refused tea or coffee; but could not avoid drawing up a chair, touching the peachy cheeks of the children held aloft for his inspection, and meeting a fire of playful sallies and kindly inquiries. As he did so, he was sensitively aware that it fell to him to break up the peace of this household. Only he knew the canker that had begun to eat at its roots.

The children borne off, Mrs Henry interrogated her husband's pleasure with a pretty: 'May I?' or 'Should I?' lift of the brows; and gathering that he wished her to retire, laid her small, plump hand in Mahony's, sent a graceful message to 'dearest Mary', and swept the folds of her gown from the room. Henry followed her with a well-pleased eye – his opinion was no secret that, in figure and bearing, his wife bore a marked resemblance to her Majesty the Queen – and admonished her not to fail to partake of some light refreshment during the morning, in the shape of a glass of sherry and a biscuit. 'Unless, my love, you prefer me to order cook to whip you up an egg-nog. – Mrs Ocock is, I regret to say, entirely without appetite again,' he went on, as the door closed behind his wife. 'What she eats is not enough to keep a sparrow going. You must prove your skill, doctor, and oblige us by prescribing a still more powerful tonic or appetizer. The last had no effect whatever.' He spoke from the hearthrug, where he had gone to warm his skirts at the wood fire, audibly fingering the while a nest of sovereigns in a waistcoat pocket.

'I feared as much,' said Mahony gravely; and therewith took the plunge.

When some twenty minutes later he emerged from the house, he was unaccompanied, and himself pulled the front door to behind him. He stood frowning heavily as he snapped the catches of his gloves, and fell foul of the groom over a buckle of the harness, in a fashion that left the man open-mouthed. 'Blow me, if I don't believe he's got the sack!' thought the man in driving townwards.

The abrupt stoppage of Richard's visits to Plevna House staggered Mary. And since she could get nothing out of her husband, she tied on her bonnet and went off hotfoot to question her friend. But Mrs Henry tearfully declared her ignorance – she

335

had listened in fear and trembling to the sound of the two angry voices – and Henry was adamant. They had already called in another doctor.

Mary came home greatly distressed, and, Richard still wearing his obstinate front, she ended by losing her temper. He knew well enough, said she, it was not her way to interfere or to be inquisitive about his patients; but this was different; this had to do with one of her dearest friends; she must know. In her ears rang Agnes's words: 'Henry told me, love, he wouldn't insult me by repeating what your husband said of me. Oh, Mary, isn't it dreadful? And when I liked him so as a doctor!' – She now repeated them aloud.

This was too much for Mahony. He blazed up. 'The confounded mischiefmonger – the backbiter! Well, if you will have it, wife, here you are . . . here's the truth. What I said to Ocock was: I said, my good man, if you want your wife to get over her next confinement more quickly, keep the sherry-decanter out of her reach.'

Mary gasped and sank on a chair, letting her arms flop to her side. 'Richard!' she ejaculated. 'Oh, Richard, you never did!'

'I did indeed, my dear. – Oh well, not in just those words, of course; we doctors must always wrap the truth up in silver paper. – And I should feel it my duty to do the same again tomorrow; though there are pleasanter things in life, Mary, I can assure you, than informing a low mongrel like Ocock that his wife is drinking on the sly. You can have no notion, my dear, of the compliments one calls down on one's head by so doing. The case is beyond my grasp, of course, and I am cloaking my own shortcomings by making scandalous insinuations against a delicate lady, who "takes no more than her position entitles her to" – his very words, Mary! – "for the purpose of keeping up her strength".' And Mahony laughed hotly.

'Yes, but was it – I mean . . . was it really necessary to say it?' stammered Mary still at sea. And as her husband only shrugged his shoulders: 'Then I can't pretend to be surprised at what has happened, Richard. Mr Henry will *never* forgive you. He thinks so much of everything and everyone belonging to him.'

'Pray, can I help that? . . . help his infernal pride? And, good God, Mary, can't you see that, far more terrible than my having had to tell him the truth, is the fact of there being such a truth to tell?'

'Oh yes, indeed I can,' and the warm tears rushed to Mary's

eyes. 'Poor, poor little Agnes! – Richard, it comes of her having once been married to that dreadful man. And though she doesn't say so, yet I don't believe she's really happy in her second marriage either. There are so many things she's not allowed to do – and she's afraid of Mr Henry, I know she is. You see he's displeased when she's dull or unwell; she must always be bright and look pretty; and I expect the truth is, since her illness she has taken to taking things, just to keep her spirits up.' Here Mary saw a ray of light, and snatched at it. 'But in that case mightn't the need for them pass, as she grows stronger?'

'I lay no claim to be a prophet, my dear.'

'For it does seem strange that *I* never noticed anything,' went on Mary, more to herself than to him. 'I've seen Agnes at all hours of the day . . . when she wasn't in the least expecting visitors. – Yes, Richard, I do know people sometimes eat things to take the smell away. But the idea of Agnes doing anything so . . . so low – oh, isn't it *just* possible there might be some mistake?'

'Oh, well, if you're going to imitate Ocock and try to teach me my business!' gave back Mahony with an angry gesture, and sitting down at the table, he pulled books and papers to him.

'As if such a thing would ever occur to me! It's only that . . . that somehow my brain won't take it in. Agnes has always been such a dear good little soul, all kindness. She's never done anybody any harm or said a hard word about anyone, all the years I've known her. I simply *can't* believe it of her, and that's the truth. As for what people will say when it gets about that you've been shown the door in a house like Mr Henry's – why, I'm afraid even to think of it!' and powerless any longer to keep back her tears, Mary hastened from the room.

But she also thought it wiser to get away before Richard had time to frame the request that she should break off all intercourse with Plevna House. This, she could never promise to do; and the result might be a quarrel. Whereas if she avoided giving her word, she would be free to slip out now and then to see poor Agnes, when Richard was on his rounds and Mr Henry at business. But this was the only point clear to her. In standing up for her friend she had been perfectly sincere: to think ill of a person she cared for, cost Mary an inward struggle. Against this, however, she had an antipathy to set that was almost stronger than herself. Of all forms of vice, intemperance was the one she hated most. She lived in a country where it was, alas! only too common; but she had never learnt to tolerate it, or to look with a lenient eye on those who succumbed: and whether these were but slaves of the nipping habit; or the eternal dram-drinkers who felt fit for nothing if they had not a peg inside them; or those seasoned topers who drank their companions under the table without themselves turning a hair; or yet again those who, sober for three parts of the year, spent the fourth in secret debauches. Herself she had remained as rigidly abstemious as in the days of her girlhood. And she often mused, with a glow at her heart, on her great good fortune in having found in Richard one whose views on this subject were no less strict than her own. Hence her distress at his disclosure was caused not alone by the threatened loss of a friendship: she wept for the horror with which the knowledge filled her.

Little by little, though, her mind worked round to what was, after all, the chief consideration: Richard's action and its probable consequences. And here once more she was divided against herself. For a moment she had hoped her husband would own the chance of him being in error. But she soon saw that this would never do. A mistake on his part would be a blow to his reputation. Besides making enemies of people like the Henrys for nothing. If he had to lose them as patients, it might as well be for a good solid reason, she told herself with a dash of his own asperity. No, it was a case of either husband or friend. And though she pitied Agnes from the bottom of her heart, yet there were literally no lengths she would have shrunk from going to, to spare Richard pain or even anxiety. And this led her on to wonder whether, granted things were as he said, he had approached Mr Henry in the most discreet way. Could he not have avoided a complete break? She sat and pondered this question till her head ached, finding herself up against the irreconcilability of the practical with the ideal which complicates a man's working life. What she belatedly tried to think out for her husband was some little common-sense stratagem by means of which he could have salved his conscience, without giving offence. He might have said that the drugs he was prescribing would be nullified by the use of wine or spirits; even better, have warned Agnes in private. Somehow, it might surely have been managed. Mr Henry had no doubt been extremely rude and overbearing; but in earlier years Richard had known how to behave towards ill-breeding. She couldn't tell why, but he was finding it more and more difficult to get on with people nowadays. He certainly had a very great deal to do, and was often tired out. Again, he did not need to care so much as formerly whether he offended people or not – ordinary patients, that was; the Henrys, of course, were of the utmost consequence. Still, once on a time he had been noted for his tact; it was sad to see it leaving him in the lurch. Several times of late she had been forced to step in and smooth out awkwardnesses. But a week ago he had had poor little Amelia Grindle up in arms, by telling her that her sickly first-born would mentally never be quite like other children. To everyone else this had been plain from the outset; but Amelia had suspected nothing, having, poor thing, no idea when a babe ought to begin to take notice or cut its teeth. Richard said it was better for her to face the truth betimes than to spend her life vainly hoping and fretting; indeed, it would not be right of him to allow it. Poor dear Richard! He set such store by truth and principle – and she, Mary, would not have had him otherwise. All the same, she thought that in both cases a small compromise would not have hurt him. But compromise he would not . . . or could not. And as, recalled to reality by the sight of the week's washing, which strained, ballooned, collapsed, on its lines in the yard – Biddy was again letting the clothes get much too dry! – as Mary rose to her feet, she manfully squared her shoulders to meet the weight of the new burden that was being laid on them.

With regard to Mahony, it might be supposed that having faithfully done what he believed to be his duty, he would enjoy the fruits of a quiet mind. This was not so. Before many hours had passed he was wrestling with the incident anew; and a true son of that nation which, for all its level-headedness, spends its best strength in fighting shadows, he felt a great deal angrier in retrospect than he had done at the moment. It was not alone the fact of him having got his congé – no medico was safe from *that* punch below the belt. His bitterness was aimed at himself. Once more he had let himself be hoodwinked; had written down the smooth civility it pleased Ocock to adopt towards him to respect and esteem. Now that the veil was torn, he saw how poor the lawyer's opinion of him actually was. And always had been. For a memory was struggling to emerge in him, setting strings in vibration. And suddenly there rose before him a picture of Ocock that time had dimmed. He saw the latter standing in the dark, crowded lobby of the court-house, cursing at him for letting their witness escape. There it was! There, in these two scenes, far apart as they lay, you had the whole man. The unctuous blandness, the sleek courtesy was but a mask, which he wore for you just so long as you did not hinder him by getting in his way. That was the unpardonable sin. For Ocock was out to succeed – to succeed at any price and by any means. In tracing his course, no goal but this had ever stood before him. The obligations that bore on your ordinary mortal – a sense of honesty, of responsibility to one's fellows, the soft pull of domestic ties – did not trouble Ocock. He laughed them down, or wrung their necks like so many pullets. And should the poor little woman who bore his name become a drag on him, she would be tossed on to the rubbish-heap with the rest. In a way, so complete a freedom from altruistic motives had something grandiose about it. But those who ran up against it, and could not fight it with its own weapons, had not an earthly chance.

Thus Mahony sat in judgement, giving rein for once to his in-grained dislike for the man of whom he had now made an enemy. In whose debt, for the rest, he stood deep. And had done, ever since the day he had been fool enough, like the fly in the nursery rhyme, to seek out Ocock and his familiars in their grimy little 'parlour' in Chancery Lane.

But his first heat spent he soon cooled down, and was able to laugh at the stagy explosiveness of his attitude. So much for the personal side of the matter. Looked at from a business angle it was more serious. The fact of him having been shown the door by a patient of Ocock's standing was bound, as Mary saw, to react unfavourably on the rest of the practice. The news would run like wildfire through the place; never were such hotbeds of gossip as these colonial towns. Besides, the colleague who had been called in to Mrs Agnes in his stead, was none too well disposed towards him.

His fears were justified. It quickly got about that he had made a blunder: all Mrs Henry needed, said the new-comer, was change of air and scene; and forthwith the lady was packed off on a trial trip to Sydney. Mahony held his head high, and refused to notice looks and hints. But he knew all about what went on behind his back: he was morbidly sensitive to atmosphere; could tell how a house was charged as soon as he crossed the threshold. People were saying: a mistake there, why not here, too? Slow recoveries asked themselves if a fresh treatment might not benefit them; lovers of blue pills hungered for more drastic remedies. The disaffection would blow over, of course;

but it was painful while it lasted; and things were not bettered by one of his patients choosing just this inconvenient moment to die – an elderly man, down with the Russian influenza, who disobeyed orders, got up too early and was carried off by double pneumonia inside a week. – Worry over the mishap robbed his poor medical attendant of sleep for several nights on end.

Not that this was surprising; he found it much harder than of old to keep his mind from running on his patients outside working-hours. In his younger days he had laid down fixed rules on this score. Every brainworker, he held, must in his spare time be able to detach his thoughts from his chief business, pin them to something of quite another kind, no matter how trivial: keep fowls or root round gardens, play the flute or go in for carpentry. Now, he might have dug till his palms blistered, it would not help. Those he prescribed for teased him like a pack of spirit-presences, which clamour to be heard. And if a serious case took a turn for the worse, he would find himself rising in a sweat of uncertainty, and going lamp in hand into the surgery, to con over a prescription he had written during the day. And one knew where *that* kind of thing led!

Now, as if all this were not enough, there was added to it the old, evergreen botheration about money.

CHAPTER TEN

Thus far, Ocock had nursed his mining investments for him with a fatherly care. He himself had been free as a bird from responsibility. Every now and again he would drop in at the office, just to make sure the lawyer was on the alert; and each time he came home cheerful with confidence. That was over now. As a first result of the breach, he missed – or so he believed – clearing four hundred pounds. Among the shares he held was one lot which till now had proved a sorry bargain. Soon after purchase something had gone wrong with the management of the claim; there had been a lawsuit, followed by calls unending and never a dividend. Now, when these shares unexpectedly swung up to a high level – only to drop the week after to their standing figure – Ocock failed to sell out in the nick of time. Called to account, he replied that it was customary in these matters for his clients to advise him; thus deepening Mahony's sense of obligation. Stabbed in his touchiness, he wrote for all his scrip to be handed over to him; and thereafter loss and gain depended on himself alone. It certainly brought a new element of variety into his life. The mischief was, he could get to his study of the money-market only with a fagged brain. And the fear lest he should do something rash or let a lucky chance slip kept him on tenter-hooks.

It was about this time that Mary, seated one evening in face of her husband, found herself reflecting: 'When one comes to think of it, how seldom Richard ever smiles nowadays.'

For a wonder they were at a soirée together, at the house of one of Mahony's colleagues. The company consisted of the inner circle of friends and acquaintances: 'Always the same people – the old job lot! One knows before they open their mouths what they'll say and how they'll say it,' Richard had grumbled as he dressed. The Henry Ococks were not there though, it being common knowledge that the two men declined

342

to meet; and a dash of fresh blood was present in the shape of a lady and gentleman just 'out from home'. Richard got into talk with this couple, and Mary, watching him fondly, could not but be struck by his animation. His eyes lit up, he laughed and chatted, made merry repartee: she was carried back to the time when she had known him first. In those days his natural gravity was often cut through by a mood of high spirits, of boyish jollity, which, if only by way of contrast, rendered him a delightful companion. She grew a little wistful, as she sat comparing present with past. And loath though she was to dig deep, for fear of stirring up uncomfortable things, she could not escape the discovery that, in spite of all his success − and his career there had surpassed their dearest hopes − in spite of the natural gifts fortune had showered on him, Richard was not what you would call a happy man. No, nor even moderately happy. Why this should be, it went beyond her to say. He had everything he could wish for: yes, everything, except perhaps a little more time to himself, and better health. He was not as strong as she would have liked to see him. Nothing radically wrong, of course, but enough to fidget him. Might not this . . . this − he himself called it 'want of tone' − be a reason for the scant pleasure he got out of life? And: 'I think I'll pop down and see Dr Munce about him one morning, without a word to him,' was how she eased her mind and wound up her reverie.

But daylight, and the most prosaic hours of the twenty-four, made the plan look absurd.

Once alive though to his condition, she felt deeply sorry for him in his patent inability ever to be content. It was a thousand pities. Things might have run so smoothly for him, he have got so much satisfaction out of them, if only he could have braced himself to regard life in cheerier fashion. But at this Mary stopped . . . and wondered . . . and wondered. Was that really true? Positively her experiences of late led her to believe that Richard would be less happy still if he had nothing to be unhappy about. − But dear me! this was getting out of her depth altogether. She shook her head and rebuked herself for growing fanciful.

All the same, her new glimpse of his inmost nature made her doubly tender of thwarting him; hence, she did not set her face as firmly as she might otherwise have done, against a wild plan he now formed of again altering, or indeed rebuilding the house; although she could scarcely think of it with patience. She liked her house so well as it stood; and it was amply big enough: there was only the pair of them . . . and John's child. It had the name, she knew, of being one of the most comfortable and best-kept in Ballarat. Brick for solidity, where wood prevailed, with a wide snowy verandah up the posts of which rare creepers ran, twining their tendrils one with another to form a screen against the sun. Now, what must Richard do but uproot the creepers and pull down the verandah, thus baring the walls to the fierce summer heat; plaster over the brick; and, more outlandish still, add a top storey. When she came back from Melbourne, where she had gone a-visiting to escape the upset – Richard, ordinarily so sensitive, had managed to endure it quite well, thus proving that he *could* put up with discomfort if he wanted to – when she saw it again, Mary hardly recognized her home. Personally she thought it ugly, for all its grandeur; changed wholly for the worse. Nor did time ever reconcile her to the upper storey. Domestic worries bred from it: the servant went off in a huff because of the stairs; they were at once obliged to double their staff. To cap it all, with its flat front unbroken by bay or porch, the house looked like no other in the town. Now, instead of passing admiring remarks, people stood stock-still before the gate to laugh at its droll appearance.

Yet, she would gladly have made the best of this, had Richard been the happier for it. He was not – or only for the briefest of intervals. Then his restlessness broke out afresh.

There came days when nothing suited him; not his fine consulting room, or the improved furnishings of the house, or even her cookery of which he had once been so fond. He grew dainty to a degree; she searched her cookery-book for piquant recipes. Next he fell to imagining it was unhealthy to sleep on feathers, and went to the expense of having a hard horsehair mattress made to fit the bed. Accustomed to the softest down, he naturally tossed and turned all night long, and rose in the morning declaring he felt as though he had been beaten with sticks. The mattress was stowed away in a lean-to behind the kitchen, and there it remained. It was not alone. Mary sometimes stood and considered, with a rueful eye, the many discarded objects that bore it company. Richard – oddly enough he was ever able to poke fun at himself – had christened this outhouse 'the cemetery of dead fads'. Here was a set of Indian clubs he had been going to harden his muscles with every morning, and had used for a week; together with an india-rubber gymnastic apparatus bought

344

for the same purpose. Here stood a patent shower-bath, that was to have dashed energy over him after a bad night, and had only succeeded in giving him acute neuralgia; a standing-desk he had broken his back at for a couple of days; a homoeopathic medicine-chest and a phrenological head — both subjects he had meant to satisfy his curiosity by looking into, had time not failed him. Mary sighed, when she thought of the waste of good money these and similar articles stood for. (Some day she would just have them privately carted away to auction!) But if Richard set his heart on a thing he wanted it so badly, so much more than other people did, that he knew no peace till he had it.

Mahony read in his wife's eyes the disapproval she was too wise to utter. At any other time her silent criticism would have galled him; in this case, he took shelter behind it. Let her only go on setting him down for lax and spendthrift, incapable of knowing his own mind. He would be sorry, indeed, for her to guess how matters really stood with him. The truth was, he had fallen a prey to utter despondency, was become so spiritless that it puzzled even himself. He thought he could trace some of the mischief back to the professional knocks and jars Ocock's action had brought down on him: to hear one's opinion doubted, one's skill questioned, was the tyro's portion; he was too old to treat such insolence with the scorn it deserved. Of course he had lived the affair down; but the result of it would seem to be a bottomless *ennui*, a *tedium vitæ* that had something pathological about it. Under its influence the homeliest trifles swelled to feats beyond his strength. There was, for instance, the putting on and off of one's clothing: this infinite boredom of straps and buttons — and all for what? For a day that would be an exact copy of the one gone before, a night as unrefreshing as the last. Did anyone suspect that there were moments when he quailed before his job, suspect that more than once he had even reckoned the number of times he would be called on to perform it, day in, day out, till that garment was put on him that came off no more; or that he could understand and feel sympathy with those faint souls — and there were such — who laid hands on themselves rather than go on doing it: did this get abroad, he would be considered ripe for Bedlam.

Physician, heal thyself! He swallowed doses of a tonic preparation, and put himself on a fatty diet.

Thereafter he tried to take a philosophic view of his case. He had now, he told himself, reached an age when such a state of mind gave cause neither for astonishment nor alarm. How often had it not fallen to him, in his role of medical adviser, to reassure a patient on this score. The arrival of middle age brought about a certain lowness of spirits in even the most robust: along with a more or less marked bodily languor went an uneasy sense of coming loss: the time was at hand to bid farewell to much that had hitherto made life agreeable; and for most this was a bitter pill. Meanwhile, one held a kind of mental stocktaking. As often as not by the light of a complete disillusionment. Of the many glorious things one had hoped to do – or to be – nothing was accomplished: the great realization, in youth breathlessly chased but never grasped, was now seen to be a mist-wraith, which could wear a thousand forms, but invariably turned to air as one came up with it. In nine instances out of ten there was nothing to put in its place; and you began to ask yourself in a kind of horrific amaze: 'Can this be all? . . . *this*? For this the pother of growth, the struggles, and the sufferings?' The soul's climacteric, if you would, from which a mortal came forth dulled to resignation; or greedy for the few physical pleasures left him; or prone to that tragic clinging to youth's skirts, which made the later years of many women and not a few men ridiculous. In each case the motive power was the same: the haunting fear that one had squeezed life dry; worse still, that it had not been worth the squeezing.

Thus his reason. But, like a tongue of flame, his instinct leapt up to give combat. By the gods, this cap did *not* fit him! Squeezed life dry? . . . found it not worth while? Why, he had never got within measurable distance of what he called life, at all! There could be no question of him resigning himself: deep down in him, he knew, was an enormous residue of vitality, of untouched mental energy that only waited to be drawn on. It was like a buried treasure, jealously kept for the event of his one day catching up with life: not the bare scramble for a living that here went by that name, but Life with a capital L, the existence he had once confidently counted on as his – a tourney of spiritual adventuring, of intellectual excitement, in which the prize striven for was not money or anything to do with money. Far away, thousands of miles off, luckier men than he were in the thick of it. He, of his own free will, had cut himself adrift, and now it was too late.

But was it? Had the time irretrievably gone by? The ancient idea of escape, long dormant, suddenly reawoke in him with

a new force. And, once stirring, it was not to be silenced, but
went on sounding like a ground-tone through all he did. At first
he shut his ears to it, to dally with side issues. For example, he
worried the question why the breaking-point should only now
have been reached and not six months, a year ago. It was quib-
bling to lay the whole blame on Ocock's shoulders. The real
cause went deeper, was of older growth. And driving his mind
back over the past, he believed he could pin his present loss of
grip to that fatal day on which he learnt that his best friend had
betrayed him. Things like that gave you a crack that would not
mend. He had been rendered suspicious where he had once been
credulous; prone to see evil where no evil was. For, deceived by
Purdy, in whom could he trust? Of a surety not in the pushful
set of jobbers and tricksters he was condemned to live amongst.
No discoveries he might make about them would surprise him.
— And once more the old impotent anger with himself broke
forth, that he should ever have let himself take root in such
detestable surroundings.

Why not shake the dust of the country off his feet? — From
this direct attack he recoiled, casting up his hands as if against
the evil eye. What next! But exclaim as he might, now that the
idea had put on words, it was by no means so simple to fend it off
as when it had been a mere vague humming at the back of his
mind. It seized him; swept his brain bare of other thoughts. He
began to look worn. And never more so than when he imagined
himself taking the bull by the horns and asking Mary's approval
of his wild-goose scheme. He could picture her face, when she
heard that he planned throwing up his fine position and decamp-
ing on nothing a year. The vision was a cold douche to his folly.
No, no! it would not do. You could not accustom a woman to
ease and luxury and then, when you felt *you* had had enough
and would welcome a return to Spartan simplicity, to an austere
clarity of living, expect her to be prepared, at the word, to step
back into poverty. One was bound . . . bound . . . and by just
those silken threads which, in premarital days, had seemed
sheerly desirable. He wondered now what it would be like to
stand free as the wind, answerable only to himself. The bare
thought of it filled him as with the rushing of wings.

Once he had been within an ace of cutting and running. That
was in the early days, soon after his marriage. Trade had petered
out; and there would have been as little to leave behind as to
carry with him. But, even so, circumstances had proved too

347

strong for him: what with Mary's persuasions and John's inter-meddling, his scheme had come to nothing. And if, with so much in his favour, he had not managed to carry it out, how in all the world could he hope to now, when everything conspired against him? It was, besides, excusable in youth to challenge fortune; a very different matter for one of his age.

Of his age! . . . the words gave him pause. By their light he saw why he had knuckled under so meekly, at the time of his first attempt. It was because then a few years one way or another did not signify; he had them to spare. Now, each individual year was precious to him; he parted with it lingeringly, unwillingly. Time had taken to flashing past, too; Christmas was hardly cele-brated before it was again at the door. Another ten years or so and he would be an old man, and it would in very truth be too late. The tempter voice – in this case also the voice of reason – said: now or never!

But when he came to look the facts in the face his heart failed him anew, so heavily did the arguments against his taking such a step – and, true to his race, it was these he began by marshal-ling – weigh down the scales. He should have done it, if done it was to be, five . . . three . . . even a couple of years ago. Each day that dawned added to the tangle, made the idea seem more pre-posterous. Local dignities had been showered on him: he sat on the Committees of the District Hospital and the Benevolent Asylum; was Honorary Medical Officer to this Society and that; a trustee of the church; one of the original founders of the Mechanics' Institute; vice-president of the Botanical Society; and so on, *ad infinitum*. His practice was second to none; his visiting-book rarely showed a blank space; people drove in from miles round to consult him. In addition, he had an ex-tremely popular wife, a good house and garden, horses and traps, and a sure yearly income of some twelve or thirteen hundred. Of what stuff was he made, that he could lightly con-template turning his back on prizes such as these?

Even as he told them off, however, the old sense of hollowness was upon him again. His life there reminded him of a gaudy drop-scene, let down before an empty stage; a painted sham, with darkness and vacuity behind. At bottom, none of these distinctions and successes meant anything to him; not a scrap of mental pabulum could be got from them: rather would he have chosen to be poor and a nobody among people whose thoughts flew to meet his halfway. And there was also another side to it.

348

Stingy though the years had been of intellectual grist, they had not scrupled to rob him of many an essential by which he set store. His old faculty – for good or evil – of swift decision, for instance. It was lost to him now; as witness his present miserable vacillation. It had gone off arm-in-arm with his health; physically he was but a ghost of the man he had once been. But the bitterest grudge he bore the life was for the shipwreck it had made of his early ideals. He remembered the pure joy, the lofty sentiments with which he had returned to medicine. Bah! – there had been no room for any sentimental nonsense of that kind here. He had long since ceased to follow his profession disinterestedly; the years had made a hack of him – a skilled hack, of course – but just a hack. He had had no time for study; all his strength had gone in keeping his income up to a certain figure; lest the wife should be less well dressed and equipped than her neighbours; or patients fight shy of him; or his confreres wag their tongues. – Oh! he had adapted himself supremely well to the standards of this Australia, so-called Felix. And he must not complain if, in so doing, he had been stripped, not only of his rosy dreams, but also of that spiritual force on which he could once have drawn at will. Like a fool he had believed it possible to serve mammon with impunity, and for as long as it suited him. He knew better now. At this moment he was undergoing the sensations of one who, having taken shelter in what he thinks a light and flimsy structure, finds that it is built of the solidest stone. Worse still: that he has been walled up inside.

And even suppose he *could* pull himself together for the effort required, how justify his action in the eyes of the world? His motives would be double-dutch to the hard-headed crew around him; nor would any go to the trouble of trying to understand. There was John. All John would see was an elderly and not over-robust man deliberately throwing away the fruits of year-long toil – and for what? For the privilege of, in some remote spot, as a stranger and unknown, having his way to make all over again; of being free to shoulder once more the risks and hazards the undertaking involved. And little though he cared for John or anyone else's opinion, Mahony could not help feeling a trifle sore, in advance, at the ridicule of which he might be the object, at the zanyish figure he was going to be obliged to cut.

But a fig for what people thought of him! Once away from here he would, he thanked God, never see any of them again. No, it was Mary who was the real stumbling-block, the opponent he most feared. Had he been less attached to her, the thing would have been easier; as it was, he shrank from hurting her. And hurt and confuse her he must. He knew Mary as well — nay, better than he knew his own unreckonable self. For Mary was not a creature of moods, did not change her mental envelope a dozen times a day. And just his precise knowledge of her told him that he would never get her to see eye to eye with him. Her clear, serene outlook was attuned to the plain and the practical; she would discover a thousand drawbacks to his scheme, but nary a one of the incorporeal benefits he dreamed of reaping from it. There was his handling of money for one thing: she had come, he was aware, to regard him as incurably extravagant; and it would be no easy task to convince her that he could learn again to fit his expenses to a light purse. She had a woman's instinctive distrust, too, of leaving the beaten track. Another point made him still more dubious. Mary's whole heart and happiness were bound up in this place where she had spent the flower-years of her life: who knew if she would thrive as well on other soil? He found it intolerable to think that she might have to pay for his want of stability. — Yes, reduced to its essentials, it came to mean the pitting of one soul's welfare against that of another; was a toss-up between his happiness and hers. One of them would have to yield. Who would suffer more by doing so — he or she? He believed that a sacrifice on his part would make the wreck of his life complete. On hers — well, thanks to her doughty habit of finding good everywhere, there was a chance of her coming out unscathed.

Here was his case in a nutshell.

Still he did not tackle Mary. For sometimes, after all, a disturbed doubt crept upon him whether it would not be possible to go on as he was; instead of, as she would drastically word it, cutting his throat with his own hand. And to be perfectly honest, he believed it would. He could now afford to pay for help in his work; to buy what books he needed or fancied; to take holidays while putting in a *locum*; even to keep on the *locum*, at a good salary, while he journeyed overseas to visit the land of his birth. But at this another side of him — what he thought of as spirit, in contradistinction to soul — cried out in alarm, fearful lest it was again to be betrayed. Thus far, though by rights coequal in the house of the body, it had been rigidly kept down. Nevertheless it had persisted, like a bright cold little spark at dead of night: his restlessness, the spiritual malaise that encumbered him had been its mute form of protest. Did he go on turning a deaf ear to its warnings, he might do himself irreparable harm. For time was flying, the sum of his years mounting, shrinking that roomy future to which he had thus far always postponed what seemed too difficult for the moment. Now he saw that he dared delay no longer in setting free the imprisoned elements in him, was he ever to grow to that complete whole which each mortal aspires to be. – That a change of environment would work this miracle he did not doubt; a congenial environment was meat and drink to him, was light and air. Here in this country, he had remained as utterly alien as any Jew of old who wept by the rivers of Babylon. And like a half-remembered tune there came floating into his mind words he had lit on somewhere, or learnt on the school-bench – Horace, he thought, but, whatever their source, words that fitted his case to a nicety. *Coelum, non animum, mutant, qui trans mare currunt.* 'Non animum'? Ah! could he but have foreseen this – foreknown it. If not before he set sail on what was to have been but a swift adventure, then at least on that fateful day long past when, foiled by Mary's pleadings and his own inertia, he had let himself be bound anew.

Thus the summer dragged by; a summer to try the toughest. Mahony thought he had never gone through its like for heat and discomfort. The drought would not break, and on the great squatting-stations round Ballarat and to the north, the sheep dropped like flies at an early frost. The forest reservoirs dried up, displaying the red mud of their bottoms, and a bath became a luxury – or a penance – the scanty water running thick and red. Then the bush caught fire and burnt for three days, painting the sky a rusty brown, and making the air hard to breathe. Of a morning his first act on going into his surgery was to pick up the thermometer that stood on the table. Sure as fate, though the clock had not long struck nine, the mercury marked something between a hundred and a hundred and five degrees. He let it fall with a nerveless gesture. Since his sunstroke he not only hated, he feared the sun. But out into it he must, to drive through dust-clouds so opaque that one could only draw rein till they subsided, meanwhile holloaing off collisions. Under the close leather hood he sat and stifled; or, removing his green goggles for the fiftieth time, climbed down to enter yet another baked wooden house, where he handled prostrate bodies rank with sweat, or prescribed for pallid or fever-speckled children. Then home, to toy with the food set before him, his mind already running on the discomforts of the afternoon. — Two bits of ill-luck came his way this summer. Old Ocock fell, in dismounting from a vehicle, and sustained a compound fracture of the femur. Owing to his advanced age there was for a time fear of malunion of the parts, and this kept Mahony on the rack. Secondly, a near neighbour, a common little fellow who kept a jeweller's shop in Bridge Street, actually took the plunge: sold off one fine day and sailed for home. And this seemed the unkindest cut of all.

But the accident that gave the death-blow to his scruples was another. On the advice of a wealthy publican he was treating, whose judgement he trusted, Mahony had invested — heavily for him, selling off other stock to do it — in a company known as the Hodderburn Estate. This was a government affair and ought to have been beyond reproach. One day, however, it was found that the official reports of the work done by the diamond drill-bore were cooked documents; and instantly everyone connected with the mine — directors, managers, engineers — lay under the suspicion of fraudulent dealings. Shares had risen as high as ten pounds odd; but when the drive reached the bore and, in place of the deep gutter-ground the public had been led to expect, hard rock was found overhead, there was a panic; shares dropped to twenty-five shillings and did not rally. Mahony was a loser by six hundred pounds, and got, besides, a moral shaking from which he could not recover. He sat and bit his little-finger nail to the quick. Was he, he savagely asked himself, going to linger on until the little he had managed to save was snatched from him?

He dashed off a letter to John, asking his brother-in-law to recommend a reliable broker. And this done, he got up to look for Mary, determined to come to grips with her at last.

CHAPTER ELEVEN

How to begin, how reduce to a few plain words his subtle tangle of thought and feeling, was the problem.

He did not find his wife on her usual seat in the arbour. In searching for her, upstairs and down, he came to a rapid decision. He would lay chief stress on his poor state of health.

'I feel I'm killing myself. I can't go on.'

'But Richard dear!' ejaculated Mary, and paused in her sewing, her needle uplifted, a bead balanced on its tip. Richard had run her to earth in the spare bedroom, to which at this time she often repaired. For he objected to the piece of work she had on hand – that of covering yards of black cashmere with minute jet beads – vowing that she would ruin her eyesight over it. So, having set her heart on a fashionable polonaise, she was careful to keep out of his way.

'I'm not a young man any longer, wife. When one's past forty . . .'

'Poor mother used to say forty-five was a man's prime of life.'

'Not for me. And not here – in this God-forsaken hole!'

'Oh dear me! I do wonder why you have such a down on Ballarat. I'm sure there must be many worse places in the world to live in'; and lowering her needle, Mary brought the bead to its appointed spot. 'Of course you have a lot to do, I know, and being such a poor sleeper doesn't improve matters.' But she was considering her pattern sideways as she spoke, thinking more of it than of what she said. Everyone had to work hard out here; compared with some she could name, Richard's job of driving round in a springy buggy seemed ease itself. 'Besides I told you at the time you were wrong not to take a holiday in winter, when you had the chance. You need a thorough change every year to set you up. You came back from the last as fresh as a daisy.'

'The only change that will benefit me is one for good and all,' said Mahony with extreme gloom. He had thrown up the bed-curtain and stretched himself on the bed, where he lay with his hands clasped under his neck.

Tutored by experience, Mary did not contradict him.

'And it's the kind I've finally made up my mind to take.'

'Richard! How you do run on!' and Mary, still gently incredulous but a thought wider awake, let her work sink to her lap. 'What is the use of talking like that?'

'Believe it or not, my dear, as you choose. You'll see – that's all.'

At her further exclamations of doubt and amazement, Mahony's patience slipped its leash. 'Surely to goodness my health comes first . . . before any confounded practice?'

'Ssh! Baby's asleep. – And don't get cross, Richard. You can hardly expect me not to be surprised when you spring a thing of this sort on me. You've never even dropped a hint of it before.'

'Because I knew very well what it would be. You dead against it, of course!'

'Now I call that unjust. You've barely let me get a word in edgeways.'

'Oh, I know by heart everything you're going to say. It's nonsense . . . folly . . . madness . . . and so on: all the phrases you women fish up from your vocabulary when you want to stave off a change – hinder any alteration of the *status quo*. But I'll tell you this, wife. You'll bury me here, if I don't get away soon. I'm not much more than skin and bone as it is. And I confess, if I've got to be buried I'd rather lie elsewhere – have good English earth atop of me.'

Had Mary been a man, she might have retorted that this was a very woman's way of shifting ground. She bit her lip and did not answer immediately. Then: 'You know I can't bear to hear you talk like that, even in fun. Besides, you always say much more than you mean, dear.'

'Very well then, if you prefer it, wait and see! You'll be sorry some day.'

'Do you mean to tell me, Richard, you're in earnest, when you talk of selling off your practice and going to England?'

'I can buy another there, can't I?'

With these words he leapt to his feet, afire with animation. And while Mary, now thoroughly uneasy, was folding up her work, he dilated upon the benefits that would accrue to them

354

from the change. Good-bye to dust, and sun, and drought, to blistering hot winds and *papier maché* walls! They would make their new home in some substantial old stone house that had weathered half a century or more, tangled over with creepers, folded away in its own privacy as only an English house could be. In the flower-garden roses would trail over arch and pergola; there would be a lawn with shaped yews on it; while in the orchard old apple-trees would flaunt their red abundance above grey, lichened walls.

('As if there weren't apples enough here!' thought Mary.)

He got a frog in his throat as he went on to paint in greater detail for her, who had left it so young, the intimate charm of the home country – the rich, green, dimpled countryside. And not till now did he grasp how sorely he had missed it. 'Oh, believe me, to talk of "going home" is no mere figure of speech, Mary!' In fancy he trod winding lanes that ran between giant hedges: hedges in tender bud, with dew on them; or snowed over with white mayflowers; or behung with the fairy webs and gossamer of early autumn, thick as twine beneath their load of moisture. He followed white roads that were banked with prim-roses and ran headlong down to the sea; he climbed the shoulder of a down on a spring morning, when the air was alive with larks carolling. But chiefly it was the greenness that called to him – the greenness of the greenest country in the world. Viewed from this distance, the homeland looked to him like one vast meadow. Oh, to tread its grass again! – not what one knew as grass here, a poor annual, that lasted for a few brief weeks; but lush meadow-grass, a foot high; or shaven emerald lawns on which ancient trees spread their shade; or the rank growth in old orchards, starry with wild flowers, on which fruit-blossoms fluttered down. He longed, too, for the exquisite finishedness of the mother country, the soft tints of cloud-veiled northern skies. His eyes ached, his brows had grown wrinkled from gazing on iron roofs set against the hard blue overhead; on dirty weatherboards innocent of paint; on higgledy-piggledy back-yards and ram-shackle fences; on the straggling landscape with its untidy trees – all the unrelieved ugliness, in short, of the colonial scene.

He stopped only for want of breath. Mary was silent. He waited. Still she did not speak.

He fell to earth with a bump, and was angry. 'Come . . . out with it! I suppose all this seems to you just the raving of a lunatic?'

'Oh, Richard, no. But a little . . . well, a little unpractical. I never heard before of anyone throwing up a good income because he didn't like the scenery. It's a step that needs the greatest consideration.'

'Good God! Do you think I haven't considered it? – and from every angle? There isn't an argument for or against, that I haven't gone over a thousand and one times.'

'And with never a word to me, Richard?' Mary was hurt; and showed it. 'It really is hardly fair. For this is my home as well as yours. – But now listen. You're tired out, run down with the heat and that last attack of dysentery. Take a good holiday – stay away for three months if you like. Sail over to Hobart Town, or up to Sydney, you who're so fond of the water. And when you come back strong and well we'll talk about all this again. I'm sure by then you'll see things with other eyes.'

'And who's to look after the practice, pray?'

'Why, a *locum tenens*, of course. Or engage an assistant.'

'Aha! you'd agree to that now, would you? I remember how opposed you were once to the idea.'

'Well, if I have to choose between it and you giving up altogether. . . . Now, for your own sake, Richard, don't go and do anything rash. If once you sell off and leave Ballarat, you can never come back. And then, if you regret it, where will you be? That's why I say don't hurry to decide. Sleep over it. Or let us consult somebody – John perhaps –'

'No you don't, madam, no you don't!' cried Richard with a grim dash of humour. 'You had me once . . . crippled me . . . handcuffed me – you and your John between you! It shan't happen again.'

'I crippled you? *I*, Richard! Why, never in my life have I done anything but what I thought was for your good. I've always put you first.' And Mary's eyes filled with tears.

'Yes, where it's a question of one's material welfare you haven't your equal – I admit that. But the other side of me needs coddling too – yes, and sympathy. But it can whistle for such a thing as far as you're concerned.'

Mary sighed. 'I think you don't realize, dear, how difficult it sometimes is to understand you . . . or to make out what you really do want,' she said slowly.

Her tone struck at his heart. 'Indeed and I do!' he cried contritely. 'I'm a born old grumbler, mavourneen, I know – contrariness in person! But in this case . . . come, love, do *try* to

356

grasp what I'm after; it means so much to me.' And he held out his hand to her, to beseech her.

Unhesitatingly she laid hers in it. 'I am trying, Richard, though you mayn't believe it. I always do. And even if I sometimes can't manage it – well, you know, dear, you generally get your own way in the end. Think of the house. I'm still not clear why you altered it. I liked it much better as it was. But I didn't make any fuss, did I? – though I should have, if I'd thought we were only to occupy it for a single year after. – Still, that was a trifle compared with what you want to do now. Though I lived to a hundred I should never be able to approve of this. And you don't know how hard it is to consent to a thing one disapproves of. You couldn't do it yourself. Oh, what *was* the use, Richard, of toiling as you have, if now, just when you can afford to charge higher fees and the practice is beginning to bring in money –'

Mahony let her hand drop, even giving it a slight push from him, and turned to pace the floor anew. 'Oh, money, money, money! I'm sick of the very sound of the word. But you talk as if nothing else mattered. Can't you for once, wife, see through the letter of the thing to the spirit behind? I admit the practice *has* brought in a tidy income of late; but as for the rest of the splendours, they exist, my dear, only in your imagination. If you ask me, I say I lead a dog's life – why, even a navvy works only for a fixed number of hours per diem! My days have neither beginning nor end. Look at yesterday! Out in the blazing sun from morning till night – I didn't get back from the second round till nine. At ten a confinement that keeps me up till three. From three till dawn I toss and turn, far too weary to sleep. By the time six o'clock struck – you of course were slumbering sweetly – I was in hell with tic. At seven I could stand it no longer and got up for the chloroform bottle: an hour's rest at any price – else how face the crowd in the waiting-room? And you call that splendour? – luxurious ease? If so, my dear, words have not the same meaning any more for you and me.'

Mary did not point out that she had said nothing of the kind, or that he had set up an extreme case as typical. She tightened her lips; her big eyes were very solemn.

'And it's not the work alone,' Richard was declaring, 'it's the place, wife – the people. I'm done with 'em, Mary – utterly done! Upon my word, if I thought I had to go on living among them even for another twelvemonth . . .'

'But *people* are the same all the world over!' The protest broke from her in spite of herself.

'No, by God, they're not!' And here Richard launched out into a diatribe against his fellow-colonists: 'This sordid riff-raff! These hard, mean, grasping money-grubbers!' that made Mary stand aghast. What could be the matter with him? What was he thinking of, he who was ordinarily so generous? Had he forgotten the many kindnesses shown him, the warm gratitude of his patients, people's sympathy, at the time of his illness? But he went on: 'My demands are most modest. All I ask is to live among human beings with whom I have half an idea in common – men who sometimes raise their noses from the ground, instead of eternally scheming how to line their pockets, reckoning human progress solely in terms of £ s. d. No, I've sacrificed enough of my life to this country. I mean to have the rest for myself. And there's another thing, my dear – another bad habit this precious place breeds in us. It begins by making us indifferent to those who belong to us but are out of our sight, and ends by cutting out closest ties. I don't mean by distance alone. I have an old mother still living, Mary, whose chief prayer is that she may see me once again before she dies. I was her last-born – the child her arms kept the shape of. What am I to her now? . . . what does she know of me, of the hard, tired, middle-aged man I have become? And you are in much the same box, my dear; unless you've forgotten by now that you ever had a mother.'

Mary was scandalized. 'Forget one's mother? . . . Richard! I think you're trying what dreadful things you can find to say . . . when I write home every three months!' And provoked by this fresh piece of unreason she opened fire in earnest, in defence of what she believed to be their true welfare. Richard listened to her without interrupting; even seemed to grant the truth of what she said. But none the less, even as she pleaded with him, a numbing sense of futility crept over her. She stuttered, halted, and finally fell silent. Her words were like so many lassoes thrown after his vagrant soul; and this was out of reach. It had sniffed freedom – it *was* free; ran wild already on the boundless plains of liberty.

After he had gone from the room she sat with idle hands. She was all in a daze. Richard was about to commit an out-and-out folly, and she was powerless to hinder it. If only she had had someone she could have talked things over with, taken advice of!

But no – it went against the grain in her to discuss her husband's actions with a third person. Purdy had been the sole exception, and Purdy had become impossible.

Looking back, she marvelled at her own dullness in not foreseeing that something like this might happen. What more natural than that the multitude of little whims and fads Richard had indulged should culminate in a big whim of this kind? But the acknowledgement caused her fresh anxiety. She had watched him tire, like a fickle child, of first one thing, then another; was it likely that he would now suddenly prove more stable? She did not think so. For she attributed his present mood of pettish aversion wholly to the fact of his being run down in health. It was quite true: he had not been himself of late. But, here again, he was so fanciful that you never knew how literally to take his ailments: half the time she believed he just imagined their existence; and the long holiday she had urged on him would have been enough to sweep the cobwebs from his brain. Oh, if only he could have held on in patience! Four or five years hence, at most, he might have considered retiring from general practice. She almost wept as she remembered how they had once planned to live for that day. Now it was all to end in smoke.

Then her mind reverted to herself and to what the break would mean to her; and her little world rocked to its foundations. For no clear call went out to Mary from her native land. She docilely said 'home' with the rest, and kept her family ties intact; but she had never expected to go back, except on a flying visit. She thought of England rather vaguely as a country where it was always raining, and where – according to John – an assemblage of old fogies, known as the House of Commons, persistently intermeddled in the affairs of the colony. For more than half her life – and the half that truly counted – Australia had been her home.

Her home! In fancy she made a round of the house, viewing each cosy room, lingering fondly over the contents of cupboards and presses, recollecting how she had added this piece of furniture for convenience' sake, that for ornament, till the whole was as perfect as she knew how to make it. Now, everything she loved and valued – the piano, the wax-candle chandelier, the gilt cornices, the dining-room horsehair – would fall under the auctioneer's hammer, go to deck out the houses of other people. Richard said she could buy better and handsomer things in England; but Mary allowed herself no illusions on this score. Where was the money to come from? She had learnt by personal experience what slow work building up a practice was. It would be years and years before they could hope for another such home. And sore and sorry as *she* might feel at having to relinquish her pretty things, in Richard's case it would mean a good deal more than that. To him the loss of them would be a real misfortune, so used had he grown to luxury and comfort, so strongly did the need of it run in his blood.

Worse still was the prospect of parting from relatives and friends. The tears came at this, freely. John's children! – who would watch over them when she was gone? How could she, from so far away, keep the promise she had made to poor Jinny on her death-bed? She would have to give up the baby of which she had grown so fond – give it back into Zara's unmotherly hands. And never again of a Saturday would she fetch poor little long-legged Trotty from school. She must say good-bye to one and to all – to John, and Zara, and Jerry – and would know no more, at close quarters, how they fared. When Jerry married there would be no one to see to it that he chose the right girl. Then Ned and Polly – poor souls, poor souls! What with the rapid increase of their family and Ned's unsteadiness – he could not keep any job long because of it – they only just contrived to make ends meet. How they would do it when she was not there to lend a helping hand, she could not imagine. And outside her brothers and sisters there was good Mrs Devine. Mary had engaged to guide her friend's tottery steps on the slippery path of Melbourne society, did Mr Devine enter the ministry. And poor little Agnes with her terrible weakness . . . and Amelia and her sickly babes . . . and Tilly, dear, good, warm-hearted Tilly! Never again would the pair of them enjoy one of their jolly laughs; or cook for a picnic; or drive out to a mushroom hunt. No, the children would grow up anyhow; her brothers forget her in carving out their own lives; her friends find other friends.

For some time, however, she kept her own counsel. But when she had tried by hook and by crook to bring Richard to reason, and failed; when she saw that he was actually beginning, on the quiet, to make ready for departure, and that the day was coming on which everyone would have to know: then she threw off her reserve. She was spending the afternoon with Tilly. They sat on the verandah together, John's child, black-eyed, fat, self-willed, playing, after the manner of two short years, at their feet. At the news that was broken to her, Tilly began by laughing immoderately, believing that Mary was 'taking a rise out of her'. But having studied her friend's face she let her work fall, slowly opened mouth and eyes, and was at first unequal to uttering a word.

Thereafter she bombarded Mary with questions.

'Wants to leave Ballarat? To go home to England?' she echoed, with an emphasis such as Tilly alone could lay. 'Well! of all the . . . What for? What on earth for?' As somebody gone and left 'im a fortune? Or 'as 'e been appointed pillmonger-in-ordinary to the Queen 'erself? What is it, Mary? What's up?'

What indeed! This was the question Mary dreaded, and one that would leap to every tongue: why was he going? She sat on the horns of a dilemma. It was not in her to wound people's feelings by blurting out the truth – this would also put Richard in a bad light – and, did she give no reason at all, many would think he had taken leave of his senses. Weakly, in a very un-Maryish fashion, she mumbled that his health was not what it should be, and he had got it into his head that for this the climate of the colony was to blame. Nothing would do him but to return to England.

'I never! No, never in my born days did I hear tell of such a thing!' and Tilly, exploding, brought her closed fist heavily down on her knee. 'Mary! . . . for a mere maggot like that, to chuck up a practice such as 'e's got. Upon my word, my dear, it looks as if 'e was touched 'ere,' – and she significantly tapped her forehead. 'Ha! Now I understand. You know I've seen quite well, love, you've been looking a bit down in the mouth of late. And so 'as pa noticed it, too. After you'd gone the other day, 'e said to me: "Looks reflexive-like does the little lady nowadays; as if she'd got something on 'er mind." And I to him: "Pooh! Isn't it enough that she's got to put up with the cranks and crotchets of one o' *your* sect?" – Oh Mary, my dear, there's many a true word said in jest. Though little did I think what the crotchet would be.' And slowly the rims of Tilly's eyes and the tip of her nose reddened and swelled.

'No, I can't picture it, Mary – what it'ull be like 'ere without you,' she said; and pulling out her handkerchief blew snort after snort, which was Tilly's way nowadays of having a good cry. 'There, there, Baby, Auntie's only got the sniffles. – For just think of it, Mary: except that first year or so after you were married, we've been together, you and me, pretty much ever

361

since you came to us that time at the 'otel – a little black midget of a thing in short frocks. I can still remember 'ow Jinn and I laughed at the idea of you teaching us; and 'ow poor ma said to wait and make sure we weren't laughing on the wrong side of our mouths. And ma was right as usual. For if ever a clever little kid trod the earth, it was you.'

Mary pooh-poohed the cleverness. 'I knew very little more than you yourselves. No, it was you who were all so kind to me. I had been feeling so lonely – as if nobody wanted me – and I shall never forget how mother put her arms round me and cuddled me, and how safe and comfortable I felt. It was always just like home there to me.'

'And why not, I'd like to know! – Look 'ere, Mary, I'm going to ask you something, plump and plain. 'Ave you really been happy in your marriage, my dear, or 'ave you not? You're such a loyal little soul, I know you'd never show it if you weren't; and sometimes I've 'ad my doubts about you, Mary. For you and the doctor are just as different as chalk and cheese.'

'Of course I have – as happy as the day's long!' cried Mary, sensitive as ever to a reflection on her husband. 'You·mustn't think anything like that, Tilly. I couldn't imagine myself married to anyone but Richard.'

'Then that only makes it harder for you now, poor thing, pulled two ways like, as you are,' said Tilly, and trumpeted afresh. 'All the same, there isn't anything I'd stick at, Mary, to keep you here. Don't be offended, my dear, but it doesn't matter half so much about the doctor going as you. There's none cleverer than 'im, of course, in 'is own line. But 'e's never fitted in properly here – I don't want to exactly say 'e thinks 'imself too good for us; but there *is* something, Mary love, and I'm not the only one who's felt it. I've known people go on like anything about 'im behind 'is back: nothing would induce them to have 'im and 'is haughty airs inside their doors again, etcetera.'

Mary flushed. 'Yes, I know, people do sometimes judge Richard very unkindly. For at heart he's the most modest of men. It's only his manner. And he can't help that, can he?'

'There are those who say a doctor ought to be able to, my dear. – But never mind him. Oh, it's you I feel for, Mary, being dragged off like this. Can't you *do* anything, dear? Put your foot down?'

Mary shook her head. 'It's no use. Richard is so . . . well, so

362

queer in some ways, Tilly. Besides, you know, I don't think it would be right of me to really pit my will against his.'

'Poor little you! – Oh! men are queer fish, Mary, aren't they? Not that I can complain; I drew a prize in the lucky-bag when I took that old Jawkins in there. But when I look round me, or think back, and see what we women put up with! There was poor old ma; she 'ad to be man for both. And Jinn, Mary, who didn't dare to call 'er soul 'er own. And milady Agnes is travelling the selfsame road – why, she 'as to cock 'er eye at Henry nowadays before she trusts 'erself to say whether it's beef or mutton she's eating! And now 'ere's you, love, carted off with never a with-your-leave or by-your-leave, just because the doctor's tired of it and thinks 'e'd like a change. There's no question of whether you're tired or not – oh, my, no!'

'But he has to earn the money, Tilly. It isn't quite fair to put it that way,' protested her friend.

'Well! I don't know, Mary, I'm sure,' and Tilly's plump person rose and sank in a prodigious sigh. 'But if I was 'is wife 'e wouldn't get off so easy – I know that! It makes me just boil.'

Mary answered with a rueful smile. She could never be angry with Richard in cold blood, or for long together.

As time went on, though, and the break-up of her home began – by the auctioneer's man appearing to paw over and appraise the furniture – a certain dull resentment did sometimes come uppermost. Under its sway she had forcibly to remind herself what a good husband Richard had always been; had to tell off his qualities one by one, instead of taking them as hitherto for granted. No, her quarrel, she began to see, was not so much with him as with the Powers above. Why should *her* husband alone not be as robust and hardy as all the other husbands in the place? None of *their* healths threatened to fail, nor did any of them find the conditions of the life intolerable. That was another shabby trick Fate had played Richard in not endowing him with worldly wisdom, and a healthy itch to succeed. Instead of that, he had been blessed with ideas and impulses that stood directly in his way. – And it was here that Mary bore more than one of her private ambitions for him to its grave. A new expression came into her eyes, too – an unsure, baffled look. Life was not, after all, going to be the simple, straightforward affair she had believed. Thus far, save for the one unhappy business with Purdy, wrongs and complications had passed her by. Now she saw that no more than anyone else could she hope to escape them.

Out of this frame of mind she wrote a long, confidential letter to John: John must not be left in ignorance of what hung over her; it was also a relief to unbosom herself to one of her own family. And John was good enough to travel up expressly to talk things over with her, and, as he put it, to 'call Richard to order'. Like everyone else he showed the whites of his eyes at the latter's flimsy reasons for seeking a change. But when, in spite of her warning, he bearded his brother-in-law with a jocose and hearty: 'Come, come, my dear Mahony! what's all this? You're actually thinking of giving us the slip?' Richard took his interference so badly, became so agitated over the head of the harmless question that John's airy remonstrance died in his throat.

'Mad as a March hare!' was his private verdict, as he shook down his ruffled plumes. To Mary he said ponderously: 'Well, upon my soul, my dear girl, I don't know — I am frankly at a loss what to say. Measured by every practical standard, the step he contemplates is little short of suicidal. I fear he will live to regret it.'

And Mary, who had not expected anything from John's intervention, and also knew the grounds for Richard's heat — Mary now resigned herself, with the best grace she could muster, to the inevitable.

CHAPTER TWELVE

House and practice sold for a good round sum; the brass plates were removed from gate and door, leaving dirty squares flanked by screw-holes; carpets came up and curtains down; and, like rats from a doomed ship, men and women servants fled to other situations. One fine day the auctioneer's bell was rung through the main streets of the town; and both on this and the next, when the red flag flew in front of the house, a troop of intending purchasers, together with an even larger number of the merely curious, streamed in at the gate and overran the premises. At noon the auctioneer mounted his perch, gathered the crowd round him, and soon had the sale in full swing, catching head-bobs, or wheedling and insisting with, when persuasion could do no more, his monotonous parrot-cry of: 'Going . . . going . . . gone!'

It would have been in bad taste for either husband or wife to be visible while the auction was in progress; and, the night before, Mary and the child had moved to Tilly's, where they would stay for the rest of the time. But Mahony was still hard at work. The job of winding up and getting in the money owed him was no light one. For the report had somehow got abroad that he was retiring from practice because he had made his fortune; and only too many people took this as a tacit permission to leave their bills unpaid.

He had locked himself and his account-books into a small back room, where stood the few articles they had picked out to carry with them: Mary's sewing-table, his first gift to her after marriage; their modest stock of silver; his medical library. But he had been forced to lower the blind, to hinder impertinent noses flattening themselves against the window, and thus could scarcely see to put pen to paper; while the auctioneer's grating voice was a constant source of distraction – not to mention the rude comments made by the crowd on house and furniture, the ceaseless trying of the handle of the locked door.

When it came to the point, this tearing up of one's roots was a murderous business – nothing for a man of his temperament. Mary was a good deal better able to stand it than he. Violently as she had opposed the move in the beginning, she was now, dear soul, putting a cheery face on it. But then Mary belonged to that happy class of mortals who could set up their Lares and Penates inside any four walls. Whereas he was a very slave to associations. Did she regret parting with a pretty table and a comfortable chair, it was solely because of the prettiness and convenience: as long as she could replace them by other articles of the same kind, she was content. But to him each familiar object was bound by a thousand memories. And it was the loss of these which could never be replaced that cut him to the quick.

Meanwhile this was the kind of thing he had to listen to.

' 'Ere now, ladies and gents, we 'ave a very fine pierglass – a very chaste and tasty pierglass indeed – a reel addition to any lady's drawin'-room. – Mrs Rupp? Do I understand you aright, Mrs Rupp? Mrs Rupp offers twelve bob for this very 'andsome article. Twelve bob . . . going twelve. . . . Fifteen? Thank you, Mrs Bromby! Going fifteen . . . going – going – Eighteen? Right you are, my dear!' and so on.

It had a history had that pierglass; its purchase dated from a time in their lives when they had been forced to turn each shilling in the palm. Mary had espied it one day in Plaistows' Stores, and had set her heart on buying it. How she had schemed to scrape the money together! – saving so much on a new gown, so much on bonnet and mantle. He remembered, as if it were yesterday, the morning on which she had burst in, eyes and cheeks aglow, to tell him that she had managed it at last, and how they had gone off arm in arm to secure the prize. Yes, for all their poverty, those had been happy days. Little extravagances such as this, or the trifling gifts they had contrived to make each other, had given far more pleasure than the costlier presents of later years.

'The next article I draw your attention to is a sofer,' went on the voice, sounding suddenly closer; and with a great trampling and shuffling the crowd trooped after it to the adjoining room. 'And a very easy and comfortable piece o' furniture it is, too. A bit shabby and worn 'ere and there, but not any the worse of that. You don't need to worry if the kids play puff-puffs on it;

and it fits the shape o' the body all the better. — Anyone like to try it? Jest the very thing for a tired gent 'ome from biz, or 'andy to pop your lady on when she faints — as the best of ladies will! Any h'offers? Mr de la Plastrier' — he said 'Deelay plastreer' — 'a guinea? Thank you, mister. One guinea! Going a guinea! — Now, *come* on, ladies and gen'elmen! D'ye think I've got a notion to make you a present of it? What's that? Two-and-twenty? Gawd! Is this a tiddlin' match?'

How proud he had been of that sofa! In his first surgery he had had nowhere to lay an aching head. Well worn? Small wonder! He would like to know how many hundreds of times he had flung himself down on it, utterly played out. He had been used to lie there of an evening, too, when Mary came in to chat about household affairs, or report on her day's doings. And he remembered another time, when he had spent the last hours of a distracted night on it . . . and how, between sleeping and waking, he had strained his ears for footsteps that never came.

The sofa was knocked down to his butcher for a couple of pounds, and the crying — or decrying — of his bookcases began. He could stand no more of it. Sweeping his papers into a bag, he guiltily unlocked the door and stole out by way of kitchen and back gate.

But once outside he did not know where to go or what to do. Leaving the town behind him he made for the Lake, and roved aimlessly and disconsolately about, choosing sheltered paths and remote roads where he would be unlikely to run the gauntlet of acquaintances. For he shrank from recognition on this particular day, when all his domestic privacies were being bared to the public view. But altogether of late he had fought shy of meeting people. Their hard, matter-of-fact faces showed him only too plainly what they thought of him. At first he had been fool enough to scan them eagerly, in the hope of finding one saving touch of sympathy or comprehension. But he might as well have looked for grief in the eyes of an undertaker's mute. And so he had shrunk back into himself, wearing his stiffest air as a shield and leaving it to Mary to parry colonial inquisitiveness.

When he reckoned that he had allowed time enough for the disposal of the last pots and pans, he rose and made his way — well, the word 'home' was by now become a mere figure of speech. He entered a scene of the wildest confusion. The actual sale was over, but the work of stripping the house only begun, and successful bidders were dragging off their spoils. His glass-

367

fronted bookcase had been got as far as the surgery-door. There it had stuck fast; and an angry altercation was going on, how best to set it free. A woman passed him bearing Mary's girandoles; another had the dining-room clock under her arm; a third trailed a whatnot after her. To the palings of the fence several carts and buggies had been hitched, and the horses were eating down his neatly clipped hedge – it was all he could do not to rush out and call their owners to account. The level sunrays flooded the rooms, showing up hitherto unnoticed smudges and scratches on the wallpapers; showing the prints of hundreds of dusty feet on the carpetless floors. Voices echoed in hollow fashion through the naked rooms; men shouted and spat as they tugged heavy articles along the hall, or bumped them down the stairs. It was pandemonium. The death of a loved human being could not, he thought, have been more painful to witness. Thus a home went to pieces; thus was a page of one's life turned. – He hastened away to rejoin Mary.

There followed a week of Mrs Tilly's somewhat stifling hospitality, when one was forced three times a day to over-eat oneself for fear of giving offence; followed formal presentations of silver and plate from Masonic Lodge and District Hospital, as well as a couple of public testimonials got up by his medical brethren. But at length all was over: the last visit had been paid and received, the last evening party in their honour sat through; and Mahony breathed again. He had felt stiff and unnatural under this overdose of demonstrativeness. Now – as always on sighting relief from a state of things that irked him – he underwent a sudden change, turned hearty and spontaneous, thus innocently succeeding in leaving a good impression behind him. He kept his temper, too, in all the fuss and ado of departure: the running to and fro after missing articles, the sitting on the lids of over-flowing trunks, the strapping of carpet-bags, affixing of labels. Their luggage hoisted into a spring-cart, they themselves took their seats in the buggy and were driven to the railway station; and to himself Mahony murmured an all's-well-that-ends-well. On alighting, however, he found that his greatcoat had been forgotten. He had to re-seat himself in the buggy and gallop back to the house, arriving at the station only just in time to leap into the train.

'A close shave that!' he ejaculated as he sank on the cushions and wiped his face. 'And in more senses than one, my dear. In tearing round a corner we nearly had a nasty spill. Had I pitched out and broken my neck, this hole would have got my bones after all. – Not that I was sorry to miss that cock-and-hen-show, Mary. It was really too much of a good thing altogether.'

For a large and noisy crowd had gathered round the door of the carriage to wish the travellers god-speed, among them people to whom Mahony could not even put a name, whose very existence he had forgotten. And it had fairly snowed last gifts and keepsakes. Drying her eyes, Mary now set to collecting and arranging these. 'Just fancy so many turning up, dear. The railway people must have wondered what was the matter. – Oh, by the way, did you notice – I don't think you did, you were in such a rush – who I was speaking to as you ran up? It was Jim, Old Jim, but so changed I hardly knew him. As spruce as could be, in a black coat and a belltopper. He's married again, he told me, and has one of the best-paying hotels in Smythesdale. Yes, and he was at the sale, too – he came over specially for it – to buy the piano.'

'He did, confound him!' cried Mahony hotly.

'Oh, you can't look at it that way, Richard. As long as he has the money to pay for it. Fancy, he told me he'd always admired the "tune" of it so much, when I played and sang. My dear little piano!'

'You shall have another and a better one, I promise you, old girl – don't fret. Well, that slice of our life's over and done with,' he added, and laid his hand on hers. 'But we'll hold together, won't we, wife, whatever happens?'

They had passed Black Hill and its multicoloured clay and gravel heaps, and the train was puffing uphill. The last scattered huts and weatherboards fell behind, the worked-out holes grew fewer, wooded rises appeared. Gradually, too, the white roads round Mount Buninyong came into view, and the trees became denser. And having climbed the shoulder, they began to fly smoothly and rapidly down the other side.

Mahony bent forward in his seat. 'There goes the last of old Warrenheip. Thank the Lord, I shall never set eyes on it again. Upon my word, I believe I came to think that hill the most tiresome feature of the place. Whatever street one turned into, up it bobbed at the foot. Like a peep-show . . . or a bad dream . . . or a prison wall.'

In Melbourne they were the guests of John – Mahony had reluctantly resigned himself to being beholden to Mary's relatives and Mary's friends to the end of the chapter. At best, living in other people's houses was for him more of a punishment than a pleasure; but for sheer discomfort this stay capped the climax. Under Zara's incompetent rule John's home had degenerated into a lawless and slovenly abode: the meals were unpalatable, the servants pert and lazy, while the children ran wild – you could hardly hear yourself speak for the racket. Whenever possible, Mahony fled the house. He lunched in town, looked up his handful of acquaintances, bought necessaries – and unnecessaries – for the voyage. He also hired a boat and had himself rowed out to the ship, where he clambered on board amid the mess of scouring and painting, and made himself known to the chief mate. Or he sat on the pier and gazed at the vessel lying straining at her anchor, while quick rain-squalls swept up and blotted out the Bay.

Of Mary he caught but passing glimpses; her family seemed determined to make unblushing use of her as long as she was within reach. A couple of days prior to their arrival, John and Zara had quarrelled violently; and for the dozenth time Zara had packed her trunks and departed for one of those miraculous situations, the doors of which always stood open to her.

John was for Mary going after her and forcing her to admit the error of her ways. Mary held it wiser to let well alone.

'*Do* be guided by me this time, John,' she urged, when she had heard her brother out: 'You and Zara will never hit it off, however often you try.'

But the belief was ingrained in John that the most suitable head for his establishment was one of his own blood. He answered indignantly. 'And why not pray, may I ask? Who *is* to hit it off, as you put it, if not two of a family?'

'Oh, John . . .' – Mary felt quite apologetic for her brother. 'Clever as Zara is, she's not at all fitted for a post of this kind. She's no hand with the servants, and children don't seem to take to her – young children, I mean.'

'Not fitted? Bah!' said John. 'Every woman is fitted by nature to rear children and manage a house.'

'They should be, I know,' yielded Mary in conciliatory fashion. 'But with Zara it doesn't seem to be the case.'

'Then she ought to be ashamed of herself, my dear Mary – ashamed of herself – and that's all about it!'

Zara wept into a dainty handkerchief and was delivered of a rigmarole of complaints against her brother, the servants, the children. According to her, the last were naturally perverse, and

John indulged them so shockingly that she had been powerless to carry out reforms. Did she punish them, he cancelled the punishments; if she left their naughtiness unchecked, he accused her of indifference. Then her housekeeping had not suited him: he reproached her with extravagance, with mismanagement, even with lining her own purse. 'While the truth is, John is mean as dirt! I had literally to drag each penny out of him.'

'But whatever induced you to undertake it again, Zara?'

'Yes, what indeed!' echoed Zara bitterly. 'However, once bitten, Mary, twice shy. *Never* again!'

But remembering the bites Zara had already received, Mary was silent.

Even Zara's amateurish hand thus finally withdrawn, it became Mary's task to find some worthy and capable person to act as mistress. Taking her obligations seriously, she devoted her last days in Australia to conning and penning advertisements, and interviewing applicants.

'Now, no one too attractive, if you please, Mrs Mahony! – if you don't want him to fall a victim,' teased Richard. 'Remember our good John's inflammability. He's a very Leyden jar again at present.'

'No, indeed I don't,' said Mary with emphasis. 'But the children are the first consideration. Oh, dear! it does seem a shame that Tilly shouldn't have them to look after. And it would relieve John of so much responsibility. As it is, he's even asked me to make it plain to Tilly that he wishes Trotty to spend her holidays at school.'

The forsaking of the poor little motherless flock cut Mary to the heart. Trotty had clung to her, inconsolable. 'Oh, Auntie, *take* me with you! Oh, what shall I do without you?'

'It's not possible, darling. Your papa would never agree. But I tell you what, Trotty: you must be a good girl and make haste and learn all you can. For soon, I'm sure, he'll want you to come and be his little housekeeper, and look after the other children.'

Sounded on this subject, however, John said dryly: 'Emma's influence would be undesirable for the little ones.' His prejudice in favour of his second wife's children was an eternal riddle to his sister. He dandled even the youngest, whom he had not seen since its birth, with visible pleasure.

'It must be the black eyes,' said Mary to herself; and shook her head at men's irrationality. For Jinny's offspring had none of the grace and beauty that marked the two elder children.

And now the last night had come; and they were gathered, a family party, round John's mahogany. The cloth had been removed; nuts and port were passing. As it was a unique occasion the ladies had been excused from withdrawing, and the gentlemen left their cigars unlighted. Mary's eyes roved fondly from one face to another. There was Tilly, come over from her hotel – ('Nothing would induce me to spend a night under his roof, Mary') – Tilly sat hugging one of the children, who had run in for the almonds and raisins of dessert. 'What a mother lost in her!' sighed Mary once more. There was Zara, so far reconciled to her brother as to consent to be present; but only speaking at him, not to him. And dear Jerry, eager and alert, taking so intelligent a share in what was said. Poor Ned alone was wanting, neither Richard nor John having offered to pay his fare to town. Young Johnny's seat was vacant, too, for the boy had vanished directly dinner was over.

In the harmony of the evening there was just one jarring note for Mary; and at moments she grew very thoughtful. For the first time Mrs Kelly, the motherly widow on whom her choice had fallen, sat opposite John at the head of the table; and already Mary was the prey of a nagging doubt. For this person had doffed the neat mourning-garb she had worn when being engaged, and come forth in a cap trimmed with cherry coloured ribbons. Not only this, she smiled in sugary fashion and far too readily; while the extreme humility with which she deferred to John's opinion, and hung on his lips, made another bad impression on Mary. Nor was she alone in her observations. After a particularly glaring example of the widow's complaisance, Tilly looked across and shut one eye, in an unmistakable wink.

Meanwhile the men's talk had gradually petered out: there came long pauses in which they twiddled and twirled their wine-glasses, unable to think of anything to say. At heart, both John and Mahony hailed with a certain relief the coming break. 'After all I dare say such a queer faddy fellow *is* out of his element here. He'll go down better over there,' was John's mental verdict. Mahony's, a characteristic: 'Thank God, I shall not have to put up much longer with his confounded self-importance, or suffer under his matrimonial muddles!'

When at a question from Mary John began animatedly to discuss the tuition of the younger children, Mahony seized the chance to slip away. He would not be missed. He never was – here or anywhere.

On the verandah a dark form stirred and made a hasty, movement. It was the boy Johnny – now grown tall as Mahony himself – and, to judge from the smell, what he tried to smuggle into his pocket was a briar.

'Oh well, yes, I'm smoking,' he said sullenly, after a feeble attempt at evasion. 'Go in and blab on me, if you feel you must, Uncle Richard.'

'Nonsense. But telling fibs about a thing does no good.'

'Oh yes, it does; it saves a hiding,' retorted the boy. And added with a youthful vehemence: 'I'm hanged if I let the governor take a stick to me nowadays! I'm turned sixteen; and if he dares to touch me –'

'Come, come. You know, you've been something of a disappointment to your father, Johnny – that's the root of the trouble.'

'Glad if I have! He hates me anyway. He never has cared for my mother's children,' answered Johnny with a quaint dignity. 'I think he couldn't have cared for her either.'

'There you're wrong. He was devoted to her. Her death nearly broke his heart. – She was one of the most beautiful women I have ever seen, my boy.'

'Was she?' said Johnny civilly, but with meagre interest. This long dead mother had bequeathed him not even a memory of herself – was as unreal to him as a dream at second hand. From the chilly contemplation of her he turned back impatiently to his own affairs, which were burning, insistent. And scenting a vague sympathy in this stranger uncle who, like himself, had drifted out from the intimacy of the candle-lit room, he made a clean breast of his troubles.

'I can't stand the life here, Uncle Richard, and I'm not going to – not if father cuts me off with a shilling! I mean to see the world. *This* isn't the world – this dead-and-alive old country! . . . though it's got to seem like it to the governor, he's been here so long. And *he* cleared out from his before he was even as old as I am. Of course there isn't another blessed old Australia for me to decamp to; he might be a bit sweeter about it, if there was. But America's good enough for me, and I'm off there – yes, even if I have to work my passage out!'

Early next morning, fully equipped for their journey, the Mahonys stood on the William's Town pier, the centre of the usual crowd of relatives and friends. This had been further swelled by the advent of Mrs Devine, who came panting up followed by her husband, and by Agnes Ocock and Amelia Grindle, who had contrived to reach Melbourne the previous evening. Even John's children were tacked on, clad in their Sunday best. Everybody talked at once and laughed or wept; while the children played hide-and-seek round the ladies' crinolines. Strange eyes were bent on their party, strange ears cocked in their direction; and yet once again Mahony's dislike to a commotion in public choked off his gratitude towards these good and kindly people. But his star was rising: tears and farewells and vows of constancy had to be cut short, a jaunt planned by the whole company to the ship itself abandoned; for a favourable wind had sprung up and the captain was impatient to weigh anchor. And so the very last kisses and handclasps exchanged, the travellers climbed down into a boat already deep in the water with other cuddy-passengers and their luggage, and were rowed out to where lay that good clipper-ship, the *Red Jacket*. Sitting side by side husband and wife watched, with feelings that had little in common, the receding quay, Mary fluttering her damp handkerchief till the separate figures had merged in one dark mass, and even Tilly, planted in front, her handkerchief tied flagwise to the top of Jerry's cane, could no longer be distinguished from the rest.

Mahony's foot met the ribbed teak of the deck with the liveliest satisfaction; his nostrils drank in the smell of tarred ropes and oiled brass. Having escorted Mary below, seen to the stowing away of their belongings and changed his town clothes for a set of comfortable baggy garments, he returned to the deck, where he passed the greater part of the day tirelessly pacing. They made good headway, and soon the ports and towns at the water's edge were become mere whitey smudges. The hills in the background lasted longer. But first the Macedon group faded from sight; then the Dandenong Ranges, grown bluer and bluer, were also lost in the sky. The vessel crept round the outside of the great Bay, to clear shoals and sandbanks, and, by afternoon, with the sails close rigged in the freshening wind, they were running parallel with the Cliff – 'The Cliff!' thought Mahony with a curl of the lip. And indeed there was no other; nothing but low scrub-grown sandhills which flattened out till they were almost level with the sea.

The passage through the Heads was at hand. Impulsively he went down to fetch Mary. Threading his way through the saloon, in the middle of which grew up one of the masts, he opened a door leading off it.

'Come on deck, my dear, and take your last look at the old place. It's not likely you'll ever see it again.'

But Mary was already encoffined in her narrow berth.

'Don't ask me even to lift my head from the pillow, Richard. Besides, I've seen it so often before.'

He lingered to make some arrangements for her comfort, fidgeted to know where she had put his books; then mounted a locker and craned his neck at the porthole. 'Now for the Rip, wife! By God, Mary, I little thought this time last year, that I should be crossing it today.'

But the cabin was too dark and small to hold him. Climbing the steep companion-way he went on deck again, and resumed his flittings to and fro. He was no more able to be still than was the good ship under him; he felt himself one with her, and gloried in her growing unrest. She was now come to the narrow channel between two converging headlands, where the waters of Hobson's Bay met those of the open sea. They boiled and churned, in an eternal commotion, over treacherous reefs which thrust far out below the surface and were betrayed by straight, white lines of foam. Once safely out, the vessel hove to to drop the pilot. Leaning over the gunwale Mahony watched a boat come alongside, the man of oilskins climb down the rope-ladder and row away.

Here, in the open, a heavy swell was running, but he kept his foot on the swaying boards long after the last of his fellow-passengers had vanished – a tall, thin figure, with an eager, pointed face, and hair just greying at the temples. Contrary to habit, he had a word for everyone who passed, from mate to cabin-boy, and he drank a glass of wine with the Captain in his cabin. Their start had been auspicious, said the latter; seldom had he had such a fair wind to come out with.

Then the sun fell into the sea and it was night – a fine, starry night, clear with the hard, cold radiance of the south. Mahony looked up at the familiar constellations and thought of those others, long missed, that he was soon to see again. – Over! This page of his history was turned and done with; and he had every reason to feel thankful. For many and many a man, though escaping with his life, had left youth and health and hope on these difficult shores. He had got off scot-free. Still in his prime, his faculties green, his zest for living unimpaired, he was heading

375

for the dear old mother country – for home. Alone and un-aided he could never have accomplished it. Strength to will the enterprise, steadfastness in the face of obstacles had been lent him from above. And as he stood gazing down into the black and fathomless deep, which sent crafty, licking tongues up the vessel's side, he freely acknowledged his debt, gave honour where honour was due. – *From Thee cometh victory, from Thee cometh wisdom, and Thine is the glory and I am Thy servant.*

The last spark of a coast-light went out. Buffeted by the rising wind, the good ship began to pitch and roll. Her canvas rattled, her joints creaked and groaned as, lunging forward, she cut her way through the troubled seas that break on the reef-bound coasts of this old, new world.

Some more Australian Penguins
are described on the
following pages

HIS NATURAL LIFE

MARCUS CLARKE

His Natural Life is the book which divulged the full reality of 'Botany Bay', the transportation 'system' to which thousands of offenders were cheerfully condemned by magistrates at the start of the last century. So literally was this a fate worse than death that convicts hanged themselves rather than suffer it. Yet Marcus Clarke's great novel is more than an enthralling narrative and a catalogue of horrors and degradations: at its best it is a classic study of human evil and of systems of repression that corrupt and imprison those who impose as well as those who endure them.

This edition is the first to print the complete original version of the novel in volume form.

Edited with an Introduction by
Stephen Murray-Smith

THE ART OF AUSTRALIA

ROBERT HUGHES

This is a comprehensive account of Australian art between the founding of the colony in 1788 and the latest developments of the 1960s.

The author, whose art column in *Nation* and whose contributions to the *Australian* proved sharp questioners of established values, traces the twin threads of the desire for independence in Australian vision and the obsessive influence of European and American models. In his view Australian painting is a phenomenon to be discussed, for good or ill, within the total context of contemporary art. He is thus led to reappraise many established reputations, and to suggest channels through which Australian painting may yet emerge as a world force.

Robert Hughes has been described by the art critic of the *Sydney Morning Herald* as 'the brilliant *enfant terrible* of Australian art and letters'.

'This book will inject into the often ungenerous and sluggish body of the Australian art world a dose of love for, and an excitement about, painting which is far more important than all the authoritative research on the size of Streeton's boots' – Eric Westbrook in *Walkabout*.

A Pelican Original